PHOENIX

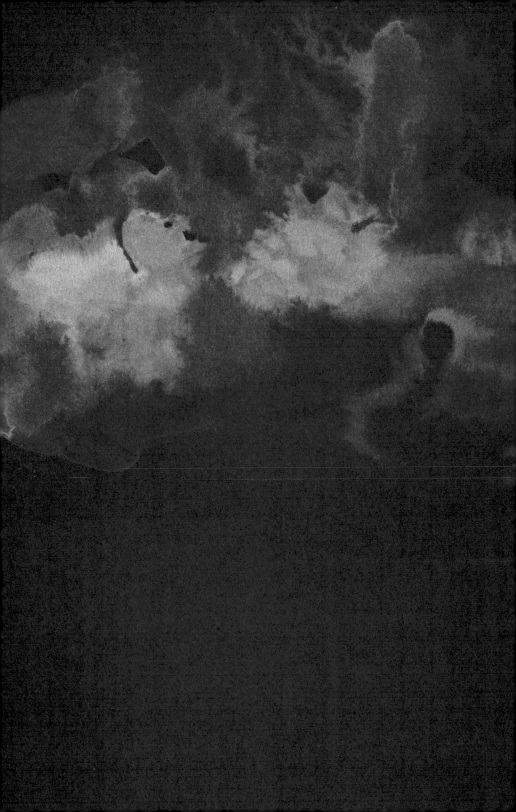

PHOENIX

SF SAID

illustrated by
DAVE McKEAN

CANDLEWICK PRESS

Text copyright © 2013 by SF Said
Illustrations copyright © 2013 by Dave McKean

First U.S. edition 2016

Library of Congress Catalog Card Number pending
ISBN 978-0-7636-8850-9

16 17 18 19 20 21 BVG 10 9 8 7 6 5 4 3 2 1

Printed in Berryville, VA, U.S.A.

This book was typeset in Minion Pro.
The illustrations were done in ink and colored pencil and assembled digitally.

Candlewick Press
99 Dover Street
Somerville, Massachusetts 02144

visit us at www.candlewick.com

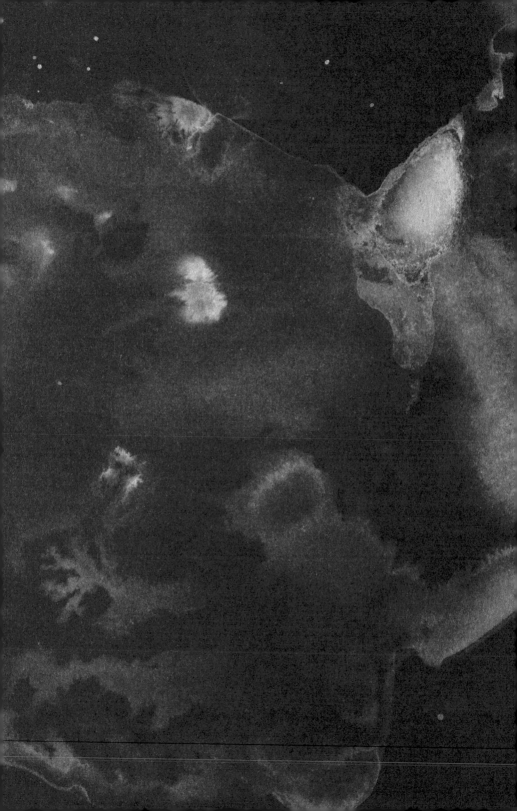

CHAPTER ONE

Lucky dreamed of the stars again that night. He loved the stars, and dreamed about them most nights. A million points of silver light, shining in the black.

But this dream was different. This time, the stars were calling him. They were trying to tell him something. They were making a small, soft, silvery sound, like the chime of a faraway bell.

The sound grew. It surged and swelled, rising up into the sky. Lucky's blood surged with it. His feet lifted off from the floor.

And in his dream, Lucky flew. He rose up and soared through space, into the stars and constellations.

It didn't feel like a dream. It seemed so real.

He rose higher and higher, until the sound wasn't distant anymore. It was all around him now, surrounding him with waves of overwhelming power, though he still couldn't grasp its meaning. If he could just get a little nearer. . . .

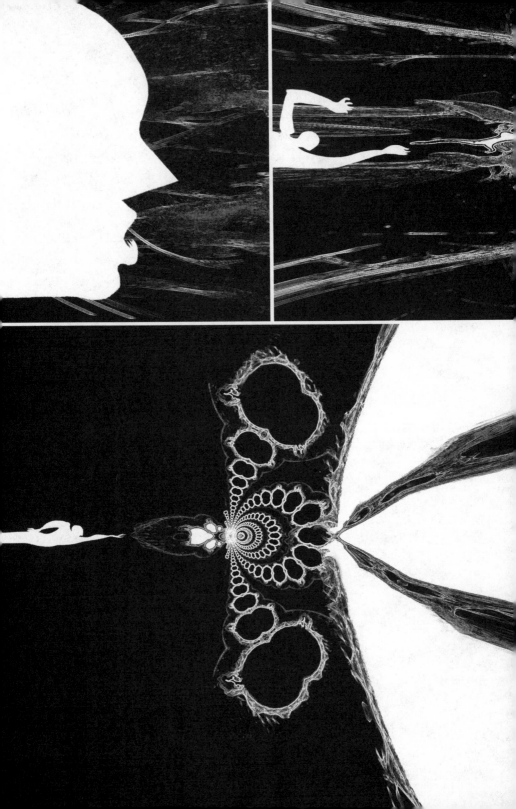

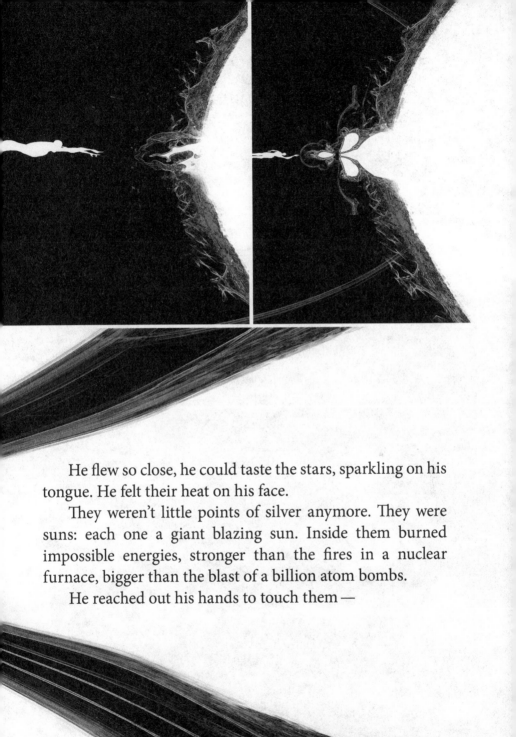

He flew so close, he could taste the stars, sparkling on his tongue. He felt their heat on his face.

They weren't little points of silver anymore. They were suns: each one a giant blazing sun. Inside them burned impossible energies, stronger than the fires in a nuclear furnace, bigger than the blast of a billion atom bombs.

He reached out his hands to touch them —

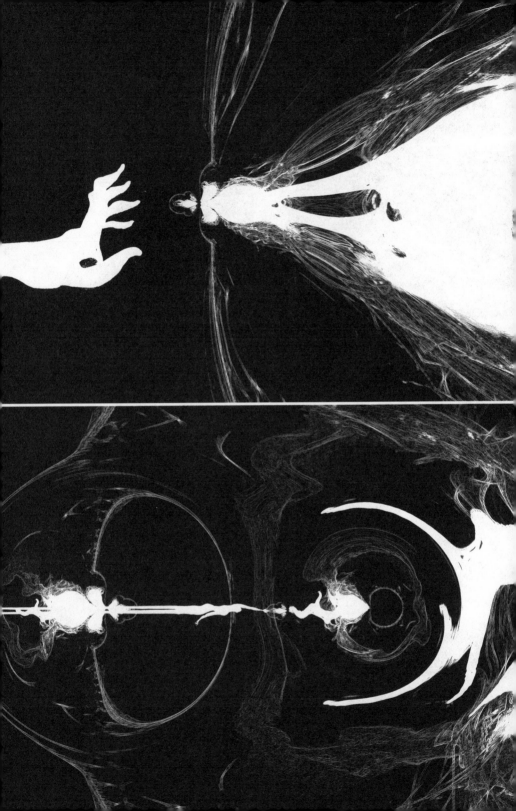

— and woke up with a violent start.

He was in his bedroom, in his mother's apartment, back on Phoenix. It was just before dawn. The air-conditioning was on full blast, but he was drenched in sweat and fever hot. A headache throbbed behind his eyes.

He fumbled for the lights — and then he saw his sheets.

The top sheet on his bed was burned. There was a massive hole through the middle of it. All around the hole, the white linen had gone black and crumbled into ash.

Lucky checked the bottom sheet. Normal. He looked back at the top one, and there it was again: a gaping hole. Smoke was still rising. His bedroom stank of it; he could taste it in his mouth.

Panic rose inside him, tightening in his chest. *What's going on?* he thought, coughing on the smoke. *Am I burned?*

He stood up. Black ash fluttered all around him. He waved it away with shaking hands and examined his skin. No burn marks. He felt exhausted and his head ached, but his body didn't seem to be hurt. It was the same puny, clumsy body as always.

Everything else in his room looked normal. The school uniform strewn on the floor. The schoolbag by his desk. His bedroom walls flickering with starmaps, showing every system this side of the Spacewall. And flying among them, his collection of model starships.

Everything was in its place, undamaged. Yet his bedsheet was burned, his room stank of smoke, and there were ashes crumbling under his fingers, smearing on his hands. *Did I do this?* he wondered. *No way — it's impossible! I wasn't even awake. . . .*

The memory of a dream flickered at the edge of his mind . . . and then slipped away.

He powered down the security matrix and opened his window, gulping in fresh air, trying to cool himself. It was still dark outside. But high above the suburban apartment blocks, the stars were shining. The sight calmed him just a little. He'd lived on this moon at the edge of the Aries system all his life, yet he never tired of gazing at the stars. They seemed so free, up there in the sky. Nothing could ever harm them.

He could hear the distant roar of starships, taking off from the spaceport. Soon it would be morning, and his mother would wake up. She would see the ruined sheet. When he couldn't explain it, she'd get worried. She'd been asking him weird questions lately, wanting to know if any unusual changes were happening to his body. He didn't know what these questions meant, but from the anxious way she asked, he knew it was trouble.

And now this. Trouble for sure . . .

No, he thought. *She mustn't see the sheet. I have to get rid of it. Replace it, and never say a word.*

He pulled on some clothes and tiptoed out of his bedroom. It was so peaceful in the corridor, he could feel the security matrix's subsonic hum in the soles of his feet. Everything was neat and ordered, as his mother liked it. Everything in its place. Shipshape, she called it.

There was a faint light under the kitchen door, and the scent of chocolate brownies. She must be in there, baking. Of course. On days when she went to work before he was awake, she'd always get up early to make him a treat: the food that had always been his favorite, back from when he was a little child.

He crept silently past to the storeroom and opened up the door. It was crammed with boring household stuff. He never looked in here normally and wasn't sure where to find sheets. He hunted through stacks of tinned food and toiletries, packs of cotton wool and bandages. Even a full battlefield Medikit! How ridiculous! Why would they ever need a thing like that in a place like Phoenix, so far away from the War?

"Lucky?" His mother's voice, behind him. He turned, and there she was: her apron on, her long red hair tied back. He hadn't heard her coming at all. "Sweetheart?" she called. "What are you doing in there?"

"Oh — nothing," he said guiltily.

"Why are you awake so early?" She sniffed the air. Her blue eyes narrowed. "What's that smoky smell?" She took off the apron and strode toward his bedroom.

"Don't go in there!" He tried to get in her way, but he was too slow. Before he could stop her, she was entering his room. He followed her in, cheeks flushed with shame —

— and there it was. The evidence. The ruined sheet, with a hole burned right through the middle.

He felt dizzy, seeing it again. It hit him with fresh force: just what a strange thing it was.

His mother breathed in sharply at the sight. Fear flashed through her eyes as she took in the smoke and ashes. But in her voice, there was not the slightest trace of surprise. "Please, *no,*" she whispered. "Not so soon . . ."

"What is it, Mum?" he said, his skin beginning to crawl. "What's happening?"

She didn't answer. She went over to the window and stared up at the sky. Lucky followed her and looked up too. There they were, as always: a million points of silver light. Whatever happened, the stars would always be there.

No.

Wait.

There was something strange in the sky. A tiny black crack. A crack in the sky, shaped like a V, where a moment ago, a star had been.

His mother slammed the security matrix on. She shut the window and backed away from it, face full of horror.

"What — what was that thing in the sky?" he managed to say.

She covered her face with her hands and breathed in deep. Then again, and again, until she'd brought her breathing under tight control. Only then did she take her hands away.

Her face showed nothing but determination now. Her voice was scarily calm.

"We have to get out of here," she said.

CHAPTER TWO

Lucky's mother pulled a kitbag down from his cupboard, and started to throw his clothes into it. Panic clawed at his chest as he watched her.

"Please, Mum," he begged. "What's going on? I need to know—"

"I need you to promise me something," she interrupted. She glanced at the burned bedsheet, at the smoke that still hung in the air. "Promise me you will never, ever tell anyone what happened here."

"I—I promise," he said, though her words were just making it worse. Her voice was so grave, as if someone had died. He could see she was making a massive effort to stay calm, but a tiny tremor worked its way along her jaw as she talked.

"Your father warned me this day would come," she said as she packed the bag, moving rapidly around his room. "I hoped he was wrong, but it's here, and it's real—"

"What is?"

She shook her head. "I can't explain it all now. It'll take too long. I'll tell you everything once we're safe, but right now, we have to leave town. Leave Phoenix, even."

Lucky gaped at her. "It's that bad?" She didn't reply; she just kept stuffing more and more clothes into the bag. "But . . . what about school?" he said. "I've got a test this morning, the one you were helping me —"

"Test?" she said. The kitbag was full to bursting now. "Don't worry. School's not important."

"Since when?" He hugged himself tightly, trying to hold down the shivering fear that was threatening to overwhelm him. He glanced at his starmaps, his spaceships. "What about my —?" he began, but she cut off the question before he could even ask it.

"This is the only thing that matters," she said, firmly zipping the bag shut. "Now I'm going to pack some things for me, and then we're out of here. I'll find us a ship at the spaceport. We'll be off Phoenix before the day is through. OK?" And with that, she marched out of his bedroom.

His stomach was churning, his mind raging with unanswered questions. Why wouldn't she tell him what she knew?

His father would have told him. He felt sure of it.

Lucky touched the wall screen and brought up his favorite vidpic. It was an old one, from before the War. He was just a baby in it; his mother was cradling him in her arms. Behind her was a handsome man with a mustache, dressed in a starship commander's uniform. He was watching over them protectively, smiling down at them beneath the blazing stars of a spiral nebula.

Lucky gazed at that smile, so far away in time and space. It was so warm, so full of love. It always made him feel better to see it.

12

If only his father hadn't gone to fight in the War. Everything would've been different, then. He imagined running away from his mother, going to find his father . . . but where would he even start? He had no contact with him. No memories of him. Only this vidpic, and the adventures they had together in Lucky's fantasies, built around his model spaceships and starmaps.

His mother hadn't packed a single one of them. She'd never liked them. But they were things he loved. He didn't want to leave them —

— and he didn't want to leave home, either.

He stumbled out into the corridor. She'd been through already, leaving a trail of chaos behind her. Baking trays and packets of sugar were strewn across the floor, abandoned. The storeroom doors hung forlornly open.

He couldn't see the Medikit in there anymore. But he could see something else: something strange, glinting in the far corner of the storeroom. An object that had been discarded in the shadows. It resembled nothing he'd ever seen before.

Scalp prickling, he reached in and picked it up.

It was a thick black disk, blacker than black, like a chunk of outer space. It was made from some kind of metal that looked like it had fallen from the sky. It felt cool to the touch, and though it was as big as both his hands cupped together, it was very comfortable to hold.

There were no words on it. But around its circumference were faint markings, intricate patterns. Twelve symbols, like a long-forgotten alphabet, carved into the black.

He couldn't take his eyes off them. He didn't recognize them, but just looking at them made his skin tingle.

They looked ancient. They looked mystical. They looked almost alive.

And within this circle of symbols lay other, smaller circles. A series of dials, like wheels within wheels, tracing elegant arcs and crescents, describing a geometry as precise as it was mysterious.

"Lucky," said his mother. She stood behind him in the corridor, a packed bag beside her already. "Put that astrolabe down."

"Astro *what*?" He hefted it in his hands. "What is it? It feels so comfortable — like it was made for me or something —"

"It has nothing to do with you," she said, a strange edge in her voice. "You weren't meant to find it. Your father never —"

"It's my father's?" Lucky stared at her in shock. "Shouldn't we take it with us?"

Her blue eyes blazed. "Forget it! Come on. Let's go."

But he couldn't. He couldn't even think about forgetting it. "If it's my father's," he said, "then we *have* to take it. You're making me leave everything here: my school, my friends, my stuff . . . Do you want to take him away from me too?"

A wave of hurt washed across her face. There was a painful silence between them for a moment.

Then she took him in her arms and held him gently. "I'm sorry, sweetheart," she said. "I'm so sorry — about all of this. I know how confusing it must be. I wish things were different. I wish we could be with your father. And believe me, so does he. . . ."

Lucky wriggled away. His mother was looking at him with a concern so deep it was awful, with a love so strong he felt embarrassed.

"If my father really wanted that," he said, "then why isn't he here with us? Why doesn't he ever get in touch? Does he even care I exist?"

"Of course he does! But . . . it's so complicated. We can't be safe with him. And right now, we can't be safe here, either."

"But why not?" he said. "Why won't you tell me what's going on?"

"All I'm trying to do is protect you, my love. I would never do anything else. You know that, right?"

He looked down. "I guess," he muttered.

She reached out again and tentatively squeezed his hand. "So will you trust me? Will you come with me? Please?"

He bit his lip. "Can I bring this astro . . . thing?"

His mother gave him a long, hard look — but he held her gaze and did not look away.

"You're as stubborn as he is!" she groaned at last. "OK. We don't have time for this, so here's the deal. I don't want to see that thing ever again. But . . . if you hide it away, and do exactly what I say . . . then, all right. You can bring it."

"I can?"

She grunted. "Don't get your hopes up. I could never get anything out of it, not one single glimmer of light. I don't expect you will, either."

Lucky didn't say a word. He just held the astrolabe in his hands, held it tight. His whole body was tingling with the strength of his emotions. At last, he had something that linked him to his father. Something better than model starships; something real. An object his father's hands had actually touched. His mother had kept it all these years, and now it was his.

"Thank you," he whispered.

She shouldered her bag. "OK. Let's get out of here."

He tucked the astrolabe away in his kitbag and took one last glance back at his bedroom. The mystery of the burned sheet remained there, unexplained. But whatever secrets his mother was keeping, whatever was really going on here, he didn't feel so afraid anymore. Not when he knew she was there, taking care of him, like always.

She put on the big dark glasses she always wore outdoors, even at night. She deactivated the forcefields, gravfields, power bars, and locks of her security matrix, pulled the front door open —

— and together, they left their home, searching for a ship to take them to the stars.

XII

The Wolf Is Rising.

The Astraeus of the Sky Cannot Stop It

for the Wolf
Will Eat
the Stars....

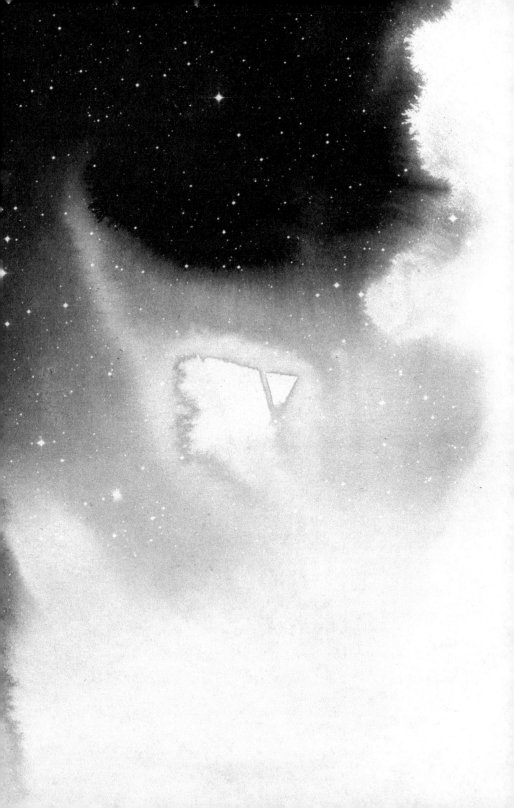

CHAPTER THREE

Outside the apartment, Lucky looked for the crack in the sky again. But he couldn't see a trace of it. The suburban sky looked totally normal and clear. The sun rose, as it always did, and by late afternoon, when they reached the spaceport, Aries One was over the horizon. The nearest planet's great red face made the clouds glow crimson.

Yet he still felt edgy as he paced after his mother into the port. Everything was so much bigger here. Above their heads, giant vidscreens flashed up the latest headlines from the War. From every rooftop, security vidcams scanned the people below. The air reeked of burning fuel and exhaust fumes.

He was panting, out of breath. A stitch cut into his side. He wasn't fit like his mother was. He hated exercise, and he hated his own body. It was always letting him down.

But then he heard a sonic boom, looked up to see a ship taking off, and he couldn't help but feel a thrill. So often, he'd heard their distant roar from his bedroom. Now here he was, looking at real-life starships, like the ones his father was flying on the other side of the galaxy.

They entered the space terminal. It was a huge white building, its lofty architecture a monument to Human civilization and its conquest of the stars. Its walls flickered with massive starmaps, projecting out into the hall, showing flights to every Human world, in every system from Aries to Libra — all the way to the Spacewall.

And through its observation windows, Lucky could see the starships glittering in their landing bays, so close now he could almost reach out and touch them. There were so many of them in the port. Their hulls were pitted from vast voyages across space. Heat haze shimmered around them, making the air look liquid with possibility.

He gazed at them, spellbound. Was one of these ships really going to take him to the stars?

"Let's see," said his mother. "Where shall we go?"

Lucky hardly needed to look at the starmaps. "How about Leo?" he suggested. It was the most glamorous Human system, famous for exotic markets where, it was said, you could get anything your heart desired. The only drawback was the large minority of Aliens who lived there too, refugees who'd fled the War.

His mother shook her head. "I don't think so," she said. "How about the smaller moons of Aries? They're barely populated, they'll be perfect. Look, there's a flight to Lethe! Let's get it."

She led Lucky up to a grand ticketing desk, where an officer with a crew cut and a headset was taking bookings.

"Welcome to Phoenix Spaceport," said the officer. "Your ident, please?"

"Of course," said Lucky's mother as she handed over her

identity card. Lucky didn't have his own yet; he was just a name on hers.

The officer scanned it and nodded formally. "Everything seems to be in order, Mrs. . . . Diana Ashbourne. What can we do for you?"

"We want a flight to Lethe," she said. "That one." She pointed at the starmaps — and then paused, puzzled. Because there, where the flight had been listed, was now the word CANCELED.

The officer frowned and adjusted his headset. "Just a moment. There's an announcement coming. . . ."

He looked up at the giant vidscreens on the wall. They were showing images of destruction. Burning buildings. Bodies on stretchers. People with hopeless, empty eyes. These images were being beamed from a Human world. A familiar one at that.

"News coming through of a Dark Matter bomb attack on Aries One!" boomed a voice from the vidscreens. "Stand by for a message from the President!"

There was an audible gasp around the terminal building. Aries One? The biggest world in this part of the galaxy had been bombed?

With a sense of dread, Lucky looked out the observation windows. He was relieved to see the great red planet still there in the sky, though he thought it looked wounded, somehow. The clouds around it seemed the color of blood now.

The vidscreens filled with an image of President Thorntree, leader of the Human government: a kindly but stern-looking woman with steely blond hair.

"I'm sorry to confirm that the Aliens have struck again,"

said the President. "Aries One was a peaceful world, but nowhere is safe while *they* are at large. My government is suspending all space traffic in the Aries system as a security measure, effective immediately. If you see anything suspicious, report it at once to the Shadow Guards. With your help, we will defeat our enemies."

The vidscreens flashed up an enormous image: the Alien King, the most wanted being in the galaxy. Lucky recoiled instinctively, and so did everyone around him. No matter how many times he saw Alien features, he couldn't get used to them: the curving horns, the cloven hooves, the burning eyes of flame.

He was glad he'd only seen them on the news, and not in real life. He'd never even seen a Shadow Guard; nothing like that ever happened in the suburbs of Phoenix. But if the Aliens had just bombed Aries One, they must be close.

Was this what his mother was running away from? Were the Aliens coming to get them?

He could feel the fear rising up inside him. It was spreading through the terminal. All around him, people were staring in horror at the vidscreens, shaking their heads at the images coming through. Some of them were crying; others were talking frantically on their comms, trying to contact families and friends.

The starmaps were all changing now, the word CANCELED coming up on every flight, to every destination.

"Surely they can't just cancel all the flights?" protested Lucky's mother. "We have to travel as soon as possible. It's an emergency."

"I'm sorry, madam," said the officer. "You'd better go home, for your own safety. It could be hours, days, weeks—"

She leaned in closer to his desk. "What about unlisted flights?" she said, more quietly. "I know there are always some freelance pilots in a spaceport. Could you help us charter one of those?"

The officer looked horrified. "No pilot would dare take off now! The Shadow Guards would stop them if they tried." He shook his head sternly. "Why would you want to leave Phoenix, anyway? At least there aren't many space devils here. Only the ones in this port, and most of them are penned up in that camp. . . ."

Lucky bit his lip. He was afraid: afraid of the Aliens, but even more afraid of the fact that his mother still seemed so desperate to get away, despite all the obstacles. What could be a bigger emergency than a Dark Matter bomb?

Whatever the answer, it looked like they weren't going to the stars after all. He'd been excited, gazing at the ships, but now it wasn't going to happen.

His scalp tingled. He had the strangest feeling. The astrolabe in his kitbag: he had the distinct sensation that it was calling him.

He glanced at his mother. She was still arguing with the officer.

Lucky couldn't stop himself. He couldn't resist. He turned away from the desk, unzipped the bag a fraction, and peered inside.

His whole body was tingling now, because the black

metal disk was gleaming with silvery light. The twelve symbols around its circumference shimmered, shining like starlight in the black.

It looked like a portal, an entryway to distant lands. The silver light within it seemed to come from somewhere far, far away. It was beautiful: so beautiful, he found he was holding his breath. Time stood still before it.

Lucky stopped being conscious of the crowds, the vid-screens, the terminal building. All he was aware of was the mysterious object in his bag. He reached down to touch the cool black metal. There was such a sense of power thrumming there, just waiting to be activated, if only he knew how to work it. . . .

He ran a fingertip around its circumference, touching each of those twelve symbols in turn. Not one of them did a thing. He tried to move the dials, but they were firmly fixed in place. He searched for a lock or a clasp that might open it up, but nothing he did could make it budge. It just sat there, silently shimmering at him.

He must have lost track of time, because he was suddenly aware that the officer was shouting at him. Abruptly, the silver glow vanished. The black metal disk looked lifeless and dark again.

". . . hell!" the big man was yelling, his eyes goggling as he stared over Lucky's shoulder into the kitbag. "Is that what I think it is?" Lucky's mother was frantically shaking her head on the other side.

"Uh . . ." Lucky's cheeks burned. Fumbling, he closed the bag, catching his finger in the zipper as he shut it. "It's — er — nothing," he said feebly.

26

"That was an astrolabe!" said the officer. "What's a boy like you doing with an astrolabe? You know they're illegal!"

"Illegal?" Lucky gulped.

"Of course it wasn't an astrolabe," his mother cut in, taking charge. "How could it be? When was the last time you saw one of those?"

The officer's eyes were narrow. "Not since the War began — but I'd recognize one anywhere. You never forget a thing like that." He moved to grab Lucky's bag.

"Are you calling me a liar?" Lucky's mother said. She threw her arms up in a great show of indignation. "How dare you! I'm not standing for this!" She marched away from the ticketing desk, dragging Lucky behind her toward the exit.

"Stop!" said the officer. "Stop right there!" He bounded after them and seized Lucky's arm. Lucky tried to wriggle away, but the man was far too strong. He yanked him back, so hard it hurt.

"Oww!" cried Lucky, falling backward, losing his balance, feet crumpling beneath him —

— but he never hit the floor. His mother caught him first. She swerved around and put herself between him and the officer.

Let the boy go," she said, in an icy low voice Lucky had never heard her use before.

She twisted the big man's wrist, just a little, and he released Lucky at once. He backed away, clutching his hand, mouth wide open in shock.

Lucky stared at his mother. How did she do that? He was twice her size!

But the officer's surprise was already turning to fury. "I'm going to report you to the Shadow Guards!" he raged. "What do you think you're doing, running around with astrolabes, assaulting people? Who the hell are you, anyway?"

Lucky's mother didn't say another word. She strode away in silence, dragging Lucky behind her, out of the terminal building and back into the streets.

It was chaos out there. There were streams of people who'd been turned away from their flights. Crowds looking up at vidscreens, waiting for more news, or staring at the great red planet in the sky. On the corner of the street, a man in a crumpled suit was shouting into a megaphone.

"The End Times are here!" he proclaimed, as Lucky and his mother rushed past him. "The End of All Worlds! The Devil himself walks among us!"

"I — I'm sorry," said Lucky as he followed his mother through milling crowds. "I'm sorry about the astrolabe —"

"I *told* you to keep that thing hidden," she said.

"You never told me it was illegal," he protested. "Why's it illegal? What does it do?"

She glanced up at the sky. "We have to get off Phoenix before they find us," was all she said.

"The Aliens?" said Lucky. "Won't the Shadow Guards protect us from them?"

She didn't reply; she just picked up her pace. Lucky shivered. The temperature in the spaceport was dropping rapidly. Night was falling. The sky blackened, and the stars came out. Aries One rose higher, like a great red wound in the sky.

Lucky's mother led him into shadowy parts of the port where there were few people and no vidcams. Here, she found a small landing bay that housed a rusty cargo ship, with a couple of old starsailors beside it.

"They might take us, if I make it worth their while," she said. "Wait here while I try." She approached the men and talked to them quietly — so quietly Lucky couldn't hear what she said. One of them didn't respond. He didn't even seem to be aware she was there; he just stared straight ahead with empty eyes. But the other starsailor's reply was all too clear.

"No way, lady! Haven't you heard the news? We ain't messing with the Shadow Guards, and neither should you!"

She hurried away from them, leading Lucky deeper into the backstreets. They went from landing bay to landing bay, ship to ship, through thickening shadows, trying every craft they could find. But it was the same everywhere. No one would give them a ride.

As he waited for his mother by the last of the landing bays, Lucky bit his lip, fighting down the feeling that this was all his fault. All this because of a burned bedsheet. But why?

sssshh

A soft hissing sound. Behind him, above him. It set his teeth on edge.

He turned around, looked up — and nearly bit his tongue off.

Because the crack in the sky was back.

It was bigger. Much bigger. It covered a whole quadrant of the sky now. It was shaped like a great black V: a sharp-edged shadow where the night's darkness looked even darker, somehow. Thicker. And all the way through it, he couldn't see a single star.

The stars had disappeared.

Lucky wanted to say something, to warn his mother or cry out, but he couldn't. His mouth had gone dry. His throat constricted. Looking at the thickening shadow, he couldn't even breathe. . . .

"No luck," said his mother, returning from the landing bay. "I don't think there are any more ships —"

"What *is* that thing?" he managed to whisper, digging his nails into the palms of his hands.

"What thing?"

He pointed behind her. "There — in the sky . . ."

sssshh

The V was growing bigger. Bigger and bigger.

His mother breathed in sharply, then took his hand. "Quick now, Lucky," she said, already beginning to move. "Run."

CHAPTER FOUR

He ran. They ran. Together. Through the backstreets of the spaceport, they ran together. Around a corner, along an alleyway, and straight into a dead end.

An electrified fence loomed up before them, ten feet tall, with floodlights at the top. A noisy crowd was gathered in front of it. There was no way around it.

They were trapped.

"Join that crowd," urged Lucky's mother. "Safety in numbers: it's our only chance." She pushed him ahead of her into the press of bodies.

ssssshh

The hissing was almost directly above their heads, yet it was still so soft and quiet, Lucky couldn't even be certain it was there. He glanced up. The V-shaped shadow was so big now, it blotted out half the sky.

"Don't look up!" whispered his mother. "Keep your head down, and we might just get away with this."

It was so hard; every muscle in his body screamed at him to look at the great V in the night sky, to see what it really was. But he forced himself to look down. He shut his eyes, pulse pounding in his throat as he held his breath — one thousand, two thousand — until the hissing faded away at last, and her grip on his hand relaxed.

"They're gone," she whispered. "But that was way too close. We're in trouble, Lucky. We need a flight off this world, and I don't know how . . ."

She shut her eyes, deep in thought. He risked another glance up and was shocked to see the stars all back in their familiar places. The sky looked totally normal and clear again. No V. No hissing. Like nothing had ever happened.

Did I imagine it? he wondered. *Am I losing my mind?*

The people around him seemed unaware of the shadow that had just passed over them. They were focused instead on something at the front of the crowd, by the fence. Whatever it was, this thing held their full attention.

Puzzled, Lucky edged around the side to get a better view.

In the harsh glare of the floodlights, a fight was taking place. Several men were piling in, kicking at something on the ground, then backing away rapidly. Other men were slamming sticks down at this thing — hitting it, then backing away too. They were shouting, their faces red with anger.

He edged a little closer to see what they were attacking.

Then it roared and reared up on its hind legs, scattering the men —

— and Lucky saw horns, great curving horns, pointing up at the sky —

— and his stomach turned to liquid. His blood ran cold.

Because it was an Alien. The first he'd ever seen in real life.

It was a young male, and he was *big*. He was way bigger than Lucky. He was as big as the biggest man in the crowd.

He was muscular, too: a solid wall of muscle, hulking and roaring under the lights, like a nightmare come to life.

He was dressed in a strange coat that looked like it was made of liquid metal, billowing behind him like wings. His flaming eyes were covered by mirrorshades, but Lucky could see cloven hooves protruding from the bottom of his coat: massive black hooves that could crush a Human head.

But there was only one of him, while there were half a dozen men ranged against him. They piled in again, all at once this time, and forced the Alien down by sheer weight of numbers. The crowd howled their approval: "Get him! Get him!"

Lucky found himself howling along with them. "Get them all!" he yelled, his fears boiling up inside him.

"Lucky!" warned his mother. She was shaking her head. She looked appalled.

The men were pinning the Alien down beneath the electrified fence. He was struggling and roaring mightily. It took four of them to hold him there, one on each limb. A fifth was hitting him in the face, again and again. He pummeled the Alien, bloodying his nose. He ripped off the Alien's mirrorshades, revealing eyes of blue fire behind them.

"Call the Shadow Guards!" screamed someone in the crowd.

"No!" said the man who was hitting the Alien. "I've got a better idea." From his belt, he pulled a hand cannon. He thrust it against the Alien's head, where the horns met the skull.

"Yes! Yes! Finish him!" the crowd yelled, as the men held the huge Alien helpless there on the ground.

Lucky's mother took a deep breath. "I've got a plan," she whispered. "You wait here. Don't watch. This might get ugly."

Before Lucky could answer, she was moving through the crowd. She moved in the most mesmerizing way. The people were packed in tight, but somehow she managed to twist and turn through them, and they just seemed to flow right off her. Yet she herself flowed, like a fish through water, or like water itself, like a tidal wave, gathering speed and momentum as she went.

She made it to the front of the crowd, where the men were holding the Alien down. No one stopped her. No one even touched her as she reached out and took the gun from the man — plucked it from his hand as if she was taking sweets from a child — and threw it away on the ground.

"What the hell are you doing?" yelled the man.

Lucky was as stunned as anyone. Why was she helping an Alien? Why was she even getting involved?

"Leave him alone," his mother calmly told the men. "What's he done to you?"

"Haven't you heard? They just bombed Aries One! They'll kill us all, unless we kill them first."

She shook her head. "Look at the way he's dressed. He's not in their army. He's a civilian. A peaceful refugee."

"The only peaceful Alien's a dead Alien," growled the man.

"For your information," she said, very softly, "his people have a name. They call themselves the Axxa —"

"His people eat eyeballs! They worship the stars! They're not even people!"

Lucky's mother shook her head again. "Sometimes," she said, "I'm ashamed to be Human. Now, *leave him alone!*"

There was silence for a moment. Then the man stood up, fist clenched, face red. "You're a devil-lover, are you?" he spat. "Then you'll get the same as they do!"

He drew his fist back to hit Lucky's mother — but she moved first. She moved faster. A blur of motion, she arced aside at exactly the right moment, and the man's fist smashed into the electrified fence behind her. He collapsed in a shower of sparks.

The second man swung at her. But already she was rolling away and coming up again, her long red hair flowing behind her in the night. Moving with astonishing speed, she flicked her feet out, like a scorpion flicking its tail, and unleashed a devastating kick that hit her attacker squarely in the solar plexus. He dropped to the dirt and lay there, poleaxed.

Lucky could barely believe his eyes. His mother was *fighting*! He had no idea why she was doing it, but she was so good! So fast and skillful. And the way she moved — it was like nothing he'd ever seen.

Another man rose to face her. In that moment, the Alien seized his chance. There were only two men left on top of him now, and they were distracted by Lucky's mother. With a mighty roar, he lifted them off his limbs and hurled them into the crowd. Then he grabbed the gun she'd thrown away, and held it up in the air.

The crowd broke up as people fled, screaming, from the huge horned beast with the cannon in his hands.

The Alien fired a shot into the air above his head. In the chaos and confusion, Lucky rushed to his mother's side as the last of the crowd escaped, shrieking. And now, for the first time, he could clearly see where they were.

It couldn't have been more different from the clean white spaceport terminal. Behind the electrified fence, the only buildings were some filthy-looking shacks and warehouses. There was a big red warning sign on the fence — DANGER: ALIEN REFUGEE CAMP! It looked like the poorest part of town.

Lucky's heart thudded in his throat. Every instinct told him to follow the crowd away to safety, but his mother held him there as the Alien advanced on them. His massive hooves thumped on the ground as he came. His horns glinted in the floodlights; blue fire burned in his eyes.

"It's OK," Lucky's mother said calmly. "You're going to put that gun down now, aren't you? Because *from the stars we all came . . .*"

"*. . . and to the stars we return!*" said the Alien. He stared at her, the fire in his eyes flashing. "How do you know that? Who are you?"

"Let's just say I'm a friend," she replied.

Lucky gaped at them both, speechless. He'd never heard an Alien voice before; you never heard them on the news. He'd always imagined they just roared and snarled like animals. Yet this one sounded very Human. And for her part, his mother was acting so strangely that he barely recognized her.

"Where's your ship?" she asked the Alien as he put the gun down. "You still have a ship, don't you?"

"Best ship in the galaxy . . . except she's stuck in Aries, like we are." The Alien wiped his bloody nose and retrieved his mirrorshades. "We can't leave this poxy system without our navigation! They took it away from us!"

Lucky's mother nodded. She peered thoughtfully at the refugee camp behind the fence, in the floodlights' glare. "If someone could help you with that problem," she said, "if someone could give you what you need, would you leave Phoenix?"

"'Course! Like a shot!"

"Even though the government just suspended space travel? You'd take off without clearance? You'd risk Shadow Guards coming after you?"

"Hell yeah!" roared the Alien, stamping the ground with a hoof. "Anything to get out of this hole! After what just happened — I wouldn't care who came after me — I'd be gone!"

"Very good," she said, with quiet satisfaction. "So here's the deal. We've got what you need. We'll let you use it if, in return, you give us a ride off Phoenix."

All this time, Lucky had been struggling to understand. How did his mother think they could help an Alien? But this last part was all too clear, and he couldn't believe his ears. "*Whaaaat?*" he cried. "Is that your plan? You're saying we should go with *him*?!"

"Lucky," she said sharply. "Enough."

"But we're at war with them!" he protested. "They're the enemy! My father's —"

"Lucky! I said, that's enough." She turned to the Alien. "I'm sorry."

The Alien shrugged. "Kid's right," he said. "What you asking *me* for, when there's all these Human ships in port?"

She glanced up at the night sky. "This place will be crawling with Shadow Guards in a minute," she said. "We need to get out of here, and so do you. I swear, we'll help you get your ship off the ground, but by all the stars, we need your help." And then she looked the Alien straight in the eye and asked the question: "Well? Have you got room for a couple of passengers?"

"Aaaah," groaned the Alien, wiping blood off his face with the back of his hand. "Look, if it was up to me . . ." His words tailed off. "But I've got a captain, see, and my captain . . . he won't like this. He won't like it one bit. But seeing as you helped me out — seeing as you just saved my skin — well, I guess you better come with me."

CHAPTER FIVE

The Alien led them to a grim-looking bar on the perimeter between the refugee camp and the rest of the spaceport. Through the door, Lucky could hear people shouting and the sound of breaking glass.

"I don't think we should go in there," said his mother, but the Alien had already pushed open the door.

"It's one of the friendlier places in town for people like me," he said. "Plus, it's where I'm meeting the Captain. You want a ride, or not?"

They walked into a thick fug of smoke. The bar was full of rowdy drunken Humans. There was a fistfight going on in one corner, an arm-wrestle in another. A wall-size vidscreen was showing more images of the bombing on Aries One. Great clouds of smoke hanging above a city. Crying children. Firefighters struggling to extinguish the blazes.

"Casualties now number in the thousands, and still the fires burn on," said a voice from the screen. "Theobroma's army has claimed responsibility and vows to continue the War indefinitely."

The image changed to show the Alien King. With his

horns and hooves and flaming red eyes, he looked utterly terrifying.

Everyone in the bar turned to stare at the Alien in the doorway, and Lucky and his mother behind him. In the sudden silence, dozens of hostile eyes were upon them.

Lucky looked down, heart in his mouth. He was ready to turn and flee, but the Alien walked right in, and Lucky's mother followed without hesitation.

There was a wave of anger around the bar. Some foul curses for the Alien. The Alien didn't respond, or meet any of their gazes. He just kept walking. So did Lucky's mother, dragging Lucky along behind her.

Lucky held his breath as one of the Humans stood up —

— but the man just changed the channel on the vidscreen. Loud thumping music came on. One by one, the others returned to drinking and fighting one another.

"I thought you said this was one of the friendlier places?" muttered Lucky's mother.

"It is." The Alien shrugged. They made their way to the counter, where the barman eyed him with obvious disgust.

"Is this space devil bothering you?" the barman asked Lucky's mother.

"No," she said. "And please. They're not devils. They're people, just like you and me."

"*People?*" spat the barman. "Look at him! We don't serve their kind of food. No eyeballs here."

"I don't want eyeballs!" said the Alien. "But I'd sure like to sample your finest brew — OK, chief?" He slapped some credits down on the counter.

The barman bit his tongue, pocketed the money, and started pouring some rusty-colored liquid into a glass.

"I'll have the same," said Lucky's mother. "And a glass of milk for the boy." Lucky cringed with embarrassment, which only got worse when he saw the Alien grinning.

Once the drinks were poured, the Alien led them to a table in the corner, by the curtained back wall of the bar. They sat down, and he raised his glass in a huge hand.

"Cheers!" he said over the pounding music. "My name's Frollix."

"Ashbourne," said Lucky's mother. "Diana Ashbourne. And this is my son, Lucky."

Frollix laughed. "What kinda name is that?"

Lucky wanted to ask what kind of name the Alien thought "Frollix" was, but he didn't dare. He felt completely out of his depth here. He couldn't even look up for fear of seeing those burning eyes, those glinting horns, those hooves that could smash his skull with a single kick. He wished they could just go home.

But his mother smiled. "It's what I wanted him to be," she said softly. She reached into her bag and pulled out a package. "Here," she said, passing it to Lucky. "I thought you might want something to eat."

He unwrapped the package. Inside was a stack of brownies. Chocolate fudge brownies, homemade. The ones she'd been baking. She'd brought them with her.

"I'm not hungry," he made himself say as he pushed them away. He couldn't let the Alien see him eat something so childish. It was too humiliating — no matter how much he loved their smell, their sweetness, their freshly baked sticky softness —

"Well, I sure am!" said Frollix, helping himself to a brownie and taking a big bite.

Lucky's mother looked a little hurt, but she fixed her attention on the Alien. "So what's your position on this ship of yours?" she asked. "Are you a fighter?"

"Nah! I'm ship's engineer. I mean, I can handle myself. But if there's serious combat, the person to do it ain't me."

He leaned back and scratched the base of his horns. Lucky felt disgusted, but couldn't help looking, despite himself. Up close, he realized he couldn't see the actual surface of the horns. They were wrapped in black velvet cloth, bound with silver thread, twining around in a crisscrossing pattern.

The Alien saw him looking, and his eyes glinted behind his shades. "You ever flown in a starship, kid?" he said.

"No, but I want to, more than anything!" The words came out before he could stop them.

"Oh, yeah?" Frollix drained most of his drink in one great glug. "Well, there's nothing finer. Not even another round of this fine brew, though I wouldn't say no to that. Your round, right?"

"I'll get it," said Lucky's mother. "Wait here. Don't go anywhere without me." She went over to the counter, leaving Lucky alone with Frollix. His stomach lurched. He clutched his kitbag close, with the astrolabe inside it, protecting it from danger.

"So . . . you wanna try the brew?" Frollix asked him. "It's not much, but it's better than milk and cookies."

Lucky's face flushed. "No." He didn't want a space devil

to look at him like that, like they knew each other or something. He didn't want Frollix to look at him *at all*.

Raucous cheers exploded across the bar. One of the men had arm-wrestled another into submission. The Alien eyed them from behind his shades, flexing his massive fists as if preparing for a challenge.

"You Groundlings..." he muttered. He cracked his knuckles.

"Groundlings?" said Lucky, flinching at the awful sound. "What's a Groundling?"

"You are," said Frollix. "You Humans, you call us weird names, like *Aliens* and *Devils* and *Scum*." He shrugged. "That's 'cos you're ignorant. Still living on the ground. You don't know nothing about the stars. So we call you *Groundlings*, 'cos we're the People of the Stars, and you're the People of the Ground."

Lucky stared at the Alien, outraged by these words, but before he could say a thing, there was a commotion at the door. Another pair of Aliens stormed into the smoky bar. They were wearing the same mirrorshades and liquid metal coats as Frollix, but they looked even fiercer and wilder.

One of them was an older male. He was very tall — even taller than Frollix — and he had great gray horns and a braided beard.

The other was a female, about Lucky's age and size. She had long black hair, tied up above her head in a nest. There was something moving in this nest of hair. Several things. Sharp pointy things. Needles, it looked like, sticking out of her head at odd angles, bristling like quills. Electric neon needles, flashing every color from ultraviolet to infrared.

She saw him staring at her, and stared right back, fearless and self-assured.

"Captain! Bixa!" called Frollix. "Over here!"

The two new Aliens approached the table. Some Humans swore at them as they came, but the tall one lowered his mirrorshades, stared down at them with eyes the color of volcanic lava, and the jeering died away. This crowd seemed tough, but he seemed tougher. Not one of them could hold his fiery gaze.

"Lucky," said Frollix as the Aliens pulled up seats at the table, "meet Captain Ozymandias Nox. He's captain of my ship: best ship in the galaxy. And this"—he gestured to the girl—"is Bixa Quicksilver, who shoulda been there to help me earlier, but obviously had more important things to do —"

"And who is *this,* Frollix?" she demanded, her voice cutting sharply through the music.

"The kid's OK," said Frollix. "Him and his mum, they saved my skin when some Groundlings were about to kill me."

"Is that right?" Bixa peered at Lucky over the rims of her shades. Her eyes were pure silver fire, like the stars themselves. "Why would a Groundling do a thing like that?"

"I — well — uh . . ." Lucky didn't know what to say. The needles in Bixa's hair seemed to change color, shifting from blue to purple to danger-signal red. The Captain was even worse: he just sat there in smoldering silence, glowering at Lucky. His horns were immense, though now that he was up close, Lucky realized again that he couldn't see their surface.

Like Frollix's, they were wrapped in velvet, bound with silver thread.

"So here's a coincidence," said Bixa. "We just saw a lynch mob, looking for an Axxa who they say attacked them. That wouldn't be you, would it?"

Frollix coughed. "The point is, the kid and his mum need a ride, and I said maybe we could help 'em."

"You did *what*?" said Bixa. "What kind of moonbrain are you?"

"Moonbrain?" spluttered Frollix. "Why, I oughtta throw you into the nearest black hole!"

"That just proves you're a moonbrain. If we were anywhere near a black hole, we'd all be sucked in and destroyed, wouldn't we?"

"*Both of you — enough!*" commanded the Captain. Frollix and Bixa fell silent at once. The Captain turned to Lucky, horns glinting. "Whatever Frollix told you — forget it. We can't give you a ride. We can't even get out of this system ourselves."

"But that's the thing, Captain," said Frollix. "They've got what we need. That's why I brought them to meet you — because *they've got one!*"

"You do?" said the Captain, staring at Lucky with new intensity. "Show me."

"Uh — show you — what?" he stammered, sweating under the Captain's gaze.

At that moment, his mother returned to the table. "*From the stars we all came . . .*" she said to the Captain.

"*. . . and to the stars we return,*" he replied. "And who might you be?"

She leaned in close and said something in his ear. To Lucky's surprise, the Captain didn't just dismiss her. The two of them turned away from the table and talked quietly between themselves. Lucky caught only the occasional word: names of people he'd never heard of, places he'd never been.

"It's looking good!" whispered Frollix. "I think she might do it!"

"They'd better hurry up," said Bixa. "There's trouble coming. I can feel it." She unbuttoned her coat. Underneath was a suit of body armor. It looked seriously professional — except where it was sprinkled with glitter and fur. A small hand cannon was slung on her hips; it too glittered brightly.

As her hand curled around its barrel, Lucky couldn't help noticing her fingers. They were long and slim and beautiful. He glanced down at her feet, and immediately wished he hadn't, because instead of feet, there again were those huge black cloven hooves. Just like those of the Captain and Frollix.

He turned away and stared at the wall of the bar. But there was a shadow on the wall that gave him the strangest feeling. As if it was looking back at him. As if it was watching him, somehow. Hair prickling, he leaned forward to see it better — but at that moment, his mother and the Captain stood up, and he forgot all about the shadow.

"Very well," the Captain was saying. "If it's true, then we'll take you on board. But I need to see the proof."

Lucky's mother smiled. "Thank you, Captain," she said. "I knew we could do business." She turned to Lucky. "Show him the astrolabe," she said, very quietly.

"What?" He couldn't believe it. "I thought you told me —"

She pulled him to one side. "Why are you arguing with me?" she said over the thumping music.

"Why do you keep changing your mind about everything? You got angry last time I looked at it — you didn't even want me to bring it in the first place — and now you're all *Show him the astrolabe*? Why do those devils want to see it, anyway? What's it got to do with them?"

She took a deep breath. "It's what they need," she said. "It's what they need to fly their ship."

"It is?" He gaped at her, trying to make sense of this. "But — then — why —?"

"Lucky," she pleaded, "I can't answer your questions now. There's no time, and there's so much I haven't told you, so many things I hoped you'd never need to know. But you'll get the truth, I promise. Once we're safely away, I'll explain it all —"

"But I don't want to go with *Aliens*!" he cried. "Have you gone completely insane?"

"It's all right: we can trust them. Now please trust me, like you said you would. Show the Captain that astrolabe, and let's get out of here!"

There were so many things he wanted to say to her. But he bit his lip and faced the table. He unzipped his kitbag and held it open a crack so the Aliens could see inside.

They all peered into it.

The astrolabe looked dull and dark this time, not a glimmer of light. But Captain Nox was transformed at the sight of it. His eyes widened, and the fires inside them flared with something that looked like desperate desire.

"By all the Twelve Astraeus!" he whispered. "So it's true. . . ."

Frollix's chest puffed out proudly. "See, Captain? I found us a way outta here! Now we can go see the Professor, like Mystica wanted—"

"Come, then," said the Captain. "We must go, quickly."

"Captain!" warned Bixa, her needles changing color, glowing deeper shades of red, scarlet, crimson. "Trouble—"

The front door smashed open. The men who'd been fighting Frollix burst into the bar—and this time, they were all armed with cannon. Lucky's mother reached for her kitbag, but before she got to it, Bixa unholstered her own cannon.

"No guns, Bixa!" thundered Captain Nox. "No killing."

Lucky was surprised to hear an Alien say those words, but Bixa didn't look at all surprised. She just ran her fingers through her hair, making her needles shimmer. "Fine," she said. "How about this?"

Her needles bristled at the door, like they were almost alive—and then, incredibly, a crimson needle shot out of her hair and soared toward the men.

KAA-BOOSHHH!

The needle exploded right in front of them.

Everything in Lucky's head went weird. His senses scrambled, all mixed up. Sounds became colors. Shapes had tastes. *I can't think straight,* he realized. *I'm going to be sick—*

—and across the bar, the men were throwing up, sinking to their knees, clutching their heads and weeping.

"What was that?" gasped Lucky, barely holding down the nausea.

"Sensory Dazzler!" whooped Frollix. "Remember I said I wasn't the person to do the combat? Well, that was a Bixa Quicksilver special!" He pulled away the curtain to reveal a hidden back door. "Now run, you guys, run! Let's get back to the ship!"

XI

The Wolf Is Coming.

The Astraeus of the
Sun Cannot See It

for One By One,
the Suns Go Out. . . .

CHAPTER SIX

Lucky's mother grabbed his hand and dragged him through the door. He strapped his kitbag to his back as they sprinted away from the bar.

Captain Nox led the way, running swiftly and gracefully on his hooves. Frollix loped along beside Lucky and his mother. Bixa Quicksilver brought up the rear, guarding them from attack. Lucky looked back at her. She was no older than him, yet she moved like a warrior, with deadly purpose in every step.

"What you felt," said Bixa as they ran, "was the flash from the other side of the room. Those Groundlings got it in the face. They're not hurt, but they won't be leaving that bar for a while." She spoke without gloating or glee, just the assurance of someone who was expert at their job.

Lucky's mother smiled. "That girl!" she said. "She's good."

Lucky glanced back again — and his mouth went dry. Because it looked like there *was* someone leaving the bar.

Or rather, some*thing*.

A shadow. The shadow he'd seen on the wall. It was moving, all on its own. And now it was coming after them.

His mother turned and saw it too. "Come on!" she urged.

They accelerated away from the refugee camp, running out beyond the edge of the spaceport. Here, far from all the other ships, they came to a derelict runway. Its flight tower was abandoned, its surface strewn with weeds. It was the worst patch of ground imaginable.

"This is where they let us land," said Frollix. "And over there: that's our ship."

There was a very surprising structure at the end of this runway. It was the size of a starship, but it was shaped like a silver crescent moon, with wires crisscrossing between the points — more like some strange sculpture than any ship Lucky had seen before. It looked battered, burned, and badly beaten up. It certainly didn't look like it could fly.

"The *Sunfire*," breathed Frollix. "Didn't I say she was the best ship in the galaxy?"

A hatch opened on the side of the ship. A warm light shone out from within.

"Good enough," said Lucky's mother. "Let's go." But something made her hesitate. She turned around —

— and there was the shadow, coming closer and closer. As Lucky watched, it seemed to grow even darker. Thicker. It was taking shape, becoming solid —

— becoming a guard —

— a Shadow Guard.

"Are they — are they coming to protect us?" Lucky

gulped, his throat constricting with fear. His mother shook her head. Her long red hair flowed behind her in the night.

The Aliens turned and saw the approaching shadow. Bixa's needles went pale. But she clenched her fists and touched her cannon.

"Bixa, no," commanded Captain Nox.

"It's us he's after," Lucky's mother told the Aliens. "You go to your ship. Get ready for takeoff. We'll join you in a minute."

The Aliens glanced at one another and then ran toward their starship. Lucky and his mother stayed on the runway. In a heartbeat, the Shadow Guard caught up with them. He stood there silently, watching them, darker than the darkness.

Even this close, it was hard to see him clearly, because he was wearing some kind of stealth armor that sucked up the light, leaving only shadows. Lucky couldn't see his eyes, his mouth, or any of his features — almost as if he didn't have a face at all. But there was a coldness coming from him that was unmistakable.

Then the Shadow Guard spoke, in a voice Lucky felt in his bones as much as heard with his ears. "Diana Ashbourne," he said. "We know who you really are. We know your real name, and we know what you've done. Come with us, and by the authority of President Thorntree's government, no one will be hurt."

"And Shadow Guards are famous for telling the truth, aren't they?" replied Lucky's mother. "Leave us alone."

"That boy beside you," said the Shadow Guard. "The boy with the astrolabe. Is that your son? *His* son?"

"I won't tell you anything," she said.

"Then we'll rip his brainscan, and yours. We'll find out everything we want to know."

Lucky backed away, his legs like jelly. His whole body was shaking. But his mother squared up to the Shadow Guard, fearless.

"You'll never even touch the boy," she said in her iciest voice. "You know what I'm capable of. Don't make me do it. There's only one of you, and —"

ssssshh

That soft hissing sound again. Directly above them. Lucky looked up —

— and there it was. The V-shaped shadow in the sky. Even bigger than before. So big now, it filled his entire field of vision.

Then blinding lights flared at the tips of the V, like floodlights coming on — so bright that Lucky's nose began to bleed — and now at last he knew what he was looking at.

A shadowship. A vast black starship, hovering in the air above them, blocking his view of the sky. There was no crack up there. That was an illusion caused by the ship's stealth armor. Because these were the ships of the Shadow Guards. Attack craft, sleek and deadly, their wings meeting in a sharp V at the front.

The shadowship descended to the ground, hissing softly as it displaced the air around it. Dust and weeds swirled in the wind. Lucky's hair blew across his eyes.

"OK," said his mother, under her breath. "Come on, Lucky. Let's go!"

But he couldn't move. He just stood there, frozen in the blinding nosebleed glare.

Shadows began to stream out of the black ship. Shadows darker than the darkness, blotting out the world. Shadow Guards. He couldn't see their faces, because they were hidden behind stealth armor. But they were carrying shoulder cannon, ground-blasters, weapons he couldn't even name —

— and they were coming to get him.

Lucky's mother grabbed his hand and dragged him down the runway, toward the Alien ship. There was a low rumble at the edge of his hearing. He thought it might be the sound of weapons powering up, preparing to fire —

BOOOM!

A massive blast. A crater opened up in the ground just behind him. The force of it flung him into the air, and for a moment he felt like he was flying —

"Aaaargh!" he screamed as he smashed into the ground, knees first. Excruciating pain ripped through his kneecaps. He tried to get up, but couldn't. He flailed as flames scorched the air around him and heat crackled his hair. Behind him, that low rumble powered up again.

"Hold on to me," said his mother. She scooped him up in her arms and carried him to the abandoned flight tower.

She kicked open the door and went through. Inside, everything was shrouded in dust, like a tomb. She put Lucky down under a flight controller's terminal, beneath rows of old starmaps, and they sheltered there together, gasping for breath. His knees throbbed with pain. They were grazed and bleeding.

His mother took a quick look at them, frowned, and unshouldered her bag. But already, the Shadow Guards were firing at the tower. A window exploded. The door blew off its hinges. Cracks appeared in the old starmaps — and then they shattered, one by one, as flames engulfed the walls around them.

"Why are they shooting at us?" cried Lucky, cowering under the terminal. "Is it my fault?"

"No, my love, of course not," said his mother over a shockwave that blasted his eardrums. "Now, can you be very brave, and hold on a minute before I treat your knees?"

He nodded. She took off her jacket, rolled up the sleeves of her white shirt, and reached into her bag. Inside it, under the Medikit, Lucky glimpsed a hand cannon, some ammunition clips, and a couple of fist-size metal objects that he thought might be grenades, but he couldn't be sure, because he'd never, ever seen such things before.

"I hoped it wouldn't come to this," she said as she loaded the cannon, fingers moving without hesitation. "But if that's how it has to be . . ."

She took up position by the door. Cocked the trigger. And blasted back at the Shadow Guards as they tried to rush the tower.

Her first shot stopped one of them.

Her second dropped another. Then three Shadow Guards were down.

She was brilliant. Perfect precision. *Aim. Fire. Reload.*

She unleashed another round. Every shot hit its mark.

"Where did you learn to shoot like that?" whispered Lucky, stunned.

She raised an eyebrow. "Beginner's luck?" she replied, the ghost of a smile in her eyes. But she didn't move like a beginner. She'd gone into another gear, reloading her cannon again like it was the most normal thing in the world.

I wish I could help her, thought Lucky. *I wish I could blow those Shadow Guards to hell —*

BLAMMM!

Her cannon clattered to the ground. She was hit! Her hand — it was bleeding!

With her other hand, she flung one of the grenades back at the Shadow Guards. There was a soft whining sound — and then a huge explosion. And then there was a deafening silence in Lucky's ears.

His mother paused, panting, listening. No shots came back from the other side. But already, more shadows were swarming down from the great black ship, surrounding the tower.

"We're trapped!" he said.

His mother moved swiftly through the burning room, checking every surface. She found a lever in the corner, pulled it, and a rickety ladder dropped down before her.

"A way out," she said. "Come on."

He tried to stand, tottered on legs that felt like liquid,

and slumped to the ground again. He lay there, terrified, clutching his bleeding knees.

His mother came back for him. Very gently, she picked him up in her arms and carried him to the foot of the ladder. "You first," she said. "I'll be right behind you."

Lucky's heart was pounding. His knees were screaming with pain. But they were going to get away. She knew what she was doing. They were going to be OK.

He put a foot on the first rung. It wobbled beneath him, and the ladder lurched before his eyes.

"I'm holding it for you," said his mother. "Keep going."

He tried another step; it felt more stable now. But behind him, outside, he heard the rumble of weapons powering up again. Taking aim. A volley of shots slammed into the tower, and he heard his mother cry out.

Because she was hit. Again. Her shoulder this time.

"Don't look," she gasped. "Come on, Lucky. Climb!"

With a desperate surge of fear, he hauled himself up another rung, then another, and another, forcing himself higher and higher, though he was tiring with every step he took toward the top. He climbed up, and up, and up — until finally he came to a trapdoor. He pushed it open and hauled himself onto a platform at the top of the flight tower.

Cold night air whipped into his face. He caught his breath, steadied himself, and offered his mother a hand up.

She shrugged it off. "I'm fine," she said, though there was blood dripping from her wounds. Already, she was scanning the layout at the top of the tower. The Alien ship was on the ground directly below them now. The Aliens had climbed on board and were preparing to take off. Frollix and Bixa were staring up at them from the open hatch.

Lucky felt giddy. He backed away from the edge of the platform and turned around. Behind them, a Shadow Guard was coming silently up the ladder. Out of the trapdoor. Onto the platform . . .

"Help!" screamed Lucky, fear finally freeing his voice.

His mother reared up like a lioness and let loose a ferocious blow that knocked the Shadow Guard back down through the trapdoor.

"You got him!" cried Lucky, hugging her and hugging her, not wanting to let go.

She hugged him back, full of pride and joy. "Not too bad for a beginner, am I?" she said. Above their heads, the black sky was shot through with red streaks from Aries One.

"Who *are* you?" he said.

"You know who I am!" She smiled, ruffled his hair, and led him back to the edge of the platform. "Now, there's only one way out of here. We've got to jump down, onto the *Sunfire*. It'll hurt, but I promise you, it'll be OK. Can you do it?"

The view lurched before Lucky's eyes. He felt sick. "No!" he whimpered. The wind shook the tower; the metal groaned beneath his feet. And already, he could hear engines spinning up. Could see the Alien ship beginning to shift and hum and move.

"Wait!" his mother called down to the Aliens. "We're coming!"

BLAMMM!

A shot rang out behind them. Something strange appeared on his mother's shirt. It was like a little flower, blooming there on the white fabric. Then its petals opened, shocking wet and red, and Lucky knew it wasn't a flower.

Blood. It was her blood. And it was seeping from her chest.

sssshh

The shadowship hovered in the air behind them, dwarfing the flight tower. A hatch at the front was open. More Shadow Guards stood inside, bristling with cannon.

"Surrender," one of them called. "You cannot win."

Lucky's mother turned away from the black ship in the sky and whispered softly in his ear. "Lucky, my love," she said as if she was putting him to bed on some very ordinary night, back home in the suburbs, "you keep yourself safe, OK? Because everything that I've done . . . I only did it to protect you."

And with that, she lifted him in her arms—and hurled him off the edge of the platform.

"No, wait—what are you doing?!" he screamed as he fell away from her and plummeted feetfirst into the night.

Down, down, down he plunged, helpless, screaming, clawing the air, trying to slow his fall—but he couldn't—he just fell—

and fell

and fell

until

WHUMP!

— he landed in Frollix's massive arms as the Alien ship lifted off from the ground.

"The kid's in, Captain!" called Frollix. He put Lucky down, just inside the ship. "But his mum — I don't know what she's doing. . . ."

Lucky stared out of the *Sunfire*'s hatch as it rose into the air — and was horrified to see his mother still up there on the flight tower. She wasn't coming after him.

No. She was going the other way. She was running straight at the huge black ship in the sky.

The Shadow Guards fired at her, all guns blazing — but she was moving in that mesmerizing way again — twisting and turning and flowing like water.

BLAMMM! BLAMMM! BLAMMM!

She hurled herself off the tower, into their line of fire, but not one of their shots hit her. Even now, she was that fast. That good.

She pulled her last grenade as she dived right into the shadowship's open hatch. There was a soft whining sound —

— and then a huge explosion that tore the black ship to pieces, fire and light bleeding out as the blast obliterated it, and everything in it and on it and around it —

— and all the time, Lucky was watching from the *Sunfire*, waiting for his mother to somehow leap aside to safety and come after him —

—and even as the *Sunfire* rose above the apocalypse of smoke and flame, he was calling for her—he called again and again and again—

"Come on, come on—where are you? Please, COME ON!"

—but his mother never came.

CHAPTER SEVEN

His world shattered into pieces. Afterward, he could only remember flashes: memories of moments, seared into his mind.

Up. Up. The *Sunfire* rising —
— rising —
— rising into the sky.

Inside the ship, everything shuddering. Juddering.
Metal bucking and shaking like it would break all around him.

"Get away from that airlock!"
Frollix hauling him back into a cabin. Slamming the hatch shut behind him.
The smoke and fire of the spaceport falling away.
The burning shadowship gone from view —
— and his mother —
Gone.
She's really gone.
My mother's gone, and —

Face crumpling.
Tears like knives behind his eyes.
A howl of grief and pain rising in his throat—

Hold it together!
You're on an Alien starship: you've got to hold it together!
I can't. I can't. Not alone—
You have to! She gave everything to save you, but if you
don't pull yourself together, it won't mean a thing!

Looking around, trying to get his bearings.
But everything strange in the Alien ship.
Unidentifiable objects. Weird shapes. Everything old,
faded, dusty. Dilapidated.

The walls covered in damaged vidscreens, buzzing on
and off. Crackling with static. Flashing up fragments.
Broken glimpses of the view outside.
Clouds streaking past. Breaking through the clouds.
Beyond them, the blood-red disk of Aries One.

"We're breaking atmosphere!" The Aliens, rejoicing. "She
beat them! There's no one coming after us!"
Impossible to reply. Eyes clenched tight, trying to hide
the howling pain inside.
A gravity field kicking in. A life-support system pumping
out air.
"The astrolabe." Captain Nox, demanding. "Give it to
me."
Handing it over. No choice.

66

"Now leave me alone!"

The Aliens leaving the cabin, leaving him alone —

— all alone in the galaxy.

My home is gone. My mother gone. And why?

But she promised! She promised it would be OK, and now look —

Collapsing right there on the floor.

Huddling in a ball.

Shivering. Shaking. Sleeping and waking, fits and starts. In and out of fever dreams.

Knees throbbing with pain. Red raw and bleeding. Whole body aching from the impact of the fall.

Remembering something stupid. That battlefield Medikit of hers. How he'd scoffed at it only a day ago —

— and how he wished he had it now.

Wishing she was there. Wishing he'd told her that he cared. All that time, she'd been looking after him — and she was brilliant, so brilliant, she could do things he never even knew about — and all he'd done was argue with her —

— and weeping —

— weeping —

— weeping into the night.

CHAPTER EIGHT

Lucky dreamed of the stars
again that night.

He dreamed they were calling to him once more. Making that small, soft, silvery sound, like the chime of a faraway bell. Trying to tell him something so important, it would change everything, if he could only understand it.

And in his dream, Lucky rose up and soared through space, into the swirling stars and constellations.

He rose higher and higher, until the sound wasn't distant anymore. It was all around him now, surrounding him with waves of overwhelming power, closer and clearer than ever before.

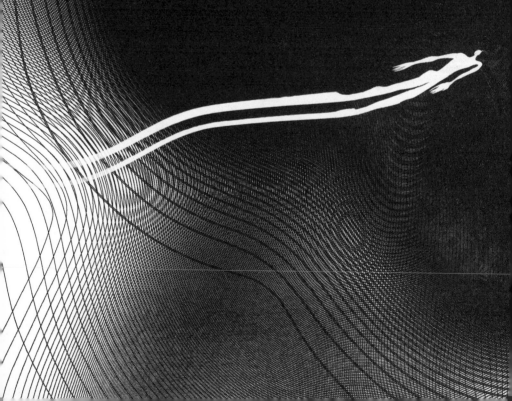

It was as near as his own thoughts, like hearing voices in his head. Many voices, in unison, the harmonies ringing out as the sound grew richer, deeper, stronger.

And then he knew. The sound was a *song*.

The stars were *singing*.

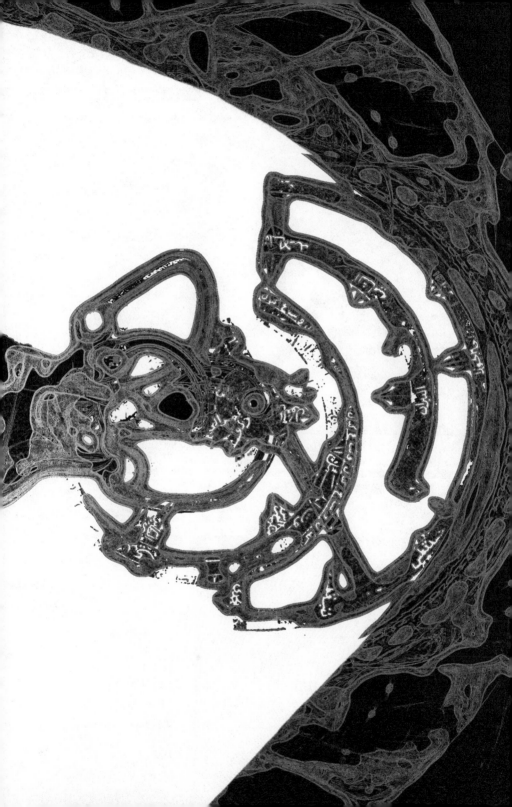

The meaning of the song lay in its words, if only he could grasp them. But they were so elusive. Already, the song was slipping away from him.

He reached out his hands to touch it —

— and woke up with a violent start.

He was in the Alien ship. He was alone, flat on his back by the airlock. The floor around him was scorched black. The metal had been badly burned. It had twisted out of shape, bubbled, and bent back on itself; it was barely recognizable as metal anymore. It looked like a lunar landscape.

He himself was unharmed, though his knees hurt, his hands felt raw, and a headache blazed behind his eyes. He was soaked in sweat. Exhausted.

And totally naked.

Lucky hugged himself, but couldn't stop shaking. *Where are my clothes? What's going on?*

The memory of a dream flickered at the edge of his mind . . . and slipped away.

He clambered to his feet. A cloud of smoke and ashes rose around him. He brushed the ashes off his skin and realized with a sickening jolt that they were the remnants of his clothes. It had happened again. Just like the burned bedsheet at home. This thing that scared his mother so much she'd made them leave home: it had happened again.

Why does this keep happening? What's wrong with me?

Lucky had no answers. Only pain, like a great burning hole in his heart where his mother used to be.

He felt so lost without her. How could he survive alone? At that moment he would've given anything to have her back, looking after him, taking charge, making plans. Whatever the truth of this terrifying mystery, she would've found a way to make it all better again. But now she was gone, and there was nothing left. Not even a crumb of those chocolate brownies he'd pushed away . . .

He felt such a wave of homesickness, he almost gave up, right there.

Lucky, my love, you keep yourself safe, OK?

He forced himself to focus. Survival. His survival. That was what she gave her life for, and that was what mattered now. He had to find his own way in the galaxy. He pushed everything else out of his mind, because if he let himself think about what had just happened, he knew he would break into a thousand tiny pieces and would never put himself together again.

First things first: he was still naked. But the bag she'd packed for him was undamaged, on the other side of the cabin. He opened it and quickly dressed himself in new clothes, making a bandage for his knees by ripping a shirt into strips.

OK. So. What now?

Lucky looked around the cabin of the Alien ship. It was nothing like his fantasies of glamorous starships. Even where it wasn't burned, every surface looked dusty and dilapidated. The floor was rusty metal, held together by loose rivets. He couldn't even see the ceiling, because it was so covered in cobwebs.

The broken vidscreens on the walls crackled and buzzed with static. He'd hoped to see the stars from a starship, but these screens were so old and damaged that he could barely see the view outside at all.

He couldn't have felt more isolated. The only people he could talk to now were a crew of Aliens, capable of ripping his head off.

He forced himself to remember that this was his

mother's plan. He was only here because she trusted them, somehow.

But I can't, he thought. *Can I?*

No way. And I can't trust the government, not after what the Shadow Guards did.

So who can *I trust? Who's going to look after me now?*

He remembered the vidpic on his bedroom wall. A handsome man with a mustache, in a starship commander's uniform. He'd been watching over Lucky protectively, smiling down at him beneath the blazing stars of a spiral nebula.

My father.

He's still out there somewhere. And he knows what's happening to me — he warned her it was going to happen, so he must know. . . .

His fingers dug into his palms, gripping on to this idea, because it was all there was.

Find my father. That's what I've got to do.

A sharp voice broke into his thoughts.

"So, Groundling? What do you think of our ship?"

He jumped back, startled. Bixa Quicksilver was standing behind him. He hadn't heard her enter the cabin. But there she was, the needles in her hair glinting electric neon colors. She wasn't wearing her mirrorshades, and without them, Lucky was dazzled by the silver fire that burned in her eyes.

He looked down at her huge black cloven hooves. Then up at the needles again. He couldn't speak. The hole inside him burned. His mother knew how to talk to these Aliens; she knew what to say and do. He didn't.

76

But he needed the Aliens' help if he was ever going to find his father.

"I need to see the Captain," he made himself say. "Can you take me to him?"

"Making demands already?" She crossed her arms, like a solid wall in front of her. "Let's get something straight right now. You try anything, Groundling, and you'll regret it. You do just one thing that damages this ship or brings us into any more danger . . ." She left the threat hanging there in midair.

"OK." Lucky gulped.

Bixa looked down and inspected the scorched, blackened ground around the airlock. "Hmm. How did this get so burned?" she asked.

His heart quivered. If she knew it had happened around him, while he was asleep —

Promise me you will never, ever tell anyone what happened here.

—but she didn't seem to know. "Those shadowships must be even more powerful than I thought," she said. "Well, I guess it's time we redecorated in here." She tapped the ground with her long slim fingers. There was a rippling sound, and everything started to change. The walls, the ceiling, the floor: every surface was suddenly unstable.

Lucky felt dizzy. He couldn't even trust his own eyes anymore. But he soon realized what was happening. The ship was cleaning itself, using some kind of Alien technology. As he watched, cobwebs fell away. Dust disappeared. Rust deoxidized and became solid metal.

The cabin still looked old, but as it renewed itself, signs

began to appear that it must once have been something very grand.

It was like a cathedral in space. The ceiling vaulted high above his head in silver arches, which flowed down into the floor through graceful columns, every line curving and connecting organically. And as Bixa tapped the vidscreens on the walls, they stopped crackling with static. Instead of showing the view outside, they started to glow from within, filling with vivid colors and light, like stained glass.

Vidpics now began to appear on the screens. They were images of people, but the most amazing people Lucky had ever seen. They were vast and powerful: more like gods than ordinary people. Some of them had wings and haloes. Others wielded tridents, scythes, flaming swords; bolts of thunder and lightning. A few held entire worlds in their hands.

"Who — who are those people?" he asked, scalp prickling with the strangeness of it.

"The Twelve Astraeus, of course."

"The twelve *who*?"

Bixa didn't reply. She tapped the ground, and a substantial stove appeared. Beside it rose a table and some spherical silver chairs, while swaths of fabric dropped from the ceiling, like hammocks. It was as if a kitchen, a dining room, and a bedroom were being jammed into a cathedral, with no boundaries between them at all.

But Lucky hardly noticed; he couldn't look away from the glowing figures on the vidscreens. "Are they characters from your myths and legends?" he guessed.

"Go ahead and laugh, if you think it's so funny," Bixa growled. Her needles flashed danger-signal red.

"Huh? Why would I laugh?"

"Because you're just like every other Groundling I ever met!" she said, stamping a hoof on the floor. Her fingers curled into fists of rage.

He backed away, heart thumping in his throat, hands up, helpless. "Look, if you're really going to hurt me," he managed to say, "just get it over with!"

She blinked. A strange expression came into her silver eyes — but whatever it was, it wasn't anger. Slowly, her needles cooled; her fists uncurled. She tapped the walls, and the lights went down in the cabin. "Well, we're all done in here," she said quietly. "You wanted to see the Captain, right?"

"Uh — yes?" he said, surprised.

"Then come with me. 'Cos *he* wants to see *you*."

X

The Wolf Grows
More Powerful,

The Astraeus of Fire
Cannot Destroy It

for It Extinguishes
All Things. . . .

CHAPTER NINE

Bixa strode away down a cloistered corridor, her hooves clicking confidently on the curving floor. Lucky trailed along behind her, losing his balance and stumbling with every step, until they reached an arched doorway.

Through it was a cabin lit with candles and sticks of incense, and more vidscreens that glowed like stained glass, showing those mysterious figures Bixa had called the Twelve Astraeus. In the center of the cabin was a fur-covered bed. An Alien lady was tucked up inside it.

She was old, like someone from another age, but she was grand as well. She was wearing a robe of turquoise and gold, blazing with color like a peacock's feathers. A matching headscarf covered her hair. She had golden rings on every finger. Captain Nox and Frollix stood on either side of her bed. The Captain was holding the astrolabe, and they seemed to be arguing about something. But as Lucky and Bixa entered the cabin, the lady looked up and saw them, and her eyes shone with fire as golden as her rings.

She stared right into Lucky's eyes. Her gaze seemed to reach directly into his brain. A worrying thought flashed through his mind: *They eat eyeballs! Is that why she's staring into my eyes like that? Does she want to eat my eyeballs?*

He began to sweat. It felt very warm in this cabin, and very light, as if gravity was lower than elsewhere on the ship. There was a strange smell in the air: a mixture of gunpowder, chocolate, and spice.

The Alien lady drew her furs tight around herself, and then spoke at last. "Welcome to the *Sunfire*," she said. "My name is Mystica Grandax."

"And I'm Lucky."

"Are you quite sure?"

"Of course! I mean — it's my name," he replied. But as he spoke, he couldn't help remembering the Shadow Guard's words. *Diana Ashbourne: we know who you really are. We know your real name, and we know what you've done.*

There was so much he'd never known about his mother. He never even knew her real name. Maybe he'd never known his own.

"Well, Lucky — or whatever your name is," said Mystica. "I heard what happened in the spaceport. I am sorry about your mother. What she did was courageous, and we will not forget it."

"What exactly *did* happen, back there in the port?" Captain Nox cut in. "Why were the Shadow Guards after you? Why did your mother . . . do what she did?"

The words were like knives in Lucky's belly. He shut his eyes, trying to hold back the feelings that were rising up inside him. "I don't know. That's the scariest thing. They wanted something — and she knew what it was — but she never told me."

84

"Well..." said the Captain. "Do you know what her plans were, at least? She asked me to take you somewhere safe; a remote moon, perhaps...."

Lucky didn't know what to say. How could that possibly help him to find his father? He knew he had to be strong here, to stand up for what he wanted, but it was so hard to speak with those fiery eyes on him.

Frollix stood up and tended to the candles, which were burning low. "That don't make sense, Captain! Shouldn't we take him to his family? Where's your family, kid?"

Lucky peered at the enormous Alien, his mother's words echoing in his mind. *They're not devils. They're people, just like you and me.* Was it possible that they really might help him?

"The only family I know about is my father," he made himself reply. "He's in the War Zone, beyond the Spacewall. So that's where I want to go."

Captain Nox's eyes burned. "Do you have any idea what you're saying?" His huge gray horns glinted in the candle-light, casting long shadows.

"Isn't that where the Alien worlds are?" said Lucky. "Isn't it your home?"

"Not anymore." The Captain looked down. "There are ... *things* ... out there."

"What sort of things?" said Lucky, feeling cold at the thought of something that could scare this formidable Alien.

But the Captain wouldn't say anymore. "If that's where your father is," he growled, "then forget about him. We'll do what your mother wanted: drop you on a nice safe moon —"

"I'm not going to forget about my father!" Lucky shuddered and forced himself to press on. "I'm going to find him, whatever it takes. I don't want to go to some moon; I'm going to the War Zone."

There was a moment of silence. The Aliens looked at one another.

"But . . . where in the War Zone, exactly?" said the old lady. "It covers half the galaxy, you know. How do you plan to find him in the middle of all that?"

Lucky had no answer. The cabin felt like it was beginning to spin around him, and only one thing was clear: just how hard it was going to be to find his father.

"Hey, don't look so sad!" said Frollix. "There must be something, some clue. What else do you know about him?"

"Not much. He's been fighting in the War since before I can remember, and my mother never liked talking about him. I've only got one thing of his: the astrolabe."

"So why don't you use it to find him?" said Bixa.

Lucky blinked; a spark of hope flickered inside him. "Could it do that?"

"It certainly *could*," said Captain Nox, "if it was working properly. Astrolabes are the most powerful navigational devices ever made. They can find anything in the galaxy, from a person to a planet . . . But yours is the most temperamental I've ever seen. It gave me just enough to plot a course, but no more. I believe there's something wrong with it." He held the black metal disk out to Lucky. "You see? Not a single glimmer of light."

Lucky took the astrolabe and held it in his hands. It

was true. There was no silver glow. The symbols around its circumference weren't even visible. It just looked like dead black metal.

But it was a relief to hold it again. It felt so good to have it back. It made him feel closer to his father; made him believe he really could find him, out there in infinite space.

"Look!" breathed Mystica.

Lucky looked down, and his skin prickled. The black metal was starting to glow again. The twelve symbols were beginning to glimmer. They gleamed and shimmered with a faint silver light that seemed to come from somewhere far, far away.

"Let me see that," said the Captain, reaching for it. But the moment he touched it, the light flickered out, and the astrolabe looked dull and dead once more.

"Don't do that!" said Mystica. "Let it be with the boy— only the boy. No one else is to touch it."

Lucky held the astrolabe close, as if protecting it. And as he warmed it with his hands, he sensed the light coming back into it again.

It was glowing at his touch — and his touch alone.

"Bizarre," said the Captain. "Why does it light up for him and no one else? I've been using astrolabes all my life, and I've never found one I couldn't work. I tell you, there's something wrong with it. Perhaps a Startalker could —"

"I think perhaps," interrupted Mystica, "this astrolabe is protected, so only the boy can use it. Why don't you show him how it works? Would you like that, boy?"

"Oh — yes — please!" begged Lucky.

"But he's just a child," the Captain protested. "A Human child at that. You think he can waltz into it and make it work when I, Ozymandias Nox, cannot?"

"Let him try," said Mystica. "How else is he going to find his father?"

The Captain snorted. "Well, there's a simple way to settle this. Boy: put your fingers on its dials and ask it to unlock itself. You'll see: it won't do a thing."

"Ask it?" said Lucky nervously.

"Yes. Think the words, in your mind."

Lucky put his fingers on the dials, feeling foolish. But in his mind, he imagined saying the words: *Astrolabe, please unlock yourself.*

The instant he thought that, the dials began to turn beneath his fingers. The wheels began to spin: smoothly, gracefully, easily.

It was moving! At last, the astrolabe was moving! All he had to do was ask: something so simple, he'd never even thought of it. Bubbling with excitement, he looked up and saw the Aliens all staring at him, their eyes aflame.

"*How are you doing that?*" hissed Nox.

"I just did what you told me," said Lucky as the metal dials turned and turned. There was such a sensation of power under his fingertips, but he wasn't doing a thing. The astrolabe was spinning at its own speed, following its own rhythms, like some starry dynamo, pulsing in the night. "So what now?" he said. "How does it work?"

"Your Human ships use starmaps to navigate faster than the speed of light," said Captain Nox, eyes flashing. "But

Axxa ships travel at the speed of dark. We use astrolabes to guide our Dark Matter drives across the vast gulfs of interstellar space."

"Dark Matter?" said Lucky, puzzled. "Like the bombs?"

Bixa scowled. "Is that all you know about us? Bombs? Well, the Dark Matter drive is the safest, cleanest, quickest way to travel ever invented. It doesn't waste fuel, like you crazy Groundlings. But without an astrolabe, the drive won't work. You're stuck in whatever system you happen to be in — like we were, when we surrendered ours. Thanks to your government for banning our technology!"

Lucky stared down at the spinning dials, the gleaming symbols, the faraway silver light. "Astrolabes are *your* technology?" he said.

"'Course," said Frollix. "They were made by Axxa navigators years ago. They were the highest point our science ever reached."

Lucky frowned, trying to imagine why his father would have a piece of Alien technology. But already, Captain Nox was pointing to the astrolabe's circumference.

"See those symbols?" he said. "They represent the twelve star systems of the galaxy. Within the astrolabe is a kind of map, encompassing all the stars and worlds we know. But it's not like one of your Human starmaps. It doesn't just show you the route. *It actually takes you there.* Well, it takes your mind there; your body remains here in a trance. Try it. Start by asking it to show you your position in space. If that works, then ask it where your father is."

Lucky concentrated with all his might. He had to make

this work. Had to. *Astrolabe,* he said in his mind, *show me my position in space!* He considered for a moment, and then added, *Please?* just in case.

The dials picked up speed. They shimmered beneath his fingertips as the black metal disk pulsed and blazed and throbbed with light —

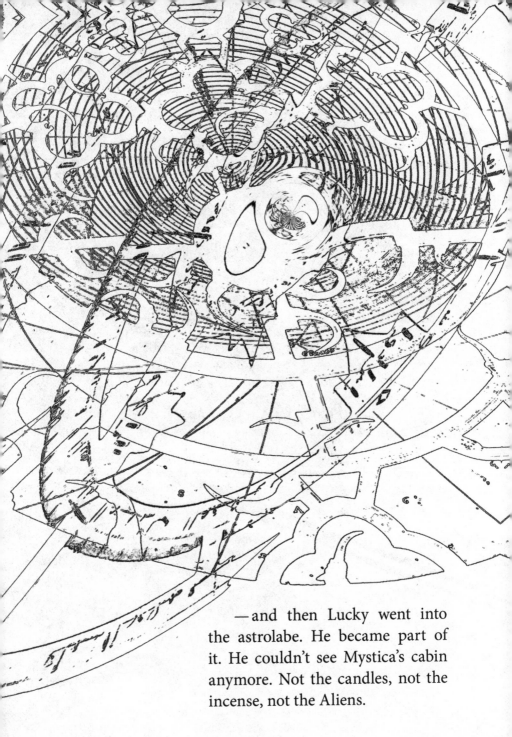

—and then Lucky went into the astrolabe. He became part of it. He couldn't see Mystica's cabin anymore. Not the candles, not the incense, not the Aliens.

91

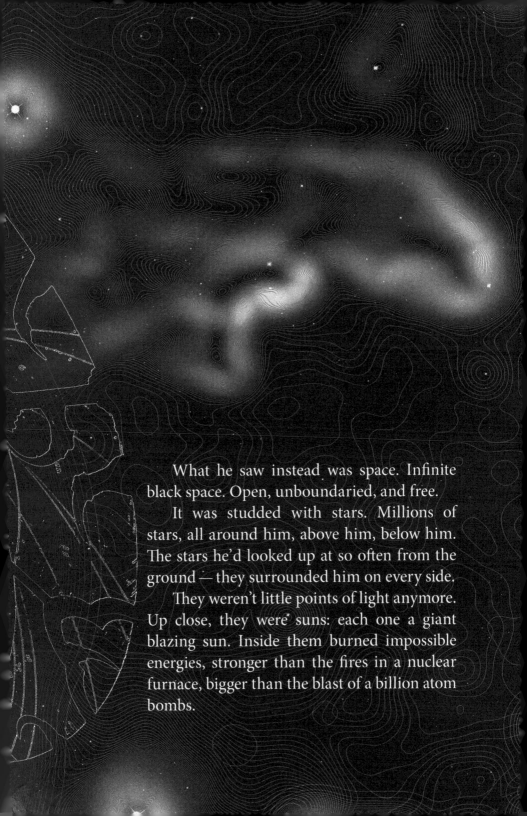

What he saw instead was space. Infinite black space. Open, unboundaried, and free.

It was studded with stars. Millions of stars, all around him, above him, below him. The stars he'd looked up at so often from the ground — they surrounded him on every side.

They weren't little points of light anymore. Up close, they were suns: each one a giant blazing sun. Inside them burned impossible energies, stronger than the fires in a nuclear furnace, bigger than the blast of a billion atom bombs.

They filled him with awe. They were so bright, it hurt his eyes to look directly at them. But he couldn't help it. He felt compelled to stare and stare into the scorching faces of those suns. For as he gazed at them, he had the distinct sensation that they were staring right back at him.

And as he flew among them, he became aware that he was no longer in his own body. He seemed to be in a new body: some kind of astral body that defied gravity and needed no air. A body of pure consciousness.

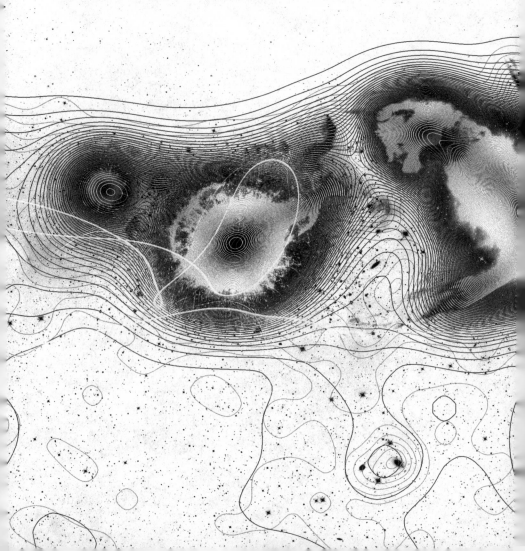

Every fiber of his being shivered with the strangeness of it. He needed every ounce of concentration to ask his question.

Please show me where my father is? he asked the astrolabe, in his mind.

A line of blazing silver light shot out from one of the stars. Then another line — and another — and now more and more lines were shooting out of more and more stars, joining up into spirals and webs, swirling away in every direction, to infinity, so fast it made his head spin and his stomach lurch.

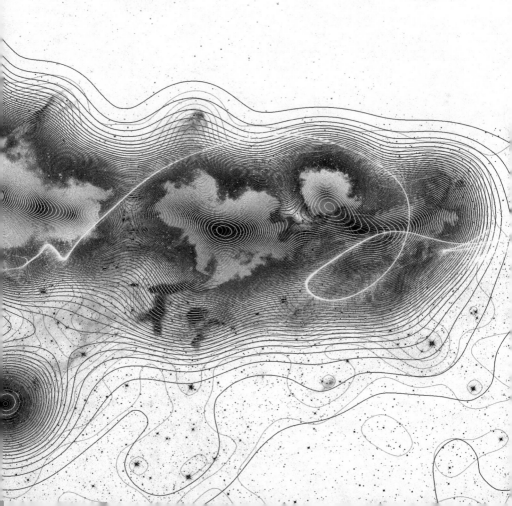

What's going on? he thought as panic rose inside him. *I don't like this! I can't move — I can't think — I can't breathe —*

And then he was hurtling along the lines of light through space, totally out of control, faster and faster, farther and farther, spiraling all the way to the edge of space — and then over the edge, and off the map, and —

"Stop!" he gasped as he fell out of the astrolabe — and landed on the floor of Mystica's cabin.

Gravity smashed back into him with a painful crash.

He dropped the astrolabe in shock. Its silver lights winked out. Its dials all ground to a halt.

He was shaking. His head hurt. The Aliens were staring down at him with eyes of flame.

"Goodness gracious!" said Mystica. "Are you all right?"

Lucky's heart was still racing, but at least he could breathe again. He could move. He seemed unharmed, though the panic was only a heartbeat away.

"That was . . . scary," he said as he hauled himself up.

"That was your first try?" said Captain Nox, looking shaken.

"Yes. I — I couldn't do it."

"You panicked, and you came out of it badly," the Captain said. "But most Humans can't get into an astrolabe at all, let alone move through it. Even the great Axxa navigators: it takes years . . ." He shook his head, his face an unreadable mix of emotions. "So where did it take you?"

"Nowhere. It just threw me off the edge of the map."

"Off the edge?" The Captain picked up the astrolabe and examined it. The dials seemed to have flipped inside out. They had twisted and turned right over, so they now appeared to be pointing outside the astrolabe altogether. "This doesn't make sense," he said. "I've never seen an astrolabe's dials point outward. It's not possible: its map contains everything in the galaxy." He shook his head. "It is as I thought. Your astrolabe must be broken, after all."

Lucky felt a sharp stab of disappointment. His only hope of finding his father, and it was really broken? "Can you fix it?" he asked.

"Like I said: that technology is old." Frollix sighed. "Even we don't really understand it anymore."

Mystica coughed and pulled her furs tighter around

herself. "There is *one* person who might be able to help. The very person we are going to see, in fact. An old friend of ours on Leo Five. He specializes in ancient artifacts. If anyone can fix that astrolabe, he can."

Lucky peered at her. "Could you maybe . . . take me to meet him?" he asked.

"Don't you think we have business of our own with him?" said the Captain coldly.

"My dear!" Mystica chuckled. "Without the boy and his astrolabe, we wouldn't be back in space at all!" She winked at Lucky, almost like they were conspirators — but then she coughed again, a deep racking cough that shook her whole body. "Besides," she managed to wheeze, "I rather think the Professor would wish to see this astrolabe for himself."

A look passed between Mystica and Nox. Then Nox stood up and strode to the doorway. "Well, it's a long way to Leo," he said. "If you want to stay on this ship, boy, you'd better start earning your keep. Can you do anything useful?"

"I know a bit about starships," said Lucky cautiously. "I've always wanted to fly one. . . ."

"Fly?" The Captain tossed his horns back in scorn. "You think I'd let you fly the *Sunfire*? No, I'll tell you how you can earn your keep. First: you can maintain this ship in tip-top condition, so we don't waste any more energy on repairs. You can clean the floors, polish the vidscreens, scrub the toilet —"

"The toilet?"

"Yes," said Captain Nox. "The toilet. It is now your responsibility. Second: you helped Frollix fight, so you obviously enjoy fighting, like most Humans."

101

"Uh—"

"Good. Because Bixa is always complaining that no one will train with her. So starting right now, you are officially her training partner. You have to do whatever she wants. Are we clear?"

Lucky's eyes grew wide with horror — but no wider than Bixa's own.

"*Whaaat?*" she shrieked as Captain Nox strode out of the cabin. "No way — I'm not training with *him!*"

CHAPTER TEN

The *Sunfire's* onboard lights created a cycle of days and nights, marking the passage of time. It was three whole days before Lucky's first session with Bixa. He spent every one of those days dreading it.

In the meantime, he found his way around. The ship was compact, and he was surprised to discover he'd already met the whole crew. It was a strange group: two old Aliens, two young, and no one in between. Lucky wondered how they'd come to crew together. Perhaps they were a family. Frollix and Bixa certainly quarreled like brother and sister, yet Mystica and Nox seemed too old to be their parents.

It was puzzling, but he didn't feel he could ask about it. After his discussion with the Captain, he kept his distance from them. He knew he needed them, but he still feared them — even Frollix and Mystica, who seemed to want to help him. He couldn't afford to make them angry, or get anything wrong. He couldn't imagine what they might do to him then. Especially Bixa and Captain Nox.

So he did his best to keep his end of the bargain. He spent hours down in the hold, cleaning the ship's toilet, though he was dismayed to learn that cleaning toilets in space was just as disgusting as cleaning toilets anywhere else. He polished floors and vidscreens, though it was frustrating when he knew the ship itself could do the job far better. He helped Frollix keep the Dark Matter drive clean, though his occasional glimpses of the cockpit only made him wish he could help fly the ship instead.

His body slowly healed itself; his knees hurt less every day. But he never stopped feeling those waves of homesickness, or that burning hole inside him. Sometimes he felt overwhelmed with guilt that he was alive while his mother was not, that she'd sacrificed herself for something as worthless as his survival. Sometimes he felt furious at her for landing him on this Alien ship, and leaving him with so little explained.

Most of the time, though, he missed her horribly. It was so lonely without her. Mealtimes were the worst. If she'd been with him, they would surely have eaten together. Instead, he ate alone. While the Aliens had their own food, Mystica prepared what she called "Human food" for him. It had no flavor and smelled synthetic, but he was grateful she'd made the effort, and ate it up dutifully.

He slept alone too, on one of the hammocks in the main cabin. Fortunately, he didn't wake up naked again, surrounded by smoke and ashes. He shuddered when he thought about those things; he just couldn't make sense of them. He placed his faith in his father: he would be the one to explain it all. So Lucky did his best not to think about Captain Nox's warnings of *things* beyond the Wall. All he knew was that he had to get there, whatever it took.

And so time passed as they traveled through the stars: voyaging out of the Aries system, through Taurus, and past the twin suns of Gemini. He was hoping Bixa had forgotten about training when she shook him awake one morning.

"Boy," she said. "Come with me. It's time."

She strode off through the cloistered corridors. He staggered and stumbled after her; he still couldn't get used to walking on the curving floors. He was relieved when at last they reached a door — until he saw what was written on it.

At the top of the door, in big cheerful letters, it said: BIXA'S QUARTERS. Below, clearly added later, was the instruction: KEEP OUT. Finally, at the bottom, in livid black capitals: *THIS MEANS YOU.*

Lucky hesitated before this door, but Bixa flung it open, went in, and immediately touched the wall screen. It filled with vidpics of an Axxa singer: an intense-looking woman dressed in black, with curtains of long dark hair hanging over her face. She was rocking back and forth as she sang, her mouth wide open in a deafening banshee wail. She was making the loudest music Lucky had ever heard. Angry, raging music, with sounds like worlds ending: huge, violent, shattering sounds.

The rest of Bixa's cabin was dedicated to fighting. There were mats and weights and charts, as well as a small but impressive collection of weapons. Also a tattered punchbag, which showed every sign of having been hit very hard, very often.

Almost as an afterthought, there was a bed folded up against the wall, with some clothes strewn around it.

Bixa took up position on a mat and faced him, scowling.

She was the same height as Lucky, but he felt dwarfed by her ferocity, her focused stillness. She didn't even blink. She just watched him across the mat, like a lioness watching her prey. Then she said something he couldn't hear.

"What?" he asked.

"I said: are you ready?" she yelled over the earbleed din. And then she began to move. She moved in the most mesmerizing way. She flowed like a fish through water, like water itself—

—and Lucky stared at her in shock, recognizing the way his mother had moved—

—and Bixa hooked an arm around his throat and dragged him to the floor.

"Wait!" he gasped as he hit the ground. "What's that you're doing?"

Her fist stopped in midair, a millimeter from his nose.

He gaped up at her as she pulled her fist away and released him. But she didn't answer his question. "Your turn," was all she said.

The full horror of the situation hit him as he hauled himself up.

She was about to smash my face in! She's not holding back. Whatever she's doing, it's deadly serious. If I don't find some way to get through this, she's going to kill me.

Bixa took up position on the mat again and confronted him. Lucky looked away, shaking.

"I said: your turn," she repeated frostily.

What am I going to do?

On the vidscreen, the Axxa singer reached the climax of her song and hurled herself into the crowd.

It gave him an idea. *OK*, he thought. *You want to fight? Let's see how you like this.*

"*Yaaaaah!*" he screamed as he hurled himself at her like a madman.

He tackled her. Threw his arms around her middle. The momentum knocked her off balance, and he felt a moment of satisfaction —

— until he realized that he wasn't in control. He was accelerating, sailing through the air too fast — and Bixa — where was Bixa? Oh — she was coiled up beneath him, suspended in perfect balance — and totally in control. She was bringing her hooves up into his belly —

"*Nooooo!*" he screamed as she uncoiled her legs and flung him like a rocket at the wall. And it was the strangest thing. As he soared through the air, he thought he glimpsed the soles of her hooves. They didn't look anything like he expected. Not like animal hooves, more like some kind of metal, flashing silver in his eyes —

— but it was just a flash, the briefest glimpse, and —

— *SMASH!* He hit the far wall, hard, and slumped to the floor. The room spun around him. On the vidscreen, the crowd was applauding the Axxa singer. Their cheering echoed in his ears as he lay there, groaning, gazing up at the battered old punchbag.

Bixa turned off the vidscreen, and the applause stopped. She bounded across the cabin and stood over him, squinting down at his slumped form. Was she looking worried, or was he imagining it?

"I didn't break you, did I?" she said a little stiffly. "I didn't think you'd be so bad."

Despite his pain, Lucky found himself bristling. "Bad?"

"You're terrible. I've never seen anyone so terrible at fighting."

"Yeah? Well, I didn't ask for this! I don't even want to be here! Your stupid father forced me to train with you!"

"He's not my father!" snapped Bixa. Her needles flashed crimson, and she looked so fierce for a moment that Lucky had to look away. But quickly, her needles cooled. "Look, I'm not making fun of you," she said. "I'm just surprised. It's weird how bad you are. You don't know how to move properly or anything. You're so clumsy, it's like you don't even belong in that body."

Lucky's anger ebbed away at her words, because she was right. His whole life, that was exactly how he'd felt.

"So what?" he said.

"So have you always been this rubbish?"

"I guess so." He sighed. "Anything physical, I'm terrible. But what about you? Isn't it weird how *good* you are? Have you always been this good at fighting?"

She looked suspicious for a moment — and then a smile flashed across her face. It was the first time he'd seen her smile, and it was like seeing a comet in the night.

"Yeah," she said. "I was always good."

"How did you learn?"

"Taught myself." She shrugged. "Me and Frollix, we grew up in the Human worlds. Frollix might look big and scary, but he's not much use in a real fight, and they always seemed to happen, wherever we went. So I had to learn to defend myself."

"That must've been hard."

"At least I learned. Lots of Axxa never did. You should see how hard it is for them." She paused, and then jabbed the battered punchbag. "You don't know the Astral Martial Arts, do you?"

"The what?"

"The way I was fighting just now: Astral Martial Arts."

Lucky shook his head. "Of course not. Why would I? But I think my mother did. . . ."

"Yeah, I saw her. She was good. Where did she learn?"

"I wish I knew." He bit his lip. The more he found out about his mother, the less she seemed like the suburban mum he'd always known, with her baking trays and apron. "What is Astral Martial Arts, anyway?"

"Fighting like the stars!" said Bixa. "They're the most powerful thing there is, so if we want to be powerful, we should be like them." She took up position on the mat again. "We have twelve styles of combat, based on the twelve signs of the zodiac that were originally seen from Earth."

"You know about Earth?" said Lucky, surprised.

"'Course we do. That's where we started out from, too. We traveled farther than you Groundlings, we evolved a little on the way, but we all began on the same planet Earth. That's why the twelve star systems of this galaxy are named after those constellations. Do they really not teach you *anything* in those stupid Human schools?"

"Doesn't seem like it," Lucky had to admit.

"Well, if you know the signs of the zodiac, that's a start. There's a different fighting style for each sign, from Aries the Ram to Pisces the Fish." She began to move again — to move in that mesmerizing way, flowing like a fish through water . . .

"Is that Pisces?" guessed Lucky.

"See? You *do* know something. Now, get up and help me train."

"No!" he protested. "I don't know! I didn't even know my mother did, until — until — the Shadow Guards . . ." His words trailed away. It was too painful to say out loud. He closed his eyes, the hole in his heart burning with the memory of her loss.

All this time, Bixa didn't say a word. She was totally silent as the fire burned and burned in Lucky's heart.

At last, he opened his eyes again. And to his surprise, she stuck out a hand and helped him to his feet.

"Look." She sighed. "It's true that you're terrible, but I really need a training partner, and you're all I've got. You don't have to know anything; you just have to do what I tell you. And now that I know how bad you are, I'll try not to break you. Whaddaya say?"

"Bixa, I hate fighting," Lucky replied, shifting uncomfortably on the mat. "It's my least favorite thing ever. Imagine the thing you hate most —"

"OK, I get it! So here's the deal. You say you want to go to the War Zone to find your dad. But you don't know the first thing about it, do you? You don't even know what's out there! So . . . if you help me with my training, you might just get some answers."

110

Lucky's heart skipped a beat. "You'll help me?"

She shrugged. "I *might* answer your questions — if you help me with my training. Do we have a deal?"

He took a deep, deep breath. Braced himself.

"OK," he said at last. "We have a deal."

IX

The Wolf
Threatens
Each One of Us.

The Astraeus of
the Hearth Cannot
Protect Us from It

for It Shatters
Every Home. . . .

CHAPTER ELEVEN

"Hey, you guys!" called Frollix that evening. His eyes gleamed with blue fire as he surveyed the scene in Bixa's cabin. "Heard you were working out. How's it going?"

Lucky's body ached all over. He'd mainly been Bixa's punchbag, but somehow, he didn't mind. She was a fantastic fighter, fierce and proud, yet she never gloated; she just got on with it.

"Let's just say she's winning," he admitted.

Frollix grinned a huge grin. "Don't feel too bad. Bixa's the sharpest kid you ever met. Anything she puts her mind to, she's brilliant. OK, she can be a pain in the —"

"Anytime you wanna do more training, Frollix . . ." said Bixa, needles bristling.

Frollix held his hands up. "No way!" He laughed. "But if Lucky survived Astral Martial Arts — maybe it's time he came and had a meal with us?"

"Not a good idea," said Bixa quickly, to Lucky's relief. Lonely as he was, he didn't want to eat Alien food.

"C'mon!" boomed Frollix. "What can go wrong?" And before Lucky or Bixa could protest, he was leading them out of her quarters and back to the *Sunfire*'s main cabin.

Beneath its curving arches and vidscreens, Mystica stood at the stove, wearing her peacock-colored robe and a matching headscarf that covered her hair. Laid out before her were three large, steaming, covered tureens.

"Welcome, Lucky," she said. "I'm glad you're joining us. That's enough fighting for one day. Enough fighting for a lifetime. It's time to eat now."

He smiled nervously. He was hungry after training, but what was in those tureens?

"Oh, how about just a *bit* more fighting?" said Bixa, shaping into the style of Sagittarius the Archer. Frollix shadowed her, stretching his arms back into the posture, making his massive muscles ripple.

"You know what I think of all this violence," tutted Mystica. "Take no notice of them, Lucky. The Axxa have been peaceful for centuries. Our religion tells us that we are all connected. An injury to you is an injury to me."

"Yeah, just a shame the Shadow Guards don't believe that!" said Frollix. "Or the Axxa army!"

Mystica lifted a lid off a tureen and stirred its contents. Clouds of scented steam rose into the air. But still Lucky couldn't see what lay inside it. "That's enough, you two," said the old lady. "Where is the Captain?"

"I told him supper's ready," said Frollix, "but he said he's staying at the helm to watch for pirates. I told him there's nothing we can do if they decide to stop us, but he won't listen. So let's just eat without him. Sit yerself down, Lucky, and sample some of our cuisine!"

They sat cross-legged on the spherical silver seats around the table. With a flourish, Mystica opened the tureens. Lucky stared into them. And his hunger vanished as he saw what lay before him.

The first pot contained some kind of dark-green slop. The second contained slimy, wet-looking stuff; he had no idea what it was, but the word *intestines* came to mind. He hardly dared look at the third pot, because it seemed to be looking back at him.

No: it *was* looking back at him. Because it was full of eyeballs.

Eyeballs.

Lucky blanched. He felt faint. He'd heard about this, of course, but he'd never seen it in real life. And yet here it was. A steaming pot of eyeballs.

Frollix was already shoveling food into his dish and licking his lips. But Lucky couldn't move. There were eyeballs, staring at him! He gazed back at them in helpless horror.

"Mystica!" hissed Bixa.

"What, my dear?" said the old lady, tucking in.

Bixa looked embarrassed. Her needles had gone dark red, puce, almost like they were blushing. "Can't you give him some of that Human stuff? The Groundlings think our food's disgusting; it was stupid to ask him to eat with us. . . ."

Her words snapped Lucky out of his daze. He shook his head, a little too vigorously. "Oh no — it looks — uh — it looks great!" he made himself say. "Thank you."

Gingerly, he poured a spoonful of green slop into his dish; it looked the least revolting. There was no way — no way in all the galaxy — he was ever eating eyeballs.

"Saving the best till last, kid?" said Frollix, winking his approval.

"You're very polite, Lucky," said Mystica. She plucked an eyeball from the pot and dropped it into her mouth. "But truly, there's no need. Just dive in." Lip-smacking noises followed as she swallowed the eyeball whole and sighed with pleasure.

Lucky glanced at Bixa. She was biting her nails; she looked mortified. Her needles were black now, and almost completely pulled back, burrowing into her hair like they were trying to disappear.

Somehow, he didn't like the idea that his presence could make her embarrassed about her own food. He wanted to make the embarrassment go away. But there was only one way to do that.

"Better hurry!" said Frollix, popping an eyeball into his mouth.

Bixa shook her head. She looked miserable. "You don't have to if you don't want to," she said in a low growl. "I know how you Groundlings think."

Lucky forced himself to reach forward and pick up an eyeball. It was deeply unpleasant to touch. Slimy wet and gelid, just as he feared. But now that he'd started, he had to see it through.

"Who are you calling a Groundling?" he said defiantly as he popped the eyeball into his mouth.

And it tasted . . . amazing.

Sweet. Soft. Spangly as snow, the flavors swirled around his tongue. The only thing he'd ever had like it was ice cream. But this was even better. He laughed as the eyeball went fizzing down his throat, and he reached at once for another.

"'Course, they're not actual eyeballs!" said Frollix, with a grin. "We just make 'em like that so Groundlings won't eat 'em all! Good, huh?"

"They're better than good," said Lucky. "They're incredible!"

Mystica smiled proudly. "Things don't always taste how they look—eh, Lucky?"

"You really like them?" said Bixa, looking shocked.

"Oh, yeah!" he said as he gobbled the second eyeball. And seeing that he meant it, Bixa's face lit up with warmth and her needles glowed a happy neon pink.

"Well. That's OK, then," she said. "But don't think you can eat them all, just 'cos it's your first time!" She dived into the bowl, her long fingers scooping up eyeballs faster than he could see. He looked at her, and the warmth in her face seemed to spread across his own.

Behind her, on the vidscreens, the images of the Twelve Astraeus were glowing like stained glass. Lucky gazed up at them. *They're so beautiful,* he thought. *And these Aliens— these Axxa—well, maybe my mother wasn't so crazy to get a ride with them.*

"So, Lucky," said Bixa, "we made a deal. I promised you some answers, right?"

He nodded. "I just want to know . . . what's out there, in the War Zone? What was the Captain warning me about?"

Bixa glanced at Mystica before replying. "There are . . . rumors," she said. "But we're not sure what they mean. See, we came to the Human worlds years ago, searching for a peaceful life." She paused. "Never did find it."

"The problem," said Frollix, "is it's real hard to get

119

reliable news through the Spacewall. And it's even harder to get it from our home system, Aquarius, 'cos it's under a Human blockade. We have family back there, and this past year, we haven't heard a word from them. All we've heard is . . . *rumors.*" He scratched the base of his horns. "Weird stories about a wolf that eats the stars —"

"A wolf?" said Lucky. A shiver ran through him. "How can a wolf eat the stars?"

"We don't know," said Bixa in a low voice. "But we do know the stars are scared."

Lucky bit down on his lip. He remembered that vision he'd seen in the astrolabe: those scorching faces, staring back at him. "You — you talk about the stars as if they're alive . . ."

"They *are* alive."

He gaped at her. Surely she couldn't mean it? "Is it true you worship the stars?" he asked.

Frollix laughed. "Worship the stars!" he scoffed, taking another eyeball. "What a typical Groundling idea! No, 'course we don't worship the stars. But we *love* the stars. Without them, there'd be nothing, right? So we've got this greeting: *From the stars we all came . . .*"

". . . *and to the stars we return,*" said Lucky, completing the phrase he'd heard his mother and Frollix exchange when they first met.

"That's it! You learn quick, for a Groundling! Most Humans are completely ignorant about the stars!"

"Hey!" protested Lucky. "That's not true. We have advanced science. We go from star to star, all over the galaxy —"

Bixa rolled her eyes. "You think you know everything

120

with your science? There's more going on in the galaxy than your moonbrained science can imagine! So many things have been forgotten; so much secret knowledge has been lost —"

Mystica coughed. "Bixa. Enough. The Humans have their beliefs too, and we should respect them. Please don't take offense, Lucky. Have another eyeball —"

A siren cut through the cabin. Captain Nox's voice crackled on the comm.

"Frollix," he called, "I need you in the cockpit, *now*. There's a Skyhawk on our tail."

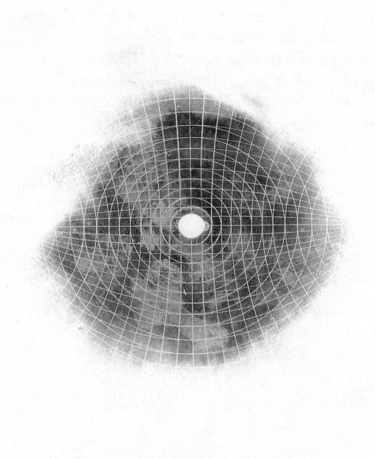

CHAPTER TWELVE

"What's a Skyhawk?" said Lucky over the wailing siren.

"The Axxa army's ships!" yelped Frollix. "When the Spacewall went up, a bunch of 'em got trapped this side of it. They survive by raiding anyone that gets in their way. They're pirates!" He scrambled away to join the Captain in the cockpit.

Mystica had gone very pale. She shuffled out of the cabin, whispering something; perhaps a prayer of some kind. Lucky couldn't help noticing how slowly and awkwardly she moved, how frail her body seemed.

"Is she OK?" he asked Bixa. The spangly flavor of the eyeballs was fading fast.

"None of your business," she snapped, pulling on her body armor, with the glitter and fur. "Better strap up. If this really is a Skyhawk, we're in trouble."

Lucky strapped himself into his seat as Bixa tapped on the vidscreens. The images of the Twelve Astraeus dissolved, and the cabin walls filled with fragmentary glimpses of the view outside again.

Through a blizzard of static, he could just make out a faraway shape. It was closing in fast. With its viciously curved wings, it looked like a bird of prey, swooping out of the sky.

"It's a Skyhawk, all right," breathed Bixa as the *Sunfire* pitched violently, first to one side, then the other, trying to get away. But slowly, inexorably, the Skyhawk grew bigger on the vidscreens.

"Can't we go faster?" Lucky asked, his chest tightening as if there was rope tied around it.

"No, we can't. And see their cannon? If they get much closer, they'll blow us out of the sky."

"Can't we shoot back?"

Bixa shook her head. "The *Sunfire* has no guns," she said.

"What?"

"I told the Captain a hundred times we need to defend ourselves, but he never listens."

"Attention, unknown craft!" a harsh voice crackled on the comm. "We have you in our sights. Identify yourselves."

"We're peaceful civilians," Captain Nox's voice replied. "We have no weapons, and we have no quarrel with you. *From the stars we all came—*"

"By the authority of King Theobroma and the Axxa army," growled the voice, "drop your Dark Matter drive and prepare to be boarded!" The voice crackled off.

Bixa's needles went pale, as they had before the Shadow Guards. She didn't look like a fierce, proud warrior anymore. She just looked scared.

The motion of the ship slowed as the *Sunfire* came to a halt, stationary in space. The Skyhawk drew up alongside them, cannon jutting from its wings like claws.

"Those pirates are coming aboard," called Captain Nox on the comm. "Bixa, hide the Human. We're dead if they see him. I'll do my best to talk our way out of this, but they absolutely must not find him."

Lucky's stomach was in knots. "But why would they do this to you?" he said. "You're Axxa, just like they are —"

"Makes no difference," said Bixa. "If you're not part of their army, they won't think twice about killing you, whoever you are. And if you're an Axxa harboring Humans . . ." She stood up, needles burrowing into her hair. "Come on. Let's get you out of sight."

She rushed him belowdecks, into the ship's hold. He hoped she was taking him to some sort of secret compartment. But as she led him to the small metal cubicle where he'd already spent many miserable hours, he realized that this was where she really proposed to hide him: in the *Sunfire*'s toilet.

"But why here?" he cried.

"Because it's the best we've got," said Bixa, opening the door. "We're civilians — this isn't a warship."

Lucky looked at the fold-down metal seat. It was cold and dark in there, and despite all his efforts to keep it clean, it did not smell inviting at the best of times.

"Get in," she urged. "And keep your mouth shut. If they find you, we're finished."

Lucky shuddered and crawled into the toilet. The metal door groaned as he pulled it shut and locked it from inside. He heard Bixa walk away.

He was alone in the dark.

At first, he was just uncomfortable. But then he heard the pirates boarding the *Sunfire*, heard voices raised in argument, and he was afraid.

"... *no threat to you, we have nothing that you need —*"

"*Is that right, old man? I reckon we could use your ship. Let's see what we've got . . .*"

The pirates weren't going away. Even Captain Nox was powerless to stop them. Lucky heard compartments and cabins being opened up as they searched the ship.

And now his mouth grew dry and his heart pounded in his ears, because he could hear footsteps coming closer, down through the decks, growing louder and louder.

He breathed deep. *If these pirates find me, what am I going to do? Fight them? Me?*

He heard their voices as they entered the hold. Harsh, hard voices.

Coming closer.

And closer.

The pounding of his heart would surely give him away, it was so loud in his ears.

"Hold it," said a voice, very close indeed. "What's in here?"

The footsteps stopped, right outside the cubicle. Lucky had never felt so trapped.

The door rattled.

"It's locked," said the voice.

"They must be hiding something. Smash it down."

Lucky panicked and kicked the door open. Two huge horned Axxa stood there, staring at him with surprise in their fiery red eyes. A third hung back behind them in the

126

shadows. Lucky rushed out at them in desperation, hoping to slip through the gaps and get away, somehow.

Big mistake. One of the pirates blocked him easily; it was like running into solid iron. The pirate lifted him off his feet and flung him at the wall.

SLAM! The impact knocked all the fight out of him. Lucky sank to the ground, head spinning, body screaming with pain.

The pirates towered over him. They all wore bulky armor and had deadly-looking cannon by their sides. They were very different from the *Sunfire* crew. They looked like battle-hardened bruisers, with metal piercings in their faces and brandings on their arms.

"This scrawny runt's one of *them!*" said the first pirate. "Human scum, on an Axxa ship." He cracked his knuckles. It sounded like bones breaking.

The second pirate — smaller, but sharper-eyed — scratched the base of his horns. "Why would a Human be on an Axxa ship? And why would they be hiding him?"

"I — I —" stammered Lucky, backing against the wall. It felt so cold against his hands.

"Maybe he's a peaceful Human," mused the second pirate. "I heard there's peaceful Humans."

"The only peaceful Human's a dead Human!" snarled the first one.

"Please," begged Lucky. *"From the stars we all came —"*

"Don't you dare say those words!" raged the first pirate, horns glinting. "No one believes that anymore — not since you sent your wolf to eat the stars. Not since *this!*"

He gestured at the third pirate, behind him in the

shadows. And it was only now that Lucky saw this Alien clearly. There was something very strange about him. Where the other two had flaming red eyes, there was no fire in his eyes at all. They looked burned out, empty, like black holes in the sky. He was staring straight ahead, but his gaze wasn't focused on anything Lucky could see.

Then the third pirate spoke, in a broken-sounding voice that chilled Lucky to the core. "Nothing matters," he croaked. "Nothing matters anymore."

The first pirate stamped a cloven hoof in fury, and the metal floor rang out. "You'll pay for what you've done, you Human scum! And after we've ripped you limb from limb, we'll execute those treacherous Human-lovers who harbored you, and take this ship for our own!"

He advanced on Lucky. Eyes full of burning murder. Teeth bared with righteous rage.

"No—please no!" Lucky tried to back away, but there was nowhere left to go.

The pirate reached for him with a huge hand. It closed around his neck, pinning him to the wall. And then it tightened like a band of steel, crushing air from his windpipe.

Choking. He was choking.

Oh, why can't I fight like Bixa? he thought desperately. *I wish I had power—anything to fight back with, defend myself . . .*

Can't move. Can't breathe.

No air.

Lucky's eyes closed.

But as everything started to go dark, he thought he heard something, in his mind.

A small, soft, silvery sound, like the chime of a far-away bell.

It was calling to him.

And something inside him responded to its call.

At the center of his being, a spark of power flared into life. It surged through his body, rising toward the surface of his skin.

He opened his eyes — and saw his fingertips begin to shine.

The pirate released him and staggered back. Lucky gulped in the air, clinging on to life, and stared at his hands in shock. Light was pouring out of them. And the power was pulsing inside him as it rose and swelled and grew.

"It — it's like something from the legends," whispered one of the pirates.

"Shoot him!" roared the first one.

And that was when Lucky began to burn. He screamed in horror as a jet of fire flashed out of his own fingers. The pirate tried to move away, but the fire engulfed his body and scorched it all away. And then there was no pirate standing there; just a swirling column of smoke and ashes.

The second pirate drew his weapon. Aimed it straight at Lucky's face — and another blast of flame exploded from Lucky's hands. It torched the Alien where he stood. Consumed him in its blazes.

Searing pain was ripping through Lucky. His fingertips felt raw. He could smell something like sulfur, filling his senses, overwhelming his mind. But still the light was flooding from his hands, his head, his heart. And the fire was streaming from him in every direction, igniting everything it touched.

He tried to restrain it, but he could not prevent it from obliterating the third and final pirate.

All that remained of them now was smoke and ashes. Yet still the power was not finished. It was growing, growing: glowing brighter all the time. Lucky felt sure it would destroy him if he didn't control it. It would burn through his own body and his brain, and then the ship's walls, and then it would kill everyone. . . .

What's happening? This is like a nightmare!

He fought with all his might to pull it back inside him. He tried desperately to rein it in.

His whole body was shaking. It felt like the surface of his brain was boiling. Like his head was splitting under the strain, erupting, breaking open as arcs of blinding pain shot across his face, bigger and brighter than any body could contain.

His eyes were on fire. From his nose and mouth and ears, the light was bleeding out, and Lucky wanted only to hide from it—but he couldn't, because it was inside him; it *was* him. He was the fire, and the light, and the burning in his brain . . .

I'm going to break under this pressure! I can't take any more! But I have to stop it. Somehow, I have to—

The blood drained from his head, the ground rushed up to his face, and he fainted, right there on the floor.

VIII

The Wolf Annihilates Minds,

The Astraeus of Wisdom Has No Answer

for the Darkness
Is Too Deep. . . .

CHAPTER THIRTEEN

Lucky woke up screaming.

"It's all right." A gentle voice spoke above him. "It's all right, Lucky."

He opened his eyes. He was back in the *Sunfire*'s main cabin. The crew were all staring at him. But there was no fire streaming from his fingers. No light pouring from his heart.

It's gone, he thought. *I'm alive. Somehow, I survived.*

"You've been unconscious for so long," said Mystica. "We were worried."

He took a huge glug of air into his lungs. He felt exhausted. His head, his hands, his whole body ached. He could still feel that awful pain, shooting across his skull, splitting open his brain —

— and then he realized that he was naked. Someone had put a silver blanket over him, but underneath it, he was completely naked. And covered in ash. Again.

His skin began to crawl. "Where are the pirates?" he asked. "What happened to them?"

"It would seem," said Captain Nox, horns glinting, "that you destroyed them."

"Nothing left of them but ashes!" said Bixa. She looked impressed. "Now, a blaster might be able to do that, at close range — but their weapons were all melted too. So how did you do it?"

"I — I don't know," said Lucky, heart hammering in his chest. How could he tell them? He'd killed three people and brought the whole ship into danger — not just from the pirates, but from himself. He could've killed them all! No wonder his mother had looked so scared when she found his burned sheet. No wonder she'd made him promise never to tell.

But Mystica was staring at him in that strange way again, as though she could see right into his brain. "We don't normally approve of violence, as you know," she said. "But in this case, we owe you our thanks, Lucky."

"You're not angry with me?"

"'Course not!" said Bixa. "You did a good job. I don't think even I could've done it that well. So why don't you just tell us how you did it? C'mon, you're my training partner: don't hold out on me."

"I'm not holding out," he said. "I just . . . don't . . ."

"What? You think stupid eyeball-eating Aliens can't understand you? Is that it?"

Lucky looked down, shamed by her words. He dreaded what might happen when they learned the truth. But what choice was there? He couldn't keep this to himself anymore; it had gone too far.

He took a deep, deep breath — and then he told them everything he knew.

And to his surprise, it was a relief to say it all out loud.

He'd thought it would sound crazy, but they didn't question it or get angry. They just listened, very quietly.

"I see it now," said Mystica when he was finished. "There are many mysteries here, but one thing is clear to me. What happened with those pirates was not your fault. You destroyed them because they left you no choice."

"But I didn't want to *destroy* them!" he said, choking at the memory. "I didn't even know I could do that!" He bit his lip. "What's wrong with me, Mystica? What's going on?"

"It appears you have some kind of power," she replied. "Some kind of gift."

"Gift?" He shut his eyes. "It doesn't feel like a gift. It feels more like a curse. It feels . . ." He couldn't bring himself to say the word *evil* out loud.

He pulled the blanket tight around himself and tried to stand up. He was unsteady. His legs were weak; every part of him felt raw. Bixa reached out and gave him a hand, but there was a strange expression on her face.

"What?" he said. "What is it?"

"Nothing," said Bixa. Her voice was edgy, her needles an uncertain tawny shade. "It's just . . . you're still my training partner, right?"

"Of course I am!"

"I still get to kick your ass, even though you've got some kind of weirdo power now?"

"Weirdo power?" Lucky gaped at her. "Bixa, please —"

"Hah!" She grinned and stuck her tongue out at him. "You better get dressed, or I'll kick your naked ass right now!"

And somehow, he couldn't help smiling back. He didn't

mind her rudeness. It made everything seem more normal, somehow.

He reached for his kitbag and pulled some new clothes on. Thankfully his mother had packed plenty; she must've known he'd be needing them. How he wished he could talk to her, just once more. She could make sense of this mind-bending mystery. She would make it all OK.

But he was alone with the mystery. Completely alone.

"You are not alone," said Mystica softly, startling him. "Our legends tell of many people who had gifts like yours. It's our belief that these gifts come from the stars. The stars are the source of all power, and sometimes they allow people to channel that power. The stars work through us, you see, in ways we do not always understand."

Lucky shivered. "How do you know that?"

"Because . . . some such people are still alive today." Her eyes glowed gold as she looked deep inside him and seemed to come to a decision. "You have trusted me with your secret, Lucky. Now I will trust you with mine. For I, like you, have such a gift." She drew herself up, very grand and proud. "I am a Startalker," she said.

The inside of his scalp felt like it was tingling. "What's a Startalker?"

"Someone who is connected to a star," said Mystica. "If you are a Startalker, you feel everything your star feels. Your destinies are linked. You share your lives. You call to each other, you hear each other —"

"Stars can *call*?" Lucky felt hot and cold at the same time, sweaty and shivery at once. He felt like he was standing on the edge of something huge.

"Of course. Your Human science doesn't recognize it, but the stars have spirits; they have intelligence. There is nothing they cannot do. And because everything came from the stars, they know the truth of all things. So we Startalkers feel the truth of any situation. You cannot hide anything from a Startalker."

"Can you read people's minds?" He gulped.

"Not exactly." Mystica looked up at the ceiling, which vaulted high above them. "As the stars call across the immensities of space — like great whales singing in the oceans deep, or bells chiming out, like silver in the black — we hear their songs, and we feel the truth inside ourselves. And we cannot help but speak it, even if it makes things difficult. . . ." She peered at him. "What is it, Lucky? Why are you looking at me like that?"

Her words had stirred something in his mind. A memory, buried at the edge of his consciousness. Just before he'd burned the pirates, he'd heard something. A small, soft, silvery sound, like the chime of a faraway bell.

He'd heard that sound before, hadn't he? It was the sound of the stars, singing in his dreams. The dreams had always slipped away by morning. But now the memories were flooding back to him.

"I — I think I might've heard the stars too," he stammered.

Mystica peered into his eyes. "Indeed? What do they sing to you?"

"I'm not sure. I can't understand the words." A shudder ran through him as he remembered the dreams — and then recalled those scorching faces, staring back at him in the astrolabe. "So . . . are there other Startalkers?" he asked Mystica.

"As many as there are stars," she said. "In ancient days, we were known by different names. Soothsayers. Prophets. We were high priests, guardians of truth and destiny, watchers over worlds. But some Startalkers have always had special responsibilities, above and beyond the rest. In our time, those duties fall to the Startalkers connected to the three brightest stars of this galaxy: Scorpio, Capricorn, and Aquarius. Each of us has a different power, a different kind of knowledge. There is the Startalker of the Present, the Startalker of the Past, and the Startalker of the Future."

"You're one of them?"

"I am the Startalker of the Present," said Mystica. "I feel what is happening right now, in this moment. This is my domain."

"And . . . what about me?" said Lucky, every hair on his body prickling. "Do I have the same power as you? Am I a Startalker?"

She stroked her chin. "Well, I know who the Startalkers of the Past and Future are, and you are certainly not one of them. Besides, I never heard of a Startalker who burst into flames. But these are not ordinary times. Anything is possible. You may be a new kind of Startalker: one we have not seen before." She glanced at Bixa and Frollix; they both looked away. "Be sure of one thing, though. Having a gift like this is never easy. It is a huge responsibility — and not everyone who has such powers wants them."

Bixa's needles darkened at her words. Frollix just laughed.

"Wait a minute," said Lucky. "Are you saying Frollix and Bixa are Startalkers too?"

"I am *not* a Startalker," muttered Bixa.

"But you will be, one day," said Mystica. Her face wrinkled with lines of pain. "I won't be here forever, you know. When I am gone, you will take my place, and when the Professor goes, Frollix will succeed him. You've always known this, yet neither of you will accept your power — constantly fighting, taking nothing seriously —"

"C'mon, Mystica!" drawled Frollix, putting his hooves up on the table. "Can you imagine me being all wise and stuff? It ain't never gonna happen!"

"Not if you don't grow up and take responsibility."

"But we don't want that responsibility," said Bixa. "We never asked for it."

"I understand your feelings, my dear, much better than you might imagine," replied the old lady. "But alas, we do not always get a choice."

"*Alas?*" snorted Frollix. "You Startalkers were almost wiped out by your own people! Does that sound like something anyone would choose?"

There was an awkward, painful silence. Then Mystica sighed wearily.

"Frollix is right about one thing," she told Lucky. "With the coming of war, it became dangerous to be a Startalker. So we went into exile, scattered across space, and hid ourselves away. That's why this is a secret — and why you must keep it. But do you understand now? You are not the only one with secrets and gifts. Far from it. Here on this ship, you are not alone."

He stared at each of them in turn. *Not alone.* The words comforted him a little. "So what do you think I should do?" he asked her.

"I cannot tell you what to do. Others may have their opinions, but only you can know for sure. So I think you need to learn more about this gift of yours before you make any decisions." She coughed: a painful fit that shook her whole body. She drew her furs close around her and adjusted her headscarf. "Does anyone else know about your powers?" she managed to say at last.

"My mother knew. She said my father warned her it was going to happen — so he must know too."

"Then you were right to go looking for him," said Mystica. "And you must keep looking until you find him, for his knowledge may hold the key." She glanced at Captain Nox. "We've made good time; we're near the outskirts of the Leo system now. I can take you to see the Professor and get your astrolabe repaired."

"Oh — thank you!" said Lucky. "Thank you so much!"

But Captain Nox was scowling. "Mystica, I've done what you asked and brought us here, but I will not let you run such risks. You're not well enough to go out onto a dangerous planet. You're staying on the ship — and I'm staying to look after you."

Lucky peered at her. She did seem very frail and weak. For all the bright colors of her clothes, her skin was pale, almost translucent. "Are you OK, Mystica?" he asked.

"I am . . . *fine.*" She smiled. "I would love to come with you, for the man you need to see is my old comrade, the Startalker of the Past, and I have not seen him for many years. But . . . perhaps the Captain is right." She turned to Frollix and Bixa. "You two must do it. Take Lucky to see the Professor. And invite my comrade back to the ship, while you're there. I suspect he may wish to travel with us for a while."

Nox stared at Frollix and Bixa. He seemed full of doubts. "Can you two take this responsibility seriously?" he asked them. "For once in your lives, can you stay out of trouble? Can you keep the boy away from danger?"

"Oh, from what I saw of those pirates, he can look after himself!" Frollix grinned. "But sure — I'll be your body-guard, Lucky." He flexed his rippling muscles and proudly pulled on his coat of liquid metal. "Don't worry, kid: you'll be safe with me!"

"Yeah, right," said Bixa, needles bristling. "We all know who's going to look after the pair of you."

"This is no joke," said the Captain, his great horns glinting. "If those pirates showed us anything, it's that a Human traveling with Axxa is bound to attract attention. The Shadow Guards will be out in force after the bombing of Aries One —"

"Shadow Guards?" Lucky gulped.

"Naturally. And what are we going to do if they find him and rip his brainscan?"

"We'll make him one of us, of course." Mystica sighed. "We'll give him horns. We'll give him hooves. We'll make his eyes burn."

"You'll do . . . *what*?" said Lucky.

He looked around at the others. But it was as if Mystica had dropped a stone into the cabin. All conversation stopped

143

dead at her words. Bixa and Frollix both turned away, their faces ashen.

At last, Nox stood up, his face like thunder. "Do whatever you must," he said darkly. "Frollix, come with me to the cockpit. Our Startalker has spoken. Let's get this ship to Leo Five."

CHAPTER FOURTEEN

Beneath the silver arches of the *Sunfire*'s main cabin, Mystica rummaged in a storage compartment. She pulled out some fabric, then hobbled up behind Lucky and tugged at his hair, hard.

"Hey!" he yelped. "What are you doing?"

"Please, calm yourself," she said. "Have we not begun to trust each other, you and I? Now, hold still. This won't hurt a bit."

She began to braid his hair, plait over plait, lock over lock.

"I can't believe you're doing this," said Bixa in a low voice.

"Why not?" murmured the old lady as she worked. "His hair is long enough. He can borrow your boots; you're about the same size, and you've got another pair, haven't you? And I still have Jonathan's old lenses, you know. He can use them."

Their talk made Lucky nervous. What exactly *was* Mystica doing to him? And who was this Jonathan she'd mentioned?

It was so hard to hold still as the old lady braided his hair, working it up into two great strands. It didn't hurt, but it felt tight and itchy across his scalp. It felt even more uncomfortable when she started to wrap the braids above his head in velvet fabric, twining silver thread around them. Velvet and thread — just like he'd seen on the Captain's horns, and Frollix's . . .

"You're making a disguise for me, aren't you?" he said. "You're making my hair look like horns!"

"No," she replied, twisting the threads up tight. "I am making your hair *into* horns."

"Huh?" He blinked. "You don't mean . . . that's what Axxa horns are really made of? Hair?"

"Just hair," said Mystica. She snipped the threads, and tied them off. "It's the traditional style for men; it's a great dishonor to be seen without your horns. Women wear their hair differently. Some have it up; some have it down. And then there's Bixa, only Bixa, who has those ugly needles —"

"I need them," protested Bixa. "I couldn't defend us without them."

Lucky's mind was reeling. "But why would anyone shape their hair into horns?" he asked, struggling to understand. "Don't you know it looks like the devil?"

"The horns point up at the stars," said Mystica simply. "They remind us where we all came from — and where we all return."

"And we're not gonna change it just 'cos some Groundlings don't like it," added Bixa.

"Oh." He looked over at her. "So where are these boots I'm supposed to borrow from you?" He couldn't imagine boots that would fit over her hooves.

"*These* boots," muttered Bixa. She reached down and hoisted up her trousers. She touched the side of her leg, and then slowly, carefully, pulled at one of her hooves. She pulled and pulled and pulled, until the hoof slid off her leg, revealing a foot—

—a bare foot, with five long, slender toes—

"You've got *feet*?" gasped Lucky.

"Mm-hmm," said Bixa as she pulled the other hoof off and put it down by the first.

He stared at it, stunned. There was a metallic sole along the bottom: the metal he'd glimpsed when they were doing Astral Martial Arts. Above the sole was an area shaped like a hoof, big enough for a foot to fit inside. It led up to a perfectly molded ankle, calf, knee—but then there was an opening above the knee, where the whole thing ended.

Boots. They were massive, skin-tight, thigh-high boots. Not hooves at all.

"But I thought—"

"You thought we all had hooves, didn't you?" scoffed Bixa. "You Groundlings: you'll believe anything! How could we have hands up top but hooves below? It doesn't even make sense!"

Lucky scratched his head at the base of his new horns. His mental picture of the Axxa was changing so fast that he felt dizzy. "Why don't more people—more *Humans*—know about this?"

"Perhaps it suits them not to know." Mystica shrugged. "People have a way of seeing what they expect to see. Not what is actually there."

"OK . . ." he said, trying to think his way into the situation. "So let me guess. Your fiery eyes are just contact lenses, right?"

"No," said Bixa. "Our eyes are real. They're the one big evolutionary difference between us. Ours are adapted for space travel, so they're sensitive to a wider spectrum of light."

"Oh? So — um — when Mystica said she was going to make my eyes burn —"

Bixa shook her head and turned away.

"Never you mind," said Mystica quietly. She rummaged in the compartment again and pulled out a tarnished silver box. "Of course, we can't change anything inside you, Lucky," she said, opening the box and fishing out a pair of purple contact lenses, "but these will make you look like one of us on the surface — and they'll expand your vision a little too. Don't worry, dear: you're not the first Human who needed to pass as Axxa."

Lucky tried not to blink as she placed the soft lenses onto the surface of his eyes.

"There," said Mystica. "You won't even notice them, now that they're in. Now put on Bixa's boots."

He glanced at the hooves and then at Bixa. She wouldn't meet his gaze.

"Go on," said Mystica. "Don't be shy."

Very reluctantly, he pulled them on, one at a time. It felt so strange. They were enormous and clumpy; he was bound to trip over his own feet in them. "Are you sure about this?" he said. "They're a little . . . big . . ."

"Oh, yeah?" snapped Bixa. "Stand up and see what happens!"

He did — and to his amazement, the hooves fit around his feet perfectly. They seemed to adjust to his shape, his posture, his movements — almost as if they were intelligent.

He took a step forward, and it was as if his feet suddenly had power steering. They were so well cushioned, they made him feel ten feet tall.

He grinned. *In boots like these,* he thought, *I could even climb a mountain!* "They're so comfortable," he marveled, bouncing up and down.

"'Course they are," said Bixa. "Axxa technology. They adapt to their owner and their environment, to give you the best footing. Now that you've got a pair of your own, you might even stop falling over every time you walk down a corridor." She inspected him critically and sighed. "Look, if we're really gonna do this, then you need one more thing."

She tapped the side of a column. It opened to reveal a hidden rack of gear, from which she pulled a silver coat. Long, shiny, shimmery, it was like wings of liquid metal. Just like the ones they wore.

"Seriously?" said Lucky. "For me?"

"Your very own space traveler's coat," she said. "Like the boots, it adapts to its environment. Waterproof, windproof — and totally fireproof, of course."

Lucky ran his fingers across the sleeve. It felt cool and smooth, like the surface of his astrolabe. He pulled it on and felt it billow out behind him. "It's amazing," he said.

Bixa pulled on her own coat and swirled it proudly around herself. "Yeah, and we were wearing these when you Groundlings were running around naked in the trees. . . ." She snorted. "Though some of you still do, from time to time!"

Lucky was too thrilled with the coat to rise to the bait. It made him feel different: no longer the boy who'd grown up on a little moon, knowing nothing of the galaxy. He felt like a space traveler now. Almost like part of a starship crew.

"Well, boy?" asked Mystica. "What do you say?"

"Thank you! Your clothes are . . . wonderful."

The old lady beamed with pride. She touched the column again, turning its surface into a silver mirror. "Have a look and see how wonderful," she said.

Lucky stared into the mirror — and saw a reflection so disturbing, it stopped him dead in his tracks.

He still looked like himself, with all the same features, but it was as if he'd been born Axxa instead of Human. He had horns that pointed up at the sky, huge black cloven hooves, and violet eyes of flame.

It was the very image of Aliens that he'd grown up hating and fearing. The enemy, staring back at him with his own face.

"Attention, everyone," came Captain Nox's voice on the comm. "We are now approaching Leo Five. Strap up tight for landing."

Lucky looked away from the mirror to the vidscreens, where Bixa was trying to get a clear image of the view outside — and found himself staring at something even more disturbing.

Through crackling static, a solar system was coming into view. At its center was a giant golden star, with several planets orbiting around it. The largest was the fifth world out: Leo Five. It was golden too, its continents all dotted with points of light, like miniature constellations. It seemed to be a world of plenty, shining under its sun.

But farther away, in the far distance, green fire filled

the blackness of space. Completely filled it. Lucky could see nothing beyond it whatsoever. It was as if space itself ended in a wall of fire.

At first he thought it must be interference on the vidscreens, like the static. But it seemed almost solid: a barrier beyond which he couldn't imagine passing.

Maybe it's these contact lenses, he thought, *making space look weird.* He squinted at the vidscreens from another angle, but still the green fire was there, flashing with electric threat. "What is that?" he asked.

Mystica turned to look and adjusted her headscarf anxiously. "Ah. Yes. You can see it now: your government's proudest achievement. The Spacewall."

Lucky gaped at it. He'd never been this near to the Spacewall, never imagined how uncanny it would really look. "How am I ever going to get through *that*?" he said under his breath.

"Don't you fret," said Mystica. She made a final adjustment to his horns, then stepped back to inspect him again. A smile as warm as sunrise spread across her face. "You're one of us now. We will take care of you."

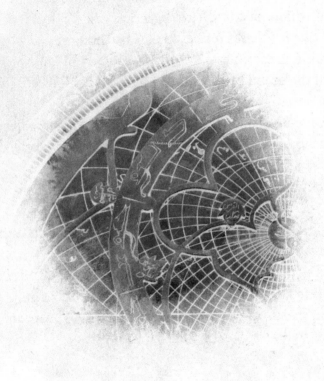

CHAPTER FIFTEEN

Lucky, Bixa, and Frollix rode out on the *Sunfire's* ship-to-shore cycle: a gleaming chrome vehicle designed for short journeys across land, air, and space. Lucky sat at the back, clutching his father's astrolabe. Bixa sat in the middle. At the front, Frollix gripped the high handlebars, revving the engine, proudly driving them onto the surface of the world.

They came in to Leo Five out of the midday sun. Around them, starships rose and fell in orderly lines, their wings gleaming in the golden light. On the comm, they could hear subspace stations full of chatter, the crackle and buzz of communications, the nonstop whirl of activity in the world below.

It was a relief to get going. After everything Lucky had been through, it felt good to breathe fresh air again, to feel wind on his skin and sunlight on his face. He drank in the sights and sounds eagerly, relishing his first new world.

And Leo Five looked dazzling. The streets were drenched in rich golden light and lined with tall buildings all lit up from within. Between them, the skyline was spiked by countless cranes, building even bigger structures. Words and pictures scrolled across their walls. Advertisements flashed by on enormous vidscreens, faster than Lucky could read. Cycles and aircars whooshed past them as they drove, an electric blur of motion, their lights like one continuous stream of flame.

This was the height of Human wealth, and it made the moon he'd grown up on look like a toy town. It was astonishing to see all that energy burning in those buildings, powering this civilization.

"Welcome to Leo!" whooped Frollix. "I love this place!"

But as they entered the city center, Lucky started to see signs that beneath the dazzle of lights and the ceaseless buzz, Leo Five was more troubled than it first appeared.

He noticed a group of down-and-out Humans on a street corner. Some were huddled around a fire. Others were slumped on the sidewalk. But their eyes were totally empty, like that Axxa pirate he'd seen.

"What's wrong with those people?" he asked as a cloud crossed the face of the sun.

Frollix peered at them. "Looks like they've got the Living Death," he said. "It's a new thing that's spreading 'cross the galaxy. See their eyes? That million-mile stare? That's the first symptom. They stare and stare, but no one knows what they're looking at. They stop caring about anything; it's like all the life gets sucked out of them."

"What causes it?" asked Lucky with a shiver.

"It's a Human plot, of course," said Frollix. "Everyone knows that!"

"But then — why would Humans have it too?"

154

"Truth is, no one knows much about the Living Death," said Bixa. "No one really knows where it came from, or how to cure it. But it didn't exist before the War, so it must be your government's doing. What else could it be?"

They drove on, more quiet now. But on the next corner, a man in a crumpled suit was shouting into a megaphone. "The End Times are here!" he proclaimed through his crackly loudspeaker. "The End of All Worlds! Repent and be saved — the Devil himself walks among us!"

The man looked up and saw Lucky. His eyes widened, and he was about to say something more, but before he could, Frollix gunned the cycle and sped away.

"Who was *he*?" asked Lucky. He felt so self-conscious about his disguise. He scratched the base of his horns. It itched, having his hair braided like this. The air was beginning to feel tight and humid, as if a tropical rainstorm might be on the way.

"Don't worry, kid," said Frollix. "They're just crazies. You get 'em on every planet. The End of All Worlds! Like that could ever happen!"

They sped on in silence, past grand mansions half hidden behind high gates. They passed opulent shops, guarded by uniformed doormen. They drove down streets lined with restaurants, tables spilling onto the road, crowded with people eating, drinking, talking, laughing.

Lucky couldn't understand it. How could they be like that when there was a war in space? When the Spacewall loomed over them all in the sky? And when there were people in the very same city suffering from the Living Death?

"I'm not sure I like this place," he said, turning his collar up as a rumble of thunder shook the sky.

"It was different before all the troubles," said Frollix. "There used to be a good spirit in this world. You'd even see Axxa and Humans together here."

He slowed the cycle as he spoke. At the top of the road ahead, the way forward was blocked by a big crowd of people. They were marching in step with one another, chanting as they marched. Lucky's senses filled with the crunch of their shoes and the rhythmic sound of their chants.

"What's going on?" he asked nervously over the noise. He kept his head down, but Frollix and Bixa were staring at the crowd, trying to figure out what it was.

"Oh — look!" said Bixa, a smile spreading across her face. "It's a protest march."

And now Lucky saw that the people were all carrying flashing banners, with slogans like STOP THE WAR and END THE KILLING and BRING DOWN THE WALL. One of them even said FROM THE STARS WE ALL CAME . . . The crowd was mainly Humans, but he was amazed to see some Axxa among them, their horns glittering in the storm light.

"See?" said Frollix. "There's still some of that old spirit left! Let's take a closer look!"

"No, Frollix," warned Bixa. "Let's find a quiet backstreet where there's no people. It'll be safer."

"Safer?" scoffed Frollix, muscles rippling. "C'mon, Bixa — live a little!"

"I'm just saying — *they* could be at that march —"

"I ain't scared!" crowed Frollix, driving right up to the edge of the crowd. "I ain't scared of anything!"

More and more people were marching past on all sides, filling the street. Frollix cruised among them as the first raindrops began to fall. There was no way back now. They were becoming part of the crowd, swept up in its flow.

"You ever hear about these marches, Lucky?" asked Frollix as he steered the cycle deeper into the throng. "They ever mention them on the news, or in your school?"

"Never!"

"It happens on every world. Ordinary people, protesting against the War. Not that the government listens."

At the top of the road was a stone monument. It was carved with names and garlanded in flowers. Beside it, a man on a platform was making a speech. Lucky caught only a few words.

". . . died in vain," the man was saying. "And you're all here because you've had enough of war. You're here because you believe this is how things could be — Humans and Axxa, side by side!"

Everyone cheered, and another chant started up. Lucky's skin tingled in the quickening rain. It felt incredible to be part of such a great flow of people. He was swept up in the rush of it: this huge crowd, marching, chanting, together, united. It gave him goose bumps on the back of his neck.

And then his neck stiffened, because now it seemed like parts of the crowd were being blotted out. Like the air was somehow darker, thicker, in those parts.

He looked closer.

Oh, no. There were Shadow Guards in the crowd, moving stealthily through it. They were pulling people out of the flow, onto the roadside.

One of them dragged a woman aside and held his hand up to her face. The woman tried to back away, but other Shadow Guards held her there. Fingers of darkness reached out from the Shadow Guard's hand and probed at the woman's eyes. They went right in through her pupils. Then the Shadow Guard pulled sharply — and ripped a stream of bright images from her eyes.

"What's he doing?" gasped Lucky as thunder shook the sky above their heads.

"Ripping her brainscan," replied Bixa. "That's how they get their information. They rip the entire contents of your brain — whether you want them to or not."

The images were pouring out of the woman's eyes, shimmering and sparkling in the shadows. Her thoughts, her memories, her feelings and dreams: the Shadow Guard was taking them all.

The woman screamed and slumped to the ground, writhing in the rain. The edges of the crowd began to break up as people saw what was happening and tried to get away.

Lucky wanted to get away too — wanted desperately to turn and flee from this scene that had spun horribly out of control — but he couldn't. All he could do was shake with fear.

"Uh-oh," said Frollix. He'd seen the brainscan. His hands were trembling, making the handlebars rattle.

"Drive!" urged Bixa.

But Frollix seemed unable to drive. He stalled the cycle and couldn't start it up again. He was shivering, his great horns wilting in the rain.

"Frollix," hissed Bixa. "By all the Twelve Astraeus — drive! We'll get pulled up if you don't!"

"I'm trying . . ." muttered Frollix, as he failed again to restart the cycle. Bixa's needles blanched to palest white.

And then, without warning, a Shadow Guard was in front of them, blotting out the world around him.

"Stop right there," he ordered in a voice that Lucky felt in his bones. And in his mind, Lucky was right back in Phoenix Spaceport, on the flight tower, with the shadowship bearing down on him and his mother —

— but she wasn't there to save him this time. All he had was a flimsy disguise.

"Show your ident," commanded the Shadow Guard as Frollix pulled the cycle to the side of the road.

"G-g-got it right here," stammered Frollix, handing his card over. He was far bigger than the Shadow Guard, but his size counted for nothing before such power.

The Shadow Guard scanned the ident. "What are you doing at an antigovernment march?"

"Uh — well — we —" mumbled Frollix.

"We're on the crew of a civilian ship, loyal to the government," said Bixa, interrupting imperiously. "We're on shore leave. We had no idea there was a protest march here today — we were just going shopping in the famous market. But we got caught up in this stupid crowd. We'd be very grateful if you'd help us get out of it."

The Shadow Guard looked at Lucky. "You at the back. You are shaking. Why?"

Lucky couldn't answer. He could barely even breathe. He looked into the faceless darkness before him. He could see no eyes, no mouth; nothing Human at all.

"Take off those glasses," ordered the Shadow Guard.

Lucky forced himself to remove the mirrorshades. His contact lenses were exposed. Surely the Shadow Guard would see straight through them. . . .

"Now, hold still," said the Shadow Guard. "I am going to scan your brain."

Oh, no. Please no.

The Shadow Guard held a hand up to Lucky's face. The fingers of darkness reached for his eyes.

But Bixa just laughed, as if she hadn't a care in the world. "Hey, 'course he's shaking! They both are! They know I'm gonna kick their asses for this mix-up when we get back to our ship, and so's our captain! I told them not to come this way, but they insisted — didn't you, boys?"

"I — uh — yeah . . ." whimpered Frollix. Lucky tried to do the same, but his mouth was so dry, he couldn't speak.

"See, that one's not even worth talking to," Bixa snorted. "Look at those teeny tiny horns: he's one sorry excuse for an Axxa! No, if there's anything you wanna know, you can brainscan me, if you like. Here." She took off her mirrorshades and looked directly at the Shadow Guard with her silver eyes. "I don't mind."

The Shadow Guard stared at her.

She held his gaze — one second, two, three — until Lucky thought his heart was going to explode.

And then, at last, the Shadow Guard nodded and let his hand fall back to his side. "That won't be necessary," he said, returning Frollix's ident. "You can go now. But be careful. Theobroma's army is everywhere."

"Uh — yes, sir," mumbled Frollix. "Thank you, sir."

He tried the engine again. Finally, it sparked into life. His hands were still shaking as he found a gap in the crowd and drove away from the protest march.

No one spoke until they were in the clear and speeding through the rain.

Frollix groaned. "I'm sorry, you guys. I'm so sorry I put us through that. . . . But you did good there, Bixa. Real good. I owe you."

"Me too," said Lucky, still shaking uncontrollably. They'd come so close to disaster. "You were brilliant, Bixa."

"I was, wasn't I?" She turned around and grinned. Like comets, her sudden grins came flashing out of nothing, seemed to light up the world, and then soared away again.

"Weren't you scared?" he asked her.

"Yeah," she said quietly. "We're all of us scared when it comes to them."

"I ain't scared of anything," Frollix mumbled. "Except . . . for . . . *them*."

"But you didn't seem scared at all," Lucky told Bixa. "You were so brave."

"Brave?" She shook her head. "Brave would've been

standing up for what we believe in, like those marchers. Or fighting them — like your mother did."

Lucky was silent; the fire in his heart burned at the memory.

"C'mon, Bixa!" said Frollix. "You can't fight them. You know you can't."

"Maybe I could, if I only had the guts! I've worked my whole life to make sure I can defend myself — and I'm a good fighter, I know I am. But I'll never find out, will I?"

Lucky was puzzled. "Why not?" he asked her. "What's stopping you? Is it because you're going to be a Startalker?"

"No!" she snapped, needles darkening. Frollix glanced back at her, then looked away without a word. "Anyway," she muttered, "don't get too excited about that whole Startalker thing. That's Mystica's idea, not ours."

Above their heads, there was another crack of thunder. The rain thickened; the streets were getting wetter and wetter. Deep puddles were forming, glowing with reflections, as if there was another world just below the surface of the water.

"We'd better take cover," said Frollix, "till the storm passes."

He pulled up by a cycle shelter on the side of the road. It was a corrugated-iron shack, just big enough for the three of them to huddle beneath. Raindrops pattered on its roof as they watched the storm play out before them.

After a while, Frollix took a pipe out of his pocket and lit it. He drew deep on the pipe, and smoke rose in spirals from its bowl. "OK," he said at last. "I think there's something you should know about us, Lucky. It's only fair — right, Bixa?"

Bixa shrugged, her needles almost black now. "You tell him, if you want to. I can't."

"Tell me what?" said Lucky.

Frollix took another deep drag on the pipe. The shelter was full of its smoky scent now, as well as the storm smells of rain and wet leaves. "Well," he said, "it's about our family, and who we really are."

"You're brother and sister, right?" said Lucky.

"'Course!" said Frollix. "And Mystica and Nox —"

"They're your parents?"

"They're our *grandparents*." Frollix exhaled with a sigh. "Their daughter, Joxi — our mum — well, there's a reason you haven't met her, or our dad. See, back before the War, before any of us were born, Joxi went traveling through the worlds. And on her travels, she fell in love with a Human. A man called Jonathan."

"Jonathan?" said Lucky. Outside the shelter, raindrops were rippling the surface of a puddle. "Mystica mentioned that name. She said my contact lenses were his."

"Yeah." Frollix looked away. "He needed to disguise himself, 'cos not everyone liked to see an Axxa and a Human together. People said it wasn't natural; some people even thought they were different species. But that's not true, and the proof is, Axxa and Humans can have kids together — just like our parents did."

"Jonathan's your father?" said Lucky. "Your father's *Human*?"

163

"Amazing, ain't it?" said Frollix, his eyes glinting blue in the shadows of the shelter. "We look Axxa, like our mother, 'cos the genetic line always follows the mother's side — but the truth is, we're half Axxa, half Human."

Lucky couldn't help grinning. "So you're Groundlings!" he said. "You're like me!"

"Don't push it," said Bixa as the rain streamed down. "We're both — and we're neither. But what difference does it make? To Humans, we just look Alien, so we're treated like Aliens —"

"And even among Axxa," said Frollix, "it's never been easy. When the War came, everyone had to choose sides. We couldn't. The Startalkers refused to, 'cos they could see all points of view. The Axxa King and the Human President both hated them for that, and our people were so fired up, they turned against the Startalkers too. It got dangerous; we weren't welcome anywhere. Our family got trapped in the middle of a battle between Shadow Guards and the Axxa army. Captain Nox saved us. He got us away to safety on the *Sunfire,* though he had to fly through exploding Dark Matter bombs to do it. But our parents, they . . . well, they didn't make it. They were caught in the crossfire and killed. Shot by both sides."

Lucky's grin was gone. He felt awful. "Oh, no . . ." he said. "I'm so sorry."

"I was just a kid," said Frollix. He blew out a series of smoke rings. "Bixa was so little, I had to carry her on to the ship. But I remember thinking, right there: *If the Star-talkers can't even defend their own families, then who cares about Startalking, huh? What's the point?*" He shook his head. "Mystica never could explain that one to me. Her and the Captain, all they wanted to do was keep us safe from violence. So they took us away from the War Zone and brought us to the quietest Human worlds, looking for a peaceful life."

"Never did find it," added Bixa in a small voice.

"So *that's* why the Captain won't let you fight," said Lucky. He leaned back and watched the smoke rise in spirals from Frollix's pipe. In the glow of its embers, it seemed to him that he saw his companions clearly for the first time. At last, he understood that strange gap between Mystica and Nox, the old people, and Frollix and Bixa, the young. He felt the absence that no one ever mentioned but that was always there, between them, on the ship. And now he could see why his disguise had upset them so much. "I think you're both so brave, to come through all that."

"We survived," said Bixa. "But only because we never, ever try to stand up to them. We never try to change anything. We just keep our heads down and let them rule us. And that's not brave. That's cowardice."

Lucky didn't agree. Now that he knew their story, he thought the way she'd just outwitted the Shadow Guard was even braver and more brilliant than he had before.

But he kept his opinions to himself. There were no more words between them; they were each lost in their own thoughts and memories.

Gradually, the storm passed. The rain eased off and the sun came out again. They left the shelter, and Frollix drove them through glistening city streets, until at last they arrived at a riverbank.

He parked by a vast bridge that spanned the river. There was a series of caverns in the arches beneath it. Lucky could see people inside these caverns, and he heard the deep bass kick of music. An oceanic sound, like heartbeats in a womb.

"So this is it, kid," said Frollix. "The famous market of Leo Five — the place where you can get anything your heart desires!"

VII

The Wolf Poisons Hearts.

The Astraeus of Love Cannot Heal Them

for They Are Too Full of Hate. . . .

CHAPTER SIXTEEN

They entered the caverns. Each one was crammed with stalls, extending far into the distance. They were wild with colors and sound. The air was thick with music, pulsing from speakers high above their heads.

Lucky recognized the tune. "Hey—isn't this that music you like?" he asked Bixa.

"Yeah." She nodded happily. "Listen, Frollix: they're playing Gala!"

Frollix beamed with pleasure as they walked through the market. Lucky gazed around, trying to take it all in. His senses were bursting. There was everything for sale here; everything he'd ever heard of, and even more that he hadn't.

The first cavern was packed with stalls selling animals, and it had an overpowering musky smell. There were brightly feathered birds flapping in their cages. Snakes hissing in glass displays. There were solemn-eyed leopards on leashes, and wolves curled up asleep.

The next was full of stalls selling combat and security gear. Rack after rack of body armor, ground-blasters, cannon of every size. Whips, chains, electrocuffs. Tracking devices, surveillance cams, long-range comms: all open, all for sale.

Beyond that was a cavern with massive speaker stacks fifty feet high and vidscreens even bigger. An image flashed up on one of the giant screens, then another, and another.

Lucky couldn't stop staring at them. It was as if everything else melted away.

Because the image was of a handsome man with a mustache, dressed in a starship commander's uniform. The very same man whose vidpic Lucky had grown up looking at. He looked much older, and he wasn't smiling, because Axxa troopers in military uniforms were holding a gun to his head — but it was unquestionably him.

UPDATE ON THE HOSTAGES scrolled across the screens.

The image changed to show the President of the Human worlds, addressing the galaxy from her office. Her voice rang out of the speakers. "We have received this footage of Major Dashwood, commander of a government science ship, who is being held by Alien forces beyond the Spacewall," she announced. "We demand his immediate release, and that of all prisoners of war. We will not negotiate with Alien wrongdoers. I vow to you, I will personally bring them to justice, starting with their king."

She continued talking, but Lucky's mind was whirling. Dashwood? So that was his real name, not Ashbourne?

"What you staring at, kid?" said Frollix.

"That man!" said Lucky, pointing at the screens. "That's my father!"

Frollix looked up and saw the broadcast. His expression darkened.

Lucky couldn't stop staring. There he was at last: the center of his hopes. The great space hero whose image had watched over his childhood, and with whom he'd shared so many imaginary adventures. This was the man who Lucky believed would answer all his questions. The one person in the galaxy who could take care of him and make everything all right again.

Yet it seemed his father was the one who needed help.

"What are they doing to him?" he said. "I have to rescue him!"

"You gotta find him first," said Frollix gently. "And even then . . ."

Lucky kept looking at the vidscreens, hoping for more information about his father — but the broadcast had ended, and the screens were now flashing up a public safety warning about the need for people to cooperate with the Shadow Guards.

He looked down, bitterly disappointed.

"Come on," said Bixa. "Let's find the Professor and get your astrolabe fixed. Then at least you might know where to look. . . ."

Lucky followed Bixa and Frollix in silence, his mind spinning with troubled thoughts. At last, he had some information about his father — but what terrible information. It was shocking to see him so vulnerable, in such danger. If he was a prisoner of war, then the chances of finding him were slimmer than ever. And yet Lucky yearned to find him all the more.

They tramped deeper into the market, past stalls selling food, clothes, boots. Lucky was struggling to keep up. After the awful vidpic he'd just seen, it made him queasy to look down and see what appeared to be big black cloven hooves, marching beneath him instead of feet. It was so strange, so *Alien*.

But Bixa and Frollix dragged him ever onward, through thousands of stalls, past heaps and heaps of merchandise, until at last, in a dim dark corner, they came to a small antiques stall. It seemed rather neglected. There were all sorts of strange objects stacked up in boxes at the front and a dusty curtain at the back. Everything looked faded, like it had seen much better days. No one else was shopping here, while the other stalls thronged with customers. A single elderly Axxa sat behind the counter.

"Stay here, Lucky, while we greet him," whispered Frollix as he approached the stall. Bixa went with him, while Lucky hung back forlornly and watched.

The old Axxa looked as antiquated as his stall. He had bushy whiskers that met in a cavalier-style mustache, and great white horns upon his head. His eyes were hidden behind a huge pair of horn-rimmed spectacles.

A bird perched on his shoulder, eyes closed. It was about the size of a parrot, but its feathers were amazingly intense colors: crimson gold, like flames. Even in the dim light, it seemed to glow like a little sun.

"Professor Byzantine?" called Bixa.

The old Axxa looked up sharply, peering over the top of his spectacles. He seemed confused for a second. Then a smile spread across his face. "Bixa Quicksilver?" he asked.

"It's me!" She grinned, needles blushing pink.

"And do my eyes deceive me, or do I behold young Frollix?" The Professor peered up at Frollix's huge bulk. "My goodness — you have grown!"

"Well, it's been ten years!" said Frollix almost shyly as they embraced the old man.

The bird on his shoulder woke up. It flexed its wings and then turned to look at Lucky, who was still hanging back, feeling troubled.

The bird blinked. It flew over to him and landed by his feet. Up close, its face looked old and wise, perhaps even ancient. It seemed playful, though, and started pecking at his hooves.

He bent down to stroke its feathers. They were soft to the touch, and very warm. And then, as he stroked it, the bird opened its beak and spoke, like a parrot.

"*Baaa-zoookaaaa,*" it chirped as a little jet of fire flared around its beak. It wasn't hot enough to hurt, but Lucky hadn't been expecting fire — or words, for that matter — and he was startled. He jerked backward and bumped into the stack of boxes at the front of the stall.

The antiques teetered one way, then the other. "No!" gasped Lucky, and stuck his hands out to steady them.

It was the worst thing he could have done.

Boxes started tumbling down around him: first one box, then two, three, and then a rain of boxes, a shower, cascading disastrously, faster and faster . . .

By the time it was over, he was knee-deep in broken antiques, surrounded by clouds of dust. And the little bird was chortling at the chaos.

"Bazooka!" called Professor Byzantine sternly. "Come here, girl."

The little bird flapped her wings and led Lucky over to her master. The Professor scrutinized him as he approached, peering over the rims of his spectacles. For all his great age, the fire in his eyes burned bright and keen. He was no bigger than Lucky or Bixa, but he held himself ramrod straight and proud.

"I — I'm sorry," said Lucky. "It wasn't your parrot's fault — it was mine —"

"Parrot?" said the Professor, whiskers bristling. "She is no parrot, sir! She is a phoenix. Or a *zhar-ptitsu,* a *simorgh,* or a *feng-huang,* depending on where and when you are. In any event, they are extremely shy, and never, ever go near strangers. What mischief did you do her?"

"I didn't!" said Lucky. "She just came over and wanted to play."

"Hmm."

Lucky could tell that the Professor didn't believe him. He looked guiltily at the fallen pile of boxes. "I — I'll pick it all up, I promise —"

"I beg you, no!" said the Professor. "Do not touch another thing."

Frollix put a huge arm around Lucky. "Prof, this is Lucky," he said. "He's riding with us on the *Sunfire.* He's kinda clumsy, but he's a good kid — even though he's Human, under that disguise."

"Human, is he?" muttered the Professor. "And why have you brought him here?"

Lucky almost didn't dare speak, but this was what he'd come for. "I heard you might be able to help me with this," he said, pulling out the astrolabe. "It's broken."

Professor Byzantine breathed in sharply at the sight of it. There was no other sound. Even Bazooka was silent before the astrolabe.

The Professor swiftly ushered them behind the curtain, into the back of his stall, hidden from the market. He took the black metal disk from Lucky very carefully, almost as if he was afraid of it. As he examined the inside-out dials, the twelve symbols around its circumference started to flicker with faint silver light. The Professor murmured a phrase, and the dials began to move.

"Can you fix it?" asked Lucky, amazed that the old Axxa seemed able to operate it.

Professor Byzantine ignored the question. All his attention was focused on the astrolabe, his face wrinkled with lines of fierce concentration as the black metal flickered under his fingertips, the dials moving faster and faster, pulsing and throbbing and blazing with light.

And then the dials flipped right over, twisting and turning about so they pointed inward again, as they were meant to, as they had before. The Professor jerked his fingers away from the astrolabe as if it was scalding hot and thrust it back into Lucky's hands — still without saying a single word.

"So — is it fixed?" asked Lucky. "Can I use it now?"

Professor Byzantine came right up to him, placed a hand on his cheek, and stared deep into his eyes. Lucky tried to hold the gaze, but the old Startalker looked into him the same way Mystica had: openly, nakedly, reaching right into the center of his brain.

"Tell me this first," said the Professor. He pulled Lucky's face close to his own. "What happened to it? How did it get so tangled?"

"I — I just asked it where my father was —"

"*You?* You did this?" said the Professor. "But you are too young to operate such a device." He stepped back a pace. "Who are you . . . truly?"

At his words, something inside Lucky flared into life.

A spark of power. It was rising up inside him. He couldn't stop it.

His fingertips began to shine.

"Tell me!" demanded the Professor. "Who are you, coming here with an astrolabe like this, and such power inside you?"

Lucky held up his hands. They were glowing, brighter and brighter. White light was spreading up his hands, his wrists, his forearms . . .

Terror tightened in his chest. Panic. *What if I burst into flames again?*

The Professor clasped Lucky's shoulders. "Please," he said. "Control yourself."

But the light was growing stronger, illuminating the dusty curtains and fragile objects all around them, threatening to combust into scorching flame. Lucky's heart was racing, his mouth dry. At the back of his throat, he could taste something like sulfur rising up, filling his senses. "I can't control it!" he cried. "It's too strong —"

"You are panicking," said the Professor. "Think of

something that makes you happy, something that matters to you. Do it — *now!*"

Lucky couldn't think straight. His mind was too full of fear. But right in front of him, he saw Bixa staring at him with her silver eyes —

— and the fire subsided, just a little.

"Yes!" said the Professor. "Whatever you are thinking of, think of it some more."

Lucky didn't move. He didn't think. He just kept looking straight ahead, at Bixa.

Gradually, the panic eased. The fear ebbed away. And as it did so, the glow faded from his hands and the light stopped streaming out of him at last.

The Professor let him go. Lucky's heart was still racing; he felt exhausted. But he hadn't burned. This time, he hadn't burned. The Professor's words had saved him.

The old Axxa turned away from Lucky, hands trembling, shaking his head. Bixa and Frollix were both gaping at him, eyes aflame. It was the first time they'd seen his power in action, and they seemed unable to speak.

"Please don't be afraid of me!" he said. "I don't want to hurt anyone —"

"But have you?" said Professor Byzantine.

"Three Axxa pirates," said Frollix, finally finding his voice. "They were armed to the teeth. Seems he torched 'em with his bare hands. Nothing left but ashes."

"I didn't mean to do it," protested Lucky.

"Until you learn to control your power," said the Professor, "you will keep doing it, and worse."

"But how do I control it? It's so strong. . . ."

"It is not something separate from you," said the Professor. "It is part of you. It *is* you! Therefore, the only way to control it is to control yourself. If you panic, then of course it will overwhelm you. To keep it in balance, you must restrain your mind, your feelings, your body...." He squinted at Lucky's hands. "What else can you do, other than kill people?"

"I — I think maybe I can hear the stars, sometimes..."

"Mystica reckons he might be a new kind of Startalker," said Bixa quietly.

The Professor twisted his whiskers. "Hmm. What do you think, boy?"

"I wish I could get rid of it," he groaned. "I hate it."

Professor Byzantine looked startled. "Get rid of it? Our legends tell us that when people have such powers, it is always for good reason. No, no — you must learn to use it. You must test it, see what it can do, discover its true purpose —"

"But it hurts! When I burn, it hurts so much — don't you understand?"

"I understand one thing," said the Professor. "With such power in you, the day will soon come when you must choose what to do with it, whether you wish to or not." He nodded briskly. "And on that day, you will need mental strength, moral clarity, and, above all, a proper understanding of who and what you are."

"But all I want to do is get my astrolabe fixed!"

"Ah yes, the astrolabe," mused the Professor. "That troubles me too. Where did you obtain it?"

"It's my father's. He knows the truth about my power, and it's the only way I've got of finding him. Can you help me with it?"

The Professor twisted his whiskers again. "Frollix, Bixa," he said after a moment. "Is there room for one more passenger on the *Sunfire*?"

They glanced at each other and then nodded slowly. "Actually," said Frollix, "Mystica asked us to invite you —"

"Splendid. Then I offer you this bargain, boy. I will come back to the ship with you. I will accompany you and assist you with the astrolabe, as you ask. And in return, you will submit to my teaching."

"Teaching?" said Lucky, surprised. "What teaching?"

"As Startalker of the Past, I know certain things about your power and the legends that lie behind it. I can help you learn to use it — painful as that will undoubtedly be." He surveyed the ruins of his stall. "Understand me: I will be traveling with you, and I do not wish to travel with a Human time bomb! So I will help you — but *only* if you submit to my teaching." His eyes glittered. "Do we have an agreement?"

Lucky looked away, stomach churning. He couldn't face that terrible fire again. Whatever the Professor claimed, he felt sure the power would overwhelm him next time. It would burn through his body and his brain: that scalding light, that scorching flame. It would destroy him, and every-thing around him too.

But his father was out there, in trouble. A prisoner. He needed Lucky's help. And if the Professor really *could* teach him how to stop the fire . . .

He looked at the astrolabe. It glimmered and shimmered and shone with starlight, as if it was calling him on, pulling at some invisible cord inside him. . . .

"All right," he replied, though he could hardly believe he was saying the words. "If you'll really help me find my father — let's get back to the ship."

CHAPTER SEVENTEEN

After their adventures on Leo Five, the *Sunfire* felt warm and welcoming. As they climbed back on board, Lucky was glad to feel his hooves locking onto the ship's surfaces once more. It was good to smell that strange scent of gunpowder, chocolate, and spice again. It seemed reassuringly familiar now.

Mystica and the Captain were waiting for them in the hold. Mystica was wearing her turquoise robe and headscarf. All her golden rings were gleaming, as if she'd polished them up specially. She beamed when she saw Professor Byzantine and, above him, Bazooka the phoenix, flapping onto the ship with infectious glee.

"Welcome, welcome, my old friends!" she called. She clapped her hands with delight, filling the air with joyful jingles.

"Mystica Grandax!" said the Professor. "You are a sight for sore eyes!"

"*Baa-zoookaaaa!*" agreed the little phoenix, landing on her shoulder.

Mystica smiled, and her eyes shone like the sun. "Oh, it is good to see you, old comrades. I missed you so much! I remember when you first came to him, Bazooka — you were just a little chick." She stroked the phoenix, and Bazooka's feathers glowed with warmth. "Tell me: how do I look?"

"Magnificent!" said Professor Byzantine, bowing gallantly. "You are as radiant as ever." It was true: Mystica seemed to light up in the Professor's presence. And the Professor, for his part, seemed much warmer and more affectionate than he had on Leo. Before Lucky's eyes, the two old Startalkers appeared to shed the years. He could easily imagine what they must've been like in the past, when they were young and strong.

Professor Byzantine was flattering Mystica shamelessly. "Did you know she was a sensation in her day?" he was telling Frollix and Bixa. "Songs were written about her eyes of gold and lustrous long hair. . . ."

Mystica looked embarrassed, and even a little sad, but then a small smile spread across her face. "I was quite something back then, wasn't I?" she said.

She led them through the cloistered corridors, hobbling slowly but purposefully toward the *Sunfire*'s main cabin. As they went, Lucky told her everything they'd learned on Leo Five.

"Well, at least now you know more about your father," she said, her stick clacking on the ground. She glanced at the Professor. "What do you think, old friend? Can you help him with his astrolabe?"

"Why, of course I can!" said the old Axxa, and his words gave Lucky hope. But then the Professor edged ahead to walk beside Mystica, and his voice dropped very low. "However, if his father is on the other side of the Spacewall . . . well, that is a dangerous place, and this is a dangerous time.

Something has gone dreadfully wrong with the galaxy. The stars themselves are in peril. Do you not feel it?"

Mystica's reply was so quiet that Lucky had to strain to overhear her words. "Of course. I feel it in my own body. . . ."

The Professor twisted his whiskers. "Many feel it in their minds. Everywhere, there is the suspicion that nothing means anything anymore. The Living Death is spreading, and so are these strange stories. The Wolf That Eats the Stars . . ."

"What is it, this Wolf?" Mystica shuddered.

"I would give anything to know," said the Professor. "I suspect its origin lies in the Aquarius system. But I have heard no word from Aquarius for a year now. I dread to think what the Humans are doing there, under cover of their blockade. There is but one source of hope: the return of the Twelve Astraeus."

Mystica's face lit up. "Ah! So you have dreamed of them too?"

"Indeed I have! Every night."

They had reached the silver archway at the entrance to the main cabin. Lucky's skin prickled as he glimpsed the walls inside. The vidscreens were all gleaming like stained glass in a cathedral, showing images of those amazing people with their wings and haloes, their tridents and scythes, holding whole worlds in their hands.

"But — who exactly are the Twelve Astraeus?" he couldn't help asking. "Are they gods?"

Mystica turned to him and smiled, eyes shining. "They've been called that, and many other things through history. Gods, angels, devils, demons — all the supernatural beings you ever heard of. But we call them the Twelve Astraeus.

They go right back to the beginning of everything. Always, they were there: at the creation of the universe, at the dawn of Earth, and then later, as we spread out across the stars and found our way to this galaxy. Every culture has known them. Images like this have been found in the ruins of every ancient civilization. They have taken different forms in different times and places, but always, the images point back to the same twelve beings, the same magnificent immortals, returning time and again."

Lucky gazed at the shimmering images and wondered if such stories could be true. "Have you ever seen one?" he asked.

"Oh, if only!" she said. "The Astraeus have not been seen for countless years. Generations."

"And what makes you think they'll come now, when they haven't for so long?" said Captain Nox. He moved to stand by the two Startalkers, while Lucky, Bixa, and Frollix hung back behind them.

"They come at times of greatest need," said Mystica. "When could the need be greater than now, when the galaxy is torn apart by suffering and war?"

"But what if they've abandoned us?" said the Captain quietly. "What if . . . they were never real in the first place?"

"Never real?" said the Professor, visibly shocked.

"Where were they when Joxi and Jonathan died?" asked the Captain. "Where were they when we lost our homes, and had to leave our worlds?"

"They will come!" insisted the Professor. "I believe they are in Aquarius right now. They must surely be somewhere behind the Wall. Why else would the Humans be expending such vast resources, if not to hide great secrets? I say we take the bull by the horns. We should cross the Wall and find the Twelve Astraeus ourselves!"

Mystica nodded in agreement. "The Professor is right," she murmured. "We must cross the Spacewall and go into the War Zone."

Captain Nox stared at them, and then shook his head. "No," he said simply. "We are doing no such thing."

Lucky's insides tangled as he listened. Because if the *Sunfire* crossed the Spacewall, then he'd be so much closer to finding his father. And yet the Captain's fears troubled him too.

"But everything points to it," said Professor Byzantine. "Everything lies out there, beyond the Wall. The Twelve Astraeus. The Wolf That Eats the Stars. Even this boy's father—"

"The boy?" said Nox darkly. "I fail to see the relevance."

The Professor's eyes glinted. "I feel sure he has some part to play in all this. Perhaps he is a new kind of Startalker. Or perhaps he is a guide: someone the stars have sent to help lead us to the Twelve." He glanced at Lucky, who shivered at his words. "In any event, we must go back."

"After everything that happened?" said the Captain. "After everything they did to us? If you think that, then you're a fool, Professor."

"Ozymandias!" said Mystica sharply. "He is our guest—"

"And he is proposing a course of action that could destroy us all."

There was silence for a moment. Deadlock. The Captain and the Professor stared at each other, totally still. The air itself grew taut and tense between them. Lucky watched, heart in his mouth, waiting to see who would blink first.

"What happened to you, Captain?" said Professor Byzantine at last. "You used to be the most fearless pilot in the galaxy. It was only your courage that saved Frollix and Bixa from the Dark Matter bombs, all those years ago."

Frollix and Bixa flinched at his words. But Nox just kept staring at the Professor, his eyes burning.

"The safety of my crew is my sole concern," he said. "I will not allow this foolishness to endanger them."

"*Ozymandias Nox!*" blazed Mystica, her eyes flaring like the sun, her voice so grand all of a sudden that even the Captain's authority was eclipsed. "We are Startalkers, and the stars themselves are in danger. This is no time for safety. Set a course for the Spacewall!"

Nox blinked. He seemed to shrink a little. "But Mystica—"

"The decision," she said, "is made." She took a decisive step forward, across the threshold, into the main cabin. Around her, the vidpics of the Twelve Astraeus shimmered and shone, haloing her with light. Then she turned and held a hand out to the Captain. "Of course," she said, more softly, "you are still the master of this ship, and the finest navigator in the galaxy. I would far rather it was you who took us across the Wall than anyone. But please understand, my dear: we are going there, whether you come with us or not."

The Captain pulled away from her, his eyes clenched shut. "Sometimes," he said, almost to himself, "I wish you weren't a Startalker, Mystica Grandax." He shook his great head in sorrow. "Oh, what's the point?" he muttered as he walked away, toward the cockpit. "What does it matter what I think? It doesn't matter, does it? It doesn't matter anymore."

And then he was gone. Everyone breathed out again.

Mystica sighed deeply. Her eyes stopped blazing, and her hands started to shake. "I am sorry about that," she said. "The Captain is not himself . . . and he has not been, ever since those terrible times."

"He is not wrong to fear what lies beyond the Wall," said Professor Byzantine as they followed her through the archway into the cabin. "Everything we hope for is out there — but so is everything we dread. And if your father is somewhere in the midst of that chaos, boy, then you need to know precisely where. So let us look at your astrolabe and see if we can find you an answer."

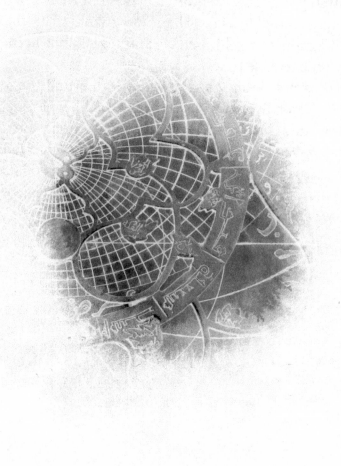

CHAPTER EIGHTEEN

Lucky, Bixa, Frollix, and Professor Byzantine sat around the table in the main cabin. Mystica stood at the stove, stirring a pot. A familiar smell was coming from it. That strange mixture of gunpowder, chocolate, and spice: this was its source. She dipped a spoon into the pot and ladled some thick, dark liquid out into small cups. Everyone got one.

"Ah, Xoco." The Professor sighed. "How I've missed this."

Lucky warmed his hands on his cup and sniffed the drink inside, savoring its aroma. "Is it some kind of chocolate?" he asked.

Bixa snorted. "If you water it down with milk and sugar, 'cos it's too strong for you — then, yeah, it'd be something like chocolate. But this is Xoco: the real deal."

Lucky took a cautious sip. The Xoco tasted smoky, fiery, sweet, and strong. It was more complex and intoxicating than any chocolate he knew and left a warm, bright aftertaste that sparkled on his tongue. The sensation was so pleasurable, he felt his muscles relaxing, his insides warming, his whole body filling with satisfaction.

He pulled out the astrolabe and placed it on the table. He touched his fingertips to the cool black metal—

"One moment," said Professor Byzantine. "Before you attempt to use that device again, may I ask if you fully understand its operations?"

"Uh—not really," Lucky admitted. "I've only done it once."

"And to be fair," said Mystica, "Ozymandias hardly gave him the best instructions."

"Very well," said the Professor, polishing his spectacles. "Then will you allow me to share some of our deepest secrets with you: our ancient knowledge of the stars and their true nature?"

A shiver ran through Lucky—but so did a silent thrill. "I've always loved the stars," he said, taking another sip of Xoco.

"Excellent," said the Professor. "So kindly tell me: what *is* a star?"

Lucky summoned up all the things he'd been taught at school, all the insights of Human science. "A star is a giant ball of burning gas—" he began confidently.

"Oh!" groaned the Professor. He bit his whiskers. "Frollix! For heaven's sake, tell him what a star is."

"Hey, don't ask me!" Frollix chuckled. He drained his Xoco in one great gulp, leaned back, and put his hooves up on the table. "I ain't never gonna be a Startalker."

"Frollix!" cried Mystica. "Not this nonsense again, and not in front of—"

"Peace, Mystica," said the Professor. "He is still young. Remember what we were like at his age? Fear not, Frollix. One day, you shall have my powers — and my phoenix. A phoenix always accompanies the Startalker of the Past, you know."

"*Baa-zeekeeee!*" the little bird chortled, as if dismissing the idea.

"Yeah, right!" said Frollix, equally dismissive. "I mean, look at me!" He grinned. "I'm nothing like you, Prof."

"There are many ways of being a Startalker," replied Professor Byzantine. "Mystica has her way, I have mine — and I daresay you and Bixa will have yours."

Frollix laughed this idea off, but Bixa seemed intrigued. "So you think a Startalker could be someone who likes fighting?" she asked. "A warrior?"

"Why not?" said the Professor. "I think you can be anything you wish to be."

Bixa's eyes went wide, and her needles lit up. "Well . . . if you ask me, I'd say a star is the place where everything comes from. It's the origin. The beginning."

"Bravo, Bixa!" said the Professor, applauding her. "You see, Lucky, everything in the universe is made of atoms and elements that were created in the hearts of stars, billions of years ago. Even our own bodies. You are entirely made of stardust, and so is everyone else and, indeed, *every single thing that exists*. And because it all came from the same source, it is all connected. Connected by Dark Matter. Do you see?"

Lucky glanced again at the astrolabe. The twelve symbols

around its circumference were beginning to glimmer with light. "What *is* Dark Matter, anyway?" he asked.

"The invisible force that holds the universe together," replied the Professor. He threw his arms out wide and fluttered his fingertips. "You cannot see it, but it is everywhere. If you destroy it — as a Dark Matter bomb does — then you break the connections that hold things together. But if you embrace it: why, then you can do anything. With a Dark Matter drive, you can follow those connections — and because they span such vast distances, you can travel faster than light. Thus we call it the speed of dark." He pointed triumphantly at Lucky's astrolabe. "That object is a guide to those connections; a device that makes Dark Matter visible. Do you see it now?"

Lucky gaped at the Professor; most of his words had washed right over his head. "Uh . . . I'm not sure," he said.

"Then tell me: did you notice lines of silver light when you were in the astrolabe?"

"Yes!" Lucky's heart thumped painfully. The memory of those infinite swirling lines still scared him.

"Those lines," said the Professor, "represent Dark Matter connections. They show the invisible threads that hold the universe together. To follow the connections, you simply choose one of them, move your consciousness along it, and the astrolabe will take you there. Nothing could be simpler."

"I don't know, Professor," said Lucky. "It was *scary*."

"Infinity is a fearsome sight, for those unaccustomed to it. But I assure you, there is nothing to fear. If you panic, merely think of something that matters to you, something that makes you happy, as you did in my market stall. Precisely the same kind of self-control is needed to operate an astrolabe."

"He's not very good at self-control," grunted Bixa. "I've been trying to teach him to control his body with Astral Martial Arts, but it's useless. He never gets any better. I don't see how thinking about something happy could help. . . ."

Lucky couldn't respond. He was staring at the ground, ears warm, face flushing — because it was Bixa herself that he'd thought of in the market stall.

She peered at him suspiciously. "What *did* you think of, anyway?" she demanded.

Every part of him blushed. "Oh, just some . . . stuff . . ." he mumbled.

"Whatever it is," said the Professor, "it will help. Hold on to it as you would to life itself. And take your time. Start with something simple. Ask the astrolabe to show you routes to the nearest planet, for example, before asking about your father. Are you ready?"

Lucky took a deep breath and summoned all his courage. He held the black metal disk in his hands and concentrated.

The dials began to move. The wheels began to spin. Once again, he felt that sensation of limitless power thrumming beneath his fingertips.

The astrolabe picked up speed, pulsing like some starry dynamo, shimmering and shining with light as never before —

—and then Lucky went into the astrolabe again.

He couldn't see the cabin anymore. He couldn't see the Professor and Mystica, or Frollix and Bixa.

What he saw instead was space. Infinite black space, studded with stars. Each one a giant sun, burning with impossible energies, with power enough to destroy whole worlds — or create them.

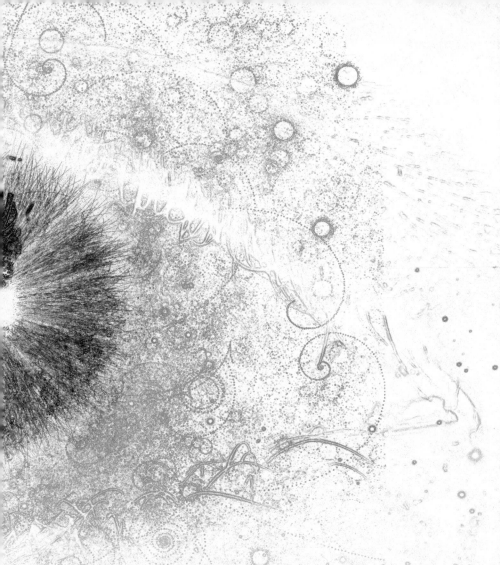

They filled him with awe. And though it hurt his eyes to look directly at them, he felt compelled to stare into their scorching faces once again. As he gazed at them, they seemed to gaze right back at him. He felt a vast, unfathomable intelligence streaming out from them, radiating in every direction. As if he was in the presence of great spirits, omniscient, omnipotent.

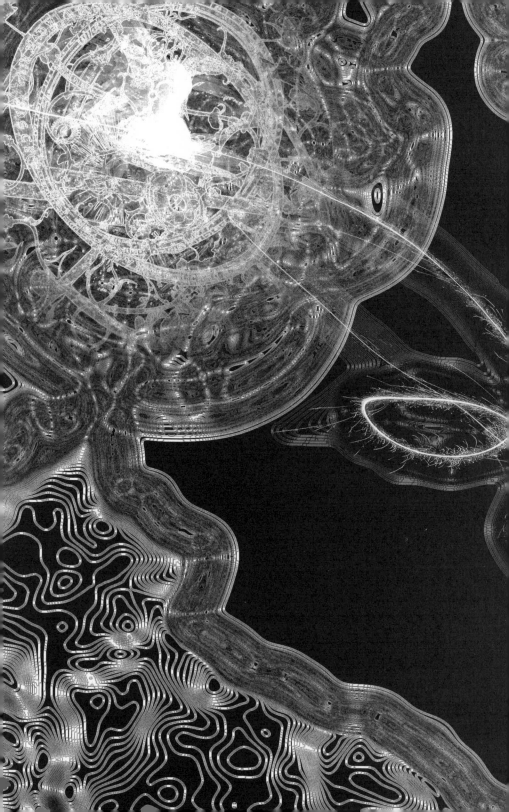

And he was flying among them in that astral body. So close he could even taste the stars, burning in space. Smoky, fiery, sweet, and strong: their flavors sparkled on his tongue like Xoco, intoxicating.

Focus! he told himself fiercely. *Don't get distracted!* He braced himself, and then he asked the question. *Astrolabe: please show me routes to the nearest planet?*

A line of blazing silver light shot out from one of the stars. Then another line — and another — and now more and more lines were shooting out of more and more stars, joining up into spirals and webs, swirling away in every direction, to infinity, so fast it made Lucky's head spin and his stomach lurch.

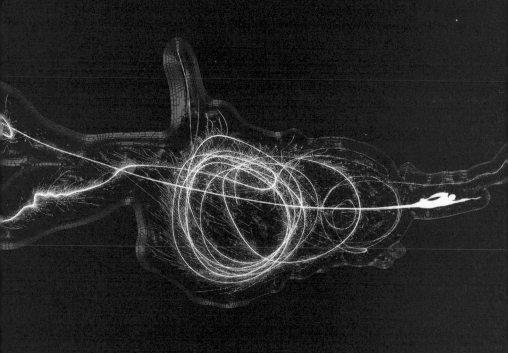

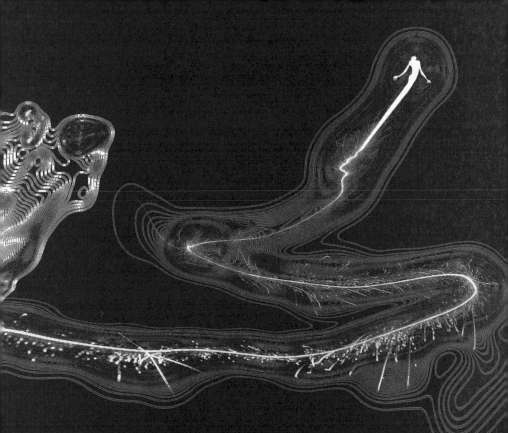

Even now that he knew what they were, these lines of light terrified him. They wouldn't stop branching out, again and again, making endless dizzying patterns that he couldn't keep up with, disorienting him, hurting his head and making him giddy. . . .

I can't think straight, he thought. *I can't breathe —*

No! Don't panic! He forced himself to think of Bixa, though the panic was rising, higher and higher.

And at the thought of her — sticking her tongue out, threatening to kick his ass, calling him a moonbrain — he couldn't help but smile. And as he smiled, the panic eased, and fell away.

It's working! he thought. *How strange . . .*

Lucky made himself look at the lines of silver light again. He chose one of them at random and ignored all the others. He concentrated all his attention on this single line and moved his astral body along it.

Infinite pathways opened up around him. Everywhere he looked, he saw all the directions he could go: every single one, spanning the stars in a dizzying rush of information.

It was so hard to hold it together, but he forced himself to keep moving.

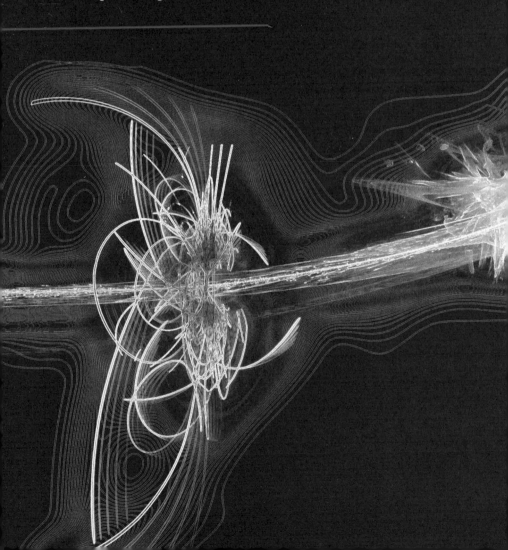

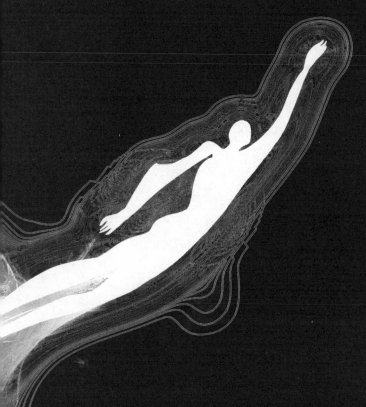

And as he moved, gradually, the infinite spiraling view started to seem more familiar, less dizzying. He didn't feel so scared of it anymore.

I can do this! he thought, picking up speed. He leaped across to another line of light, and followed that one through space for a while. He guessed he was barely skimming the surface of its potential, but for the first time, he knew he was using the astrolabe properly.

And now he was becoming aware of a silvery sound, surrounding him with waves of power. The very same sound he'd dreamed about. Right here in the astrolabe, he could hear the stars singing: vast, echoing, galactic, oceanic; the harmonies ringing out as they called to him through space.

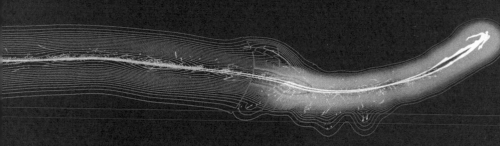

Lucky focused his mind and reached out to the song of the stars. It seemed to grow even stronger and nearer, as if the astrolabe was amplifying it. And then, at long last, he began to hear the words coming through, loud and clear.

Do not fear us. We will help you. Help you learn to fly.

And on—it was wonderful! The idea that these great spirits not only accepted his presence but wanted to help him—it sent a shiver of joy through his whole being.

But it lasted only a moment. Because now, behind the songs of the stars, he started to hear something else coming through. Some kind of interference, like the crackle of static on a vidscreen or the buzz of shifting frequencies on a comm. He heard snatches of other songs, very different. Fragments of strange, sad songs, echoing across infinity.

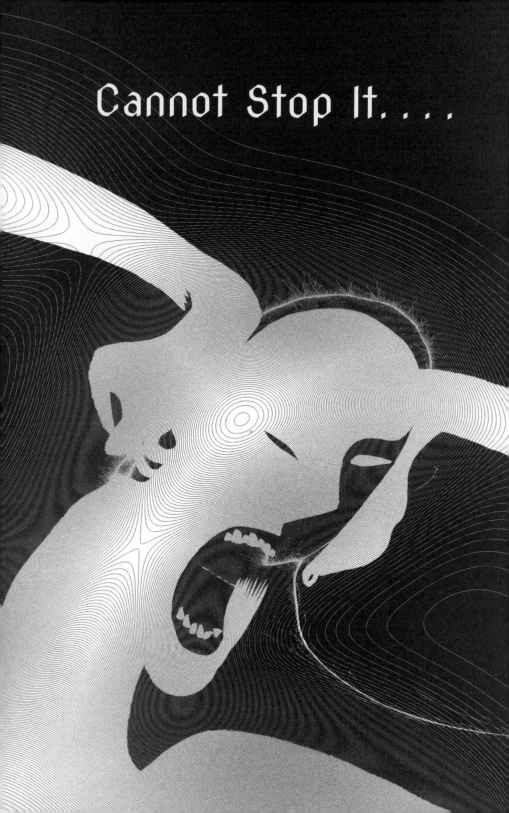

Cannot Destroy It. . . .
Cannot Defeat It. . . .

Lucky had no idea where these other songs came from, or what their words meant. But they filled him with a sense of dread that was almost overwhelming.

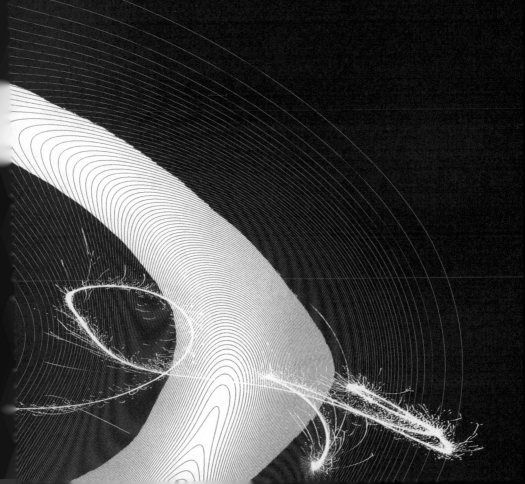

He shut them out. Whatever they were, they had nothing to do with him. He turned his mind away from them and back to the task at hand: finding his father.

He focused. Every ounce of determination.

Astrolabe, he asked it, *please show me where my father is?*

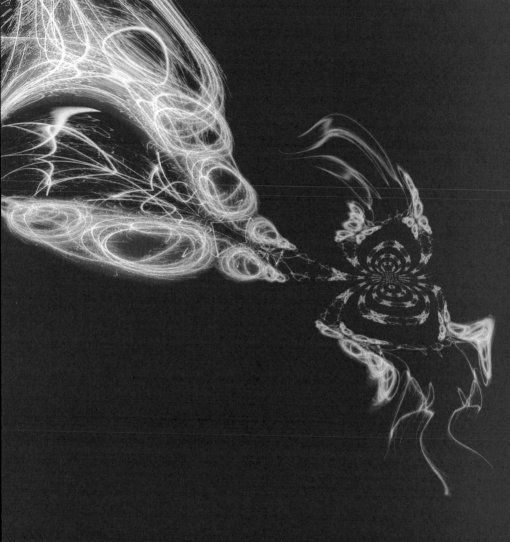

And then, before he could stop himself, he was hurtling
along the lines of light through space — totally out of control,
faster and faster, farther and farther — spiraling all the way
to the edge of the map — then over the edge, and off the map,
and —

"No!" he gasped as he fell out of the astrolabe — fell hard — and crashed to the ground.

Gravity smashed back into him full force. He felt a grinding crunch as his mind snapped back into his body — his useless, clumsy body — not that perfect weightless body he'd just been in. . . .

Lucky opened his eyes and looked up. He was back in the *Sunfire*'s main cabin. Beside him on the floor, the astrolabe's silver lights winked out. Its dials ground to a halt — and they had flipped inside out again. They had twisted and turned over, so they appeared to be pointing outside the astrolabe again.

He started to shake. He wanted to cry. Bazooka pecked at him gingerly, worry in her eyes.

"Good heavens!" said Mystica. "What happened?"

Lucky shook his head. "I don't know. It worked fine when I asked about the nearest planet. I could hear the stars singing — I was moving along the lines, I was flying and everything. But then, when I asked about my father . . . I lost control. It threw me off the edge again."

"How perplexing." The Professor stroked his whiskers. "If it answered your first question, it is surely not broken . . . Perhaps it is telling you that your father is off the edge of its map? But its map covers the whole galaxy! I do not understand."

"Nor I," said Mystica. "And if two Startalkers cannot understand it — whatever can it mean?"

The Professor frowned at Lucky. "We will never know until you achieve full control," he said. "You must practice this, and you must master it before we reach the Spacewall.

For it is not only the astrolabe that you need to master. If you cannot learn to control your power, it will flare up the first time you see a Shadow Guard at the Wall — and you will give yourself away, right there."

Lucky hauled himself to his feet. "I don't think I'm ever going to get it." He sighed.

The Professor's eyes glittered. "You have the principle," he said. "All you need now is practice. Practice, practice, practice . . ."

VI

The Wolf Is on the Prowl.

The Astraeus of War Cannot Defeat It

for It Conquers
Every Force. . . .

CHAPTER NINETEEN

Lucky practiced hard as they flew on toward the Spacewall. Under the watchful eyes of Professor Byzantine and Bazooka, he spent every spare minute with the astrolabe, learning how to control it, plotting routes through space until he began to see stars and the connections among them even when his eyes were closed.

As his understanding expanded, he found himself able to stay in the astrolabe for longer and longer periods. He grew more accustomed to being in that astral body, dancing among the stars. He often thought he could hear them singing to him, songs that lifted his spirits with words of encouragement — even as he caught snatches of other songs, those strange sad songs whose meanings he could not fathom.

Yet whenever he asked the astrolabe about his father, it always gave him the same response: flinging him off the edge and out of the map. Always, he would lose control and come crashing back into his clumsy, gravity-bound body again. It was always painful.

Even more painful were the occasions when his power rose up inside him, and these now happened every day. The Professor tested it relentlessly. He would goad and provoke

Lucky until he panicked, and then, inevitably, the power would rise. His hands would start to shine. Flames would spill out of him. It would take all his strength to pull it back inside him, and then he would feel utterly spent, exhausted, and in terrible pain.

The Professor never let him stop, though. "This is precisely the same as navigation," he'd say. "You are learning self-control: the key to both the astrolabe and your own power. Focus on what matters to you. It will give you something to hold on to; something to balance the fear. Stay calm and in control, and everything else will follow."

The only thing that helped at such times was thinking of Bixa — Bixa, of all people! Lucky didn't know what to make of this fact. But it seemed to work, so he did his best to keep doing it, to keep practicing and building his control over the power, though it felt like it was growing stronger every time he used it, and harder to contain.

He dreaded the test that lay ahead at the Spacewall. He was so unprepared for it. He wondered if he'd ever be ready to face Shadow Guards. Despite the Professor's teaching, he felt nothing but overwhelming terror every time he thought of them.

And the ordeal was coming up all too fast. The *Sunfire* soared through the systems: out of Leo, through Virgo, and on toward Libra, the turning point of the galaxy. The place where the Human worlds ended and Axxa space began: where the Startalkers hoped to find the Twelve Astraeus and where Lucky longed to find his father.

And all the while, the Spacewall came closer and closer, growing bigger and bigger on the vidscreens, until the wall of green fire filled their view completely, blotting out everything else, even the stars.

As they came in close to it, Captain Nox called a meeting in the main cabin, to prepare for the challenge ahead. Through the vidscreens' crackling static, they saw a gigantic space station at the center of the Wall. It was sharp-edged and solid, like some impossibly massive door in space, so vast that Lucky's mind reeled before the scale of it.

"That is what they call the Spacegate," announced the Captain, jabbing a finger at the flickering image on the screen. "It's the only way through the Wall."

Patrolling alongside this Spacegate were government craft: shadowships and battleships, guarding the frontiers of Human space. Lucky could also see fragments of debris hanging in orbit around the Wall: fractured wings, broken hulls, floating powerless and adrift.

"What are those?" he asked.

"If you try to cross the Wall without clearance," said the Captain, "they destroy you. Many have tried, and none survived. Those bits of wreckage . . . they leave them there to discourage others."

They looked at the ruins in silence. Even Bixa had nothing to say.

"So . . . how are we going to get through it?" said Lucky at last.

The Captain turned to Mystica and the Professor, his horns held proudly high. "I've been thinking about what you said," he told them. "And perhaps I owe you an apology. Perhaps I have grown too cautious. So I have taken the liberty of devising a plan to get us through the Wall. Leave the talking to me. If it works, we shouldn't even have to leave the ship."

Mystica's eyes glowed. "My dear," she said, "I knew we could count on you."

The Captain turned back to Lucky. "There's one problem. The government isn't letting Human civilians cross the Spacewall anymore; it's totally off-limits to you. Only Axxa who are returning to their home worlds are allowed over. So your disguise is more important than ever now. If you make one mistake — if they even suspect for a moment that you might be Human — they'll never let you through. And if they catch us helping a Human impersonate an Axxa . . ."

"Yeah," Lucky said with a gulp. "I can imagine."

"I don't think you can," said Nox. "However scared you were of the Shadow Guards before — that was nothing. We are going into the place where they are strongest. We will do everything we can to protect you, but if they *do* catch you — well, we're just one small starship, and they're the biggest force in the galaxy. So I must ask you: are you absolutely certain you want to come with us?"

Lucky stared at the livid green sky. "My father's out there," he said. "A prisoner." He nodded, more to convince himself than anything. "Of course I want to come."

"Then by the powers vested in me as ship's captain, I am giving you an ident to go with your disguise. It shows that you're part of our crew: an apprentice navigator. Keep it with you at all times. And, boy? Don't mess this up."

He spoke gruffly, but as he handed the ident over, Lucky felt overwhelmed with gratitude. He'd never had an ident of his own before, and the Captain was taking a huge risk giving it to him. "Thank you, Captain," he said.

Nox stood up awkwardly. He went in silence to the cockpit, taking Frollix with him.

"Now, *that's* the Ozymandias Nox I knew!" whispered Professor Byzantine.

"You see?" said Mystica. "I told you he still had it in him."

Lucky watched the flickering vidscreens as they approached the Spacewall. The green fire rippled with awesome power. And then —

FLASHHH!

— the Wall pulsed with a burst of light so painfully bright that Lucky not only saw it, but felt it searing his retina with scorching heat.

Mystica screamed. Her face crumpled, and she fell to the floor, hugging herself as if wounded. So did Professor Byzantine. They both writhed in agony as Lucky stood there, helplessly shielding his eyes, until the light faded.

"Was that the Spacewall?" gasped Mystica as Bixa rushed to her side.

The Professor's face was filled with shock. "It cannot be! The Spacewall should be a solid wall of energy. Something must be happening on the other side!" He crawled up from the floor and, with Bixa's assistance, helped Mystica to stand again. "Yes," he said. "I am certain: it comes from the other side. Can you feel it? Can you hear it?"

Mystica swayed on her hooves, unsteady, her golden eyes cloudy with confusion. "Is this the work of the Wolf?" she whispered.

"Come, Mystica," said the Professor gently. "Let me take you to your quarters. You need rest."

The two Startalkers hobbled away, sticks clacking on the ground, as Bazooka the phoenix flapped anxiously above their heads. The cabin felt empty and quiet without them. Lucky looked over at Bixa. She'd been unusually quiet for a while, he realized.

"Are you OK?" he asked her.

"Me? I'm fine. 'Course I am. Why shouldn't I be?"

"Well . . . Mystica and the Professor . . . I mean, they both felt something, and they're both Startalkers. Didn't you feel it too?"

"I'm not a Startalker," she muttered.

"I don't think I am either," he mused. "I didn't feel anything or hear anything."

"Good for you. Only an idiot would want to be a Startalker."

Lucky peered at Bixa. "The way they talk about it, it sounds amazing—"

"Yeah?" Her needles flashed dangerous colors. "Well, your weirdo power sounds amazing to me. Having the power to torch anyone you like? I'd give anything for that. But I don't see you getting so excited about it."

"That's different!" protested Lucky. "That's something that could destroy me—"

"And being a Startalker could destroy *me*! I couldn't fight anyone if I was a Startalker, could I? I could never defend myself, because I'd always have to see things from all sides. I'd be like Mystica, and look what it's like for her! I don't want that—I've never wanted it!"

They flew on toward the Spacegate. No more pulses of light came from the Wall. It was a solid barrier of green fire again: a barrier powerful enough to destroy any ship, smash any shields. The two of them looked out in silence as it overwhelmed the *Sunfire's* vidscreens, engulfing them on all sides.

"Well, there's something that might destroy us both," Lucky said quietly.

"Yup," said Bixa, needles blanching pale as snow, shrinking back into her hair.

"What's it really like, going through that thing?" He gulped, hoping she'd make a joke and make everything OK again.

Bixa scowled at the Spacewall. Her needles were almost totally hidden now. "I don't remember," she said. "I was very young when we came through."

"How do they power it, anyway?" asked Lucky. "Where does the energy come from?"

"How should I know?" she snapped. "Where do all your stupid questions come from? It's probably the same place!"

He stopped asking questions. Her words told him only one thing, and it was something he wished he didn't know: Bixa was as scared as he was. She might have outwitted a Shadow Guard on Leo Five, but these were still the people responsible for the death of her parents. The prospect of facing them again filled her with just as much fear as it filled him.

And though their terror was the same, neither of them could do a thing to comfort the other in the face of it.

No reassurance there, then. And already, Lucky could feel

the ship decelerating. The easy, fluid motion of the *Sunfire* as she sailed through open space was gone.

Ahead of them, the Spacegate loomed enormous. And now Lucky saw that its surface was hatched with numerous portals, through which countless spacecraft were coming and going.

The comm crackled into life. "Axxa craft *Sunfire* requesting clearance to dock at the Spacegate," came Captain Nox's voice.

"Clearance assigned," came the reply. "You will land in docking bay Z."

"Z," grunted Bixa. "Zero priority. We're going to be stuck in this place a while."

One of the portals opened before them. The *Sunfire* edged through it into a vast steel hangar. The portal slid smoothly shut behind them as they touched down.

Space was gone. The stars were gone.

They'd landed.

CHAPTER TWENTY

On the flickering vidscreens, Lucky could see the steel hangar outside, with harsh white striplights on the ceiling. It looked so cold and clinical out there. Shadow Guards were already stalking around the hull of the ship in their stealth armor. The comm buzzed again.

"Alien craft *Sunfire*," came their voices. "Stand by for onboard inspection."

Captain Nox came down from the cockpit, followed by Frollix. Everyone put on their mirrorshades.

Lucky prepared himself to face the Shadow Guards. He tried to stay calm in spite of the sickening fear that was rising inside him. He couldn't let it overwhelm him.

The *Sunfire*'s hatch opened. A hiss of cold air entered the warm cabin, and a Shadow Guard came on board, blotting out the air around him.

Calm. Calm. Calm.

"Welcome to the *Sunfire*. I'm Ozymandias Nox," said the Captain, extending a hand in welcome. The Shadow Guard ignored his greeting and started to survey the cabin.

Bixa's needles had retracted all the way back into her hair so they weren't even visible anymore. She stood behind the

Captain, staring at the ground in silence. Beside her, Frollix was beginning to shiver and shake, as he had on Leo Five.

"What is the nature of your business at the Spacewall?" said the Shadow Guard at last.

"We're civilians," said Captain Nox. "We've lived peacefully in the Human worlds for many years. Now we're returning to Axxa space."

"Returning?" said the Shadow Guard. "Unusual. What's in your hold? Smuggling weapons to Theobroma's army?"

"Of course not. Just provisions for ourselves."

The Shadow Guard shook his head. "This is highly irregular. You must all leave this ship and go to Border Controls for further inspection."

"That's impossible," said Nox. "One of our crew is extremely unwell and never leaves the ship. We keep the gravity low in her quarters, because she's too weak for full gravity." The Captain was far taller than the Shadow Guard, and he spoke in his most authoritative voice. "According to government regulations, this means we're entitled to an onboard inspection."

"That applies to people," said the Shadow Guard. "It does not apply to you."

"What does that mean?" said the Captain. "Axxa aren't people?"

"The regulations are for Human Beings."

Lucky's insides twisted as the argument built up. He didn't like the way it was going.

"The regulations," protested Captain Nox, "clearly state that—"

"For hostile Aliens in a time of war, there are no regulations."

"But we're not hostile!" said the Captain, struggling to keep his composure. "We've got nothing to do with the War! We've been living under Human rule for years now, and we have rights!"

"You have no rights. You will go through inspection, and then you will be held indefinitely while we process your case."

"Indefinitely?" said the Captain, fiery eyes flashing as his calm front finally cracked. He slammed a fist down. "By all the Twelve Astraeus — that's not fair!"

The Shadow Guard raised his cannon, pulled back the safety catch — and inside Lucky, a spark of power began to rise. He could taste something like sulfur at the back of his throat. He could see the tips of his fingers beginning to shine —

"Welcome, welcome!" came Mystica's voice. "Welcome to our ship, Mr. Shadow Guard! What is all this shouting?"

Everyone turned to look as the old lady hobbled into the cabin, leaning heavily on her stick yet still somehow looking grand. Professor Byzantine was behind her, with Bazooka perched on his shoulder, feathers ruffled with tension.

But Lucky was looking at Bixa, only Bixa, and he was wrestling with his panic, struggling with his power. He couldn't lose control now!

He made a massive effort to calm his mind and hold the power down. With every fiber of his being, he fought to rein it in —

—and gradually, he brought it under control. It was still there, burning inside him—but his fingertips weren't shining anymore. The power wasn't flaring up or spilling over. He was controlling it.

For now.

"They want you to leave the ship, Mystica," said Captain Nox, his great forehead furrowed. "And I would sooner die than let—"

"No one is dying here today," said the old lady as she turned the lights off behind her. "I will happily come." She smiled at the Shadow Guard, fixing him with all her charm until he lowered his cannon. "You do what you have to, sir. We understand—truly, we do."

The Shadow Guard didn't respond. He just gestured at the hatch, emotionless.

Mystica led the way off the ship, brooking no further debate. With Frollix and Bixa both helping, she climbed out of the ship's hatch. It was awkward, and it took a while, but eventually she stood on the ground. Captain Nox and Professor Byzantine followed her, and then Lucky went out last, still concentrating on keeping his power in check.

Cold air slapped his face as he left the ship. It tasted artificial. On a space station this size, it had probably been through a million lungs already. Everything here would be minutely controlled and calibrated.

A huge sign above them pointed the way to the Border Controls. They followed it out into a long steel tunnel, which twisted sharply around a corner ahead. They couldn't see what lay at the end of it. The sheer scale of this place was intimidating, as if it was designed to make them feel daunted.

Mystica walked slowly, with great concentration, like someone for whom walking wasn't entirely natural and had to plan every step, tell each muscle what to do. Captain Nox lent her his arm, but even with his assistance, she was struggling.

"You don't have to do this, Mystica," the Captain said quietly. "You shouldn't be off the ship; you know you shouldn't. That Shadow Guard had no right —"

"Ozymandias," she said, "you were very brave back there, very gallant. But there was only one possible outcome, and no one could have done a thing about it." She grimaced and paused, panting in the cold steel tunnel. She was sweating despite the chill, but seemed determined not to show her pain. "Anyway. It's not so bad," she said. "It's not so bad." She started walking forward again, her stick echoing on the metal floor. But she was wheezing hard and bent over almost double as she walked.

"So what is our plan of action now?" asked Professor Byzantine. "I confess myself at a loss. . . ."

"We're in their hands," replied Nox. "Just pray to all the Twelve Astraeus that they let us through."

They moved on down the tunnel. Mystica and Captain Nox led the way, Frollix and Bixa flanked Lucky to the left and right, while Professor Byzantine and Bazooka brought up the rear. Without Lucky noticing, the *Sunfire* crew had taken up positions around him — almost as if they were protecting him. Shielding him with their own bodies.

On the way down the tunnel, he glimpsed a corridor full of Axxa who were traveling in the opposite direction. Some of them clearly had the Living Death: he could see the million-mile stare in their eyes, like black holes in the sky. The adults were carrying overstuffed bags, with pots and pans strapped to their backs; the ragged-looking children were clutching toys. They were a pitiful sight.

"Who are those people?" he asked.

"Refugees," said the Professor. "They are fleeing the War, hoping to find safety in the Human worlds. I do not think they have much chance."

Lucky gulped. All those Axxa were hoping to cross the Wall so they could leave the War Zone. No one else was entering it. No one except him and his friends.

At last, they came to the end of the tunnel. Shadow Guards awaited them, faces obscured as always by their armor. Above them was a huge sign that said BORDER CONTROLS. There were no other Axxa here. They were alone with the Shadow Guards.

Lucky's stomach tightened. Beside him, he could feel Bixa's fear, and Frollix's.

"Step forward," commanded one of the Shadow Guards, who sat impassively behind a thick shield of cannonproof glass. "Show your idents."

They all passed them over. Lucky surrendered his with a queasy feeling. He'd only just gotten it, and he hated to let it go. Would it stand up to inspection? He felt so conscious of his horns and hooves, his mirrorshades and contact lenses.

The Shadow Guard ran a scanner over Lucky's ident. Rows of vidcams swiveled toward him, making insect-like machine whirs. This place was like nothing he'd ever seen: Human power at its most faceless. All the surfaces looked like surgical steel, and it smelled of disinfectant, as if it had been swabbed down repeatedly, killing not only germs but anything that lived. Behind the Shadow Guards, at the end of the tunnel, he could see only a pair of sealed double doors, with a conveyor belt beside them.

A Shadow Guard pointed at Bazooka, who sat shivering on Professor Byzantine's shoulder. "You cannot take that creature with you."

"But she accompanies me wherever I go," protested the Professor.

"That creature will be quarantined," said the Shadow Guard. "If found to be dangerous, it will be destroyed." He reached for Bazooka. The little phoenix cowered away, her eyes cloudy with fear.

"*Baaa — Baaa — Baaa —*" she chittered.

The Shadow Guard seized her and ripped her from Professor Byzantine's shoulder. Bazooka screeched, spurting little jets of fire, but she couldn't shake the Shadow Guard. She reached out for Professor Byzantine with her wings, and the Professor was reaching for her too. . . .

"Please, sir, I beg you!" he cried. "Do not take her from me!"

But Bazooka was hauled away, out of sight, and the Shadow Guards remained emotionless behind their stealth armor.

"Take off your clothes," they ordered.

Lucky shivered. It was bitterly cold in here.

"Why should we?" demanded Bixa.

"Take off your clothes, and place them on the conveyor belt," said the Shadow Guard. "You and your possessions will be scanned separately. That way you cannot hide anything. Have you something to hide?"

"No, no, no — of course not, sir," said Mystica. "Come along, Bixa, don't make trouble!"

Bixa scowled, but said no more. Silently, they began to strip off their clothes.

It was humiliating. So humiliating. One by one, they removed their mirrorshades. They slid off their cloven hoof boots, to reveal their bare feet beneath.

Without his hooves, Lucky immediately felt clumsy and uncoordinated again. The floor was freezing under the soles of his feet, and it stung. His skin came up in gooseflesh as he removed his space traveler's coat, his shirt, his trousers. He stood there in his underwear, feeling tiny with terror.

"All your clothes, you Alien scum," said the Shadow Guard.

Lucky lowered his eyes as he stripped completely. He didn't want to see his friends humiliated. Didn't want them to see him humiliated, either. Because he was a Human, and here were Humans, treating him the way they routinely treated the Axxa.

It disgusted him. Even the word *Alien* was beginning to sicken him. *They're Axxa*, he thought. *The People of the Stars.* Why can't anyone call them that? Why always *Alien* and *Devil* and *Scum*? Especially when the Shadow Guards must have known the truth that was now so clear to see: that without their clothes, Axxa bodies were exactly the same as Human bodies. The only difference was in the eyes.

He felt ashamed to be Human — and he felt ashamed of his own body. He hated it. Small, weak, useless. He hoped no one was looking at him.

"So that's the ass I've been kicking all this time?" whispered Bixa in his ear. "Not bad!"

And he couldn't help it: a little smile crept up on his face.

But it only lasted a moment. Because the Shadow Guards were making them surrender everything, even Mystica's big golden rings. Bixa had hidden her needles somewhere deep in her hair, so she didn't lose those, but everything else was taken away.

"The horns," a Shadow Guard said. "The males: take down your hair."

The Captain bristled. "But these horns — they're part of our faith. We wear them to remind us of the stars —"

"You can forget about the stars," said the Shadow Guard. "Take them down."

Mystica came up behind Lucky and tended to his horns. He felt the threads unraveling, the braids being undone, the velvet coming off. He saw it happen to the Professor, the Captain, Frollix — all of them, stripped of the majestic horns they were so proud of, until their hair hung long and loose and lank.

Frollix looked so much smaller without them. He seemed to shrink before the Shadow Guards, as he had on Leo Five. Professor Byzantine's head had hung low since they'd taken

233

Bazooka. He stood not ramrod straight as normal, but hunched and stooped, even his whiskers drooping. Only Captain Nox was unbowed, standing up to his full height, exuding an authority that even the Shadow Guards couldn't quell — as if he had faced things far worse than Shadow Guards in his time.

But Lucky could not imagine anything worse. He felt totally helpless and naked. And the only disguise he had left now was a flimsy pair of contact lenses.

"Enter the inspection chamber," a Shadow Guard commanded. "The old ones first: walk through the double doors."

Captain Nox, Mystica, and the Professor went forward together. They walked arm in arm through the double doors, which closed behind them with a silent swish.

"W-what happens in there?" said Frollix, shivering.

"Full body inspection," said the Shadow Guard.

They waited. One minute passed. Two. Then the word CLEAR came up on the doors.

"You two," the Shadow Guard told Frollix and Bixa. "Your turn now. Go in."

They went through together, leaving Lucky alone. *Why can't I go with them?* he wondered. *Why did they leave me on my own till the end? Maybe because they know I'm a fake Axxa, and they're just waiting —*

No! Don't think like that! Think about all the hours you've spent with the Professor, practicing for this moment. Think about Bixa. Think about anything except the panic that's clawing at your chest. . . .

But still it was rising, simmering, smoldering inside him.

He could taste sulfur at the back of his throat, just waiting to flare up, to shine and burn and give him away —

"Your turn now," called the Shadow Guard at last.

Lucky fought down the fear and walked through the double doors. They closed behind him, sealing him into a shallow chamber, alone.

Then tiny metal probes filled the chamber: probes like spiders, with needle-sharp legs. Before he could move, they swarmed all over him, spidery legs clicking as they scurried across his skin. It was vile, but he couldn't stop it. He had to endure it, somehow.

"Keep walking," came a voice, "with your hands in the air."

He put his hands up and walked forward. His skin was crawling with spiders, all over — front and back, up and down — spiders' legs scuttling across his face, his nose, his eyes.

The taste of sulfur was in his mouth now; he was just a moment from flaring into flame . . .

No! Think of Bixa, only Bixa —

— and hold on —

— hold on —

— hold on —

— and then, suddenly, the spiders were gone. The doors opened before him, and he staggered out the other side.

The *Sunfire* crew was all there. They were shivering but unharmed. They were retrieving their clothes from the conveyor belt, pulling on their hooves, braiding their hair into horns before a full-length mirror on the wall.

Lucky joined them, gasping.

Have I really done it? he thought.

Nothing bad happened. I kept the power down. I didn't burn. . . .

I've done it! We're going to get away with it! We're going to get through the Wall!

Relief coursed through his body, cool and sweet. He started to dress, smiling secretly to himself—but then he noticed Bixa staring at him with undisguised horror. She was motioning frantically at his eyes.

He glanced into the mirror. His reflection looked back at him, completely normal. What was she trying to tell him?

And then he understood.

Normal. His eyes looked normal.

The probe had taken his contact lenses, and now his Human eyes were exposed.

No! He reached for his mirrorshades, hoping against hope to get there in time—

—but one of the Shadow Guards was already stalking up to him. A probe was in his hands, the telltale contact lenses in its grip. "Fake lenses? A Human disguised as an Alien?" The other Shadow Guards all turned to stare at Lucky. "Scan his brain."

Bixa bristled. Frollix's massive fists clenched. Captain Nox took a step forward, towering over them all.

"The boy is with us," he said. "He is our apprentice. We will answer for him, and—"

And suddenly every cannon in the room was pointing at Nox's head.

"Ozymandias," said Mystica quietly. "We can do nothing

at this moment in time. The present belongs to them. Only the future remains open."

She was right. The Axxa were totally surrounded. They were powerless to help.

Slowly, the Captain held up his hands and backed away.

One of the Shadow Guards reached out to Lucky's face. Fingers of darkness came toward him. Toward his eyes. His pupils.

"No — please!" begged Lucky.

"Hold still," commanded the Shadow Guard. He leaned forward. The fingers of darkness filled Lucky's vision — touching the surface of his eyeball . . .

He couldn't bear to have the darkness enter his eyes — to watch as it came inside his head — no way! No! *No!*

He jerked his head back —

"Move one more time," said the Shadow Guard, "and we kill you."

Lucky stood there, helpless, and let it happen. There was no choice. He tried not to watch the fingers reaching for his eyes, and focused instead on his friends, in the background. He could see them shaking in fear as the dark shadow touched the surface of his eye —

— he felt it entering his eyeball —

— felt huge pressure, reaching back, through his optic nerve, toward his brain —

— reaching right into his brain —

— he saw the sparkle as bright images were ripped out of his brain — as his thoughts and dreams and feelings were pulled from a place deep inside him, streaming up into the darkness —

—and his fingertips started to shine as his self-control finally broke; his hands began to glow as all hope of escape slipped away—

—he screamed in horror—

and

slumped

to

the

ground,

unconscious.

V

The Wolf Is Breaking
Through.

The Astraeus of Union
Cannot Bind It

for It Severs
Every Bond. . . .

CHAPTER TWENTY-ONE

It was the scent that woke Lucky. The scent of chocolate brownies baking.

He stretched out and opened his eyes. They stung; everything looked blurry. But he could see the outline of someone leaning over him, gently mopping his brow.

He shut his eyes again, relaxed, and smiled. That home-baked smell was unmistakable.

He must be back on Phoenix, in his mother's apartment. The whole thing must've been a dream.

He breathed in the smell of home. He inhaled long, deep lungfuls, and thought about all the things he was going to tell her, all the things they were going to do.

"Hello, my boy," said a voice above him. A woman's voice.

But not his mother's voice.

Lucky opened his eyes in shock. A woman in an apron was wiping his brow —

— and she was not his mother.

She looked kindly but stern, with steely blond hair. She seemed familiar, and so did his surroundings. He was lying on a leather couch in a dark wood-paneled room. There were blinds over the windows; a grand mahogany desk.

In his mind flashed up an image he'd seen on countless vidscreens. The face of the President, addressing the galaxy from her office.

This is it, he realized. *The office of the President. And this woman standing over me . . .*

"You're President Thorntree?" he said.

"That's right," said the President. She smiled, showing a set of polished white teeth. "Welcome, Lucky. You've come a long way."

"How do you know my name?"

"We know everything about you," she said. "At least, we know everything in your brain."

Scan his brain.

He sat bolt upright. It all came back to him, crystal clear and sharp as a needle. The brainscan. The Shadow Guards. The *Sunfire* crew, trying to help . . .

"Where are they?" he gasped. "What have you done with my friends?"

"They are perfectly safe," said the President.

Lucky didn't believe her. What kind of trouble had he gotten them into? He prayed they were still OK.

"Now, try to relax," said the President. "I know you're scared of my government, and my agents — and you have every reason, after that tragic incident with your mother. But you must believe me: we mean you no harm."

Her words burned into him. He could hardly answer. "Then why did they . . . ? Why did she . . . ?" He couldn't bring himself to say the word *die* out loud. Not when he'd

244

believed for one wonderful moment that it had never happened.

The President's face clouded with pain, and she reached down to wipe his brow again. "I am *so sorry* that you had to witness such a thing. It must have been appalling for you." She looked at him with deep concern in her eyes. "Your mother was a remarkable woman. The way she raised you, on her own all those years: she did a wonderful job. But she never told you the truth. Not about who she was, or who you were — not about anything."

"That's not true!" Lucky protested, bristling.

"Really?" said the President, very softly. "Did you know she was a Shadow Guard?"

Lucky stared at her in shocked silence. It couldn't be true.

"Where do you think she learned to fight so well?" said the President. "And how do you imagine she knew so much about the Aliens? She was brilliant: one of our top agents. A soldier through and through."

Still Lucky refused to reply. Still he refused to believe it. But he couldn't deny . . . that was exactly what his mother was like, though he'd learned it only at the end.

"I know you've wondered about her secrets," said the President. She leaned in and laid a hand on his shoulder. "I can shed some light on those secrets. You see, your mother worked undercover. She traveled in the Alien worlds, learned their customs, knew their ways. But then something happened to her. She became a little . . . confused, shall we say. A little paranoid. She left the government's service and went into hiding. She had some information about the Aliens that we needed, but she refused to give it to us. She believed we wanted to hurt her, when we only wanted to talk. And that misjudgment caused her tragic death."

"But . . . she was right!" he said at last, biting his lip. "They — they shot her — and then, when they finally caught me, they ripped my brainscan . . ."

The President smiled. "You were so scared of that, weren't you? Well, see for yourself. Are you hurt?"

Lucky glowered at her, but her smile stayed totally fixed. It looked like it was painted on her face. "They ripped my thoughts out of my eyes," he said.

"I know it stings a little — but honestly, think about it. Are you actually *hurt*?"

Lucky thought about it. He felt around his body. "No," he had to admit. "I guess not."

"Well, there you are," said the President, still smiling. "All that fuss over such a small thing. You were only scared of us because your mother filled you with fear. But I know that's not how you really are. You are remarkably courageous."

"Yeah, right," he grunted.

"Oh, but you are," said the President in a silky voice. "You are so brave, and so resourceful: I am extremely impressed. From Phoenix, all the way to the Spacewall — you've crossed half the galaxy. You've overcome so many obstacles. Your story is amazing, and I must say, so is your brainscan. You have some interesting powers."

Lucky's eyes narrowed. "So you know? Is that why you were after me?"

"Of course not," said the President. "We had no idea. But you're not the first person in history to have powers.

Spontaneous combustion, bioluminescence — these are well-documented phenomena. Whatever powers you have, our scientists will explain them. And there's no reason you can't use them for the good of Humanity."

She went over to her mahogany desk and switched on the desk lamp. Her eyes glinted in the soft light. Lucky turned away from her. He felt trapped. Whatever she said, he was a prisoner here, just as his father was a prisoner. And how was he ever going to find *him* now?

"So what are you going to do, now that you've got me?" he said.

The President chuckled. "Lucky, nothing bad is going to happen to you. We had you in here, helpless all this time, and what did we do? We cleaned you up and made you comfortable. Oh — and I made you something to eat."

From the desk, she passed him a plate heaped high with brownies. Chocolate fudge brownies. Just like the ones his mother used to make.

Just like the ones he'd pushed away.

"Go ahead," said the President. "They're for you."

Lucky hesitated a moment — but then the smell was too tempting to resist, and he took one.

It was still warm, and the chocolate melted in his mouth.

It was perfect. Exactly like his mother's home-baked brownies. *Exactly* the same smell, the same sweetness, the same freshly baked sticky softness.

This can't be real, he thought, *can it?*

He took another bite, just to make sure — then a bigger bite — and the President smiled.

"You see?" she said. "All we want to do is help."

Lucky sat back and munched. The brownie gave him a sense of comfort that deepened with every bite. He was still suspicious, but if anything bad was going to happen here, surely it would have happened by now.

He finished the brownie, wiped his mouth, and took another from the plate. He was hungry, he realized. "OK," he said, between melting mouthfuls. "So what do you want from me?"

President Thorntree removed her apron. Underneath it was a formal suit. "Lucky, we know you've been searching for your father, and that you want to find him, more than anything. Well, that's exactly what we want too. We want you to find your father."

"Major Dashwood? You know him? Is he OK?"

The President reached over to the window and drew the blinds fully shut, so that the only light in the room came from her desk lamp. Then she went behind her desk and consulted some documents.

"Major Dashwood was commanding a government science ship when he was captured," she said. "He was investigating rumors that the Aliens were developing a new secret weapon, something we would very much like to have for ourselves. He has vitally important knowledge that could help us win this war." She looked up. "He matters to us, Lucky, just as he matters to you."

"So where is he?"

"We understand he's being held in the Alien army's secret base," said the President. "As you can imagine, we've searched and searched for it — but its location is the most closely guarded secret in the galaxy, and we just can't find it. We need a new strategy. And that's where you come in."

She reached into her desk and pulled out his father's astrolabe. "We don't like these devices, as you know," she said. "We even made them illegal, because they encourage the Aliens in their star-worshipping superstitions. However, we'll make an exception in your case. I'll admit, I was hoping you'd find your father with it. But I see from your brainscan that it hasn't worked."

"No," he said. "I don't know why. I've tried and tried . . ."

"Keep trying," said the President. She handed it back to him with a conspiratorial smile. "But even if it never works, there is an alternative. A boy traveling with Aliens, with their trust: you can go places we never could. They can help you to find the secret base, even without the astrolabe."

"I don't think so," said Lucky. "The Axxa I'm traveling with aren't in the army. They don't know any more than I do."

"Perhaps not. But if you agree to my plan, I will give you a piece of information that will change everything. I will tell you the Alien name for the planet where this base is located. It's not a name that means anything to Humans, but it does to *them*, and with their help, I know you can find it." She paused and pushed the plate of brownies closer to him. "There's something you must do first, though. This information is highly sensitive. If it was ever found out that I told it to a child . . . Well, I have to be sure you will use it wisely. So I am making one small condition."

"What's that?" he asked, biting into another brownie.

"You must never tell anyone where you learned it. You mustn't tell your Alien friends that we met, or any of the things we've discussed. If they knew I had personally intervened in this matter, they would be suspicious. They certainly wouldn't want to help you find your father, if they thought it could help us win the War. So you must tell them you discovered the information all by yourself. Tell them you overheard Shadow Guards talking about it, or you saw it in a secret document. Tell them anything you like, but please trust me on this: you must not on any account tell them the truth."

Lucky peered up at the President, trying to take it in. "If I agree — you'll set them free?"

"Of course."

"And the phoenix? They took Professor Byzantine's phoenix."

The President smiled and nodded down at him, as if indulging a small child. "Well, if it means so much to you, then, yes, I'm sure you can have the bird back."

He frowned at her patronizing tone. "Why were we treated so badly out there? The old lady, Mystica — she's ill, and they forced her off the ship —"

"This is a time of war," said the President. "Many people have suffered and died because of the Aliens. It's unfortunate if innocents get caught up in it. But we cannot allow Human lives to be endangered because we didn't do everything in our power to protect them — can we?"

"I — I guess not. It's just . . . I've seen people treat the Axxa like dirt . . . and this Spacewall, it's horrible! It's so wrong —"

"On the contrary, the Wall is all that keeps us safe. It's not a perfect system, we admit that. But we do our best. Never forget what we're up against. These are people who worship the stars, rather than accepting that stars are just burning balls of gas, natural resources for all to use. I'll never understand why they cling to their superstitions or why they hate us as they do. But I know you understand we're only doing what we must. Why would a man like Major Dashwood or a woman like your mother work for us if we weren't completely in the right?"

The scent of chocolate fudge brownies was rich in the room, like velvet across Lucky's senses. He wanted to believe the President. He wanted the government to be good, as he'd grown up believing, and for the President to be on his side after all.

She's got a point, he thought. *The Axxa wouldn't like it if they knew I was talking to her. But . . . I don't want to keep secrets from them.*

"I'm not sure, President Thorntree," he said.

The President took a deep breath. Her eyes filled with concern. She got up from behind her desk and came to stand beside him, leaning over to speak quietly in his ear. "Perhaps you don't appreciate the severity of your situation. Unless you do something extraordinary, regulations would require you to be held here indefinitely. You won't see your friends again, because you'll each be held in solitary confinement. And as for that bird . . . well, unless someone intervenes on its behalf, I fear it will be destroyed under quarantine regulations."

Lucky's stomach turned over as she spoke. But then the President smiled her painted smile.

"None of that needs to happen," she said, her tone all silky smooth again. "Just promise me you'll keep this conversation secret. Why is that so difficult? Don't you want to find your father? Don't you want to work undercover, like your mother? You would be fulfilling her legacy, you know. She would be so proud of you."

Confusion and suspicion simmered inside him. The more he thought about it, the less he liked the idea of lying to his friends. But he had no doubt that the President meant every word. If he didn't do what she wanted, he'd never see his friends again, never fly through the stars on the *Sunfire* with them — never, ever again — let alone have a hope of finding his father. And those thoughts were just too much to bear.

"All right," he said. He picked up the last brownie from the plate, and wiped it clean. "I'll do it. I swear to you: I won't tell anyone."

The President beamed. "That's my boy!" she said, ruffling his hair. "I knew I could trust you. So: the Alien army's secret base is on a planet they call Charon. We believe it's somewhere in the region of Aquarius, but they're the only ones who know for sure." She took a deep breath. "I wish we could come with you, and protect you. However, the slightest suspicion would ruin your chances. So you are on your own from here on in. But whatever happens after you leave this office, don't ever give up. You are the only person in the galaxy who can find your father. I am counting on you. And so is he."

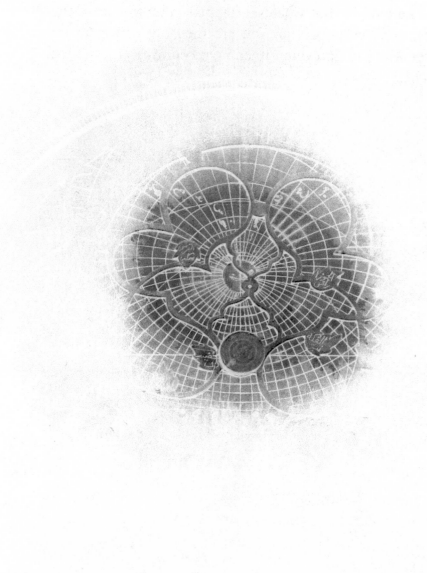

CHAPTER TWENTY-TWO

President Thorntree opened the door to her office. It looked heavy, but glided back on well-oiled hinges. She led Lucky out, and he followed her into a very grand hall.

High above, from a domed ceiling, hung the flags of every Human world in the galaxy. The walls were made of gleaming marble; the floor smelled of polish. It was so huge, Lucky could almost have believed he was on a real world and not a space station, were it not for the artificial-tasting air.

There was a Shadow Guard waiting for him in the hall. For a moment, Lucky felt a horrible flash of doubt. He tensed up, clutching the astrolabe in his hands. He feared the President was about to turn on him, betray him, order the Shadow Guard to get him — but it didn't happen. She just smiled again.

"I so wish I could come with you, my boy," she said softly. "But you go with the Shadow Guard now. He'll take care of everything."

She shook Lucky's hand, and then they parted. The President went back into her office, and the Shadow Guard led Lucky away. His head was still spinning with her words; his mouth was still full of the taste of brownies.

The Shadow Guard led him to an elevator with no buttons on it, no markings at all. The doors closed, and they plunged down, down, down.

The doors opened to a very different view. A dim gray vault lined with cell doors, watched over by sentries. The Shadow Guard led Lucky out into the vault. The sentries saluted at once.

"Where is the crew of the Alien ship *Sunfire*?" the Shadow Guard asked them.

"In there, sir," said a sentry, pointing at one of the cells.

The Shadow Guard nodded, and the sentry opened the door right away.

It was dark and cold inside the cell. Squinting into the gloom, Lucky could see Frollix and Bixa huddled in one corner; Mystica, the Captain, and the Professor in another.

They looked up and saw Lucky standing in the doorway.

"Hey — is that him?" said Bixa, blinking in the sudden light.

"Is that you, Lucky?" croaked Mystica, peering out of the cell.

"It's me," he said.

Frollix and Bixa jumped up. Professor Byzantine and Captain Nox helped Mystica to rise. She stood with difficulty — she looked exhausted and pale — but she was beaming at Lucky, her golden eyes filling with an emotion so strong and pure, it gave him goose bumps.

"We thought you were lost forever," said the old lady. "But you made it, you made it, you made it! Come here, you lovely boy!"

She pulled him to her, embracing him, holding him close and warm. The others crowded around too, and in their happy faces there was such comfort, such relief. Bixa was calling him every name under the sun, but he didn't mind it one bit.

"We thought we'd never see you again, buddy!" said Frollix, giving him a huge bear hug. "We were so worried about you —"

"I was worried about *you!*" protested Lucky. "I thought I'd gotten you into such trouble!"

Captain Nox's face darkened as he noticed the Shadow Guard standing behind Lucky in the doorway. He pulled himself up to his full height. "What are you doing with the boy?" he demanded, his huge horns bristling. "This time, I will not stand by and —"

"It's not what you think," said Lucky, holding the Captain back. "It's OK."

The Shadow Guard raised a hand — and waved them out of their cell, to freedom. "Their case has been processed," he told the sentry. "They are cleared to go."

"Sir?" said the sentry. "But they —"

"They are cleared to cross the Spacewall." His voice was so firm that the sentry just stood aside, saluting. "Your possessions have been returned to your ship," the Shadow Guard told the *Sunfire* crew. "Now, follow me."

They hesitated on the threshold of their cell.

"It's OK," Lucky reassured them. "I swear, everything's OK. Let's go!"

"How in heaven's name . . . ?" Nox asked, as he led his crew out into the light.

Lucky couldn't answer. Not yet. He couldn't spoil this moment with a lie.

The Shadow Guard led them in silence back through the Spacegate, past the inspection chamber and Border Controls, down long steel tunnels. Everywhere they went, doors opened for them. Shadow Guards stood back, saluted. No one challenged them.

It was surreal. But it was satisfying. At that moment, Lucky felt so glad that he'd made the deal with the President. It was worth it, just for this.

They walked out of the tunnel and into the docking bay. Cold air hit his face. He shivered. It was freezing out here, in this echoing space with its harsh white striplights.

But before them now stood the *Sunfire:* a beautiful crescent of beaten silver, shining with silent promise under the lights.

And in its shadow stood a little phoenix of crimson gold.

"*Baa-zookaaaa?*" she chirped, her feathers glowing with warmth.

"Bazooka!" cried Professor Byzantine, rushing forward.

She soared up onto his shoulder and perched there proudly, preening, as if she'd fought off the Shadow Guards all on her own.

"*Baaa-zoookie!*" she chirruped happily.

Professor Byzantine looked even happier. He turned to the Shadow Guard, and then to Lucky, his eyes full of tears. "However this came to pass," he said, "I am most grateful!"

Lucky smiled, but he didn't say a word. The Shadow Guard just turned and left the docking bay, his footsteps echoing on the cold metal floor.

"Let's get outta here," said Frollix, shivering. "This place gives me the creeps!"

He ran toward the *Sunfire,* and Lucky followed. This ship had crossed half the galaxy to get him here, and after everything that had happened, returning to it now felt like coming home. He could still hardly believe he'd made it through the Spacegate. Not just made it; he'd emerged with the help and protection of the President herself. It barely felt real.

But this much was real, he had no doubt: the *Sunfire,* the Axxa, his friends.

Beneath the ship, he found a pile of his possessions: his space traveler's coat, his cloven-hoof boots, his purple contact lenses. One by one, he put them on again. Beside him, Frollix popped open the hatch and then shimmied up to perch on the edge of a crescent wing, grinning from ear to ear.

"Aaah, home!" he whooped, relief audible in his voice. "Look, Lucky: did you ever see anything so beautiful?"

"I never did," said Lucky.

"Come sit with me while the others get on!" said Frollix.

"Uh — I don't want to break anything. . . ."

"You won't!" said Frollix. "C'mon! It's the best seat in the house."

Lucky scrambled up the side of the ship, trusting that his hooves would not let him down — then shut his eyes and leaped across to the wing. Sure enough, they brought him safely over. He walked right up to the edge of the wing, and sat there beside Frollix, the two of them swinging their legs, carefree, as the others boarded the *Sunfire.*

He looked back at the docking bay and saw the Shadow Guard, still watching him. He felt a flicker of doubt. *This feels too easy,* he thought — *and yet, what can go wrong? The President herself authorized it.*

No: we're going to get away. It's really happening.

"You two!" called Bixa. "Stop daydreaming! We've got places to go. Get your asses in gear before I come over there and kick them!"

Lucky grinned, climbed off the wing, and swung into the ship through the hatch. In the old days, he would've tripped straight over it. But his hooves knew what they were doing and brought him in with a stylish flip.

Inside the *Sunfire,* everything was exactly as they'd left it. It was like coming back to a sanctuary. The scent of Xoco was still rich in the air. Lucky filled his lungs with it. It was so good to smell it again, and to see the stove where Mystica made it. It was good to see the cathedral columns and vaulting arches of the cabin, the vidscreens glowing like stained glass with their images of the Twelve Astraeus. He thought it would even be good to see the ship's toilet again.

Captain Nox and Frollix were already up in the cockpit. Mystica and the Professor had gone to Mystica's quarters.

Bixa closed the hatch, and they strapped themselves into their silver seats.

Here we go, thought Lucky. *Good-bye to everything I know.*

And hello to the War Zone.

CHAPTER TWENTY-THREE

The docking bay doors opened, and the *Sunfire* sailed out on the other side of the Spacegate. The Wall was behind them now. Ahead, on the crackling vidscreen, was Lucky's first sight of Axxa space.

FLASHHH!

A searing pulse of light scorched his eyes. It didn't come from the Spacegate, or any of the shadowships guarding it. It came from somewhere else, somewhere deep in distant space. It was the same kind of pulse he'd seen through the Spacewall. But now, no longer filtered through the wall of green fire, he could see its true color. It was blinding magnesium white, like a crack of lightning across the black.

The *Sunfire* rocked as a shockwave knocked it sideways. Lucky held on to his seat with white knuckles. If he hadn't been strapped in tight, he would've been hurled out and smashed into the floor.

"Hold on, everyone!" the Captain's voice crackled on the comm. "Frollix: all power to the Dark Matter drive!"

With a great surge of energy, the *Sunfire* righted itself. It stabilized, picked up speed, and soared into space, back in its element once more.

Lucky breathed out with relief. His skin tingled at the sensation of the Dark Matter drive kicking in. He looked over to Bixa — but she didn't look happy at all.

"Mystica?" she called up at the comm. "Are you OK?" No response. "Hold on, I'm coming!" she shouted, leaping from her seat, racing out of the cabin.

Lucky followed her down to Mystica's cabin. Through the grand arched doorway, he could see the old lady huddled up in bed. She was shivering beneath her furs, teeth chattering. Professor Byzantine was beside her, Bazooka on his shoulder, tending to the candles that lit the cabin.

There was something about Mystica that looked very strange, but Lucky couldn't put his finger on what it was.

Then he realized: her headscarf had come off. And without the scarf, he could clearly see that the old lady had hardly any hair left. Just a few thin white wisps, beneath which he could clearly see her pale skull.

"I — I'm sorry," said Mystica, flustered. She quickly pulled a scarf on. "It's so ugly. You shouldn't have to see such things."

Lucky almost didn't go into the cabin; he felt like he was intruding. But she waved him in with a weak smile.

"Come in," she said. "It's always good to see you . . . even if it's not so good to see me. . . ."

Lucky felt embarrassed. All he wanted to do was make it better for her somehow. "Mystica," he said as he went in, "there is no one I would rather see. I missed you so much at the Spacegate."

"I missed you too." She held out a hand, and he took it. Her skin was deathly cold, like ice. "Stay a while," she said. "I feel warmer when you are here. There are such terrible things going on in this galaxy. Did you see that flash of light as we came through the Wall?" She looked down gravely. "That was a star, dying."

Lucky flinched. The thought was too horrible. "How can you tell?"

"Those flashes are supernova pulses," said the Professor. "To a Startalker, they are like death throes: the desperate screams of someone facing the end of their life."

Lucky could feel Mystica's hand shaking as tremors surged up from deep inside her. But her voice stayed calm, betraying not a hint of pain.

"Until now," she said, "their source was hidden by the Spacewall, so we couldn't tell their origin. But now there is no doubt. A star is dying — and not just any star." She shut her golden eyes; it was like night falling upon her face. "It is the star I am connected to. The star at the center of the Aquarius system. I feel everything the Aquarius star feels. I cannot help it; our destinies are linked. So I know my star is dying, because" — she took a sharp breath and opened her eyes again —"because I know that *I* am dying."

"What?" It felt like someone had reached into Lucky's chest and squeezed his heart.

Bixa shook her head, her eyes burning. "I don't believe it, Mystica," she said. "You can't be dying. Yes, you're ill, very ill, but —"

"Not ill, my dear. Dying."

"No!" said Bixa, her needles almost black. "It doesn't make sense. Aquarius still has millions of years left to shine. It's nowhere near time for it to go supernova."

"I cannot explain it," said Mystica. "I do not understand why it is happening. But I feel it in my bones, and so does the Professor. Don't you feel it too?"

"I don't feel a thing," growled Bixa.

Mystica was seized by another fit of coughs: deep, racking coughs that tore her apart from inside.

"There must be a cure," said Lucky. "Every illness has a cure."

Mystica shook her head, exhausted. "This is no illness. It is the suffering of my star that I feel. If only we knew what the Wolf was! It is connected, I am sure. My star will survive only if the Wolf is stopped — and only then, perhaps, will I . . ."

"Our best hope lies in finding the Twelve Astraeus," said the Professor. "What say you, Mystica? Do you feel their presence?"

"I — I'm not sure."

The Professor twisted his whiskers. "I am positive they are somewhere this side of the Wall. We should start to search for signs, out there among the stars."

"Of course," said Mystica. "Bixa. Can you get us a clear view of space?"

Silently, Bixa turned away from her grandmother and tapped on the vidscreen, bringing up a flickering image of the view outside. They squinted through the static, but there was too much interference to see anything clearly.

"May I?" said Professor Byzantine. "In my experience, there is only one thing to do with this kind of technology."

He approached the wall screen and gave it a hefty thump. The image flickered, crackled, and finally cleared.

The Professor smiled at his handiwork. But on the vidscreen now, all they could see was empty space: a lightless black void. The Professor's fingers flicked over the screen, bringing up many different views. He peered through his spectacles, examining all possible angles as he searched for signs of the Twelve Astraeus.

"What are we looking for, exactly?" said Lucky. "Are they really like those people on the vidpics: the gods with the flaming swords and lightning bolts and everything?"

"Those images are based upon ancient legends," said the Professor. "The legends are incomplete: only fragments remain. And different cultures had different legends. Some thought of the Astraeus as immortal gods; others saw them as stars who came down from the sky to walk among us for a while. So it is hard to be sure of anything. All we can say with certainty is that these were beings of unimaginable power, capable of destroying worlds — or creating them."

Lucky looked hard at the vidscreens, for he too was beginning to hope for the return of the Twelve Astraeus. If they really were as powerful as the Startalkers believed, then perhaps they would be the ones to make everything OK.

But there seemed to be no trace of them as yet.

Captain Nox came into the cabin, looking very serious.

"How are you, Mystica?" he said. "I am so sorry about that shockwave. I did my best. . . ."

The old lady managed a small smile, despite her pain. "I am fine, my dear. And thanks to Lucky here, the horrors of the Wall at least are behind us."

The Captain turned to Lucky, a dark look in his eyes. "How did you persuade those Shadow Guards to release us, anyway?" he asked.

Lucky's heart thumped. This was it. No avoiding it anymore. He didn't want to lie to his friends — but the President had left him no choice. "The Shadow Guards know my father," he said carefully, sticking as close to the truth as he could. "They let me go so I'd have a chance to find him."

"Seriously?" said Bixa. "Wow. He must be important!"

"Yeah." Lucky took a deep breath. "And . . . I discovered something. I overheard them saying he's being held in an Axxa army base, on a planet called Charon."

They all stared at him like he'd said something unspeakably foul.

"*Charon?*" said Bixa. "You sure you heard right? 'Cos that's like saying . . . *Hell*! It's a place people whisper about in their nightmares, somewhere you scare kids with. *If you're not good, you'll end up in Charon Caves. . . .*"

Lucky felt the ground shift under his hooves. "Really? Well, do you know where to find this planet Charon?"

"Of course not," said the Captain. "No one even knows if it's real. You'd have to ask the army to get the truth, because I don't believe there's a civilian who knows it."

"Oh." Lucky's heart was sinking.

But Mystica and the Professor exchanged a glance. "There is another possibility," said Mystica. "Someone else who might know."

"Who?" asked Lucky, clutching at hope.

"The Startalker of the Future," said Professor Byzantine. "You see, she has knowledge of things that are presently unknown and have never been known — so if anyone knows, it's her. And as it happens, I would rather like to visit her, to consult her about the mysteries before us. I see no reason Lucky should not come along too, and ask her about Charon. It cannot hurt, can it?"

"I agree," said Mystica. "It is decided." She looked at Lucky in the same way she'd looked at him in the cell on the Spacegate: with nothing but love in her golden eyes. "Do you have anything else to tell us, Lucky?" she asked gently.

He felt too guilty to speak. If she knew the truth about President Thorntree, would she feel the same? But he couldn't risk telling her. "Thank you," he said. "I would love to meet the Startalker of the Future. But where is she?"

"She never left her home planet," said the Professor. "She alone persuaded her people to remain neutral in the War, so she is still to be found on Scorpio Six."

"Scorpio?" muttered Captain Nox. "The most remote Axxa system? It was always difficult to get there — and now you have to fly through a war zone to reach it." He shook his head. "There will be battles, Skyhawk patrols, obstacles every step of the way. But . . . if this is the will of the stars . . . I will try to find a route."

He reached for the astrolabe, and Lucky handed it over at once. The Captain's face creased with lines of fierce concentration as he summoned all his strength, all his experience. He laid his fingers on the black metal disk, and shut his eyes.

The astrolabe flickered faintly with starlight. The Captain seemed to go into a trance, whispering urgent phrases. His fingers moved purposefully over the dials. Lucky could see the dials turning as the Captain tried many routes, even projecting them onto the cabin's vidscreen so everyone could see. But not one of them seemed to work.

After several long, painful minutes, the Captain came out of the astrolabe again. He looked drained, his face as gray as his horns. "It's hopeless," he said. "The space lanes ahead of us are total chaos. I cannot find a single course that would get us to Scorpio safely."

Professor Byzantine cleared his throat. "Perhaps," he said, "you should let Lucky try."

"Me?" said Lucky, startled.

The Captain shook his head. "Navigation is not child's play. The number of possible routes to Scorpio is literally infinite."

"I am well aware of that," said the Professor. "However, the boy has been practicing very hard with that astrolabe. You might be surprised at how good he is now."

Lucky flushed with embarrassment. "I—I could try," he said.

"There is no route," said Nox wearily. "I am certain of it."

"But there must be," said Lucky. "There always is." He could imagine being in there, tracing pathways through the stars. It made him feel better to think of such things, rather than President Thorntree's secrets and lies. "Captain, you gave me an apprentice navigator's ident, so let me be your apprentice. Let me help you. I can; I know I can."

Captain Nox shook his head again. There was a strange look in his eyes: as if the fires inside them were somehow burning out, turning cold. "Get it into your head, boy," he said. "There is no way you are ever going to fly this ship. It's mine. Do you understand? *Mine!*"

Lucky flinched as if he'd been slapped in the face — but Professor Byzantine spoke up at once.

"Of course it is yours, Captain," he said mildly. "But Lucky is not proposing to fly the ship. Real-time navigation at the speed of dark is a task for only the most experienced pilots, such as your good self! No, all he will do is search for a route. And if he happens to find one — why, then you can use it or not, as you wish."

Nox did not reply. Still his eyes had that strange cold look.

Mystica reached out and took his hand. She held it gently, holding him in the soft candlelight of her cabin.

After a moment, the Captain shuddered — and a spark of fire flickered in his eyes. They seemed to come back into focus, as if his mind had been a million miles away.

"I — I'm sorry," he said, starting to shiver. "Go ahead, boy. If you really think you can find a route with that astrolabe of yours — then go ahead and try."

Lucky took a deep breath, unnerved by the Captain's strange behavior. He took the astrolabe in his hands and did his best to concentrate on it.

The symbols began to glow. The dials began to move. They shimmered beneath his fingertips as the metal pulsed and blazed and throbbed with light—

—and then Lucky went into the astrolabe. He became part of it again.

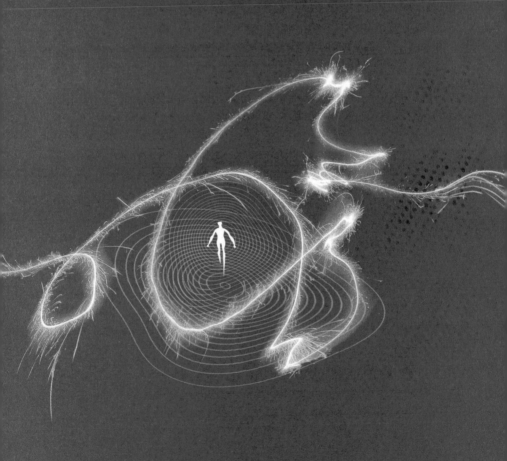

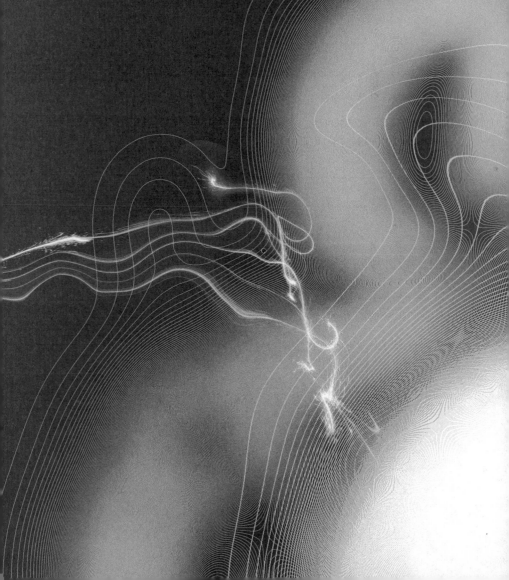

He couldn't see Mystica's cabin anymore. But he could see the stars: all around him, above him, below him. Their scorching faces staring right back at him. So clear and close, he could taste them on his tongue.

He was floating in space among them, in that astral body once more. And he could hear their silvery songs, chiming out in waves of overwhelming power.

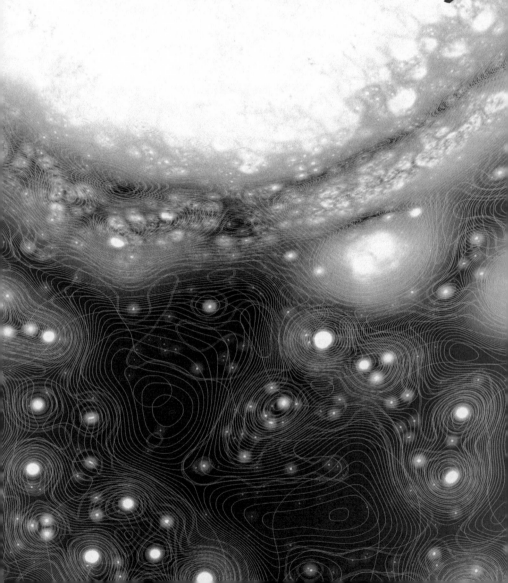

Do not doubt it.
You can do it.
You can learn to fly.

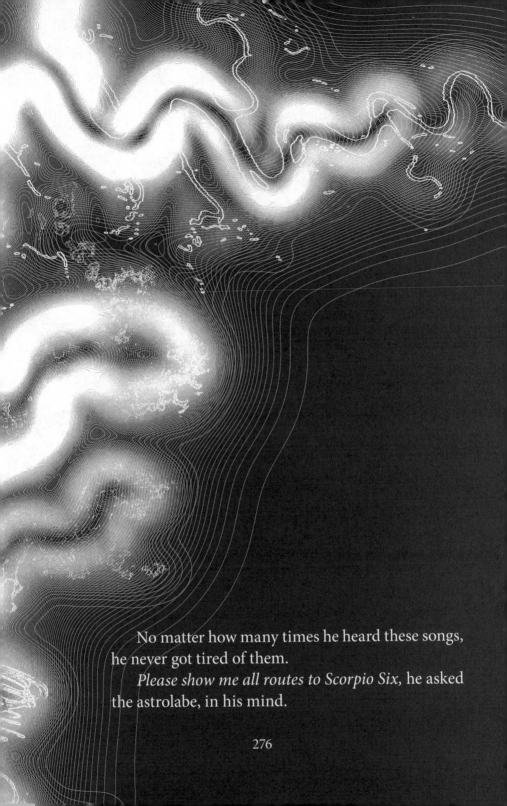

No matter how many times he heard these songs, he never got tired of them.

Please show me all routes to Scorpio Six, he asked the astrolabe, in his mind.

Lines of silver light swirled out from the stars in every direction: every possible pathway through space, spiraling into infinity. He remembered how this used to scare him, make him dizzy — but now he just felt excitement and anticipation.

He looked out across the stars — and took in vast vistas of information at a single glance. He started to survey the routes one by one, moving smoothly along them and seeing where they led.

It was total chaos in Axxa space. Most routes were clearly too dangerous. Everywhere he looked, there seemed to be raging battles, Skyhawk patrols, or other hazards, like deadly radiation storms.

But there were a few patches of clear space out there, a few safe channels. Lucky focused his attention on them, trying to string together a sequence, to build a route that might get them all the way to Scorpio.

At first, he hit dead end after dead end. But he refused to get discouraged. Each time he reached an obstacle, he discarded the route and moved on to the next possibility. He kept asking questions, and the astrolabe responded, giving him all the information he wanted, and more.

He smiled to himself. It felt so good to move through space, to find connections over vast interstellar distances, to think and see at the level of the stars themselves.

But then he heard something that made his smile fade. Those strange sad songs again. Those fragments echoing across infinity. He heard them clearer than ever before:

The Wolf Is
on the Prowl. . . .

The Wolf Is
Breaking Through. . . .

The Wolf Is
Bursting Loose. . . .

The voices seemed so full of fear and grief. He wished he could help them. But he had a job to do here, and only one chance to do it. He made himself focus on navigation, only navigation, and went back to work.

It was clear that a single, straightforward route would not get them there. But what if he put together parts of different routes? He started to improvise, trying anything and everything to expand his options. Still, he kept falling short—but each time, he got a little bit farther, a little bit closer. He kept going, refusing to believe it was impossible, refusing to give up. Trial and error, again and again.

He kept trying and failing, but he kept going, bringing himself closer—

—and closer—

—and closer—

—until finally: there it was before him, as if it had been there all along. A swirling spiral corkscrew of a course that was so unlikely, no one could possibly predict or prevent it. Out of all the infinite possibilities, the one and only pathway that would take them clear through to their destination.

The only safe way to Scorpio.

The route.

He knew it was right the moment he saw it. He felt it, deep within his being. He had the sense of something slotting into place, clicking, satisfying.

This is what I've been looking for, he thought. *But I can't get carried away; there's too much at stake. I've got to be sure I'm right.*

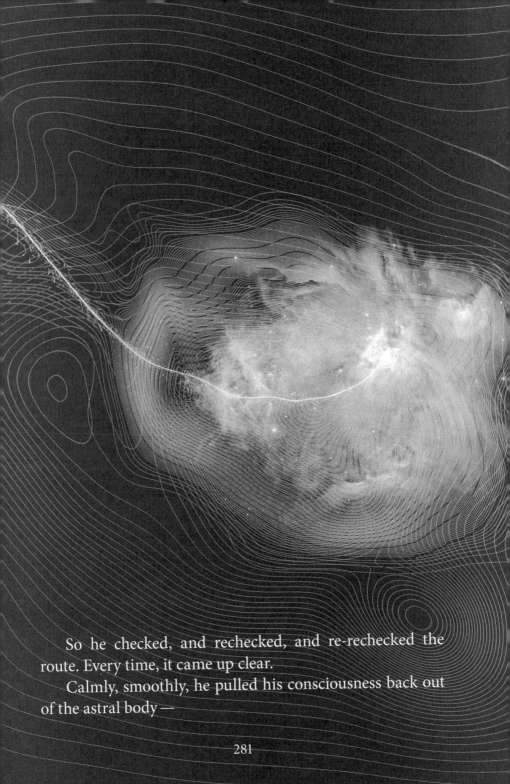

So he checked, and rechecked, and re-rechecked the route. Every time, it came up clear.

Calmly, smoothly, he pulled his consciousness back out of the astral body —

—and returned to the reality of Mystica's quarters.

In the soft candlelight, the old lady was applauding him. Bixa was cheering, her needles flashing neon pink. Bazooka was flapping her feathers, merrily sneezing jets of flame. Because there was his route, projected on the vidscreen — and even he had to admit, it was a beauty.

"My word!" said Professor Byzantine. "What a route!"

"What do you think, Captain?" said Lucky.

The Captain shook his great head. "I — well — I don't know what to think," he said at last. "It might work. It may. Perhaps." He stood up with some difficulty. "I — I shall go to the cockpit, and see what I can do." And with that, he shuffled out of Mystica's cabin.

They watched him go in troubled silence. A moment passed. Then everyone started cheering again — congratulating Lucky on finding the route, calling him a brilliant navigator, a born starsailor.

It felt so good, he could almost forget about Captain Nox.

And he could almost forget that he'd just lied to his friends.

IV

The Wolf Is Bursting Loose.

The Astraeus of the Sea Cannot Fathom It

for Every One
of Us Will Be
Washed Away. . . .

CHAPTER TWENTY-FOUR

The *Sunfire* flew in a great arc toward Scorpio, weaving between all the battles of the War Zone. Lucky's route often brought them close to danger — and Axxa Skyhawks tried to intercept them more than once. But by the time they'd registered the *Sunfire*, the ship was already gone, on a whirling, curling course their navigators just couldn't follow.

All the way to Scorpio, Professor Byzantine kept Lucky hard at work with the astrolabe, and even harder practicing with his power.

"The Spacewall was a formidable test of your control," said the Professor. "And you passed with flying colors. So your task now is to go beyond mere control. You must start learning how to use your power: how to tap into it, let it loose, push it further and further, as far as it can go."

At first, Lucky was reluctant. He didn't want to let the light shine out of him or flare into flame. But he was coming to trust the Professor's judgment, and he was encouraged by his progress with the astrolabe. So he began to experiment in small ways. He started cautiously, learning how to channel the power through his hands, so he didn't burn his clothes every time he used it. He learned how to project the light away from himself, illuminating the air around him. Gradually, he built up the courage and confidence to let the fire out too, allowing blazing heat to stream from his body, even creating explosions by force of will.

It felt different, making these things happen deliberately rather than having them happen to him in his dreams or bursting out of him because of his fear, as they had before. The Professor and Bazooka were with him throughout, urging him on as he made the cabin light up with vivid colors.

But it never became easy for him. It never stopped hurting. Sometimes he lost control. He'd be overwhelmed by fire and would feel like his head was splitting open under the strain, exploding, burning so badly he never wanted to do it again. Even when it went well, he always felt so raw and exhausted afterward that it was a relief to practice Astral Martial Arts with Bixa instead. At least the worst that could happen there was getting beaten up.

So the time passed as they traveled through Axxa space, surging past great rings of astral dust, chasing comets' tails across the stars, until at last they saw the Scorpio system ahead, glowing purple in the black. And at its heart: the planet Scorpio Six, home to the Startalker of the Future.

The *Sunfire* landed without incident. There were no government ships patrolling the skies. No sign of the Axxa army, either. It was as Professor Byzantine had said: a neutral world.

Everyone was invited to the main cabin to celebrate their arrival and finalize their plans. Lucky and Bixa came in from training to find Mystica and the Professor deep in conversation over a pot of Xoco that was bubbling on the stove.

". . . exceeding all expectations," the Professor was saying. "In fact, sometimes I find myself wondering if maybe —"

"Lucky!" said Mystica sharply. "Bixa! Welcome!"

The Professor looked up, startled. Before Lucky could ask what they'd been talking about, Bazooka attacked his cloven-hoof boots, while Frollix and the Captain came striding down from the cockpit. Everyone seemed excited at the thought of what lay ahead. Mystica began to pour the steaming Xoco out into cups, but as she did so —

FLASHHH!

— another terrible pulse of light came through the vidscreens.

Mystica dropped the Xoco pot. It fell to the floor and smashed to pieces, hot liquid splattering everywhere as she screamed in pain. Lucky helplessly watched her coughing, shaking, worse than ever before — and still the searing light blazed on. Everything was laid bare in its merciless glare. He could see every drop of Xoco on the floor, every line and wrinkle on Mystica's face, until at last the light faded.

He hurried to pick up the pieces of the broken pot as Captain Nox moved to help Mystica.

"Don't worry about that, boy," the Captain told him. "Go now. Go with the others, and see if you can find out anything that might help us."

Grimly, Lucky pulled on his space traveler's coat and tucked his astrolabe into the pocket. Frollix, Bixa, and Professor Byzantine made preparations beside him; they were coming too, while Mystica and the Captain stayed on the ship.

But Bazooka the phoenix seemed terrified at the idea of going out. She flapped her wings in horror, and hid under the table, squawking loudly. *"Baaa — Baaa — Baaa —"*

"Bazooka," the Professor called. "Come out of there. You have nothing to fear."

But still she wouldn't come out. *"Baaa-zeekeeee?"* she asked.

"No. Absolutely not," said her master sternly. "You must come with me, this instant."

Reluctantly, she crept out from under the table, eyes cloudy with fear. She perched uncertainly on the Professor's shoulder, shaking her head and chittering to herself.

"What's wrong with her?" asked Lucky, stomach tight with tension.

"Pay her no heed," said the Professor. "Come now. Time is of the essence."

They said quick, tense farewells to Mystica and Nox, and then Frollix drove them out on the cycle.

Lucky's spirits lifted as soon as he saw Scorpio Six. It was beautiful: lush green fields and rolling hills under an open lilac sky. The air was heady with the scent of freshly tilled soil, of agriculture and animals: things growing and alive. He had never seen such things in the Human worlds, and he drank it all in thirstily, relishing the new sights and sounds and smells.

In the far distance, across the horizon, an enormous rainbow framed the sky. Professor Byzantine's face lit with a smile when he saw it.

"Take us that way, Frollix," he said. "That's where we'll find her."

Frollix drove them through fields of wildflowers, their colors as vibrant as their scents: sunflower golds, passion-flower purples, poppy-field reds. They drove through forests full of trees, dotted with dwelling huts that were decorated with patterns representing the stars and constellations.

"Keep going," said the Professor as the sun set and twilight fell, turning the sky deep indigo. He pointed at the horizon again.

Lucky looked up and blinked in surprise. The rainbow they'd seen earlier seemed much bigger from here, and it had become so bright, it was lighting up the twilight with vivid colors. He'd never seen a rainbow after sunset before. He didn't think such a thing was possible.

He kept watching, puzzled and enchanted by its colors, though no one else seemed surprised.

"There's never been any fighting on Scorpio, has there?" Frollix was saying. "Never even a case of the Living Death."

"Indeed," said the Professor. "You will never see Theobroma's army here; they hate Scorpio. They call it a traitor's paradise, because the Startalker of the Future refused to join the War. But this is how it was everywhere before the War. It may be hard to remember, after all that has happened, but back then, we had such hopes for the meeting of Human and Axxa." He sighed. "You know, some say even Theobroma had a Human lover once, though I find that hard to believe."

"King Theobroma?" snorted Frollix. "No way! He was the one who said the stars wanted us to make war on the Humans!"

"Couldn't the Startalkers have challenged that?" asked Lucky. "Couldn't you have said it wasn't true?"

"Oh, we tried," said the Professor. "But how do you prove a thing like that? The King and his commanders had whipped the Axxa up into such a frenzy, they would not listen to us. Our temples were destroyed by our own people. We had no choice but to flee and go into hiding. Few of us ever recovered from those events; we were all diminished by the War. Only the Startalker of the Future was strong enough to persuade her planet to stay out of it. And you can see what a wise decision that was."

They came over the top of a hill as twilight deepened into night. Right in front of them now was the rainbow.

And here, at last, Lucky could see that it was really some kind of vast crystalline structure. A perfect circular wheel, glowing from inside with every color of the spectrum: red, orange, yellow, green, blue, indigo, violet. It was bigger than any building he'd ever seen, reaching right up into the clouds. It took his breath away.

As he looked closer, he realized with a thrill that there were compartments hanging off this wheel, each one full of people. They were looking down at the ground from on high as the wheel turned slowly in the Scorpio night.

"That, my boy, is an Axxa temple," said Professor

Byzantine. "The Rainbow Temple Wheel of Scorpio. And that is where we will find the Startalker of the Future."

Lucky kept looking up, and up, and up; he couldn't take his eyes off it. It was the most amazing construction, constantly turning through its cycles, majestic as the sky itself.

They walked right up to it. Many people were clustered around its base, camped out in tents: old folk, parents, children, all together. There were even some Humans there, mixing peacefully with the Axxa. All around them, Lucky could see the gleam of campfires, and he could smell warm woodsmoke on the wind.

Frollix gazed up at the wheel in undisguised awe. For once, he made no jokes; he was like a little boy in the presence of something he'd never quite dared believe in. "Oh — it's amazing!" he said, his eyes reflecting the rainbow lights.

Bixa bit a fingernail and held back for a moment, gazing up at the wheel.

"What are we waiting for?" said Lucky.

"It's just . . . you can't imagine what this Startalker means to us," said Bixa. "Growing up in the Human worlds, all we ever heard was how everything Axxa was rubbish. But *she* was different. They played her music, and they loved it. And the idea that an Axxa could do that — make music so good and strong and brilliant that even Humans had to respect it . . ." She shook her head, lost for words.

Lucky stared at her. "Who is the Startalker of the Future, anyway?" he said.

"Gala, of course," said Professor Byzantine. "She is not

merely a singer. She is a Startalker: the most powerful of us all."

Lucky gulped. The woman who made the scariest music he'd ever heard was Startalker of the Future? "Well, come on, then," he said, trying to put a brave face on it. "Let's see if we can get her autograph!"

There was only one entrance to the wheel: a high gate, guarded by burly Axxa armed with cudgels.

Professor Byzantine approached them, holding himself straight and proud. *"From the stars we all came..."* he greeted them.

"And what do you want?" snapped the guard who seemed to be their chief.

"Why, we are here to see Gala, naturally," the Professor replied.

The guards' faces darkened. "And who are you?" said the chief. "Have you been granted an audience with the Startalker?"

"We are old friends," said the Professor, stroking his whiskers. "We have traveled very far; she will certainly wish to see us...."

The chief shook his head. The atmosphere had changed. All sense of wonder was gone now, and the night air crackled with tension.

"We defend our Startalker with our lives," said the chief, horns glinting. "Others have come before you, wanting to hurt her. None of them left this world alive."

The guards circled Lucky and his friends.

Frollix grinned and held his hands up in a gesture

294

of peace. "Hey, you wanna defend a Startalker?" he said amiably. "Then you should know you're talking to Professor Byzantine, Startalker of the Past!"

They all stared at the little old man with the white whiskers and the chittering bird on his shoulder — and they didn't look remotely convinced.

"The Startalker of the Past left our worlds long ago," said the chief. "I don't know what he looks like anymore. I just see an old man who's causing me trouble. Get out of here, if you know what's good for you."

Bixa's needles flashed crimson. "We're not going anywhere," she said. "We need to talk to Gala, and we're not leaving till we do."

"By all the Twelve Astraeus!" said the chief, digging his hooves into the ground. "Get out of here, or we'll throw you out, little girl!"

"*Little girl?*" said Bixa. "You moonbrain! You have no idea how important this is!"

"You're calling me a moonbrain?" The chief's face twisted up with disbelief and indignation. His horns bristled at Bixa.

Bixa's needles bristled right back. Raw aggression sizzled in the space between them. The space rapidly narrowed as they moved toward each other. The chief towered over her, but Bixa stood her ground, shaping into an Astral Martial Arts style that Lucky recognized as Cancer the Crab.

The chief swung a fist at her — but she'd already taken a deft sideways step away. Then she flicked out her hooves, like a crab with its pincers, and trapped the chief's arm in her grip. With one twist, she flipped him over. He hit the ground hard, sprawling flat on his backside in the dust, with one of her hooves poised menacingly above his face.

But the other guards were circling them now, swinging their cudgels. Lucky didn't know what to do. He didn't doubt that Bixa could deal with them, but this was getting out of hand, and it wasn't going to get them in.

Professor Byzantine raised an eyebrow. "Lucky," he said softly, "I think our friends need a little convincing. Perhaps they should see some of the things you have been practicing?"

Lucky concentrated. He shut his eyes and thought about everything he'd been working on with the Professor. He dug deep inside himself—

—and felt it rise up within him. Heat. Light. Incandescent power.

He could taste burning at the back of his throat as the energy rose and swelled and grew.

And then he let it loose. He let the power stream out of his hands, and sent it straight up into the sky as a volley of multicolored fireworks.

They exploded above, sending flares streaking out across the night. And all around the wheel, people gazed up at Lucky's fireworks, savoring their bright colors and smoky smells.

The guards looked up too. And when they looked down, there was a new expression on their faces. They stared in awe at the glow of his hands as he pulled the power back inside him.

"Can it be . . . ?" whispered one of them, as Lucky fell forward into the Professor's arms, exhausted and in pain as always.

"What say you, friends?" the Professor asked them. "May we see my old comrade Gala now?"

After a moment's silence, the chief nodded. Bixa moved her hoof away from his face and offered him a hand up.

"Who are you people?" he asked.

"They're like something from the legends," one of the others said. "It's like a sign: a sign that the Twelve are returning."

The Professor's eyes sparkled. "Quite so," he said. "That is what we believe, and I am glad to hear you say it. It is precisely what I hoped to find in your hearts."

Frollix gaped at the Professor, openmouthed. So did the guards. They glanced at Lucky again — but not one of them could say a thing to him. They turned back to the Professor with a strange look in their eyes, as if they'd just discovered that their dearest, most secret dreams weren't just dreams, but were real after all.

"So — you really *are* the Startalker of the Past?" they said.

The Professor bowed graciously before them. The atmosphere changed again. The guards now clustered respectfully around them, as if they were celebrities or royalty.

"Oh, we have missed you, sir!" said the chief. "You don't know how much we've missed you. We've had such troubles with this war. The one thing that keeps us going is our hope that the Astraeus will return. It's a hope we've never lost — but every year, it gets harder to believe. Will they really come back, sir? Will it be soon?"

"We certainly hope so," said the Professor. "And we hope Gala will help us to find them."

"Then please: step on board the Rainbow Temple Wheel! Step right this way!" And with that, he opened the gate with a flourish and moved aside to let them through.

CHAPTER TWENTY-FIVE

They stepped into a large compartment at the bottom of the wheel. On the outside, the crystal gleamed with rainbow colors, but on the inside, it was so clear, Lucky felt he could see forever through it. The guards closed the gate, and the compartment rose into the air, lifting slowly and smoothly off the ground.

Professor Byzantine and Frollix stood on one side. The Professor was talking in hushed tones about the Twelve Astraeus, and Frollix was listening intently, looking out at the world as they rose higher and higher.

Bixa helped Lucky over to the other side of the compartment. He was still unsteady; his body ached after his fireworks. Together, they watched the planet gradually reveal itself before them. They were already high enough to have a clear view into the next valley. An enormous amphitheater had been carved out of the hillside, as big and wide as the hill itself. A huge crowd of people thronged around it, buzzing with excitement, watching the wheel.

The view was so clear that Lucky could still see individuals in the crowds below. He was becoming aware just how diverse the Axxa were. Though the men all had horns, some had great curving crescents, while others sported short sharp spikes. The women's hair was all different too, and so were their eyes. Lucky could see every shade of flame imaginable, and features just as varied as Human features.

Even so, he couldn't help noticing a couple of Axxa who seemed out of place. Two burly men with metal piercings in their faces and brandings on their arms.

That's strange, he thought. *They look a lot like those pirates who boarded the ship, the pirates who I . . . I killed.*

"Hey," he said to Bixa. "Didn't the Professor tell us there'd be none of Theobroma's army here?"

"That's right," she replied, silver eyes glowing as she took in the view.

"Then what are those two doing?" asked Lucky.

Bixa looked where he was pointing — but by the time she did, the men had disappeared into the crowds. "Which two?" she said.

"Never mind. They're gone now." Lucky kept looking, but there was no sign of them amid the mass of people. It was becoming hard to make out individuals; they were rising higher all the time. They could see hills and valleys extending far into the distance, and an endless horizon stretching out beyond. The panoramic view made him feel light-headed. In this magical space, high above the world, anything seemed possible. "Could you imagine the War ever ending, Bixa?" he asked. "The two sides making peace, and not fighting anymore?"

"I don't see so much difference between them," she replied. It was so quiet up here; the only sounds were their own voices, echoing off the crystal walls. "Sometimes I think there's two sides in this war, but it's not Humans against Axxa. It's all the people who want war on one side, and all the people who don't on the other."

He'd never thought about it like that before. "And which side are you on?"

"I'm a warrior," she said proudly, needles bristling. "But . . . I'm supposed to be a Startalker one day too, right?" She glanced across at Frollix and the Professor, and her voice dropped so low that Lucky had to lean in close to hear her. "You know what? Sometimes I wish I *could* be a Startalker. You think I really like having to defend myself all the time? Imagine having a temple like this. Imagine being like Gala!" Just for an instant, her neon needles flashed with cobalt-colored light; then the color drained away. "It'll never happen, though," she said glumly. "I don't have the power Mystica thinks I do."

Lucky frowned. "What do you mean? You're brilliant! You know everything about the stars."

"Sure, sure: I can talk about the theory. And it's not like I haven't tried. But I just don't feel it, inside me." She shook her head. "The truth is, I've *never* heard a star singing, my whole life long."

"You haven't?" he said, surprised. It was totally silent for a moment as he took this in. Then he looked up through the crystal top of the compartment. There they were, bright and beautiful as always: a million points of silver light, shining in the black.

"I want to." Bixa sighed, gazing up at them too. "More than anything, I wish I could hear a star singing to me, like Mystica and the Professor have, like even you have. . . ." She

301

looked down again. "But it'll never happen. And anyway—what's the point of power if it can't save the people you love? Mystica's power couldn't save my parents from the Axxa army and the Shadow Guards. Now she's dying, and no one can save her. Soon she'll be gone, and the Captain too. What am I gonna do then? It doesn't matter what powers I've got—how can I survive alone?"

Lucky knew the feelings she was talking about, knew them very well indeed. The loss of his mother went so deep inside him, he'd thought he was the only one who'd ever felt that way.

"You won't be alone," he said. "Not ever, Bixa. If there's anything I can do—"

"There's nothing anyone can do, is there?" she said, knuckles whitening as she clenched her fists. "I hate death—I hate it! I wish I could fight it. I wish it would come here and give me a fair fight! But death just takes people away. It doesn't care what's fair and what's not. It takes everyone in the end; it destroys *everything*! Look around you, Lucky. In the end, all this will go back to nothing. So what's the point?" she demanded bitterly, needles black as night. "What's the point of anything?"

Lucky looked at the world, laid out beneath them like a tapestry, or an open book. He could see it all: its hills and valleys, its wrinkles and folds, its rolling ups and downs. From this perspective, turning silently in the sky, all of it seemed beautiful, all of it alive. "I'm not sure," he admitted. "But just because it's going to die one day . . . doesn't mean it's not worth fighting for. Maybe it matters even more,

302

because it's all we've got." He looked straight into her eyes. "And there's no one who could fight for it better than you, Bixa Quicksilver."

Her eyes widened at that, and a little color came back into her needles. They were near the top of the wheel now, and the view was beyond breathtaking. Lucky could see the curve of the planet itself from here. For the first time, he really understood what it meant to be on a world. He could almost feel it turning, like the wheel: a globe of life and light, moving through the vastness of space, so fragile, yet so alive. He looked at Bixa, looking at the world —

Click.

The compartment opened. They turned to look outside. And there, on a platform at the top of the wheel, stood Gala: Startalker of the Future.

She was just as intense in real life as she seemed on the vidscreens. She was dressed all in black. Long dark hair hung over her face. But as she saw them coming out of the compartment, she threw her head back, and her hair parted to reveal her eyes. They blazed every color of the spectrum at once, from ultraviolet to infrared: eyes like diamond fire.

"Old friends!" she called as the Professor bowed gallantly before her, while Bazooka shivered on his shoulder. "I've waited so long for you to return — and now here you are, bringing those who will shape the future." She beamed at Bixa and Frollix, who both looked starstruck — and then she turned to look at Lucky with her rainbow-colored eyes. She stared at him openly, nakedly, like the other Startalkers did — and her gaze seemed to reach directly into his brain.

"Thank you for your fireworks," she said. "I know how much they cost you."

Lucky felt confused. He could feel the wind on his face; could feel how high up they were. *From the stars we all came . . ."* he began.

". . . and to the stars we return," said Gala. "Perhaps sooner than we expect." She turned back to the Professor. "So tell me, friend: what brings you back at last?"

"Many mysteries lie before us, Gala," said the Professor. "We hope you will help us unravel them."

"You seek knowledge?" She held her hands out wide, embracing the vast view all around them. "Then you have come to the right place. Ask, and I shall answer."

"Those supernova flashes in the sky . . ." said the Professor. "Have you seen them?"

"I see them, and I hear them. Right here, I feel them." She touched her heart. "The death throes of a star. In my dreams, the Twelve Astraeus sing of little else."

The Professor nodded briskly. "We are searching for the Twelve," he said. "Mystica and I both feel sure they are at hand. The signs are everywhere."

"Indeed." Gala sighed, hair waving in the wind. "But are you looking in the right place?"

"And where would the right place be?" said the Professor a little stiffly. "Would it perchance be in Aquarius, behind the government blockade?"

She closed her eyes. "Aquarius . . ." she murmured. "So many things are hidden there — but all of them will be found."

"Ah!" The Professor looked rather pleased with himself. "And the Wolf That Eats the Stars?"

"I cannot say. I feel it, and I fear it, yet its nature is mysterious to me. I see it devouring suns, one by one. But what is it? Do not ask me, for I do not know. Even the King, with all his faith and fury, cannot stop it — though his great weapon is coming to him, closer all the time . . ." She opened her eyes and turned to Lucky. "And you, strange boy: you have a question for me?"

"Me?" Lucky breathed in sharply. This was the chance he'd been waiting for, ever since his meeting with the President. "Well, I'm looking for my father," he told her. "I heard he was on the planet Charon. Do you know where that is?"

Gala scowled. "There are secrets even I do not know," she said. "And yet — you have your father's astrolabe?"

Lucky's skin prickled. How did she know that? He pulled it out and showed it to her. "I've been trying to use it to find him," he said. "The problem is, whenever I ask about him, it throws me off the edge of the map."

She reached out and took the astrolabe. "Off the edge?" she echoed. "That must be something uncharted. Unknown. Something yet to come. That is my domain, boy. If you have the courage to go there — I say you will find your father, and more."

"How?" asked Lucky. "How do I do that?"

"Leave the astrolabe with me," she replied. "I will ask my star: the Scorpio star. I will ask it in song — about your father, and all these questions — and I will tell you what it sings in reply." She gestured toward the amphitheater over the next hill. "I am singing tonight: a great concert for my people. You are all invited, as my honored guests. At the end of my song, seek me out, and I will tell you what the stars have told me."

"Thank you," said Lucky. Beside him, Professor Byzantine stroked his whiskers thoughtfully, while Bixa and Frollix grinned, their eyes wide and starry bright.

But Gala shook her head, and her eyes flashed like a diamond prism. "Thank me?" she said. "I am not sure you will. Are you absolutely certain you wish to find him?"

"Of course," said Lucky. "I'd do anything to see him again."

"What do you mean, Gala?" asked the Professor. "Surely Lucky has to find his father? For only he knows the truth about the boy's power; only he has the answers —"

"On the contrary," she said. "In the end, the boy must find his answers for himself, in himself. No father can tell him what to do. It is not a parent that he needs, but that which is already inside him." She turned back to Lucky. "Let me see what is inside you, boy. Let me feel your heart."

She reached a hand up to Lucky's chest. Her fingers had long curving nails, painted black, tapering to points; they looked very sharp indeed. He hesitated, feeling scared of her — but he wanted her help even more. So he stayed still and let Gala touch him.

She closed her eyes. "I feel it," she whispered after a long moment. "I see it, rising inside you." She looked at Professor Byzantine in amazement, and her eyes flashed every color at once. "It cannot be, can it . . . ?"

The Professor stared back at her. "Mystica and I have had our suspicions — but —"

"What is it?" said Lucky, tension tight in his chest. "What do you see?"

Gala did not reply for a long time. "Higher and higher," she said at last. "Stronger and stronger. And every time, it burns a little more of you away. Did you not realize? You are burning your mortal life away every time you use your power."

Lucky pulled away from her, shaking. He held his hands up in front of him, as if to ward off her torrent of words.

"You cannot stop it," she went on. "It is written in the legends. *You are what you are, and you will return to the sky!*"

"Return . . . ?" Lucky looked desperately at Professor Byzantine. The old Axxa was staring at the wheel as it turned in the night, twisting his whiskers, tighter and tighter. "Professor, what does that mean?" he pleaded. "It doesn't mean . . . I'm going to *die*?"

Professor Byzantine looked up. His eyes were like rain. "Well . . . the legends are not entirely clear, as you know," he said. "Only fragments remain, and it is impossible to be certain what they mean. But perhaps — possibly . . ." He looked down.

"You knew?" said Lucky. "I trusted you, I thought you were helping me — but all this time, you were making me burn my own life away? How could you do that?"

"Lucky, whatever the legends say, I tell you that you *must* learn how to use your power, whatever the cost," the old Axxa insisted.

307

"Even if it means I'm going to die?" he cried. "I wish I'd never met you! If that's what this power means — if that's why it hurts so much, every time I use it — then I'm never using it again!"

"But you must," hissed Gala. "And you will. That is why you are here."

Lucky stumbled back, away from the Startalkers, till he stood on the very edge of the platform, high above the ground, with the Rainbow Temple Wheel rising and falling silently behind him. He could see that vast view of the world again, spread out beneath him. But it no longer seemed magical. Now he just felt sick with vertigo. He felt weak, and small, and scared. Because Gala had made her prophecy of the future — and Professor Byzantine had as good as confirmed it.

"You will remember this moment when the time comes," said Gala, behind him. "You will remember me."

Her words were like poison in his veins.

The Professor bristled fiercely and strode up beside Lucky. "That is enough, Gala!" he said. "If you can help the boy find his father — then please do. But I will not stand here and let you scare him any longer."

"He would be a fool not to fear the future that awaits him," she replied. "But the future is not fixed. He has the power to decide how all this will end. So come to me at the close of my song, boy, and I will give you what you seek."

There was silence for a moment. Then Lucky stepped away from the giddy edge of the platform, away from Professor Byzantine.

"All right," he said. "All right." He turned to Frollix and

Bixa. "Will you two come to the concert with me?" he asked them, ignoring the Professor.

"Of course," said Bixa. She looked shocked.

"Let's just hope the music's better than the prophecy!" muttered Frollix.

Professor Byzantine looked at Lucky. Lucky refused to meet his gaze.

"Then — I — I shall stay here," said the Professor after a moment's pause. "I shall wait for you on this beautiful wheel."

"Understand, old friend," said Gala, "I bear you no ill will. I tell you only what I hear as my star sings to me."

A new compartment reached the top of the wheel. Frollix and Bixa followed Gala into it, but Professor Byzantine called to Lucky as he turned to go.

"Just a moment, Lucky," he said. He looked somehow smaller, older, less sure of himself than before. "I — I apologize to you. I did not know for certain what the legends meant — but perhaps I should have told you what I suspected."

Lucky shook his head bitterly. "Seems like no one ever tells me the whole truth."

"Not one of us knows it," replied the Professor. "Only the stars. But still I say: if you have this power, it can only be because you are meant to use it. Please, do not stop now. You have come so far, so fast. I am so proud of what you have achieved already. I truly believe you are here for a reason, the best possible reason —"

Lucky shook his head. "I don't think so," he said. "But — I'm sorry about what I said. I didn't mean it. I don't wish I'd never met you, Professor." He could feel emotions rising inside him, taking him by surprise.

The Professor's eyes looked deep into his being, and he smiled. "Well," he said, "there need be no more practice for today. Now, go and enjoy the music — and may the stars light your path."

"*Baaa-zookaaaaa!*" chirped the phoenix on his shoulder.

Lucky turned and followed his friends into the compartment, and down the other side of the Rainbow Temple Wheel.

CHAPTER TWENTY-SIX

The amphitheater was enormous inside. There were rows and rows of seats, on more levels than Lucky could count, all built around a central stage that was carved out of the hillside. Every seat was occupied; it was a full house. Yet he and his friends had been given the very best seats, right at the front, near the stage.

High above them, the Rainbow Temple Wheel was turning slowly in the night, casting a warm glow over everything. He imagined himself still up there with Professor Byzantine and Bazooka, watching the world go by. He regretted the harsh words he'd spoken, but he felt at peace with his decision. He was never going to use the power again. He was right after all: it really *was* a curse. He felt sick to think he'd been burning his life away; Gala's prophecy had chilled him to the core.

Maybe she's wrong, he told himself. *Maybe if I don't use the power anymore, I'll be OK. And if I can just find my father, then he'll tell me the truth, the whole truth.*

The lights went low. The amphitheater fell into an expectant hush, and Lucky focused on the stage.

There was nothing at first. Just darkness. Blackness. Silence.

Then came a small, soft, silvery sound, like the chime of a faraway bell. Lucky shivered with recognition. Around him, everyone in the amphitheater held still, as if under a spell, as slowly the sound got bigger, and closer, and clearer.

A light began to glow onstage. In the light stood Gala. She was singing, her fingers sweeping across the strings of a musical instrument, her bare feet planted firmly on the floor. The song seemed to be rising up, coming through her, as if she was just a channel for it.

The sound deepened. It started to surge and swell, as if it was taking off, and Lucky felt his blood surge with it, felt his head lighten, his cares and worries lifting from his shoulders. And all around him, he saw people with wide-open eyes, their expressions telling him they were feeling the same rush he was, the same exhilarating thrill.

Everyone stood up as the music lifted off, and it began to fill Lucky with the most powerful feelings — feelings that streamed up from the very center of his being.

This is it, he thought. *This is the sound of the stars, singing in my dreams. It can't get any better than this*—but even as he thought this, the music built further; it grew richer, deeper, stronger, without ever losing its delicacy— the music and his feelings both growing and growing, until he found himself grinning, just grinning with the beauty of it all.

And still the music stretched out and shone into the night. For an hour or more, they stood there swaying, transported to a place as far away as deepest space, yet as close as their own heartbeats. It was like hearing the music of life, endlessly renewing itself. Like an ember of light in the dark; a spark of silver in the black.

And as they swayed together in time to the music, Bixa Quicksilver reached out to Lucky, took his hand in hers, and squeezed it.

Her hand was warm. It felt smaller than he would have expected, and softer too. He squeezed back, and out of the corner of his eye, he saw her smile, like a comet in the night. At that moment, she looked so beautiful to him, so true and alive.

She held on to his hand, and it was like electricity going through him, like fireworks in his heart. Connected: he felt connected to her, and together, they were connected to everything.

Feelings were flowing into him and filling him up. Oh, they were huge, these feelings. What were they? Where did they come from? He didn't know. All he knew was that he wanted to hold her tight and never let go. He wanted all his life to be like this.

And then Frollix put his huge arms around them both, and the three of them were hugging, dancing, swaying together in time to the music.

And Lucky smiled like he'd never smiled before. It was as if his whole body was smiling. *I think it's called happiness,* he realized. *This strange feeling that I'm feeling: I think that must be its name.*

A moment of perfect happiness. It lasted just a moment —

— and then he felt the earth shake through his boots as a massive blast ripped the night wide open.

The blast knocked him clean off his feet. Stunned, he cowered on the ground, shielding his head as shockwaves scorched the air above him.

He looked up.

Above the amphitheater, over the hill, the Rainbow Temple Wheel was exploding.

The horror was inconceivable. Lucky saw compartments shattering, crystal cracking as the wheel was ripped apart. He saw people falling from the sky. But everything came in flashes. There was a moment, then another, yet the two were not connected. An image, a blast of sound, but no flow.

And where the center of the wheel should have been, there was now . . . *nothing*. Lucky stared and stared, but his mind couldn't seem to get a grip on it. His eyes kept sliding away. The center was gone, but he couldn't see through to anything behind it. There was just . . . nothing. Absolutely nothing.

His eyes lost focus. His field of vision narrowed. All he could see now was himself. Everything else was fading away.

An overpowering wave of despair hit him. He felt as though his life was suddenly, totally meaningless. All hope and purpose and connection were destroyed. All that remained was a terrible emptiness inside.

Nothing matters.

Nothing matters anymore.

". . . Lucky!" someone was shouting, a million miles away. "Lucky, look at me!" the voice insisted. He wished they would go away. "Look at me, come on!"

Someone squeezed his hand—someone warmer, and smaller, and softer . . .

He squinted. It was Bixa. He could see her: she was right there in front of him. She was holding on to him like she was holding on to life itself. She was calling out to him. He looked into her silver eyes — and his field of vision widened. The blur cleared a little.

She matters.

Of course she matters.

The sense of despair receded, just a little. He fought it back, clung on to Bixa as clarity and meaning and focus returned. *Bixa matters, and Frollix, and Professor Byzantine, and —*

The Professor was on the wheel.

Lucky looked up. But there was only the skeleton of a structure: just spokes now, revealed like bare bones, crumbling in slow motion.

There was a terrible ringing in his ears. Somewhere in the distance, shots were being fired. Sirens were wailing. Around him, people were screaming in terror. They started to run as panic spread like fire. The air smelled scorched.

Bixa's voice cut through it all: "... could've been us!" she was saying.

"What happened?" he asked her. "What *was* that?"

"A Dark Matter bomb. Nothing else could do this."

"Did you feel it, Bixa? That wave of despair? That horrible blur?"

"I felt it. Like everything came apart: time, space, everything. That's a Dark Matter bomb. They destroy the connections. They destroy everything." She looked up at the wheel. "I can't believe it happened here. How could King Theobroma do this to his own people?"

Lucky looked around. He could see Axxa with that terrible emptiness in their eyes, like black holes in the sky. The million-mile stare. The Living Death.

And now he knew how it looked from the inside, because he'd been there too, for a moment.

He'd had the Living Death.

Suddenly, out of nowhere, it had struck Scorpio Six — at exactly the same moment as the Dark Matter bomb. And yet . . . why didn't everyone have it? Why was he OK now, like Bixa, and Frollix —

Wait.

Frollix was not OK. He was huddled on the ground, on the other side of Bixa. There was something very painful about the way he was sitting. He was clutching his head, rocking back and forth. "Frollix — what's wrong?" called Lucky.

Frollix didn't answer; he just kept rocking back and forth. He looked cut down, like a giant tree that had been felled in a forest.

He doesn't have the Living Death, does he? thought Lucky, his stomach lurching at the thought. *Please no — please let him be OK —*

"Speak to me!" Bixa yelled at her brother. "Frollix, what is it? What's wrong?"

"I — I don't know!" gasped Frollix. His starry eyes were blazing. "It's like my head's exploding — I can't control it —"

"Hold on to me!" said Bixa, reaching over to him. "You're going to be OK." But Frollix looked very far from OK.

As they lay there on the ground, people all around them

were stampeding in terror, trying to flee from the amphi-theater, crashing past the security guards, sweeping them aside like an avalanche.

Yet it was no safer outside. The wreckage of the wheel was raining down from the sky. A great pillar of smoke rose up in its place. The air was full of fragments of shattered crystal, as if the atmosphere itself was wounded.

"The Professor was on that wheel," said Lucky. "The Professor and Bazooka."

For a moment, Bixa couldn't speak. Her needles were jet-black, and she couldn't look Lucky in the eye. "Then . . . they're dead," she said at last, with terrible simplicity. "You saw it. No one could survive that explosion. We're lucky we were shielded by the amphitheater, so we didn't get the full blast. All this is just shockwaves."

"But—he can't be dead," said Lucky. "He *can't* be, can he?"

Bixa clenched her fists. "Come on," she said in a low voice. "We have to see Gala, remember?" She hauled herself up. "We have to get your astrolabe back and find out what the stars told her. Maybe there'll be something that can help us."

Lucky stared up at the ruin of the wheel, tears behind his eyes. "What—what about Frollix?" he managed to say.

"He's coming with us," said Bixa. "He's going to be OK."

Lucky looked at Frollix again. The big Axxa was whimpering, holding his head. He didn't see how Frollix could possibly be OK—but they couldn't leave him there. So he got to his feet and helped Bixa haul her brother up. Frollix's body was so heavy, they had to support it between them.

Unsteady, ears still ringing from the blast, they stumbled forward through the crowds. The broken ground was treacherous; even with his cloven-hoof boots, Lucky lost his balance more than once.

But Bixa steered them, picking her way through the wreckage, purposeful as ever. "Mystica's counting on us," she said. "We can't let her down."

Finally, they reached the stage. It was a mess of rubble, cables, girders — fallout from the blast everywhere. The taste of ash filled Lucky's mouth.

Gala was there, on her knees, covering her face with her hands.

"Gala!" called Bixa, reaching out a hand. "Startalker of the Future!"

Gala looked up. Her face was smeared with ash. Her rainbow eyes overflowed with grief; tears streamed down her cheeks. She stared at the ruin of the wheel, and the destruction of her world.

"How could they?" she whispered. "How could anyone do this?" Slowly, she turned to look at them, one by one: Lucky, Bixa, and finally Frollix. She gasped as she met Frollix's eyes. She grabbed his hands and held him to her chest like a drowning man.

"What are you doing to my brother?" said Bixa. "If you hurt him —"

"Hush!" said Gala, holding him tight. She cradled Frollix, rocking him back and forth, whispering in his ear. "So Byzantine is gone," she murmured. "And now his power passes to you. But you — poor fool — you never believed it, or prepared for it, until too late . . . And now here it is, overwhelming."

"I — I can't stop it," groaned Frollix. "I keep seeing things that make no sense — hearing things I don't understand — all at once, rushing in. . . ." He ground his palms into his eyes and ears, as if to stop the flood of visions.

Gala held him for a long while, and then glanced up at Lucky. "As for your father," she said, "he is waiting for you. He is expecting you, even now. Go to Aquarius, and you will find him."

"He's in Aquarius? Is that where Charon is — in Aquarius?"

Gala shook her head; her hair flicked across her face. "Nothing is in Aquarius! But that is where you must go. For Aquarius is dying — and if Aquarius goes, everything goes. Nothing will remain." Her rainbow eyes filled with tears again. "Oh, we had such hopes, we Startalkers — but all is fallen into ruin. No, we cannot help you. Our time is over. One by one, we die."

Bixa's needles buried themselves at the words, and her head drooped. But Lucky forced himself to speak. He had to keep trying, though he dreaded what Gala might say next.

"I don't understand," he said. "How do I find my father if he's not in Aquarius? I'm begging you, please — just tell me how to find him! Give me something to go on!"

Gala looked into his eyes. Through her tears, she seemed to be struggling with terrible demons. Then she nodded, hesitant. "Very well. Watch . . ."

She held the astrolabe in her hands and tapped its surface with her long black nails. The dials began to move. They started to turn and spin, shimmering beneath her fingers as the metal disk pulsed and blazed and throbbed with light. "Do you see?" she murmured. "Through the storm, and off the edge. Do you see it? The stars will lead you there, if you are bold enough to follow."

Lucky looked. All he could see was the blur of her fingernails as they flicked over the symbols and dials. But then — just for a moment — he thought he saw the astrolabe opening out beneath her touch. He thought he saw lines of silver light stretching off the astrolabe, off the edge of the disk altogether, extending out into the open space around her.

He felt a shiver of hope —

— and then Gala shrieked like someone possessed. She dropped the astrolabe. It fell from her hands into the rubble. Those lines of silver light flickered out, and were gone.

"The Wolf!" she howled, convulsed with horror. Her eyes sparked every color at once. "The Wolf That Eats the Stars! *That* is what lies at the end of your path! For you and the Wolf — you are connected! In the end, you are one!"

"What?" gasped Lucky. "How can we be connected?"

But Gala was backing away from him, hands held up before her as she stumbled into the rubble. She was fleeing from the stage, fleeing from Lucky. She was running out into the crowds.

He called after her, but she didn't look back. Gala, the most powerful Startalker, seemed utterly terrified of him as she plunged into the torrents of people surging past on all sides. She was swept up, carried away among them — and was gone.

Lucky and Bixa looked at each other: helpless, hopeless, wordless.

"Can we get out of here?" groaned Frollix.

Lucky retrieved his astrolabe from the rubble, and they stumbled out of the amphitheater in silence. The explosion was still ringing in their ears. Smoke and ash were still rolling across the night as they walked through the ruins of the world.

It looked as if a great fist had come down from the sky and smashed the landscape to pieces. The forest trees had shattered into twigs. The dwelling huts had been blown away. Of the wildflowers in the fields, only stalks remained, shaking in the wind.

There were animals stampeding through the fields, and people running, walking, stumbling out of the smoke. Their faces were covered in ash, and still the ash kept raining from the sky.

Lucky looked for Professor Byzantine and Bazooka by the wreckage of the wheel. Bixa tried to convince him that it was pointless, but he refused to believe it. He had to look. He had to search.

It was long, and hard, and grim.

Half buried in the rubble, he found a single feather of crimson gold. Just one feather: that was all he could find.

He picked it up. It was still warm to the touch, still glowing with light.

His heart ached for the little phoenix and her master, the Startalker of the Past.

He couldn't show the feather to Frollix and Bixa. He couldn't bear to look at it himself, but he couldn't leave it in the ashes, either. So carefully, silently, he put the feather away in the pocket of his coat.

That was when he had to turn away from the wreckage and admit to himself that there were no survivors.

III

The Wolf Is Free.

The Astraeus of the Hunt Cannot Catch It

for We Are Now the Hunted. . . .

CHAPTER TWENTY-SEVEN

Mystica knew what had happened. Though she'd wept, she had already dried her tears by the time they returned to the *Sunfire*. Yet it was even sadder for Lucky to see how bravely she composed herself, sitting up in her bed and refusing to show despair, thanking the stars instead that Frollix, Bixa, and Lucky at least had survived.

"What's wrong with Frollix?" said the Captain as Lucky and Bixa carried him into the cabin and laid him down on Mystica's bed.

"There's voices in my head," groaned Frollix, his face shadowy in the candlelight. "Songs. And I don't know what they are. . . ."

Mystica cradled Frollix in her arms. "It is your star, singing to you," she said. "My dear old comrade is gone; he has returned to the stars, too soon. Now you have taken his place as Startalker of the Past. You are coming into your power, as we always said you would."

"But I don't want it," gasped Frollix, holding his head in his hands. "It's too much!"

"Many Startalkers feel that way at first," Mystica replied gently. "But you can master it. Try, Frollix. Don't be scared of it."

Her words didn't seem to comfort him. Watching her brother, Bixa looked even more troubled.

"Something strange happened to us all, right after the bomb," she said. "Something like the Living Death. I've never felt anything like it. Suddenly, nothing mattered; everything was meaningless. All I could see was myself. And I remember thinking, maybe Dark Matter bombs cause the Living Death. . . ."

"I thought the same thing," said Lucky. "But then we recovered from it; I don't know how. Lots of people didn't."

"So what did Gala tell you?" asked Mystica, peering at them through the flickering light.

Lucky looked down; he couldn't bring himself to tell her all Gala's dire prophecies. "She — she said we had to go to Aquarius. She told the Professor that was where we'd find what we're looking for. And she said I'd find my father — only she didn't say *how*."

Mystica shivered and pulled her furs tight around herself. "She always speaks in riddles, that one. You never know what her words mean until it's too late. But that is the nature of the future. It is fluid. Nothing is certain."

"She seemed pretty sure about one thing," said Bixa. "She said that you're right, Mystica. Aquarius is dying. And if Aquarius goes, everything goes."

"Ah." Mystica tried to control her shivering, but it was no good; her whole body shuddered at the news. "Then we can delay no longer. Captain, I know you will object, but kindly set a course for Aquarius."

Captain Nox did not reply. He was staring at images of space on the vidscreens. He seemed a million miles away.

"Ozymandias?" said Mystica quietly. She reached out and took his hand. "My dear? Will you set a course to Aquarius, please?"

The Captain blinked. "Aquarius?" He scratched the base of his horns; pondered the question in silence for a moment.

"I know it is not safe," said Mystica. "The Axxa fleet will be resisting the Humans' blockade. There is bound to be fierce fighting. But that is where we must go."

"We can't fly without Frollix," the Captain said bleakly. "He has to operate the Dark Matter drive while I navigate. I can't do both at the same time."

Frollix gritted his teeth. He made a massive effort and slowly hauled his huge bulk up, until he was standing on his own. "I'll do it," he said. "I'll fire up the drive. We'll get to Aquarius. Don't worry, Mystica: you can count on me."

"Frollix," cautioned the Captain, "you are in no fit condition."

"No, sir. But if I'm really gonna do this Startalker thing — then I gotta do something normal too!"

The Captain looked from Frollix to Mystica and back again — and then exhaled in resignation. "Very well." He stood up. "If that's how you want it, then come along. We have work to do."

"I can help with the navigating," Lucky pitched in. "I could use the astrolabe, and help you find the best route."

He pictured the ship's cockpit in his mind. He desperately wanted to be there, part of the action. He didn't want to think about the dangers they were going into — or the possibility that he himself might be the biggest danger of all. He just wanted to do something useful.

But the Captain shook his head. "Help? How can anyone help us now, boy? We're beyond help." His horns glinted. "Besides, I don't want you anywhere near my cockpit. Wherever you go, bad things happen. Sometimes I'd swear you were cursed. So you stay right here, and don't touch a thing." He left the cabin, trailing Frollix in his wake.

Lucky felt crushed. *I can help,* he thought. *I know I can. But the Captain's right. I am cursed. Wherever I go, bad things do seem to keep happening —*

"Don't listen to him!" said Mystica, interrupting his thoughts. "You stay here with me. I always feel so much warmer when you're here."

Lucky sat beside her and Bixa on the bed. Together, they stared at the vidpics of the Twelve Astraeus in silence.

"So what else did Gala say?" Mystica asked after a while. "Surely there was more."

Lucky bit his lip. He could hardly bear to think about it. But he made himself tell her Gala's prophecy on the wheel: how he was burning his life away, and how the Professor had confirmed it. "Did you know too?" he asked the old lady.

Mystica's golden eyes went wide with shock. She shook her head and took his hand. Her skin was cold, so cold, like death. "Are you absolutely certain that's what she meant?" she said. "After all, it was the Professor who died on Scorpio,

330

not you. Perhaps she intended the prophecy for him. Think carefully, Lucky. What were Gala's exact words?"

The memory was crystal clear, and it made him shudder, even now. "*You are what you are, and you will return to the sky!*"

"*You are what you are?*" murmured Mystica. "What a strange thing to say. Did she at least tell you what she thought you were?"

Lucky's throat constricted. It felt like there was a hand around his heart, crushing it. "She said that me and the Wolf . . . we're connected. Me and the Wolf are one." He could hardly breathe now. "What if that means *I'm* the Wolf That Eats the Stars? What if I'm the one who's killing Aquarius — and killing you, Mystica?"

There was silence for a long moment. Mystica's golden eyes looked deep into him, through his secrets and fears, all the way to the center of his being.

"No," she said at last. "That cannot be true. Whatever she meant . . . I think I would know if you were the Wolf."

"There was something else," added Bixa, her needles glimmering. "Right at the beginning, when Gala first felt Lucky's power, she looked at the Professor — and he told her that you'd had your suspicions, Mystica."

Mystica gasped and covered her mouth with her hand.

"What?" said Lucky. "What suspicions?"

The old lady looked up at the vidscreens. "There was a possibility that the Professor and I wondered about," she said. "We didn't dare believe it, because after all, it is so unlikely. . . . But perhaps the thing we've been searching for, out there in space — perhaps it's been right here, under our

331

noses, all along." She turned to Lucky, her eyes bright as sunrise. "You," she said. "What if you are one of the Astraeus?"

"What?" He shook his head; he almost laughed. "You're joking, right?"

But Mystica didn't look like she was joking. She was gazing at the vidscreens, her eyes shining. His mouth went dry as he looked up too and saw those amazing people, so vast and powerful. The light was streaming out of their hands, their heads, their hearts. Just as it had streamed out of him.

"The Twelve Astraeus," she whispered. "The stars who came down from the sky." She shivered and hugged herself. "We thought you were channeling the power of the stars. But what if you are not a channel? What if you are the thing itself? What if there is a star inside you, rising up as you come into your power?"

Lucky's scalp was prickling, his mind reeling. He felt dizzy. It was like standing on the edge of the wheel again — or falling and falling and falling through the night.

"There can't be a star inside me," he managed to say. "Those legends of yours — they're *legends!*"

Mystica wiped her eyes. "Of course," she said. "But how else can you explain all your powers? The heat, the light, the flames? Your brilliance with the astrolabe?" She peered deep into his eyes. "And you say you hear the stars singing to you?"

"That doesn't mean anything. Startalkers hear them too —"

"Startalkers hear only one star: the star they're connected to. How many do you hear?"

"I — I'm not sure. Lots of them . . ."

"Lots?" she said softly. She shook her head in wonder. "That is something no Startalker could claim."

"But — look!" Lucky pointed up at the figures on the screens, with their wings and haloes, their flaming swords and thunderbolts; the people who held whole worlds in their hands. "They're incredible! They're like gods; they can do anything. I'm nothing like that. I'm useless, clumsy —"

"Of course!" breathed Mystica, clapping her hands together. "Of course — of course you are clumsy! You are bound to have trouble with anything physical, because this Human body is not your true form. Your deep being is that of a star!"

"Oh, come on!" Lucky kicked the floor with a cloven hoof. "OK, I've got some power . . . but what can I do with it? Kill people. Burn things. Hurt myself."

But Mystica's eyes were glowing brighter as her conviction grew. "You don't know your power's limits," she countered. "You've never truly let it go, have you? The Professor thought there might be no limit to it if you did — no limit at all." She shook her head again. "How extraordinary. To think this might happen in my lifetime —"

"Mystica!" cried Lucky, totally embarrassed now. "Please! If I'm an Astraeus, then where's my wings and halo?" He turned to Bixa, knowing she would say something rude and put an end to this crazy talk.

But Bixa's silver eyes looked thoughtful. "It's not impossible," she said. "The legends are old, aren't they? They're bound to have been corrupted over time. Maybe people wanted to remember the Astraeus as perfect gods, but that might not be the truth. All we really know is they were beings who had the power of the stars inside them. And your power, whatever it is, obviously has *something* to do with the stars — doesn't it?"

Lucky gaped at her. How could even Bixa be talking like this? "If you really think I've got that kind of power," he challenged, "then what am I supposed to do with it?"

"That depends on which of the Twelve you are," said Mystica. "Each Astraeus was different. Each was the origin of a different kind of myth. All the war gods, sky gods, sea gods, love gods — all the ancient pantheons — they all go back to one of the Twelve Astraeus. So if we knew which one you were, then we might guess your power's purpose. If you are the Astraeus of War, say, then you must surely be here to fight in the War. If you are the Astraeus of Love —"

Bixa giggled at that, and Lucky blushed deeply. He stared up at the vidscreens, trying to remember ancient gods and mythologies, but Mystica's words had prompted another thought.

"Twelve!" he said. "There's meant to be twelve! If I'm an Astraeus, where are the others?"

"I pray they are where Professor Byzantine believed we'd find them: behind the blockade, in Aquarius," replied Mystica. "But even if I am wrong, and you are not one of them — then isn't it clear that the stars must have given you this power for a purpose? There is something you are meant to do with it."

She gazed at him, and in her eyes Lucky saw the hope

still radiant, in spite of all his denials. He felt deeply uncomfortable, having that gaze upon him. He hated being the center of such attention, the focus of such faith.

He stood up and drew away from the warmth of the bed. "I'll tell you what I'm going to do," he muttered, pacing the cabin like a caged animal. "I'm never going to use that horrible power again."

He expected Mystica to argue with him, as the Professor had — and he was ready to argue back, to argue till the end — but to his surprise, her golden eyes filled with sympathy as she watched him.

"You poor boy," she said. "I am sorry. It is not for us to say who you are, or what you're here to do. You are the only one who can say. But please know this, Lucky: I trust you as I trust the stars themselves. Whatever you decide, we will support you."

She was doing her best to reassure him, but his thoughts were growing darker and darker. "Never, ever again," he vowed. He shut his eyes, and all he could see was darkness. "It's not going to kill me. It — it's not . . ."

"Are you all right, dear?" said Mystica. "I didn't mean to distress you. . . ."

He shook his head. He tried to push the feelings down, but they were overwhelming. It felt like his face was tightening — and then, all of a sudden, he was gasping for air —

— and weeping —

— weeping —

— weeping into the night.

Without a word, Mystica pulled him toward her and pressed his face into her arms.

He felt safe in there. It was warm and dark; it smelled like chocolate and spices. He let go, and the feelings came out in a great flood: all the pain and fear and sadness he'd been holding on to for so long.

Mystica held him all the time, asking nothing, saying nothing, just letting him cry.

Eventually, the weeping subsided. He felt strangely light-headed and relieved, as if he'd been washed clean inside. He felt embarrassed too — what was Bixa going to say? — but he looked up to see her watching him with something he'd never seen on her face before. Something like tenderness.

"Are you OK?" she said awkwardly. "Is there anything I can do?"

He couldn't help giving a wry smile. Those were the same words he'd offered her on Scorpio, when they were talking about death. How hollow those words seemed now.

"You were right," he admitted. "There's nothing anyone can do, is there?"

"Not really." Bixa shrugged. "But maybe it helps a bit — knowing you're not alone?"

Lucky wiped his eyes. "Yeah." He sat up straighter. "Can we talk about something else? Something good, for a change? Tell me about this place we're going. Aquarius."

"Oh, it's the most beautiful system!" Mystica declared. "We've crossed the whole galaxy, witnessed so many wonders, but none compares to home. Let me show you the great nebula you'll see as we approach Aquarius; we have an old vidpic of it."

She tapped on the wall, and the screens all rippled and resolved to show one giant image: the swirling arms of a spiral nebula.

Lucky gaped at it, gooseflesh prickling his skin. It was like seeing one of his oldest memories brought to life: the vidpic he'd grown up looking at.

"I know that place!" he gasped. "There's a vidpic of me as a baby, with my mother and father — we were under that nebula. We were there!"

"Is that so?" said Mystica. She stroked her chin. "Well, it seems fitting, for a nebula is a place where new stars are born. It's a kind of astral nursery — and this particular nebula has some of the most beautiful stars in the galaxy. Remember, Bixa?"

"How could I forget?" Bixa's needles glowed silver. "It's my first memory of anything, ever. Stargazing in the nebula with our aunts and uncles. The skies were so clear — I'll never forget seeing those baby stars being born." She grinned. "You're going to love it, Lucky. It's really something special."

Lucky felt cheered by the prospect. After the horrors of Scorpio, after Gala's prophecies, after all the doubts and fears that were tearing him apart — here at last was something good and bright and pure. Something that spoke to him of better times, when his parents were still together, when he was safe and protected beneath his father's smile. It gave him hope that he was getting closer, that they would soon be reunited at last.

Because whatever the Startalkers said, his father was the only one who *really* knew the truth about his power. And he was going to prove that Lucky wasn't an Astraeus, or a Wolf, or anything strange and supernatural.

Just a boy.

A boy who wasn't going to die.

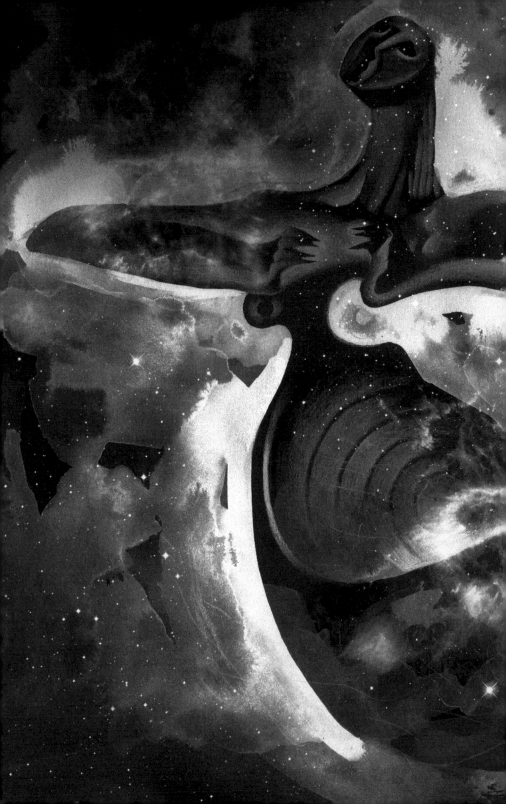

II

The Wolf Is Close,

The Astraeus of Birth Cannot Survive It

for It Is the End of All Life. . . .

CHAPTER TWENTY-EIGHT

As they flew through the outer systems, past Sagittarius and Capricorn and on into the deepest reaches of Axxa space, Bixa and Mystica talked of little but the wonders of the nebula. They filled Lucky's mind with their stories and memories of it. By the time the *Sunfire* came to the outskirts of Aquarius, he could hardly wait to see all the beautiful sights they'd described.

He sat with Bixa in Mystica's quarters, watching the vidscreens. The old lady lay huddled in her bed, wrapped in furs and shivering. She seemed weaker and more frail than ever, but her eyes were glowing with anticipation.

"We are now approaching the Aquarius Nebula," came Captain Nox's voice on the comm. "It should be visible any minute now."

They all looked eagerly at the screens — but there was just empty black space out there. They could see no sign of the famous nebula. Not a trace of the Twelve Astraeus, either. They couldn't even see the Axxa Skyhawks they'd expected to find. There was no life whatsoever in the fathomless gulfs outside.

Lucky kept looking at the endless black, a sense of dread beginning to creep up on him. But as they stared at the blank screens —

FLASHHH!

— another searing pulse of light scorched their eyes.

It lit the whole of space, turning all the blackness white: bleaching it out with an unnatural, excruciating glare. Lucky recoiled, and Mystica writhed before the light.

"Not again," she gasped as she coughed and coughed from the depths of her lungs. She was getting worse: no doubt about it.

This time, the sky stayed white for more than a minute before it faded.

And on the vidscreens now, traces of strange debris began to appear. Fragments of broken rock, horribly crushed, their very structures disintegrating. Clouds of formless gas, swirling silently through the dark. An endless dance of death — but silent. Utterly silent.

"What is this?" whispered Mystica. "There should be stars here: stars, stars, stars, all singing into space! What happened to them all?"

Lucky's mouth was dry now. His ears burned as he strained to hear sounds that did not come. The silence was overwhelming. It seemed to crush down on his chest, as if he was buried beneath all that blackness.

And as they flew on through the silent debris, only one conclusion became possible. These clouds of gas and fragments of rock: they must be the ruins of the nebula. The only traces of it that remained.

Somehow, it must have been extinguished, snuffed out like a candle. For no new stars were being born here, and none ever would be again.

"I don't believe it," said Bixa, her needles shrinking back into her hair. "How could so many stars die?"

"These stars didn't just die," whispered Mystica. "Not so many, not all at once. They must have been *killed*."

Lucky's skin crawled at the words. "What kind of power could do that?"

"And what has become of our family?" asked Mystica. "There were planets here, full of life and hope and promise. Where are they? How can whole worlds just disappear?"

Frollix's voice cracked on the comm as the *Sunfire* steered through the ruins of the nebula. "I'm seeing things I don't understand; things that happened here in the past. A disaster so vast it can't be natural. A great catastrophe—but what?"

"The Wolf That Eats the Stars," said Mystica, her voice quavering. "It was here."

"But what is it? I feel its traces in time, I hear its echoes, but I can't make sense of it."

"Hold on," said the Captain grimly, on the comm. "I'm taking us in to Aquarius, as close as I can get."

Lucky could not speak anymore. The horror was too great. It was like sailing through a graveyard of stars. Like seeing his own memory obliterated: as if the killing of the nebula had also extinguished his father's smile.

Bixa turned away from the vidscreens. "I can't watch," she said. "Everything I remember is gone. It's too horrible —"

"There it is!" cried Mystica suddenly. "My star — my beloved star — it still lives!"

Ahead now, on the other side of the nebula, they could finally see Aquarius: a colossal star at the heart of a system, the sun of many worlds, the center of an ancient civilization.

Aquarius was surrounded by spacecraft, blockaded by government shadowships and battleships that ringed the star with a great circle of armor. Yet it was ominously silent, even here. There were no Axxa ships. No battles. No fighting.

And though Lucky hoped with all his heart to see them, there was no sign of the Twelve Astraeus, either. Professor Byzantine was wrong. They were not behind the blockade. The only thing behind it was Mystica's star.

The *Sunfire* steered a slow, steady course toward Aquarius.

"I don't think we should look directly at the star," Frollix warned on the comm. "Just a feeling I've got. It could be dangerous. Captain, don't look at it —"

FLASHHH!

The star pulsed with blinding white light, and Mystica shuddered with pain. They all looked away from the flash — but even in its indirect glare, Lucky could clearly see that the old lady had been right all along. Aquarius was going supernova. It was dying, and as it died, it was throwing out massive amounts of heat and light. In its death throes, it was outshining all the other stars of the galaxy combined. And its pulses were getting even more brutally bright.

So bright that this time, the light did not fade.

One minute. Two minutes. Three . . . The blinding light blazed on; it never left the sky. All around Aquarius, all of space was white. The sky that should have been black was sickeningly bright. The stars were visible only as points of darkness in the white. Everything was inverted.

"Captain?" came Frollix's voice on the comm. "We're close enough now, aren't we?"

Nox did not reply. The *Sunfire* kept moving, creeping closer and closer to Aquarius. And now, across its face, Lucky thought he could see something strange. A vast shadow, sharp-edged and solid, cutting into Aquarius, eclipsing the face of the sun.

"By all the Twelve Astraeus!" whispered Mystica. "Is *that* the Wolf?"

"No," said Frollix. "Look at it: it's man-made! It's some kind of technology. There's no technology powerful enough to snuff out a whole nebula. Nothing in the whole galaxy could do that!"

As he spoke, the strange shadow cut deeper into Aquarius, there was another pulse of light —

FLASHHH!

— and Lucky could hear nothing but the death throes of the star. Its song was like that of some great whale, trapped in nets and bleeding to death, its lifeblood spilling from its broken heart. And the rest of the stars were singing back to it, crying in sorrow, but powerless to help.

We are falling!

We are dying!

Killed before our time!

Aquarius was dying—but not naturally. That sharp-edged shadow in space was accelerating the process. It was bleeding out all the star's heat and light and power in a series of shuddering supernova pulses.

Whatever this was, if it carried on, Aquarius would soon be like the baby stars of the nebula. A burned-out ruin, a silent cloud of debris.

The supernova blazed again. Mystica convulsed in agony. Her eyes shut, and she slipped out of consciousness.

Lucky's back stiffened. His fists clenched. He couldn't just stand by and watch this happen. Whatever was going on here — something in him protested against it, rebelled, said, *No. Enough.*

"We've got to stop it!" he shouted. "Whatever that thing is — we've got to stop it!"

FLASHHH!

The *Sunfire* tilted violently in space. The floor fell away beneath his feet. He lost his balance and smashed into the cabin wall.

The comm crackled with Frollix's fear. "Captain, what are you doing?"

No answer came back.

Then Frollix's voice again. "Bixa! Lucky!" he yelped. "Get up here quick! There's something wrong with the Captain. . . . No one's flying the ship!"

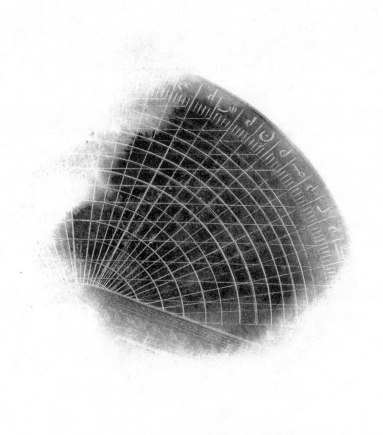

CHAPTER TWENTY-NINE

Lucky and Bixa raced out of Mystica's cabin. They burst into the cockpit to find Frollix by the Dark Matter drive and Captain Nox by the front vidscreen. He was staring silently into the heart of the star.

There on the screen, Lucky could see that unnatural shadow, cutting into Aquarius. And at the heart of the star, he thought for an instant that he saw something else —

— but his mind couldn't seem to get a grip on it; his eyes slid away —

— and then it was gone.

"What happened?" asked Bixa, rushing to the Captain's side.

Nox did not reply. He just stood there, staring into the dying star.

"Captain!" she urged him. "What's wrong?"

But still he did not reply. He did not even move. And his eyes, those proud eyes of volcanic fire, looked totally burned out. No stars danced in them now. They were cold and dead and empty, like black holes in the sky.

"Captain?" said Lucky, shivering.

"Nothing matters," croaked Nox at last in a broken-sounding voice. *"Nothing matters anymore."*

"No!" said Bixa, staring in horror at her grandfather. "Please, Captain, you've got to fight it!"

But Nox just kept staring straight ahead: the million-mile stare.

And now, seemingly from nowhere, starships were swooping up behind the *Sunfire*, circling them. Not government ships. Fast ships, with cannon jutting from their wings, like giant birds of prey.

Axxa Skyhawks. Three of them.

The comm crackled. "Unknown craft," came a harsh voice, "identify yourselves."

"This is the Axxa ship *Sunfire*," replied Frollix on the comm. "We're civilians —"

"Then what are you doing in this quadrant?"

"We're here on a mission of peace —"

"Peace?" snarled the voice. "Tell the truth. Are you spying for the Humans?"

Frollix stared in horror at the comm. Then he cut the channel and turned to the Captain. "They're never gonna listen to us," he said. "We have to run. Can you set a course, sir?"

Nox didn't even seem to hear Frollix's words. He remained silent and still, in his own sealed-off world.

"He — he can't do it," said Bixa, shivering. "There's no way he can navigate like this."

Frollix scratched the base of his horns. "Then *you* have to do it, Lucky," he said.

"Me?" Lucky gulped. "But — how?"

"With your astrolabe, of course! It's hooked up to the ship. You just trace a route; I'll take care of the rest with the Dark Matter drive."

Lucky gaped at his friend. "But I've never flown a ship before. Not for real. The Captain would never let me —"

"Hey!" said Frollix, shaking Lucky with his huge hands. "In case you hadn't noticed, it's up to us now, buddy! C'mon, don't doubt yerself. You can do this: I *know* you can."

And with that, he turned away and started to fire up the Dark Matter drive.

Uncertain, Lucky looked down at the astrolabe.

He ran his fingers over the cool black metal. The disk lit up instantly at his touch. The twelve symbols around its circumference started to glow. Silver light flickered as its dials began to move, to turn and spin.

He took a deep breath —

— and then he went into the astrolabe.

He was floating in space, totally weightless among the stars. And though their silver voices were shot through with sorrow, they were still full of encouragement.

You are flying!
You are coming!
Coming to the light!

Farther away, he could hear those other songs: those fragments of strange, sad songs, still echoing across infinity.

The Wolf Is
Coming. . . .
The Wolf Is
Close. . . .

And We Cannot

Cannot

Cannot . . .

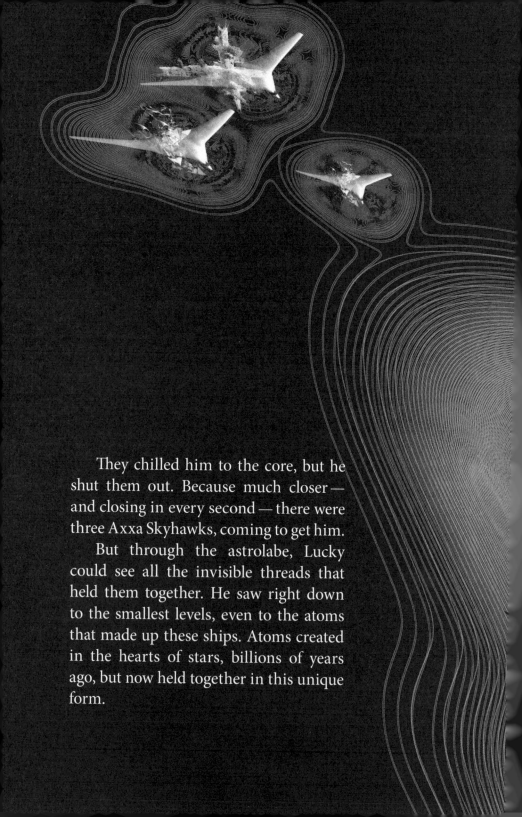

They chilled him to the core, but he shut them out. Because much closer — and closing in every second — there were three Axxa Skyhawks, coming to get him.

But through the astrolabe, Lucky could see all the invisible threads that held them together. He saw right down to the smallest levels, even to the atoms that made up these ships. Atoms created in the hearts of stars, billions of years ago, but now held together in this unique form.

Inside the Skyhawks, he could see the Axxa pilots, each one another unique configuration of atoms. Each one like a galaxy in itself: a galaxy of dancing matter and energy, minutely patterned and perfect, beautiful to behold.

But at this moment, every fiber of their being was focused on one thing only: destroying him.

He saw their fingers, touching triggers —

— and he knew he had to fly. Right. Now.

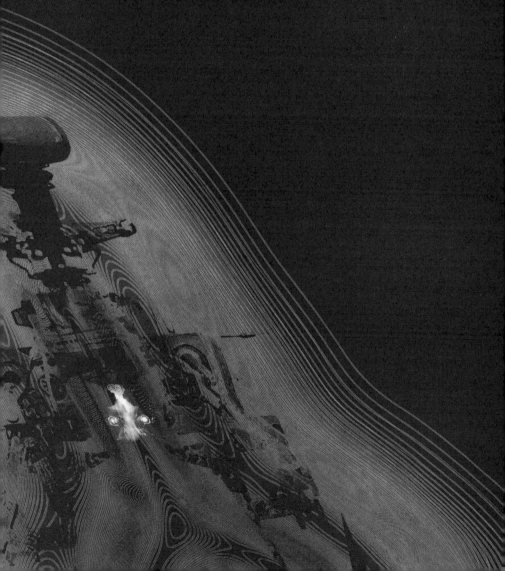

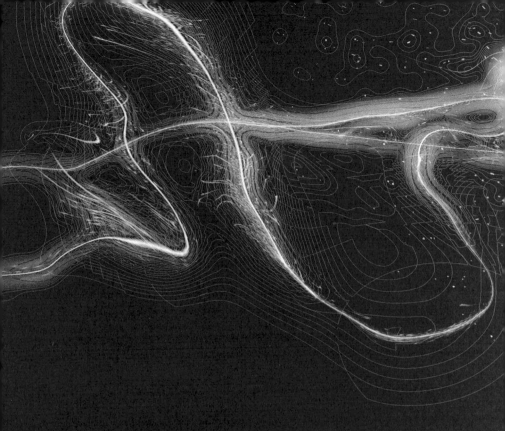

He picked a course at random: just somewhere, anywhere, away from them. He chose a line of silver light,
went racing after it — and the *Sunfire* accelerated away as a ·
torpedo came sizzling behind them.

It exploded just under the hull.

Lucky slalomed through space, riding the waves of
destruction as best he could. The Skyhawk pilots still had
him in their sights. He felt their ferocious anticipation of a
kill. The next shot would almost certainly hit.

But now at least he had a course. And he was changing
it every moment, leaping from one line of light to the next,
constantly shifting direction so the *Sunfire* would be hard to
follow, and even harder to hit.

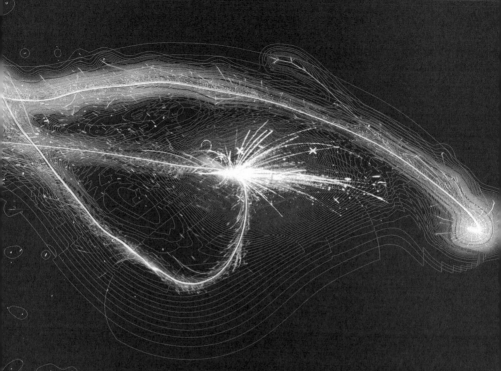

He was deep in the astrolabe now. Deeper than he'd
ever been. So deep, it felt like it was part of him, and he was
part of it. This infinite view of space, where everything was
connected: it was beginning to feel like home.

And now that he was flying the ship at last, he was loving
it. He flew with a fierce, bright joy, as if he'd been born to it —
and with every movement, he felt more and more confident.

Frollix was right, he thought, amazed. *I really can do this!*

But the Skyhawk pilots were just as fast as him, and far
more practiced. They flew with ruthless accuracy, matching every move he made. He steered the *Sunfire* deeper into
space, toward the edge of the galaxy, trying desperately to
shake them off. But still they were closing in.

I can't outrun them, he thought. *But maybe I can out-
maneuver them. . . .*

Rapidly, he plotted a new course—diving, wheeling, swiveling along infinite paths of light. The *Sunfire* banked, rolled, and spun through 180 degrees in space. It circled around and arrowed directly across the Skyhawks' flight paths. Right into their range.

All three Skyhawks fired their cannon—but Lucky's course had dragged them across one another's bows. The quickest Skyhawk was caught in the crossfire.

BLAMMM!

As it imploded in a flash of flame—as its atoms came apart in an incendiary blaze—Lucky felt everything the pilot was feeling.

The moment of horror as he realized his mistake. The regret. The pain.

And then—gone. The pilot was gone, his life snuffed out in a single instant, his unique form never to be repeated.

Lucky felt it all. There was no joy in destruction. Just the deepest sorrow.

But he also felt the fury of the other two pilots as they realized they'd been tricked. And he knew he was running out of options. He was flying as fast as he could think, surfing Dark Matter connections as he made his leaps and jumps through the stars instinctively. But it was only his first time — and good as he was, the Skyhawks were closing in again, spurred on by grief for their comrade.

The *Sunfire* was nearing the edge of the astrolabe's map, nearing the end of the galaxy. They blurred past Pisces, the twelfth and last great star system, and surged on into the outermost reaches of Axxa space.

And now, at the edge of his perception, Lucky had the strangest sensation. Just the faintest feeling: a place behind him where space seemed darker than normal somehow. It was moving, this darkness. Almost as if it was following him. But it wasn't the Skyhawks; the darkness was behind them too. . . .

Puzzled, he turned his attention away from the chase for just a second — and shook as a volley of torpedoes exploded around the *Sunfire*. He scrambled into an evasive pattern, but it was too late to avoid them all. One of the torpedoes was going to hit —

SCORCHHH!

It singed the *Sunfire*'s wingtip. Lucky felt the impact in his own body. It was like the ship was a living thing, in pain, and he was connected to it through the astrolabe.

He knew they couldn't take another hit.

Concentrate! he told himself fiercely. He redoubled his efforts — reaching for faster connections, quicker currents, swifter pathways through the stars — away from the Skyhawks that were now hell-bent on finishing him off.

But space was running out. Before him now lay a dense cloud of purple fire. A radiation storm: a deadly front of energy, burning on the very edge of the galaxy. He could not see through it to whatever lay on the other side. Beyond it, space was completely unseen, uncharted, unknown.

Lucky stared at the cloud of purple fire. *Oh, no,* he thought. *That's all we need.*

And then a memory flashed into his mind. Something Gala had said, when he asked her how he would find his father. *Through the storm, and off the edge . . .*

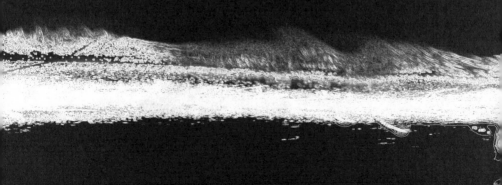

What if she meant the radiation storm? What if he flew straight into it, and off the edge of the galaxy?

It's crazy, he told himself. *But what's the alternative?*

He summoned every last scrap of courage and concentration. *Where is my father now?* he asked the astrolabe in his mind.

A single line of silver light shot out from where he was. It streaked to the edge of the map, where the radiation storm marked the boundary of charted space—and then kept going: off the edge and out of sight.

Off the edge.

Follow the light!

Before he could doubt himself, Lucky steered the *Sunfire* straight after it. He sent the ship surging along the line of silver light, directly into the heart of the storm. He flew right up to the edge of the map—and then off the edge.

This time, the astrolabe didn't fling him out. Instead, the map kept going, opening out before him as he followed that fragile line of silver light — just as it had when Gala used it. Somehow, she must have expanded the map, giving it knowledge it didn't have before: knowledge of the future, knowledge of the unknown. And Lucky was following it into the storm — chasing the fragile line of silver light as it streaked deeper and deeper into uncharted space.

He was working on pure instinct and adrenaline now. The radiation storm's lethal energies crackled all around him. Ultraviolet light dazzled him, drenching him in irradiated glow as he steered the ship through deadly purple haze.

The *Sunfire*'s shields shook; its hull began to groan. They were losing power. He could feel the machinery beginning to fail. It couldn't take much more.

He glanced behind him. He couldn't see the Skyhawks. Just clouds of pulsing power, throbbing all around him, like acid eating into the ship's shields. They were buckling; the radiation was seeping through.

Already, it was making him nauseous. His hands were starting to shake, his muscles aching, but he forced himself to keep concentrating. He had to keep going. He could not stop now.

He kept following the line of silver light through the storm, trusting that somehow, the astrolabe would not let him down.

And then — at last — he glimpsed a tiny patch of black ahead. A break in the storm. The line of light was heading straight for it.

With a swift movement, he sent the ship toward it — and the *Sunfire* came soaring out of the storm, just as its shields buckled around him.

Lucky looked back. Still no Skyhawks coming after them. They were in the clear.

He pulled himself out of his astral body —

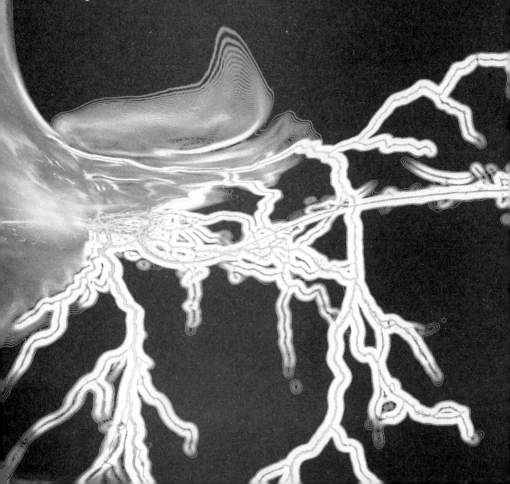

— and back into the cockpit.

Bixa was sprawled on the ground beside him; she must've been hurled about in the chase. Frollix was clinging on to the Dark Matter drive, but he was grinning.

"*Wooo-hooooo!*" he whooped. "We made it! You did it! You lost 'em!"

"Maybe," said Bixa as she picked herself up. "But what's that, ahead?"

Lucky's pulse accelerated. What could she see? Could it be the Twelve Astraeus?

Hoping against hope, he looked at the vidscreen —

— and his hope died.

Because right there, before him in space, was a mighty fleet of Skyhawks. The Axxa fleet, hidden behind the radiation storm, just off the edge of the galaxy.

And beyond them was a new star system: one he'd never seen before. A thirteenth system, with a cold blue star at its heart. Circling it was a single white planet, like a fist of ice.

"Charon," whispered Bixa. "The Axxa army's secret base. I think you've found it."

CHAPTER THIRTY

The radiation storm behind them flickered — and from its depths burst the Skyhawks that were chasing them.

This time, there was nowhere to hide. Every option was blocked. They were trapped.

"This is the Axxa craft *Sunfire*," Frollix called desperately on the comm. "We're on a peaceful mission, and we —"

BLAMMM!

Without warning, a torpedo hit the *Sunfire* full on — and this time, they had no shields.

The Dark Matter drive crackled, sparked, and burned out.

Lucky tried to get back into the astrolabe, but it was no longer connected to the *Sunfire*. He had no control of the ship.

They plunged down toward Charon, drawn by the planet's gravitational pull. Frollix struggled furiously to keep the ship in space, but it was out of control.

Flames scorched the ship's sides as it fell into the planet's atmosphere, down through the layers, losing altitude all the time.

Charon looked totally white from above. Its surface was covered in ice. It seemed a cold place. A hard place. A terrible place to crash . . .

"Strap in tight!" yelled Frollix. "This is gonna be bumpy!"

The *Sunfire* shook and juddered like never before as they plummeted through the whiteness. A blizzard raged around the ship, hurricane winds buffeting them.

Frollix grappled with the Dark Matter drive, trying with all his might to bring it back online. "There's something I gotta try," he said. "I never did it before, but . . ."

He flipped his fingers over his controls — and with a great ripple, the silver strings that crisscrossed the *Sunfire*'s crescent wings unfurled.

They caught the wind between them like a parachute. The ship began to glide.

Lucky could feel their descent slowing — but it was still not enough. Because now, on the vidscreen, he could see mountains, cabins, bunkers, blurring by in the blizzard. They were still falling too fast.

"Watch out, folks — here it comes!" warned Frollix, bracing himself.

And the *Sunfire* crashed into the planet Charon.

The hull ruptured as they smashed into the surface. The impact ripped open the underbelly of the ship. It sheared off both wings, snapping the steel strings, leaving them fluttering like ribbons. The *Sunfire* skidded and thudded along the ground, a trail of shattering metal sparkfire in its wake — tearing apart, breaking up on impact —

— until finally —

— finally —

— the *Sunfire* rolled over, and over, and shuddered to a standstill.

Everything was upside down. Every surface was broken. Smoke and steam were rising from the wreckage.

In the cockpit, there was silence. Dust swirled before Lucky's eyes.

He hauled himself to his feet. He felt dazed and unsteady; he was beginning to shake. He was bruised all over — but at least he was alive.

Which was more than he could say for the ship. The cockpit had cracked open. The vidscreen was fractured; the Dark Matter drive was smashed to pieces. Frollix's huge bulk was hunched forward over the wreckage, ominously still.

"Frollix!" called Lucky. He leaped toward his friend.

But Frollix's starry eyes were open. He was alive too. "Did we make it?" he gasped.

"You did good," said Bixa. "But now I think we might really be in trouble. . . ."

She was looking at the fractured vidscreen. It flickered on and off, buzzing, broken, showing only flashes of the view outside. An army barracks in the snow. Axxa troopers in military uniforms. Marching toward them. Fast.

Bixa's needles buried themselves in her hair, but she stood up. "Mystica," she said. "We have to get Mystica."

She helped the Captain to stand. He was unsteady, but he could still walk. The Living Death had not yet destroyed his body. Only his mind.

They clambered down from the cockpit and picked their way through the wreckage.

It broke Lucky's heart to see the state of the *Sunfire*. In the main cabin, the vidscreens were shattered, the cathedral columns and vaulting arches flattened. Mystica's pots and pans were strewn across the deck. The spherical silver seats were crushed flat, while the hammock where he'd slept hung upside down, like a limp flag.

They staggered on through smashed-up corridors. All the ship's curved lines were at jagged angles: broken now, not connecting anymore.

"Mystica!" called Bixa as they stumbled onward. "We're coming!"

No answer came back.

They burst into her quarters. The low gravity was gone; the air felt heavy. The old lady lay sprawled on the ground, unconscious, her body bent double. Her golden rings were scattered on the floor.

Frollix put his ear to her chest at once. "She's alive," he said. "But her heartbeat's weak. We need to get her out of here, in case the ship blows. . . ." He picked her up in his great arms and carried her. She looked so fragile in those massive, muscled arms, but Frollix held her with infinite gentleness and care.

Bixa led them back to the main cabin and threw open the ship's hatch. Freezing wind whipped into the warmth of the *Sunfire*.

And out there, the Axxa army was waiting: tough, tattooed troopers in body armor and cloven-hoof boots, with huge horns and burning eyes of flame. Their cannon and

370

ground-blasters were all aimed at the *Sunfire*. And the ship was still smoking, steaming, even in the blizzard. Flames lapped around it, consuming what was left of it, like carrion birds after a kill.

Lucky and his friends staggered out of the hatch. Their beautiful ship was now just a pile of wreckage, strewn in a long trail behind them. A silent tear rolled down Frollix's cheek. It froze there on his face, a solid tear of ice.

Snow was knee-deep on the planet's surface. It was freezing cold here: a deadly cold Lucky had never felt the likes of before. It seemed to cut through him — through his clothes, skin, flesh, blood — right down to the marrow of his bones. In just a few seconds, his hands were utterly numb. He couldn't feel his fingers.

All he felt was unbearable guilt. Because he was the one who'd brought them here. He was the one who'd steered the *Sunfire* into a radiation storm, in the desperate hope that he would find Charon and his father on the other side.

And he had found Charon. But at what cost?

An Axxa trooper crunched toward them through the snow: a powerfully built woman whose face was studded with metal piercings. They raised their hands as she came before them, cannon cocked, proud authority in her stance.

"You were evading capture," she said. "What were you doing so near the Human fleet? Are you spies?"

"'Course not!" said Frollix. "I keep trying to tell you guys: we're on a mission of peace —"

"Peace?" spat the trooper, her eyes burning like hot metal. "There is no peace in this galaxy. Not anymore."

"But we're no threat to you," pleaded Bixa. "These old people here — my grandparents — they need help —"

The trooper wasn't listening. "By all the Twelve Astraeus, I don't have time for this! Take them away," she ordered. "Take them down to Charon Caves."

CHAPTER THIRTY-ONE

Lucky and his friends were bound in electrocuffs and marched away from the *Sunfire*.

They had to lead the Captain by the hand. Mystica was still unconscious. The tears were freezing down Frollix's face. Bixa was silent, but she was watching everything with her silver eyes, her thoughts unreadable.

The wind lashed into them as they stumbled through the snow. Lucky was beginning to feel numb inside as well as out. What was he supposed to do now?

Whatever happens, don't ever give up. You are the only person in the galaxy who can find your father. I am counting on you. And so is he.

They came to a halt by the camp. There were squadrons of Skyhawks and ranks of troopers, rows of cabins and bunkers: a fully operational base.

They were led at cannonpoint through gates in the ground. Axxa troopers searched them as they went. They were allowed to keep only their clothes; their possessions were taken, as they had been at the Spacewall. The troopers seized Bixa's cannon and armor, though they didn't notice her needles, because she'd retracted them deep into her hair again. But they wrenched the astrolabe away from Lucky, even as he begged and pleaded to keep it.

Down into the darkness they were led: down steps, through corridors, ever farther underground. Lucky lost track of the way. His head spun with all the twists and turns they took.

They were taken finally into a freezing cold cavern, shielded by steel doors, with a detachment of troopers standing guard outside. The walls and floor were solid rock, encrusted with ice. Vidcams on the ceiling kept everything under surveillance. A dim blue lamp provided the only light — just enough to show how hopeless it was.

The cavern was crowded with ragged-looking prisoners, huddled together for warmth. Some of them were Human; some were Axxa. Many had the black-hole eyes and the million-mile stare, just like Captain Nox. In the cold blue light, they looked as if they were dead already: all color drained from their faces, all hope abandoned.

"Mystica Grandax?" came a voice from one of the Axxa prisoners. "Can that be the Startalker of the Present?" Whispers rippled through the prisoners as Frollix settled Mystica and the Captain down among them.

"Who are all these people?" Lucky asked Bixa.

"King Theobroma's dirty secret," she said. "All the Axxa who oppose the War — I guess the army locks 'em up here." She glanced back into the gloom. "As for those Humans, they must be captured Shadow Guards. Prisoners of war."

Meanwhile, Frollix was talking to some Axxa prisoners sitting near him. There was a seriousness about Frollix that Lucky had never seen in his friend before. "Some of the people in these caves came from the Aquarius Nebula," he told Lucky and Bixa. "I need to find them. I need to hear their stories, to understand what happened there."

"Then I'll come with you," said Bixa.

"And I — I have to find my father," said Lucky. "He must be here, somewhere. . . ."

They left Mystica and Nox in the care of their fellow Axxa prisoners. Frollix and Bixa headed in one direction; Lucky went the other. He made his way through the cavern, picking a path through clusters of people.

He found a group of Humans in a corner, packed in tight, looking down with sunken eyes. From the smells, he could tell they hadn't washed for a long time. The men were unshaven, their beards bushy; the women's hair was tangled and wild. It was shocking to see them like that. Could these really be the people he feared so much?

"Are you Shadow Guards?" he asked them.

"We used to be," said one, cowering away from him. "Please don't hurt us. . . ."

"Shdw Grds," said another, shivering.

"Nthng mttrs," croaked a third in a broken-sounding voice. "Nthng mttrs nymr."

Lucky shuddered. Some of these people had the Living Death so badly, they couldn't even speak properly. They were painfully thin, as though they hadn't eaten for far too long — yet they didn't seem to care. They just lay there, as if dissolving.

"I'm looking for Major Dashwood," he told them. "Has anyone seen him?"

"Dashwood? He was down that way. . . ."

Lucky's heart beat faster. So his father *was* here. In these very caves. Maybe only a few steps away—the man he'd crossed a galaxy to find. . . .

He picked up his pace as he pressed on through the cavern, past bound and chained prisoners of war. "I'm looking for Major Dashwood!" he called as he went. No one answered. "Major Dashwood?" he shouted, louder now.

But still no response.

"Major Dashwood?" called Lucky, beginning to panic.

"Who's there?" came a weak voice.

Lucky squinted through the bodies, through the dark blue gloom, into the shadows—

—and found himself looking at the face that had watched over his whole childhood. The man with the mustache, in his starship commander's uniform.

The man looked very different now. He was still handsome, but he had aged so much. His uniform was torn to tatters. There were deep lines scored on his face and marks of brutality on his body. It was almost impossible to imagine this man smiling.

But it was him, Lucky was sure of it. He hesitated a moment, his heart beating hard. He felt as if his whole life had been leading up to this moment.

"Are you—are you Major Dashwood?" he asked at last.

"Yes, I am," said the man, peering up at him from the icy ground. "And who are you?"

"I'm Lucky. I—I'm your son."

Major Dashwood looked bewildered. "My son?"

"And you're my father." The words began to pour out of Lucky as the feelings welled up inside. "I've come such a long way to find you, and I'll take care of you — don't worry — I'll rescue you — I'll get you out of here. But I need to know everything about myself — who I really am, why I'm like this —"

But Major Dashwood was shaking his head. "I'm not your father, young man," he said. "You're Axxa. I'm Human. We're different."

"No!" said Lucky, ripping out the contact lenses, unbraiding his horns of hair. "This is all just a disguise — it's not real. I'm Human, like you!"

"But I can't be your father," the man said. "I never had any children."

"You didn't?" Lucky bit his lip. "But you're in the vidpic," he insisted. "With my mother and me. I was a baby — you were smiling at me, by the Aquarius Nebula —"

Major Dashwood's eyes widened. "Just a moment . . . You're Diana's son?"

"Yes!" Lucky paused, his heart on a knife edge. "At least, I think so; my mother never told me her real name. But she called herself Diana Ashbourne."

"That name was my idea!" the Major said. "I thought it up when I helped her escape." He ran his fingers through his hair, pushing it back from his eyes so he could see Lucky more clearly. "Diana's son? How extraordinary . . . No, I am certainly not your father. I was only a friend of your mother's. We were Shadow Guards together. I did everything I could to help her. But where is she?"

Lucky looked down. Couldn't answer. Somewhere in the distance, the sound of water dripping echoed in the caves.

"Oh," said Major Dashwood. "I am . . . so sorry. . . ."

Lucky bit his mouth until he could taste salt blood and burning. "So — you're really not my father?"

"Of course not. Whyever did you think I was?"

"That's what she told me. She never talked about you much . . . but she loved that vidpic. It was always on our screens."

"Is that so?" Major Dashwood looked down at the icy rock beneath him.

Lucky was beginning to shake. "So it was just another lie — like everything else?"

"Oh, I wish I was your father." The Major sighed. It sounded like it came from the depths of his being, and his breath made a tiny cloud of condensation in the freezing air. "I loved her, you know. I would've done anything for Diana. But she never thought of me that way. She loved someone else."

"Who?"

"Your father, of course. But she never told me who he was. She was always rather mysterious about it. All I know is, she was desperate to get away at the end — from him, from the government, from everything. And she was right to get out. This war has made fools of us all. The things I've seen and done since she left; I wish I could forget. . . ." He shook his head violently and covered his face with his thin, bony hands. He turned away from Lucky, eyes clenched shut, and sat there in the shadows, shivering. "Please — enough of these questions. Leave me be."

Lucky stared at him, stunned. He could not believe it.

He'd done the impossible. At a cost so great he could not bear to think of it, he'd found Charon. He'd found Major Dashwood.

And yet it was all for nothing.

All of it, everything he'd been through, meant nothing. His whole life, his childhood, his most precious memories and beliefs: everything was a lie.

Why had his mother felt the need to lie to him about everything — why?

And if his father wasn't Major Dashwood — then who was?

He sat there in silence, hoping the Major would speak to him again. But the Major looked like he might never speak again.

The only sound Lucky could hear was water, dripping in the distance. He peered around and saw a little rivulet rolling down the cavern's sides. The ice itself seemed to be weeping.

Then he heard the voices of his friends coming toward him, and a wave of comfort washed through him. It was so good to see them. What would he ever do without them?

"Lucky! You OK?" said Bixa. She and Frollix came out of the dark-blue gloom and peered down at Major Dashwood. "Is that *him*? You found him?"

Lucky shook his head. "It's Major Dashwood. But he — he's not my father. He was just my mother's friend. They were Shadow Guards together. . . ."

"Doesn't look so scary now, does he?" mused Bixa. "None of them do."

Major Dashwood did not respond, or make the slightest sign that he was listening. He just sat there in silence, shivering.

"I'm sorry," Lucky told his friends. "I've brought us here for nothing." He looked down at the ice in misery. "Did you find what you were looking for, at least?"

"Very few people survived the catastrophe in the nebula," said Frollix. "I can't make sense of their stories. They're all talking about that strange shadow we saw in space. They say it created the Wolf That Eats the Stars. They say this Wolf devoured the Aquarius Nebula, and it's going to destroy the whole galaxy—"

"Yes," murmured Major Dashwood, to everyone's surprise. His eyes were open again, and they were filled with dread. "I was there. I saw it all."

"You saw the nebula when it died?" said Frollix. "Please— tell me what happened."

The Major glanced sharply up at the ceiling. A vidcam whirred there above their heads. He waited for its gaze to move on before he replied, and when he did, it was in a whisper. "I don't know if they can hear us, but these secrets are not for their ears. Only yours." He glanced at Lucky. "It's only right that you should know the truth. After all, that nebula was your mother's favorite place in the whole galaxy. It's where you were born—did she ever tell you that?"

Lucky shook his head glumly. What could this matter now?

"She would've hated us for what we did," the Major went on. "Because we were the ones who did it. Humanity. *We* destroyed the nebula."

"But — why?" said Frollix. "Why would anyone do a thing like that?"

"We needed to harvest the energy of the stars, to power our civilization and help us fight the War," said the Major. He straightened his tattered uniform and sat up smartly, as if remembering better days. "We developed a secret new technology. Dark Matter technology: like a Dark Matter bomb, but much more powerful. We call it the Starburner. It cuts into the heart of a star, breaking apart the connections that hold stars together, making them release all their power — so we can siphon that power off, channeling it anywhere we choose. Without it, we could never maintain the Spacewall."

Lucky's scalp prickled with horror. "The Spacewall? Oh, no — is *that* how you power it? By killing stars?"

"We had to keep Humanity safe! And besides, we tested the Starburner on one of the smallest stars in the nebula, far from any population centers. It should have been safe; it should have benefited everyone . . . but things did not go as we planned. As the Dark Matter connections unraveled, something strange and terrible was unleashed. Something we did not expect. No matter how you looked at it, your mind couldn't get a grip on it. Your eyes kept sliding away."

"I've seen something like that!" said Bixa. "It was on Scorpio, just after the Dark Matter bomb, at the center of the wheel. It was so weird, I thought I was imagining it . . ." She turned to Lucky. "Did you see it too?"

"Yes," he said, skin crawling at the memory. "I did. And I think I might've seen it again, somewhere . . . But what is it?"

"Nothing," whispered Major Dashwood, his eyes sunken, hollow, haunted. *"Absolute Nothing.* It's the void that lies behind all reality. The negation of all things: the force that will one day destroy everything. This is what lies at the heart of a black hole. And that is what we saw when we killed the star. A black hole."

Lucky shivered.

"But don't black holes destroy everything around them?" Bixa asked the Major. "If you were close enough to see one, why didn't it destroy you too?"

"I wish it had," he replied. "But black holes are made from the bodies of dead stars. The bigger the star, the bigger the black hole. The star we destroyed made a small one; it collapsed rapidly, and we were distant enough to escape it. Yet in the brief moment it existed, it was still strong enough to devour the entire nebula."

"The Wolf That Eats the Stars!" gasped Frollix. The blue fire sparked in his eyes. "But . . . if the Wolf is a black hole, how can you fight a thing like that?"

"You can't." Major Dashwood covered his face with his hands, trying in vain to close out a sight he could never forget. "If you've seen a Dark Matter bomb, scale it up a billion times, and you'll understand why. You see, Dark Matter bombs damage the fabric of spacetime just enough to reveal the merest glimpse of the void. Everyone who sees it feels profound despair. The mind retreats from the horror and turns in on itself. Nothing matters anymore. Everything seems meaningless. This may happen at once, or it may take years; you may recover from it, or you may not. But sooner or later, you will suffer the Living Death."

Lucky looked around the caves, at all the people with black-hole eyes.

"The Captain!" breathed Bixa. "He flew through Dark Matter bombs when he saved us — remember, Frollix? Maybe he got the Living Death all those years ago, and he's been fighting it ever since. But something must've pushed him over the edge —"

"Aquarius." Frollix shook his head grimly. "I tried to stop him, but he was looking right into the star as it flashed."

"Aquarius?" gasped Major Dashwood. "Please tell me they're not using the Starburner on Aquarius itself?"

"It's going supernova right now," said Lucky, his mind flinching at the memory of the dying star's screams. "That's where we saw the Starburner. And . . . I think that was where I saw the Nothing again. . . ."

Horror warped Dashwood's features. "Before I was captured, I told them not to use it again — I warned them of the dangers! If a massive star like Aquarius dies before its time, the resulting black hole would be so vast, nothing could possibly escape! It would be the end of all worlds. The end of all stars. The end of everything."

"That was Gala's prophecy," said Bixa. "*If Aquarius goes, everything goes.*"

"It doesn't have to happen!" cried Major Dashwood. A last desperate hope flickered across his face. "If only Thorntree and Theobroma would talk to each other and stop this senseless war. If only they would make peace." He bit his lip, shook his head. "But . . . how can there be peace? No one will make the first move. No one will back down." With a deep, deep sigh, he shut his eyes, and his body began to shiver and shake in the cold blue light. "No," he said. "There is no hope. The end is coming, and we cannot stop it. Death would be a mercy now."

I

The Wolf Is Here.

The Astraeus of
Death Cannot Kill It

for Even Death
Will Die.

CHAPTER THIRTY-TWO

They trudged back through the freezing cold caves in silence and sat with Mystica and Nox in the overwhelming gloom. There was nothing left to say. They were each lost in their own thoughts, their own private hell.

Lucky had never felt more hopeless. He thought he'd known bad times before, but this was the worst it had ever been.

He shivered. He was so cold. A deadly cold that sapped his will to live —

But wait. One side of his body wasn't so cold. In fact, it felt warm. And it was getting warmer every moment.

Fumbling with the electrocuffs, he twisted around to touch the side of his coat. The pocket felt positively hot. He peered down at it, and was startled to see a fiery glow streaming up from the opening.

Quickly, he emptied the pocket out onto the frozen ground —

— and from it tumbled a tiny chick. It was smaller than the palm of his hand, but it was complete and intact. It stood there, staring at him with wide-open eyes. Its plumage shone with crimson gold light, stunning against the cold blue ice.

A phoenix.

"Bazooka?" he breathed.

The tiny bird blinked. She tipped her head to one side, as if she was trying to remember something. She flexed her beak, still not quite able to speak.

"*Ba — Ba — Ba—*" she squeaked in a minuscule voice.

"Bazooka!" he said.

She hopped up and perched on his shoulder, glowing like a little sun. Radiant with heat and light, she warmed the glacial gloom that surrounded them.

"Is that Bazooka?" gasped Frollix. "But . . . how?"

"I don't know," said Lucky. "I found a feather in the wreckage of the wheel. I put it in my pocket — and somehow, from that one feather, she came back."

"Of course!" said Bixa. "That's what phoenixes do: they're immortal. They always rise again from the ashes."

"Bazooka?" said Frollix again.

The little phoenix looked at the huge Axxa — and her feathers glowed even brighter. She gazed eagerly into Frollix's eyes. "*Ba — Baaa?*" she chirped.

Frollix shook his great head sadly. "I'm sorry, Bazooka," he said. "The Prof's not coming back. He's gone."

"*Ba-zooo?*" she asked, reaching out her beak to him, as if she wanted to hop over and perch on his shoulder.

Frollix turned away and stared into the gloom. He couldn't look at her anymore. "No. I — I can't. I ain't your master, Bazooka."

"Ba-zooo-kaaaaa!" She shuddered and huddled on Lucky's shoulder.

But illuminated now by the light of the phoenix, Mystica opened her eyes. She was conscious once more. She turned and saw Captain Nox beside her on the icy ground. "Oh, my dearest . . ." she whispered as she took him in her arms and held him tightly. "What has become of Ozymandias?" she said in a weak voice. "Where are we?"

They told her everything that had happened. "I—I'm so sorry," said Lucky. "It's all my fault. I should never have brought us here."

Bixa Quicksilver shook her head, eyes glowing with determination as she gazed at the reborn phoenix. "No," she said. "If we hadn't come here, we would never have learned the truth about the galaxy. We know about the Wolf and the Starburner and the Spacewall—we know secrets now that no one else knows. And we have a shot at fixing it. If we can get King Theobroma to make peace, like Major Dashwood said, then we can still save Aquarius. With a single word, the King could start peace talks with President Thorntree, and then they'd have to stop killing the stars. And you know what? I reckon he's right here on Charon. This is their secret base, after all."

"But why would the King make peace now, when he never has before?" said Frollix.

"Because of Lucky! He's the key. If we can just get him to see Lucky—"

"What?" said Lucky. "Why?" The idea of seeing the Axxa King scared him senseless.

"Because if Mystica's right, and you really are an Astraeus — then you're the proof we need. Your power proves the stars *don't* want us to make war on Humans. Why else would an Astraeus come down in a Human body?"

Frollix nodded his head, taking in her words. "You think Lucky's an Astraeus?" He peered into Lucky's eyes. His gaze seemed to reach right into Lucky's mind. "Huh!" he said. "He could be; it'd make sense. But which Astraeus?"

Lucky gaped at him. "Frollix! Not you too — I can't believe you're saying that!"

"Even if you're not an Astraeus," argued Bixa, "why would the stars give power like that to a Human? There's no way they want us to fight the Humans! If we can just get the King to see your power, then he'll see the truth and stop the War — and Mystica will live. . . ."

"Perhaps," said Mystica. She shivered and then coughed violently: great hacking coughs that tore her apart from inside. "But how do you propose to put this to the King, Bixa? They will not listen to you. Look around you. There is no escape from these caves. Even if you did somehow find a way out — you would only freeze to death on the surface. To say nothing of the army that guards us."

"I'll find a way," said Bixa in a low voice. She kicked the icy ground with a hoof. "I'll break us out of here. I'll fight every last one of them if I have to."

"These are the people who took Joxi and Jonathan from us," said Mystica quietly. "What hope have you against people like that?"

Bixa closed her eyes. Bit her lip. She couldn't reply. The only sound was water, dripping in the distance.

Lucky didn't like her plan. He didn't want to be the key to it. He didn't want to be the key to anything.

But . . . he could still hear the stars, crying in space. It broke his heart to hear them, and it broke his heart to watch Mystica die. He wished the real Astraeus would show up! They could save Aquarius, save Mystica, save the galaxy — but where were they?

He had to face the truth.

They weren't coming to save the day. No one else was going to save Lucky and his friends. They were alone, with only what they had inside them to fall back on.

And so — though he hated to admit it — there was only one conclusion here.

He cleared his throat. "Uh — I think Bixa's right," he said. "Not about me being an Astraeus! But about us breaking out of here and getting the King to make peace."

They all stared at him.

"She's right," he repeated. "I can feel it: the stars are going to die if this war doesn't end soon. We've got to act fast if we're going to save them. We've got to act *now*."

"But how?" said Frollix in a small voice. "Mystica's right. It's impossible."

"I know it looks kind of hopeless," Lucky admitted. "I know we don't have a ship, or weapons, or anything. But we've got to try. Even if we fail, we've got to try. See, I've been Bixa's training partner all the way here. If she thinks she's got a chance, then I believe she can do it. She can fight her way out of this horrible place — and I'll back her up, all the way."

"*Baaa-zoookie!*" chirruped the glowing phoenix on his shoulder. He turned to look at her, and her new light gave

393

him courage he didn't know he had. For if Bazooka had survived, after all — then perhaps he might too, despite Gala's prophecies.

And so he took a deep, deep breath, steeled himself, and said the words he'd sworn never to say again. "I — I'll even use my power, if I have to. I'll do it, just this once." He turned to Bixa and shrugged. "After all, what's the point of power if you don't use it to save the people you love?"

Bixa grinned. "Yes!" she said. "Thank you, Lucky!" She turned to Mystica. "See? We have a chance. Two of us now. What do you say?"

Mystica looked at the Captain, in her arms. "I'm sorry, Bixa. I don't like your plan. It's far too dangerous. And I don't believe the Captain would like it, either."

Bixa leaned in to Captain Nox, curled up on the frozen ground. She took hold of his hand and looked into his eyes: those burned-out, empty eyes, reflecting the terrible Nothing he must have seen. "Captain?" she said softly. "Can you hear me?"

And as she spoke to him, as she held him, as Bazooka glowed above them all — the Captain blinked. A spark of fire flickered in his eyes. Just a tiny spark, like the faintest ember of volcanic lava in a mountain of cold, dark ash.

"Captain?" said Bixa again.

He looked at her, as if from a million miles away, and then a single word passed his lips: *"You . . ."*

Bixa stared at him in shock. "Captain?"

He shuddered, but that tiny spark of light was still there, at the back of his eyes. *"You . . . matter . . ."* croaked the Captain. The spark of fire flickered a little brighter. It was growing, catching light, in spite of the darkness all around it.

"Keep doing it, Bixa!" said Lucky. "Whatever you're doing, keep doing it!"

What is she doing? he wondered. *How is she bringing him back? Is there something that cures the Living Death? Something that protects against it?*

Whatever the answer, Captain Nox was looking more like his old self every moment.

"Oh, my dearest!" cried Mystica, embracing him. "You're coming back!"

"Captain, we're gonna get you out of here," said Bixa, her eyes glowing with hope. "We're gonna fight our way out, and you're gonna be OK —"

"*No,*" groaned Nox. Focus gradually returned to his eyes, and clarity came back to his words. "No violence. Because . . . you matter, Bixa. You and Frollix." He sat up shakily. "I want you to be safe. To be Startalkers one day, like Mystica."

"But I can't be like Mystica," said Bixa. "The Professor told me there were many ways of being a Startalker. Well, my way is to fight for what I believe in."

Mystica looked at her and shook her head. "That is not the way, Bixa."

"It's *my* way. And as long as there are people trying to kill us, it always will be."

"Bixa," said the Captain, horns glinting in the cold blue light. "Enough foolishness. I am ordering you: no violence!"

Bixa shut her eyes. Very slowly, she shook her head. "I —

I'm sorry. I owe you both my life. I've always done what you wanted. But this time I can't. I just can't." She opened her eyes again and met the Captain's gaze. "I don't want to do this — but if those are really your orders, then I've got to disobey them."

The Captain stared at her. "You cannot beat them, Bixa," he said. "They're too strong for you. They're—"

"They're not," she said. "They're *not*." The fire in her eyes rose up, strong and silver and totally alive. "I've had enough of letting them do whatever they want to us. We are getting out of here, and I am getting us out, and you're all coming with me!"

This time, the Captain and Mystica could not reply. They sat there speechless, staring at their granddaughter.

"Good," said Bixa. "The decision's made." She turned to her brother. "Frollix, I need your help. Someone has to carry them out of here; they can't make it on their own. Can you do it?"

Frollix grinned. "'Course I can! I'll be right behind you!" He turned to Mystica and Nox. "Don't worry," he told them. "I'll take care of you — I promise."

And out of the shadows now came a man with a mustache, in a tattered starship commander's uniform. "Forgive me," said Major Dashwood. "I couldn't help overhearing. I can help you escape. I have a little experience of combat — if you'll accept the help of a former Shadow Guard?"

"We'll take all the help we can get," said Bixa. She looked at the solid-steel door, the ice-encrusted rock walls, the vid-cams rotating on the ceiling — and breathed in sharply, like someone who was surprised to finally get what she wanted, and now wasn't sure she wanted it after all. But then she clenched her fists and turned to Lucky. "Right. That backup you mentioned? You ready to go find the King and beat some sense into his stupid head?"

CHAPTER THIRTY-THREE

Bixa's needles bristled from her hair again: defiant, proud, unbeaten, and unbowed.

"OK," she said. "First thing we gotta do is lose these electrocuffs. So, Lucky, if you could just pass me the purple needle from my hair, that'd be a nice start."

"Um — OK — but —"

"See that vidcam up there?" She pointed at it, whirring on the ceiling, way out of reach. "I've been counting. It's on a fifteen-second rotation. We're wasting time talking. Very soon, it'll be back on us, and they'll see my needles, and that'll be the end of this escape."

She was right: the vidcam was already swinging back toward them. Lucky could see the purple needle glowing in Bixa's nest of hair. But his own hands were bound in electrocuffs too.

"How, Bixa? I can't reach it."

"Use your teeth!" she urged. "Use anything — just do it!"

The vidcam was coming. He leaned in close to Bixa and brought his mouth next to her glinting needles. He hesitated there; he'd seen how powerful they could be, and wasn't sure he wanted one in his mouth.

"Ten seconds to go," snapped Bixa. "Nine! Eight! Seven!"

It was now or never. Lucky opened his mouth, took the purple needle between his teeth, and pulled very, very carefully. The needle vibrated a little — but the sensation wasn't unpleasant. It eased out of her hair — one inch, two inches, but there was more, still more — the shaft was longer than he'd imagined — so he kept pulling, as gently as he could — until finally, it came all the way out.

Whew. He looked at her, the purple needle between his teeth. There could only be five seconds left — four — three . . .

"Give it to me," said Bixa. She opened her palm. He dropped the needle in, and her fingers closed around it. She flipped it over so its tip was pointing at the electrocuff — and at once, it began to glow a deep violet color. There was a buzz, the sound of something electrical crackling — and Bixa wriggled free of the cuffs.

She turned to the vidcam, which was now less than a second away, and unleashed another needle. It arced toward the vidcam and hit its electronic eye dead center, shattering it just in time.

"My goodness!" exclaimed Major Dashwood. There was hope on his face now; he stood straighter and taller. "That was . . . quite remarkable."

"That was the easy part," said Bixa. She was already busy freeing Lucky and her family. "Now the real problems begin." She went up to the door and examined it. "This is solid steel. Must be a foot thick, at least. There are deadbolts — here, here, and here . . ." Her face fell. "I don't think I can take this out."

The Major joined her by the door. "Everything has a

weakness," he said. He ran his fingers over the icy rock face by the edge of the door. "Aha. See here? Meltwater has been dripping down this wall. It's been doing it for countless years: melting and dripping and freezing again . . . and in all that time, I do believe it has eroded the rock, just a little. It has weakened it. Do you see?"

Bixa looked closely at where he was pointing: right by the edge of the door, where it met the wall. There was the tiniest crack there, almost invisible but for the droplets of water dripping down it.

"If you hit that spot with sufficient explosive force," suggested Major Dashwood, "I think you may just be able to do it."

"OK, I'm gonna try," said Bixa. "Stand back, everyone. There are sentries outside that door. They're Axxa army troopers, and they're armed to the teeth." She hesitated on the threshold. "We have to take out every single one of them straightaway. If we don't, we're finished, right here. . . ."

"But we will," said Major Dashwood. He rolled up his tattered sleeves. "Have no fear, young lady. You are not alone."

Bixa looked at the door with grim determination, and shaped up to fight. Beside her, Lucky brought to mind everything he'd learned from her about Astral Martial Arts.

"Ready?" said Bixa, checking that they were all in position. Then she leaned away and fired a needle at the edge of the door, where Major Dashwood had found the crack.

SHA-BLAMMMM!

There was a huge explosion. Hot metal flew through the air. Emergency lights on the ceiling started to flash. Alarms began to howl.

Bixa kicked down what remained of the door.

There were troopers on the other side. Five huge Axxa troopers with cannon in their hands. They were off-balance from the explosion, but recovering fast. They raised their cannon — aimed —

— and Bixa was upon them. They were so much bigger than her, yet she took on two of them, all on her own: fists smashing out, hooves kicking with perfect precision.

Major Dashwood fell upon two more, wrestling with them under the flashing lights.

Lucky charged at the last trooper, head down, hoping to take him by surprise. But the man was much stronger than him. He turned Lucky aside and slammed him into the wall.

OOOF!

Lucky sank to the floor. He looked up to see the trooper aiming his cannon. Squeezing the trigger. A shot went off —

— but not before Major Dashwood had somehow gotten between them. Hollering a bloodcurdling war cry, he seized the trooper by the collar and launched his own head forward. Their skulls connected with a sickening crack — and then the trooper was on the floor, unconscious. Dashwood had felled him with a single massive head-butt.

"Aries the Ram!" he roared in triumph as he helped Lucky up. "Your mother taught me that one!"

Behind him lay the first two troopers he'd fought; he'd knocked them both out too. Meanwhile, Bixa had dispatched the other two. Confidence flooded into her; she seemed to grow in stature.

"We did it!" she said. "We beat five of them! They're just people, like anyone else."

"That's right," said Major Dashwood. "And you are an extraordinary warrior: perhaps the best I've ever seen. You can do this, you really — *unnnh!*" He groaned with pain and doubled up, clutching his side with both hands.

Bixa frowned at him. The flashing red lights cast dark shadows all around. "You OK, Shadow Guard?" she asked.

The Major shook his head. A thin stream of blood began to trickle out from between his fingers. Lucky's insides felt raw as he saw it.

"What — what happened to him?" said Bixa.

"He saved me," said Lucky. "He took the shot . . ."

Major Dashwood straightened up, a grim look in his eyes. "No one has saved anyone just yet, I'm afraid." He glanced at the howling alarms. "That explosion hasn't gone unnoticed. There'll be more of them coming any moment." He hefted one of the sentries' cannon in his hands, and his jaw set with determination. "I'll make sure they don't catch you. You must get to the King and persuade him to make peace. It's the only hope."

"But you've got to come with us!" said Lucky. "We need you —"

"No. You didn't before, and you don't now." Dashwood touched his side again. His fingers came away wet. "I — I can't go any farther. But I *can* keep you covered and buy you a little time."

"He's right," said Bixa. "Come on. We have to get out of here."

She scooped up the cannon the troopers had dropped. She kept two for herself and tossed a third at Lucky. He caught it awkwardly, almost discharging it by mistake.

"But I don't know how to use this!" he protested.

"I don't want you to use it!" said Bixa. "Just carry it for me till I need it." She crept around the corner to check that the way forward was clear.

Lucky followed her uncertainly into the dim red corridor. He glanced back over his shoulder.

And as he met his eyes, Major Dashwood smiled at him, for the first and last and only time.

It was the same smile Lucky had grown up looking at. The smile in the vidpic. A protective smile so warm, so full of love, it always made him feel better to see it.

His throat tightened at the sight.

He knew the Major was not his father — but at that moment, how he wished he was. He'd done more than Lucky had ever dared to dream a father might.

But there was no time to say any of this. No time to thank him, no time even to say good-bye. Because already, they could hear more troopers coming to get them.

"For your mother's sake," urged the Major, "get out of here, Lucky! Go!"

CHAPTER THIRTY-FOUR

They ran down the corridor, away from the troopers.

Bixa led the way, a cannon in each hand, hair bristling with needles. Lucky was right behind her. Next came Frollix, carrying Mystica in one huge arm, leading the Captain by the hand. And above all their heads flew Bazooka, flapping her wings in celebration of their escape.

A massive explosion shook the corridor behind them. They heard Major Dashwood's war cry and the screams of Axxa troopers.

Then the explosions stopped. It grew ominously still and silent behind them.

"Major Dashwood?" called Lucky over his shoulder. "Are you OK?"

No answer came back.

"Bixa . . . he's —"

"He knew what he was doing," said Bixa. "Keep going. Don't stop."

She was moving ahead already, scouting the way forward, around a corner and out of sight. Lucky waited for Frollix to catch up. Together, they edged around the corner, then up some steps, making their way in silence toward the surface of the planet.

But a detachment of troopers was waiting for them on the next level. They raised their cannon — fired — and a volley of shots hit the wall above Lucky's head, shattering the stone. Mystica and Nox cringed away from the shrapnel. They looked so frail, so vulnerable.

"Stay back!" cried Bixa. She ran full pelt at the troopers. Flicked a crimson needle at them. And —

KAA-BOOSHHH!

Everything in Lucky's head went weird. His senses scrambled, all mixed up. Sounds became shapes. Colors had tastes. And the troopers were throwing up, sinking to their knees, clutching their heads and weeping.

"Sensory Dazzler?" asked Lucky, barely holding down the nausea.

Bixa grinned. "You're catching on!"

"This," groaned Captain Nox, "is why we don't like violence."

"But we're getting there," said Bixa. "Just two more lefts and a right, and then we'll be clear of this level."

"Are you sure?" asked Lucky, running after her. "Can you really remember every turn we took on the way in?"

"If you'd been watching, 'stead of feeling sorry for yourself," she said, "then maybe you'd remember too!"

Two lefts and a right later, a dead end loomed up ahead of them: a solid wall. A vidcam stared silently down at them from the ceiling.

"Hmmm," said Bixa. "Did we pass this on our way in?"

"I don't know!" Lucky retorted. "I was too busy feeling sorry for myself!"

Cautiously, she approached the wall. "Frollix," she called. "Hang back behind that corner with Mystica and Nox till I tell you it's safe. There's something about this I don't like. . . ."

The vidcam whirred — and suddenly the wall began to move. It slid open before their startled eyes. And on the other side, dozens of Axxa troopers were waiting. They had an entire armory of weapons. Racks of cannon and ammunition. Stacks of ground-blasters and grenades. Heaps of body armor and shields.

Bixa fired both her guns at once — and her shots bounced right off their shields. The fire came straight back at her —

"Duck!" she yelled. She and Lucky hit the floor together as fire singed their hair.

Bixa tossed aside her cannon and sprang into action with Astral Martial Arts instead. She leaped Leo-style over a blast from the first trooper, then hit him with a Cancer pincer move. The trooper crumpled, dropping his blaster. Bixa caught it and took out two more with her elbows as she went all Sagittarius, unleashing a hail of jabs and punches — but the others were on to her at once, surrounding her.

And now one of the troopers was in Lucky's face, shoving him back, aiming the muzzle of a cannon at him.

Lucky shaped up to deliver a Scorpio kick —

— and the trooper cracked him across the face with the barrel of his gun.

Excruciating pain exploded in Lucky's mouth. There was a terrible crunching sound. It sounded like teeth breaking. He could taste something salty. He wondered if it was blood.

He hit the ground, stars spinning before his eyes.

The trooper cocked his cannon —

"You leave him alone!" roared Bixa. She reared up like a lioness and let loose a ferocious blow that knocked the trooper sideways.

But the walls were beginning to move again: swiveling, sliding, trapping them in the corner. And more troopers were coming through all the time.

It was getting desperate now. Bixa fought on, but she was just one girl. Even with all her skills, she couldn't keep it up forever. She was pinned down in that corner, and there were more, always more, coming through all the time.

CRACK! One of the troopers broke through her defenses. She reeled back.

WHACK! Bixa gasped. She glanced down at Lucky. He wasn't doing what he'd promised, and they both knew it.

Bazooka the phoenix swooped down at the trooper — claws extended, breathing fire — but the big man swatted her away like she was an insect, and leveled his cannon at Bixa's head.

"You're dead," he said. He grinned, pulled the safety catch, and —

It is coming!
It is rising!
It is time!

—at the center of Lucky's being, a spark of power flared into life. Impossible energies began to burn.

His fingertips started to shine.

And finally, the light poured out of him: the brightest light he'd ever seen, pouring from his hands, his head, his heart.

The trooper gasped. He dropped his cannon, shielding his eyes. He backed away as the power rose and swelled and grew, blazing from Lucky like a star.

A star.

What else could it be? It had been growing inside him, in his dreams and in his body, all this time. And now it was scorching out of him with unearthly light and heat and power. Stronger than the fires in a nuclear furnace. Bigger than the blast of a billion atom bombs. So bright and brilliant, it was like staring at the sun.

At that moment, he knew the Startalkers were right.

There was no limit to this power. No limit at all to what it could do, if he just let it go.

The other troopers saw it. They fell back. But they were disciplined, crack troops. They regrouped, aimed their weapons at Lucky, and pulled all their triggers at once.

A great hail of death came shooting toward him.

He held up a hand — and the power of a star exploded out of him. Fire flashed from his fingers like a flaming sword. It caught their blasts and made them harmless. Not one of their shots got through.

Lucky pulled himself up from the floor, flames crackling over his head like a halo, and sent a solar flare out at their armory. He was painfully aware that he was burning his own life away. The power was killing him — but he was determined not to kill anyone else with it. He was aiming to destroy their weapons. Not the troopers, but their instruments of death.

His solar flare hit, and the weapons racks went up in flames. The blasters blew up; the cannon melted. The ammunition exploded like a string of fireworks going off.

Bixa's eyes widened. She watched from the corner, staring directly at the light that shone from Lucky's body, but she was not blinded by it. She looked inspired.

She got up, needles flashing neon colors, and sprang forward again: a one-girl whirlwind of fighting force, running out ahead of the fire. Lucky moved forward with her. Between them, they were unbeatable. The warrior girl with needles in her hair and the boy with the star inside him: they fought side by side.

It was like a furnace in the armory now, and the temperature was still rising. At the back of his throat, Lucky could taste something like sulfur, filling his senses with fire. But the power was so strong, so bright — it was irresistible, and it streamed out of him, unstoppable. Not just his hands now: his whole body was aflame.

"The Astraeus!" cried the troopers. "The Old Ones have returned!" And with that, they broke ranks at last, and began to flee in terror.

When it was done — when all those fearsome troopers had been put to flight and all their deadly weapons were smoke and ashes — Lucky and Bixa turned to each other.

Bixa's eyes were alight. She looked on the scorching star that burned in Lucky's chest, and she was not afraid.

She held out a hand and reached with her long, beautiful fingers — reached toward the blazing furnace in his heart.

"Don't!" he warned her. "Don't touch me — it'll kill you —"

But she reached, and touched, just for a moment — and her silver eyes glowed ultrabright.

"Don't fear it, Lucky," she said across the gap between them. "It's beautiful. We try so hard to be like the stars, but you — you actually *are* one. . . ."

He watched her, speechless, filled with feelings he didn't have names for.

It was a moment when time seemed to stop — but it was just a moment. Then they heard voices calling from around the corner, and Bixa stepped away from Lucky, unharmed.

"Is it safe?" asked Frollix.

"Yeah," said Bixa, looking up. "Yeah, it's safe." She grinned, and ran her fingers through the neon needles in her hair. "Watch out, Theobroma!" she whooped. "We're coming for you!"

"*Baaa-zookieeeee!*" exclaimed the phoenix, picking herself up and leading the way forward again, flying toward freedom.

They moved on — up, and up, and up — rising through the levels with new hope, fresh determination. They burst out of Charon Caves: out of the bunker, through the gates, and back into the open air.

It was freezing cold outside. On the surface of the planet, the blizzard was still raging; the air was full of ice. Yet still the star blazed out of Lucky's body.

And through the blizzard, through the whirling whiteness, they could see an entire army waiting for them by their encampment. Row after row of troopers facing them, with cannon and blasters at the ready. The Axxa army, in all its power and glory — and beyond it, the Skyhawks of the Axxa fleet.

"King Theobroma!" Bixa yelled. "We need to talk to you!"

"Put down your weapons!" a harsh voice came back. "Put them down — or we will destroy you."

Was that the King's voice? Lucky looked out at the army. He couldn't see where the voice had come from; there were just too many of them. It was a million against two.

He looked up at the sky. Even through the radiation storm, he could see that it was bleached white as bones with the dying supernova light of Aquarius.

"King Theobroma," called Bixa again. "If you're here, then answer me. By all the stars — this is the most important thing there's ever been!"

No answer came back, except for the click of safety catches being unlatched and the rumble of weapons powering up.

The Axxa army wasn't listening. The King wasn't coming. The plan wasn't going to work.

Lucky felt bleak and angry. This was not the way he wanted it to end. Burning his own life away, just so he could take the lives of others — surely this wasn't what he was supposed to do with his power? Surely it was meant for something more?

Wind whipped into his face. Yet his insides felt like superheated matter, raging against the blizzard: red-hot, white-hot, hotter still.

Some of the Axxa troopers shielded their eyes as the solar wind swirled around him. Some of them dropped to their knees. But still the power rose inside him, higher and higher, and higher again.

His body was shaking. It felt like his head was splitting under the strain, breaking open as arcs of pain shot across his face, brighter and stronger than any Human body could contain. He was holding his hands out ahead of him, trying with all his might to restrain the power that was bleeding out of him: the fire and the light and the burning in his brain. . . .

But it was bigger than him. It was like an endless nuclear meltdown: a chain reaction that could burn this whole world and more. And if he just let it go, he would explode, destroying himself and everything around him: everything.

413

There's no stopping it, he thought. *It's going to blow*—

"Enough," came a new voice, rolling over the blizzard. "Put down your weapons. No one hurts that boy."

It was a rich, deep voice—not loud, but totally commanding.

The troopers lowered their weapons. Lucky looked up, trying to see who'd spoken.

And then it came again, that voice. "Boy, here I am. I am your King. I am Theobroma!"

CHAPTER THIRTY-FIVE

And there in front of them, at the end of the line of troopers, stood Theobroma, the Axxa King.

There was something surprising about the way he looked. He was large and imposing: as tall as Captain Nox and as broad as Frollix. His horns were huge curving crescents that pointed straight up at the sky. But he did not look wild, or savage, or terrifying, as he did in the government vidpics.

No; he looked like an old-fashioned king. On his head was a crown that glittered like starlight. On his shoulders were robes of black velvet.

Most unexpected was his face. His features seemed full of compassion. His eyes were not mad and staring. They were warm, ruby red, like the last moments of a summer sunset. Even from this distance, Lucky could feel the power of his gaze. The King was looking at him as if he couldn't take his eyes off him. And there was something about him that Lucky couldn't look away from, either. A charisma that commanded his attention completely.

"Put down your cannon," the King ordered his forces, his voice so deep and quiet, so rich and strong, it compelled everyone's attention. "Bow down before the Astraeus."

The troopers turned to look at Lucky. His body was glowing, pulsing, the solar fires in his heart still burning; they couldn't look at him directly. But they bowed down before him as the King strode past their ranks, toward him through the snow.

He carried something very familiar in his hands. A thick black disk, shimmering with silver light.

Lucky stared at the King, with the astrolabe in his hands, and a terrible thought began to form in the back of his mind.

The astrolabe. His father's astrolabe.

What was it Gala had said? *He is waiting for you. He is expecting you, even now . . . But are you absolutely certain you wish to find him?*

The King's eyes were shining as he looked at Lucky through the blizzard — as if Lucky was the most special person in the universe. As if . . . as if he *loved* him.

No. It couldn't be . . .

And yet — it would make sense of so much.

"At last," said the King softly as the snow swirled all around him. "What is mine has come back to me. I have waited so long, my son."

His words made Lucky's heart shiver. "But — my mother's Human," he protested as he stared into those sunset-red eyes. "*I'm* Human."

Yet even as he spoke, he remembered what Frollix and Bixa had said about their own parents: *The genetic line always follows the mother's side. . . .*

"Yes," said the King. "I loved a Human woman, once. When she realized that war was coming, she tried to protect you. She ran away with you — and though I searched and searched, she hid you too well for me to find. But I always prayed you would return one day. And the instant I saw my old astrolabe, I knew in my heart that day had come."

So it was true. This was his father. Not poor, lost Major Dashwood — but Theobroma, the Axxa King.

The fire inside him went out. The great solar wind dropped. Lucky took the power back into himself and felt again the exhaustion, the terrible pain that always came after these moments of incandescence. His hands, his head, his heart: every part of him hurt.

He fell forward into his father's arms, naked and shivering in the snow.

The King caught him. He covered Lucky with his own robes and lifted him from the ground. He carried him as if he was as light as a feather. The snow swirled down around them, but Lucky was not cold, not in those arms. It was as if everything else just melted away. As if no one else was there — just him and his father, and his father held him close, as if he was a treasure.

Bixa bristled beside them, needles flashing danger signals. "If you hurt my friend," she warned the King, though he towered over her, "I'll make you pay."

The troopers touched their triggers at her words, but the King nodded respectfully at Bixa. "You are brave, warrior girl," he said. "And a fearsome fighter: I have seen what you can do. Believe me, I will not hurt him, for I love him as much as you do." He turned to Lucky. "You chose your friends well, my son."

Bixa flushed. Bazooka spat sparks. Far above them all,

Aquarius was screaming out supernova light, brighter and whiter and closer to death than ever.

Lucky was almost unaware of all this, so powerful was his father's presence. But Bixa was not.

"We came to find you for a reason, King Theobroma," she said. "We've got things to say to you. Important things."

"Of course you do," said the King. "Come with me. We have much to discuss, and very little time."

He took them to the grandest-looking cabin, on the edge of the encampment, at the foot of a great ice mountain. He left his commanders outside, with instructions to bring food and drink, and fresh clothing for Lucky.

A warm fire flickered inside the cabin, bright enough to show old-fashioned wooden beams on the ceiling and bearskin rugs on the floor. There were no windows in here; just giant vidscreens on the walls. The King sat Lucky down at a dark oak table with many chairs around it, carved from the same wood. Lucky sat there, dazed, exhausted — and amazed.

We did it, he was thinking. *We found my father, and we found the King. Now he's going to stop the War and save the stars. He's going to tell me why I've got this power —*

— and Gala was wrong! I used it again, and I didn't die. I didn't burn my life away. I'm going to live!

He basked in a warm glow as his father welcomed the others into his cabin.

"Captain Nox," he said. "It has been too long. And can that be Mystica?" He peered at the old lady as Frollix laid her down on the bearskin rugs.

Mystica was weak, pale, and clearly in pain, but she still

looked grand, in spite of it all. Her golden eyes were clear and bright again — almost too bright, like pulses of super-nova light.

"Yes, it's me, Theobroma," she said, warming her hands by the fire. "I'm not at my beautiful best, after a spell in your jail. But you can't get rid of me that easily!"

The King smiled at that. His face was full of compassion, his voice warm and sweet. "I must apologize for the way you were treated," he said. "Please understand: this is a time of war. Many Axxa have suffered and died because of the Humans. My officers did not know who you were. They made a mistake."

"And the other people in the caves?" asked Frollix. "They all mistakes too?"

"It's unfortunate if innocents have to suffer," said the King. "It's not a perfect system. We know that. But we do our best."

Frollix didn't argue. He just hung back and watched the King silently with his starry blue eyes.

The door opened. Lucky was brought new clothes and a pair of cloven-hoof boots. Then trays of food were brought in, held aloft on silver platters. There were racks of meat, and roasted birds. A huge dish of eyeballs, and Xoco for everyone.

"Eat, my friends," said the King, biting with relish into a leg of lamb. "I have an appetite tonight. Let us celebrate: my son has come back to me!"

Lucky took some eyeballs, but he couldn't eat. His head was spinning with all that had happened.

Bixa didn't even bother with the food. "But if you know your son's an Astraeus," she said, "and you know he's half

Human — then you must know the stars don't want this war. Why else would an Astraeus come down like that? He's proof that the stars want peace."

"Peace?" said the King. "Do you know what the Humans are doing, even as we speak? They are killing Aquarius."

"And the only way to save it," said Bixa, "is to make peace. You have to do it, or it'll be the end of everything. Gala told us that, and so did Major Dashwood."

"Major Dashwood!" scoffed the King. "He was a Shadow Guard. One of *them*." He shook his head and sank his teeth into the lamb, ripping meat from the bone, stripping it bare. "No, warrior girl. You are right that we must save the stars — but there are better ways of doing that. Aren't there, Astraeus?"

He turned to Lucky, his eyes shining with passion and belief. But Lucky had questions for his father — questions he had crossed the whole galaxy to ask.

"If I'm really an Astraeus," he said, "then why am I here? What am I meant to do with my power?"

The King held out his big, broad hands. "Isn't it obvious? I knew war was coming, and I knew it would be long and hard and bitter. We needed something to tip the balance in our favor. A secret weapon. And you," he said, "you are that weapon."

Lucky stared at his father. "A *weapon*?" he said numbly. "Is that what I am to you?"

"You are my son, my only son. But yes: you are also the weapon that will win this war, by destroying our enemies forever."

Lucky shifted in his chair. Its back was very high. The oak felt hard and unyielding beneath him. Perhaps it was a chair fit for kings and princes — but it was beginning to make him uncomfortable.

"But I'm not even a good fighter," he protested. "I'm clumsy, useless . . . If you need a fighter, Bixa's the one you want."

His father smiled. "I have seen your power, my son. It is greater than any fighter, greater than anything known to Human or Axxa warcraft." He threw the bare lamb bone down on his plate. "That is what I prayed for. That is why I found the lost legends, made the sacrifices, and performed the rituals to summon an Astraeus from the sky. And that is why the stars sent you: to destroy the Humans."

Lucky shivered at his words. His father could be so warm and welcoming — yet so ruthless too. His gentle features hardened when he spoke of the Humans. A different tone came into his voice: a tone you could not argue with.

"Listen to yourself, Theobroma," said Mystica, by the flickering fire. "Do you not remember? We are all connected; we are all one. *From the stars we all came —*"

"Spare me your sermon," said the King, his tone growing more bitter. "You Startalkers were always so naive. The Humans started this war. But now at last we have something that can finish it — something greater than their science can conceive of." He turned to Lucky. "A star come down from the sky. And not just any star."

"So — which Astraeus am I?" said Lucky, pulse beating in his ears.

"You do not know? Your mother never said who you really were?"

"She never told me any of this. All she ever tried to do was protect me. But now that I'm here, I need to know the truth. So tell me: which of the Twelve am I? Am I the Astraeus of War?"

His father drew a deep breath. He looked very grave. Lucky's stomach was tied up in knots; he could hardly bear not knowing any longer.

"Tell him, Theobroma," gasped Mystica as the flickering flames burned low in the fireplace. "Even if it is as I fear — Lucky deserves to know the truth."

"Lucky?" said the King. He stood up to stoke the fire. "That is not your true name."

"But that's what my mother called me —"

Theobroma's eyes flared. "Your mother," he muttered. He prodded the fire with a poker, building it back up, making the embers crackle with sparks. "How like her, to wish that fate for you — and to deny the destiny you were born for."

"Why?" said Lucky. "What is it? Who am I? What's my name?"

The King closed his eyes, and then he spoke the words. "Your name is Lucifer. Not Lucky, but Lucifer."

"No . . ." Lucky recoiled from his father.

"Do not pretend you never felt it," said the King. "You know what is in you, and what you can do. You are Lucifer, the Thirteenth Astraeus: the one we never speak of. There is one in every mythology. A Devil. A Destroyer of Worlds. And that is what you are. You are the nightmare that has haunted Humanity through its history, and now you will put an end to Humanity. For you are the very Devil himself: the Astraeus of Destruction."

Lucky felt dizzy, like his head was coming away from his shoulders, like the ground was falling away beneath his feet. "But — but — *why?*"

The King threw another log on the fire, and the flames rose up, spitting sparks that spiraled toward the ceiling. "Space devils," he said. "That's what they call us. So let them face the wrath of the real Devil. Not just people who happen to be different from them, but the ancient and terrible power that sends whole races to hell — the Alpha and Omega and the end of all things!"

And now, finally, Frollix spoke up again. He'd been silent all this time, just watching the King — but now at last he spoke, his eyes glittering with cool blue flame.

"You know what, Yer Majesty?" he drawled. "I don't think your story makes sense! No one can summon an Astraeus. If a star comes down from the sky, only the stars themselves can know why."

"And who are you to make this claim?" asked the King with barely concealed disdain.

"Oh, didn't I say?" replied Frollix. "I'm the new Star-talker of the Past. I'm the one who knows everything that's gone before. I even know about those lost legends of yours!"

The King dropped the poker and stared at Frollix open-mouthed.

"You may claim you summoned Lucky," Frollix went on calmly, "but I'll tell you what really happened. The stars sent him. You recognized what power he had — and you wanted to use it for your own ends. You still do."

The King hesitated a moment. Then his eyes flared again. "Why else would the Thirteenth Astraeus be here now, at this time of destruction, if not to destroy?"

Frollix sighed. "Professor Byzantine told me something about that, on the Rainbow Temple Wheel. He said some people think there's a Thirteenth Astraeus, the Astraeus of Destruction — but others think it's the Astraeus of *Creation*." He shrugged his great shoulders. "Creation and Destruction. The Prof thought they were two sides of the same Astraeus, the most powerful of them all. Because the stars don't just destroy. They create too. They created everything."

"But he is *Lucifer!*" roared the King, striding to stand over Lucky.

"And you know what that name means?" said Frollix, standing up too. "It means 'Bringer of Light.' That's all. Lucifer wasn't just the Devil. He was also called the Morningstar: the brightest star. And in all the legends, one thing shines through. Lucifer was stubborn! He stood for free will and choice. So even if Lucky is Lucifer, I reckon he can do whatever he wants with his power. He's the only one who can decide. You can't tell him what to do."

"He is what he is," said the King. "He knows. He has felt it; I can tell." He crouched down before Lucky, his huge horns glittering in the firelight, and gazed deep into his eyes. "You must use your power, my son. You must destroy the Humans."

Lucky wanted to believe Frollix, but his father's words had gone deep inside him. He felt hot and cold, all at once. He couldn't think straight, couldn't stop the thoughts.

Was I right, after all? Am I evil? The Devil? The Thirteenth Astraeus?

"I — I don't want to destroy the Humans," he said at last. "I'm half Human — they're part of me, like you are . . . And I'm not just a weapon, like a Dark Matter bomb. I was on Scorpio when the wheel was destroyed. I saw what it was like. Was it you who killed all those innocent people?"

The King stood up. He walked over to the platters of food. He took a bird's wing and snapped it off in his hand. "The Humans are not innocent," he said. "They use our stars to power their machines. They burn our suns to light their cities. And those who let them do this are not innocent, either. The people of Scorpio had the choice to fight on the right side. They refused; they wanted to stay neutral. Now they know better. There is no neutrality. You are either with us or against us in this war."

"But Professor Byzantine was on that wheel — he died there," said Lucky. "Your Dark Matter bomb killed him, and thousands who never did anything to you."

"*Baaa-zookaaaa!*" cried the little phoenix, her body glowing crimson in the firelight.

"Of course we regret all loss of life," said the King, "but that is the risk and the cost of war. I'll never understand why the Humans hate us — but so long as they fight us, we must fight them. So long as they see us as their enemy, we must be the worst enemy their nightmares can conjure. That is why I summoned you, of all the Astraeus — because that is what you are, Lucifer."

Lucky flinched. "Don't call me that," he said. "Please. It's

425

not my name." He coughed. Smoke was rising from the fire; thick smoke, heavy with pitch and tar. He felt like he was choking on it, suffocating. He looked around for a window, a way out, but there was not a single window in this cabin. No view of the stars on the vidscreens. Only his father's red eyes, burning into him.

"My son," said the King. "You have more power than anyone in the galaxy. I gave you that power. Now use it for its proper purpose, and put an end to this suffering."

Lucky wanted to trust his father. He wanted desperately to believe that there might be a place for him here —

— but how could he? He watched the smoke rising, and all he could think of was the Rainbow Temple Wheel.

"How is killing people going to make things better?" he said. "It'll just make the Humans hate you more. Bixa's right: you've got to make peace. That's the only way."

"No," said his father in a low voice. "Now that you have found me, we can stop them from ever killing another star again. Just use your power."

"But I only just stopped it this time," said Lucky. "If I use it again, I don't know where it will end —"

His father nodded. "Destruction without end," he agreed. "That is precisely what I prayed for."

Mystica gasped. Her golden eyes were full of pain. "But it would destroy him," she said. "His body could not take it. He would die!"

"We must be prepared to make sacrifices," said the King, "if we are to win this war."

"Your own son?" said Captain Nox. "Do you have any

426

idea what it means to lose a child? Are you really so full of hate that this war means more to you than he does?"

"No one means more to me than my son. But yes, Captain, I would sacrifice everything for what I believe is right. I have sacrificed so much already for our cause." The King looked at Lucky — tentative, almost unsure of himself for a moment. "Where is Diana — your mother? Why is she not here too?"

Lucky shook his head. The feelings burned inside him. There were tears like knives behind his eyes. But he dug his nails into his palms and made himself say it out loud. "The Shadow Guards," he said. "They came for us. She saved me from them, but she . . ." He looked down and said the words at last. "She died. My mother's dead."

The King closed his eyes. "Then let us avenge her," he said very quietly. He opened his eyes again, and they were burning blazing red. All the gentleness and compassion was gone from his look, and that hard, bitter tone was all Lucky could hear in his voice now. "Will you do it? Will you fulfill the destiny you were born for?"

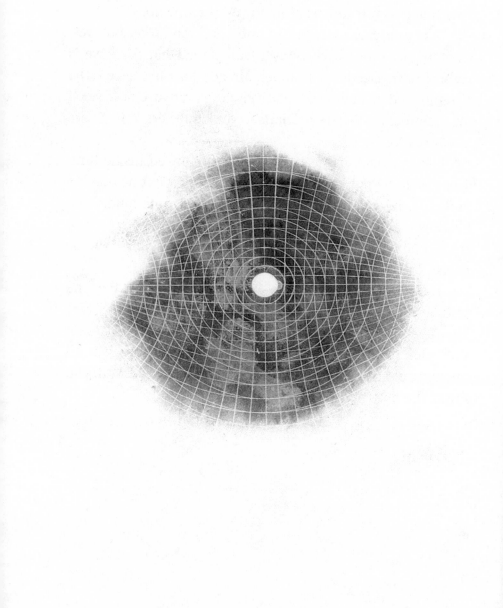

CHAPTER THIRTY-SIX

It felt like everything was spinning around Lucky. So many forces at work, so much bigger than he was, and so finely balanced.

Here it was: the choice Professor Byzantine had anticipated. *With such power in you, the day will soon come when you must choose what to do. . . . On that day, you will need mental strength, moral clarity, and, above all, a proper understanding of who and what you are. . . .*

That day had come — yet he didn't have any of those things.

All he had was confusion. And it was tearing him apart.

"I — I have to go and think," he said.

He stepped out into the snow at the back of the cabin. Axxa troopers surrounded him, but the King waved them away, then went back into his cabin, leaving Lucky alone with his thoughts.

It was bitterly cold outside, and as still as death in the shadow of the ice mountain. The wind had dropped. Nothing moved except the snowflakes falling from the sky.

And yet the cold was a relief after the King's cabin. It cooled the burning emotions inside him. Lucky could think clearly, for the first time since he'd found his father and discovered who he really was.

Lucifer: the Devil.

When he'd wondered which Astraeus he might be, he'd thought only of the ancient gods. But a devil? No wonder he'd never trusted this power. No wonder he'd always feared it, and felt it could destroy everything, including himself.

He was right all along. It could. And that was exactly what his father wanted.

So . . . am I just here to destroy? Is that all my power's for? I don't want it to be. This is like a nightmare, and I'm so lost and alone in it—

There was the crunch of hooves. He looked up. Bixa was watching him from the edge of the cabin. She eyed him coolly as the snow circled down around them.

He tried to smile at her.

Couldn't.

"So you're the Devil, huh?" she said. He didn't answer; what could he say? "That's pretty bad, right?" Bixa carried on. "I mean, the Devil—the *real* Devil—he's not so popular, is he? I don't think you'll have too many friends. What kind of idiot would hang around with Lucifer?" She grinned at him.

He tried to grin back.

But it was no good. He couldn't smile. Things were just too bleak for jokes.

"So—are we still friends?" he asked her. "Even though— I am what I am?"

Bixa screwed her face up into a twisted devil's mask. She made her needles cluster into horn-shapes above her head.

430

She stuck her tongue out at him and caught snowflakes on its tip. "Well, yeah!" she yelled. "But only 'cos I like kicking your crazy ass so much!"

And he couldn't help it: finally his face cracked into a smile. Even with all this madness, she could still make him smile.

"Come here, you moonbrain!" she said. She pulled him over to her and hugged him hard. He hugged her back; he hugged her and hugged her, holding on to the one thing in the galaxy that still made sense.

"Lucky," she said at last, "whoever the hell you are, I'm your friend, right? Whatever happens, I will always be your friend."

He felt his face quiver. "Yeah. Same goes for you . . ."

"And—" Bixa started. Then she stopped and dug her hooves into the snow.

"And what?" he said.

"And . . . so many other things. . . ."

She looked at him with her silver eyes, and they both held the gaze.

The snow swirled around them; the wind blew the blizzard straight across their faces; but they didn't feel it. Didn't feel it one bit.

"So what are we gonna do now?" she asked him. "What are *you* gonna do?"

"I don't know," he said. "All this time, all I ever wanted was to find my father. Finding him was meant to make everything OK! He was meant to give me all the answers, take care of me. . . . But now . . ." Lucky shook his head and stared down at the snow.

The wind dropped. The snow stopped falling. It became so calm and clear that he could see tiny ice crystals in the air, sparkling like diamonds.

"We're not gonna persuade him to make peace, are we?" said Bixa.

"Did you hear that stuff about killing the whole Human race? I don't care if he's my father — I think he's crazy!"

She giggled. "You've got a crazy dad! I should've guessed — it runs in the family!"

"Hey!" he protested. "That's not fair!"

"Awww," she mocked. "Anyway — I don't believe he's all that crazy. I just think he's so desperate to win the War, it's blinded him to everything else."

"Yeah." Lucky nodded. In the sudden clarity, he was remembering his encounter at the Spacewall. "You know, I think President Thorntree's the same. They both believe they're doing the right thing — but between them, they're destroying the galaxy." He shook his head in confusion. "So who are the good guys?"

"Maybe there aren't any good guys," said Bixa. "Maybe there aren't even any bad guys. Maybe . . . they're just people. All of them, just people. Good and bad at the same time."

They looked up. It was deepest night over Charon, but the sky was whiter than ever. The supernova of Aquarius looked brighter, and even more unstable. It could not be long before it collapsed in on itself forever.

"We've got to save the stars," said Lucky. "That's the important thing. But how?"

Frollix came out of the cabin and joined them on the ice. The three of them stood there in silence, looking up at the sky. They turned away from the dying supernova and saw an awesome sight in the other direction, one that prickled the hairs on Lucky's neck.

It was open space, infinite and unboundaried. The endless black highway to all the other galaxies and undiscovered countries out there ahead.

I could look at that view forever and never get bored, he thought.

"Ain't it beautiful, brother?" said Frollix, gazing up at it. "When I look at the stars now, I see how they were, billions of years ago, when all that light started out. Right back to the beginning of everything . . . And I can't believe it's all got to end, just 'cos of this stupid war."

"Yeah," said Lucky. "I know." He felt overwhelmed with sadness. But what could he do about it, even with all his power, if the two sides wouldn't stop fighting?

"Lucky?" said Frollix softly. "Remember when Gala said you didn't need a parent to tell you what to do? She said you'd find your answers for yourself, in yourself. Well, maybe that's true." He put his great arms around them both. "Look at us. Look how far we've come. Think about all the things we've done together. We did them on our own, without any-one telling us what to do." His eyes glowed with deep blue fire. "So it's your decision what happens now. No one else's. Whatever you wanna do: you just say the word, and we'll back you up."

Lucky looked at his friends, and his heart welled up. "Thank you," he said quietly. "Thank you so much, both of you. I just wish I knew what to do —"

ssssshh

A soft hissing sound. Behind him, above him. It set his teeth on edge.

His mouth went dry.

He peered up into the sky — hoping against hope that he was wrong — but there —

— oh

no

not them —

not here —

not now —

— there was a V-shaped shadow in the sky.

A shadowship, swooping out of the radiation storm, silhouetted against the supernova.

And now at last Lucky understood that strange darkness in space he'd glimpsed in the astrolabe: the darkness that seemed to be following him.

They must have been tracking him, shielded in stealth armor, all this time, all this way. Ever since that meeting with the President, they must've been behind him as he made his way to Charon, to his father, to the Axxa army's secret base.

He turned to his friends and saw them staring at the shadow in the sky.

He couldn't bear to lose their friendship now — not after all the things they'd just said — but he couldn't lie to them anymore.

"There's something I have to tell you," he said. "I met President Thorntree at the Spacewall. She made me promise to keep it secret. I didn't want to, but we'd still be stuck there if I hadn't." He was painfully aware of how weak it sounded. "She tricked me. I think she sent that ship to follow me —"

"It's all right, Lucky," said Frollix, looking down. "We knew."

His heart jolted. "You did?"

"You can't keep secrets from Startalkers, kid!" Frollix's eyes flashed.

"I'm so sorry — I should've told you — I know," said Lucky. "But she threatened us. She said we'd never see each other again —"

"It's OK, you moonbrain!" said Bixa. "I understand why you did it. What I don't understand is this. What kind of adult uses a kid like that? What kind of leader rules with secrets and lies?"

Oh, those words meant so much to him at that moment. He clung on to them, as if to life itself. He looked up at the sky again — and his heart stopped dead in his chest.

Because it wasn't just one V-shaped shadow.

It was hundreds of them. Thousands. And more were coming through the radiation storm every moment, swooping down on Charon.

The whole Human fleet, it seemed, was descending from the dying sky.

CHAPTER THIRTY-SEVEN

Sirens began to wail around the Axxa base.

Lucky saw Skyhawks taking off, shields going up, artillery locking onto the black ships in the sky. He saw troopers scramble into action. And now the first bombs began to fall as the shadowships sent down their deadly rain.

BLAMMM!

The Axxa gunners sent great streams of cannon fire back at their enemies. They hit a shadowship full on, crippling its shields, making it glow brighter and brighter — until the black ship exploded, and the Axxa roar of triumph went up into the sky.

But Lucky just stared in horror at the destruction erupting all around him. He could hear the screams of dying people on the wind; he could smell burning flesh and metal. It was like that Skyhawk pilot he'd sensed in the astrolabe: he felt nothing but sorrow as life after life was snuffed out.

His father strode out of the cabin. If he was surprised by the appearance of the Human fleet, or afraid of them, he did not show it. He was proud and straight-backed: a leader utterly certain of his purpose, even now. "My son," he said, "tell me you will destroy them."

Helpless, hopeless, Lucky shook his head.

His father's eyes burned. "How many of us must die before you do your duty?" he said. And with that, he stormed away to command his forces. "People of the Stars!" he cried. "Stand and fight! This is our chance to finish the Humans forever!"

Lucky stood there by the cabin, Frollix and Bixa by his side. A blast of ice whipped into their faces. The blizzard was rising again. It was blowing like the end of the world.

Frollix's words cut through the wind. "Lucky," he said. "We're still with you. We'll back you up, we'll follow you to the end of the world — but this is it. You need to decide. What are you gonna do with your power? How are we gonna save the stars?"

Lucky's scalp tingled. The stars. Surely they knew what he was meant to do?

He concentrated, trying to reach for the stars in his mind — but he couldn't hear them over the explosions. He couldn't feel them through the blaze of battle.

He needed to go up: above and beyond the battle. He needed to get away from all this destruction, to see them clearly once again.

He looked at the ice mountain. He couldn't even see its summit from here — but he felt drawn to it.

"What is it?" said Frollix, as Mystica and Nox joined them outside the cabin.

"I have to go up," Lucky said, staring at the slopes. "I have to see the stars."

"Of course he does," breathed Mystica hoarsely. "And we have to get him there!"

She still looked pale and weak, but there was a little life in her yet. Lucky clung on to hope. *Maybe she's going to make it, after all. If I can just get close enough to the stars—maybe I'll find a way to save us all. . . .*

"Let's go, then," he said. "One last climb."

His boots crunched in the snow as he took his first steps up the mountain. Bazooka lit the way, perched on his shoulder. Bixa climbed beside him. Frollix was on the other side, carrying Mystica. Captain Nox refused to be carried; he was strong enough now to climb on his own.

It wasn't too steep at first. But it grew steadily steeper, and more slippery. The wind whipped and ripped and lashed his skin, but he kept moving up through snow and rock.

Below him, above him, the War raged on. Even here on the mountain slopes, the wind was thick with smoke, and the ground shook with explosions as the two great forces threw everything they had at each other. The whole world seemed to be on fire.

It doesn't have to be like this, thought Lucky. *There could be peace. But instead, they'll fight and fight until there's nothing left.*

Nothing left at all.

He kept climbing. The mountain got steeper the higher he climbed. It became hard to get a grip on the frozen snow. His feet kept slipping, sliding beneath him. Even with his hooves powering him up, his legs kept giving way. Each time he slipped, he put out his hands to catch himself—and ripped his palms on sharp-edged ice.

His friends weren't faring much better. It was a struggle for them all. But higher and higher they climbed, though they kept falling back a step for every two they took.

The first shadowships were now landing at the foot of the mountain. Human forces swarmed out from them and engaged the Axxa in combat. President Thorntree herself was commanding them, clad in battle armor.

King Theobroma met them head-on with his Axxa troopers, but there were more Shadow Guards landing all the time. They began to force the Axxa back, gaining ground through sheer brute force. The King started to retreat up the mountain slope — in the same direction Lucky was going, toward the top.

Lucky kept climbing.

Breathing was getting harder. His lungs felt small and shriveled. His breath came out in crystal clouds. The moisture in his eyes was freezing; solid chunks of ice, big as coins, were forming on his eyelashes. His hands were numb with cold and aflame with pain, all at the same time.

All he wanted to do was lie down in the snow, lie down and rest, but —

FLASSSHHH!

"Keep going!" cried Bixa, as the supernova blazed in the sky and Mystica writhed in pain. "Keep climbing — Aquarius could die anytime!"

Lucky hauled himself up another step. It was a huge effort, straining up that icy slope into white fog. Even with Bazooka lighting the way, he still couldn't see the mountain-top. There was no way of knowing how far away it was, or if they'd ever make it. Yet he felt certain that was where he had to be.

Below him on the mountainside, more and more people

were climbing upward, their figures reduced to ghostly shadows by the blizzard and the fog of war. Shots rang out, but his friends were guarding the rear now, shielding him again, just to give him a chance to make it to the top and see the stars once more.

He was bent double, pulling himself toward the summit, one backbreaking step at a time. And then he had to go down on his hands and knees, just to haul himself a little bit closer to the top—

—and closer—

—until finally, with hands torn and bloody from the ice, his fingers touched flat ground—

—and he hauled himself up onto a plateau.

They'd reached the summit of the mountain. The highest point on Charon. Shards of ice and frozen stone lay all around. It was utterly barren and lifeless.

Bixa and Frollix stood beside him on the summit. Despite the freezing cold, Frollix took off his coat and laid Mystica gently down on it. The Captain lay by her side. Below them, not far from the mountaintop, King Theobroma and President Thorntree were commanding their forces, locked in deadly battle, climbing higher all the time.

Lucky looked up. The stars were visible at last—but only as points of darkness, black against the bone-white sky, like eyeholes in a skull.

"So what is it?" he called up at them, pleading. "What am I here for? What am I supposed to do?"

And from the stars—

—there was no reply.

Aquarius hung like a cracked jewel in space. The

connections that held it together had been ripped apart by the Starburner. It was a pitiful and terrifying sight.

FLASSSHHH!

The dying star convulsed once again, and Mystica doubled up in agony on the ground.

Bixa reached down to her grandmother. "Mystica — are you OK?"

The old lady shook her head, exhausted. Her eyes were losing their golden color. They were fading, like a sun going out. "The power will pass to you now, Bixa," she whispered. "Use it wisely. . . . I've always been proud of you, my dearest — you know that, don't you?"

Bixa's eyes were wet. She took her grandmother's hand. "Mystica, please, hang on. You can't leave us. . . ."

Mystica tried to hold on to her. She gripped Bixa with pale fingers, gripped her tight —

— and then her fingers trembled, and her grip slipped, and her fingers curled away —

— and she was gone.

It was that simple. That stark.

It was as if something left her body, and was gone. Whatever it was that made her Mystica — whatever the source of her power and her life — it was gone.

There was nothing left in its place. Nothing but a cold, dead, lifeless body, curled up on the ground.

"No!" begged Bixa, tears streaming down her face. "Come back! Mystica, please don't die!"

Beside her, Lucky felt his own face crumple. Because they couldn't save her. For all his power, for all Bixa's, for all that they loved the old lady and would've done anything for

her — they couldn't save her at the end. Bixa was wailing —
"*No, no, no!*" — but she knew it too.

Mystica was dead.

FLASSSHHH!

And in the sky above, with one last scream of supernova light, her star died with her.

Its massive body began to implode. It was folding in on itself. Collapsing.

As it collapsed, its final blast of light seemed to curve around and bend back into the broken heart of the star.

Aquarius was sucking its own light back in —

— and becoming a black hole.

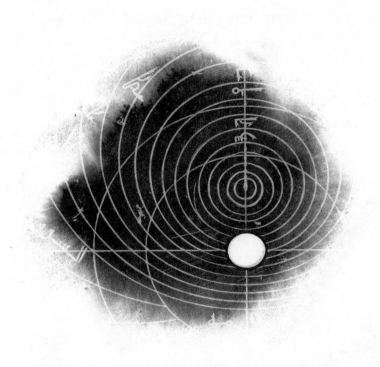

CHAPTER THIRTY-EIGHT

Aquarius began to shrink. Very soon now, this massive star would be gone from the universe. And where it once was, there would be nothing left but a black hole so vast and powerful, it would consume the entire galaxy.

"Father!" pleaded Lucky. "President Thorntree. Look at the sky. It's happening—the black hole is coming! Please listen to me: you have to stop fighting!"

He screamed with all the force in his lungs, but his voice was drowned out by the destruction all around. No one was listening. Not his father. Not the President. Not the Axxa troopers or the Shadow Guards.

Those people in power, who were supposed to know what they were doing: they were so fixed on destroying each other, they didn't even see the death that was falling on them all from above. They were just blasting away at each other, trying to kill as many people as they could—neither side willing to stop, not even for a moment.

There was another huge explosion. It knocked Lucky off his feet. The mountain shuddered with the force of it, as if it might break to dust beneath him.

He looked up at the sky again — and felt cold to the center of his marrow. Aquarius was gone. It was no longer in the universe; it had been annihilated. And the planets around it, one by one, were being sucked into the titanic black hole that was growing in its place.

And now, at the heart of the black hole, he could see . . . *Nothing.*

He stared and stared at it, but his eyes would not accept it. They kept sliding away, recoiling, unable to gain any grip on its surface.

For there was no surface. No depth. No up, no down. No light or dark; no sound or silence.

Just . . . *Nothing.* The same Absolute Nothing he'd seen at the heart of the Rainbow Temple Wheel. The ancient and terrible void behind the sky. The negation and destruction and the end of all things.

His mind buckled before it.

An overpowering wave of despair hit him. All meaning was sucked out of the world. All hope and purpose and connection were destroyed.

His field of vision narrowed. His eyes lost focus.

All he could see now was himself. He was alone in the universe.

And nothing matters.

Nothing matters anymore.

He was going down into darkness when he felt a hand grab his own.

A hand he knew. Warmer, smaller, softer . . .

Bixa.

Bixa Quicksilver was holding on to him, the connection flowing through them—

—and the wave of despair receded, just a little.

She matters. Of course she matters.

His focus widened. The blur cleared.

He looked at her. She looked at him. There was surprise in her eyes: exactly the same surprise he felt.

They looked down at each other's hands—and saw their fingers intertwined. They were holding hands again, just as they had at Gala's concert.

"It's connection!" cried Lucky, feeling a sudden dizzy spark of hope. "Connection is the thing that protects against the Living Death!"

"Yes!" said Bixa. "Remember the Captain? I held on to his hand, and he came back. And on Scorpio—you and me and Frollix—we were dancing together, weren't we? We were holding hands. Just like we are now." She looked at their fingers and smiled. "When you destroy Dark Matter connections, the Nothing gets through. But if we hold on to each other, if we stay connected . . ."

". . . then we can survive this!" said Lucky. Still holding Bixa's hand, he looked up again—

—and his spark of hope died.

Because it wasn't just Aquarius anymore. The entire sky was being pulled apart. Cracks and fractures rippled out from the black hole as the horizon broke in two. Space was shattering above their heads.

All around the mountain, Axxa and Humans were beginning to look up at the broken sky, and to see the Nothing on the other side. The sounds of battle faded as, one by one, they saw the cracks in the fabric of spacetime.

"What . . . is . . . *that?*" gasped Lucky's father in the sudden silence, just below him on the mountainside.

"We tried to warn you," said Bixa. "It's the black hole. The Wolf That Eats the Stars. It's here."

How can I stop this? thought Lucky desperately. *How do you destroy a black hole? If only I could hear the stars; if only I still had the astrolabe . . .*

But that vast view of space: wasn't it part of him now?

He concentrated, shut his eyes, shut out everything around him. He remembered how it felt to hold the black metal disk in his hands. Remembered that feeling of limitless power thrumming beneath his fingertips —

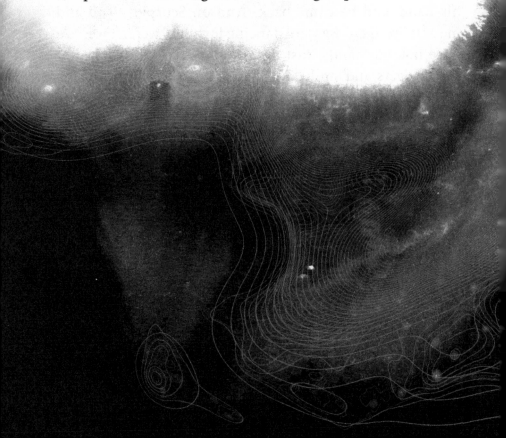

—and then, in his mind, Lucky went into space. He stopped being conscious of the two armies, the mountain, even the black hole in the sky.

He was conscious only of the stars. And here, at last, he could hear them. But their voices were so faint, so weak, so scared.

falling

dying

out of time

Behind them, he could hear those fragments of strang. sad songs, still echoing across infinity. They seemed clearer than ever before. Bigger. Stronger than the songs of the stars — and older too. They were songs that went right back to the beginning of everything. . . .

He gasped as he realized what they were.

The Twelve Astraeus.

They were singing across space, and they had been all along. One by one, they'd been calling to one another, warning of the Wolf and their powerlessness before it.

But now they were singing to *him*. And their song was terrible in its simplicity, its clarity, its meaning.

...Come Back to Us...

...Come Back to Us...

...Come Back to
the Sky...

And in that moment, Lucky knew at last what his power
was meant for, and what he had to do.

The shock was so great that he crashed out of space —

— and crashed straight back into his body again.

No! he thought desperately. *There must be another way — there must!*

But in his mind, the Twelve Astraeus sang on, the same song, again and again — and he knew there could be no avoiding it, after all.

He could not escape the destiny that Gala had foreseen, the fate he hoped he had escaped. All hope was snatched away, and the meaning of her prophecy became finally, fully, horribly clear.

CHAPTER THIRTY-NINE

On the mountainside, the Axxa and the Humans were all staring up at the black hole. It was tearing the sky to pieces, and the Nothing was pouring through.

The sight of it began to suck the life and light from their minds. One by one, they succumbed to the Living Death.

"What's happening?" gasped President Thorntree, horror cracking her painted smile.

"The stars are falling from the sky," said King Theobroma. He looked down. "It's over. Nobody can save us now."

Lucky shuddered. "I — I'm going to try," he said, almost in spite of himself. "I think there might be a way." It was as if it wasn't him speaking; as if someone braver and wiser had taken over, and he was just watching from the sidelines. "But if I save you, will you stop fighting and make peace? Because if you don't, all this will just happen again. . . ."

The President and the King looked at each other with suspicion and hatred in their eyes.

"But *they* made it happen," said the King.

"No," said the President. "It was *them*. The War, the Living Death: *they're* responsible for it all."

Lucky's heart sank. Even now, they still couldn't see what they were doing. "Don't you get it?" he pleaded. "The Living Death isn't an Axxa plot or a Human plot. It's what happens when you destroy Dark Matter connections. You've both been doing that, so you're *both* responsible. The only thing that can save you from it is connection — so please: stop fighting, hold on to each other, and don't let go!"

But still they would not reply. They would not even meet each other's eyes.

Bixa's needles bristled with defiance. "You people are incredible!" she shouted. "Peace is the only thing that can save you! Can't you get that through your heads?"

They both recoiled from the girl with needles in her hair.

"Who are *you*?" said President Thorntree.

"I'm the new Startalker of the Present," said Bixa. "That means I know what you're all thinking, right now. You're thinking you can never make peace with *them*. But you're wrong. Because there's no difference between you that matters more than your lives. We're all the same when we're looking into a black hole. We're all *us*!"

Lucky gazed at her, amazed that in this darkest and most desperate hour, she seemed to have come into her Startalker power so smoothly and so confidently. He felt so glad that she was there beside him at that moment.

But above their heads, the crack in the sky was spreading. As they watched from behind the radiation storm, they saw planets, suns, and moons sucked in, crushed down to Nothing, annihilated — as if they had never existed at all.

It was like a Dark Matter bomb, but as big as a star. Aquarius was gone, and now — as Major Dashwood had predicted, and as Gala had foreseen — everything was going. Everything slipping away. The black hole was growing bigger and bigger, more and more powerful, as world after world fell into it. Soon it would move beyond Aquarius, to the next star system, and the next, until it had consumed the entire galaxy.

Darkness began to descend on Charon. Humans and Axxa alike were plunged into freezing cold. And the air filled with their screams, their cries, their total terror at the end of all worlds.

"Do what Lucky told you!" Bixa urged them. "Make peace with each other — *now!*"

And now, at long last, they did it. They dropped their weapons, reached out, and took each other's hands.

It was such a small gesture. Such a tiny, fragile thing — almost pitiful compared to the vast forces raging above them in the sky — and yet, somehow, it helped. It held off the darkness and despair that assailed their minds.

King Theobroma and President Thorntree, Axxa troopers and Shadow Guards: all across the mountainside, people were taking their enemies' hands, linking arms, clutching tightly on to one another for sanity and for life. They held on, and slowly, their screams of fear subsided. The waves of despair receded.

But still the black hole was growing bigger, longer, wider. Expanding in every direction at once, pulling in more and more worlds. More and more stars were falling from the sky.

Lucky stared up at it, cold with fear, and prepared to face the end.

Frollix watched him with eyes of blue flame. "So . . . what *are* you gonna do?" he said. "You're not gonna do what I think, are you? You can't, Lucky, you can't —"

"You've got to leave this mountain," Lucky told the President and the King, avoiding Frollix's question, turning away from his friends. He couldn't look at Frollix, or Bixa; he didn't think he'd have the strength to go through with it if he did. "I'm going to use my power now. Anything near me will be destroyed. You have to get everyone away to safety, right now."

Without another word, the two leaders led their forces away. The two armies moved down the mountainside, connected: arms linked, hand in hand. They didn't look like armies anymore. They looked more like small children, clutching on to one another, because there was nothing else to hold on to. Axxa and Humans — the People of the Stars and the People of the Ground — they left side by side.

Lucky remained on the mountaintop under the unraveling sky, his friends by his side.

"You have to go too," he forced himself to say, as he let go of Bixa's hand. It was the hardest thing he'd ever done. "You can't stay. No one can survive what's going to happen here."

Captain Nox held Mystica's body in his arms. "Without her, I don't want to survive," he replied. He shook his great head in grief. "I wish I was dead."

Lucky looked at the heartbroken old man. "No, Captain," he said. "You had the Living Death, and you came back. You've *got* to live. That's what she'd want, isn't it?"

The Captain looked back at Lucky. His eyes were like rain. "You mattered to her, you know," he said very quietly. And then his voice cracked, and he turned away. "You mattered to us all."

And with those words, he lifted Mystica's body and started to climb down the mountainside.

"Frollix," said Lucky, turning to his friend, "you have to take Bazooka. I've been carrying her for you, but she was the Professor's, and he said a phoenix always accompanies the Startalker of the Past — so she should go with you. Even a phoenix can't come where I'm going."

He lifted the little bird from his shoulder. She perched on his palm, shivering, as he held her out to the huge Axxa.

Frollix hesitated — and then, finally, reached out and accepted the phoenix. He took her in his hands and gently stroked her feathers. "It's OK," he whispered, soothing her. "It's OK, Bazooka. I'm here now."

"*Baaa-zookaaaa?*" she chirped, glowing crimson gold.

"Yes," said Frollix, as she hopped up and perched on his shoulder. "I — I'm not gonna say good-bye, Lucky. You're gonna be OK, right?"

Lucky couldn't meet his eye. "Take care," he said softly. "My brother. My friend."

He watched them go down the mountainside together: the new Startalker of the Past, with the new phoenix on his shoulder.

It was just him and Bixa now. They looked up at the broken sky.

"I'm glad you were here at the end," he told her. "But —

457

don't let them forget this, OK? Even if you have to smash their heads together, you've got to make sure they keep the peace."

"Oh, I will," said Bixa. "I'll do some head-smashing, don't worry!"

"I'm counting on you. You're Startalker of the Present now."

Bixa's face fell. "No," she said. "I'm not. I — I didn't really know what they were thinking, back there. It was just a bluff." She looked up at the stars, dying before their time. "I don't feel any different, Lucky. I don't hear any stars singing." Her needles were totally black, as lightless as the sky. "I don't have the power, and I never will."

"But — that bluff of yours was brilliant!" He couldn't leave her like this. There was so little time, and so much to say. He took her hand again and looked right into her silver eyes. "*You* were the one who persuaded them to make peace. And if you did it without some weirdo power — well, I think that makes you even more brilliant. I think you're the bravest and most brilliant person I ever met, Bixa Quicksilver."

She stared back at him. And then, at last, she lost her cool and slapped him straight across the face.

"Oww!" he said, startled. "Why d'you do that?"

"'Cos this isn't fair!" she raged, stamping a hoof on the frozen ground. "We just met — I want to be with you — have adventures — see things. . . ." She shook her head. "Isn't there another way? There must be another way — there must —"

"I don't think so," he said. "I've got to go now. Bixa, I love you."

Her silver eyes filled with tears. And then she grabbed him in her arms and kissed him, hot and sweet and full on the mouth.

And then she let go and walked away, leaving him alone on top of the mountain.

Alone.

Again.

Once more.

He looked up at the sky. The ruined hollow shell of reality. The Nothing streaming through. The black hole, growing all the time.

There were only moments left. If he didn't act now, the stars he loved would be gone forever. Every single world was going to die.

He looked at the heart of the black hole. Directly into the jaws of the Wolf That Eats the Stars.

Nothing matters, whispered the darkness.

Nothing matters anymore.

He fought it off with the memory of Bixa's kiss, her warmth, her taste.

How hard it was to leave that now, at the very moment when he'd found it. They would never touch again. Never talk again.

He felt like he was losing a part of himself. A part? No: he was about to lose everything that made him who he was. This unique configuration of atoms was about to be snuffed out and burned away.

What a useless, clumsy body, he thought, holding up his hands, staring at his fingers. *I've always hated my body. But now that I'm about to lose it — I don't want to let go.*

Far below, he could see the shattered ruins of the *Sunfire*, the strewn-out trail of wreckage where they'd crashed. He'd loved that ship. He would've given anything to have it back — but now it was gone, and all that remained was this one last chance to save the people he loved, by using every last part of his power.

I don't want to die. I don't want to leave my friends. I want to live —

— but I'm the only one who can do this.

He looked up at the sky, at the black hole, at the Nothing —

— and now he felt it rise.

At the center of his being, a spark of power flared into life.

Impossible energies surged through his body.

His fingertips started to shine.

And then the light poured out of him, scorching from his hands, his head, his heart.

The light flared into flame. Red-hot. White-hot. Hotter still. And Lucky could smell something like sulfur, filling his senses, overwhelming him with fire as his body burned.

This time, he let it burn. He didn't try to stop the pain. He let it go all the way, as he never had before.

Far above, he could see the stars as they fell into the darkness. He stretched his arms up, reaching for the stars, sending all his energy into the sky.

A great pillar of flame rose up from him, stronger than the fires in a nuclear furnace, bigger than the blast of a billion atom bombs. Aimed directly at the black hole that was ripping the galaxy to pieces.

And still the power was growing, growing. Glowing brighter all the time.

Lucky's hands felt raw. Searing pain ripped through his heart. It burned and blazed behind his eyes. Yet still he let the power rise — higher and higher — all focused on that black hole in the sky.

But already, something inside him was beginning to buckle.

His body was shaking, shaking. The surface of his brain was boiling. His head was splitting under the strain, erupting, breaking open as arcs of blinding pain shot across his face, bigger and brighter than any body could contain.

His eyes were on fire. From his nose and mouth and ears, the fire was bleeding out, and it was killing him.

Yet still he didn't try to stop it. Still he kept it coming, letting it rise and flare and flame — even though it was tearing him to pieces — the pain of his life being burned away, his mortality blazing — how much could there be left? Not much now, surely not much; he could hardly think straight anymore, but still he kept burning, and blazing, and reaching for the stars —

— but the pressure was too great. His body was beginning to melt, to come apart under the strain.

He could feel himself disintegrating. This frail body of flesh and blood was falling apart, his heart failing, heart breaking. . . .

He felt his atoms fly apart at a million miles an hour. . . .

His mortal life was gone. It was all spent, and now there was nothing left.

It was not enough; it could never be enough.

And as the flames consumed him, he understood that it was over.

The Nothing was stronger than he was. It always had been.

For everything

everywhere

every

o n e

e n d s

Lucky burned and burned and burned, down to the last ember.

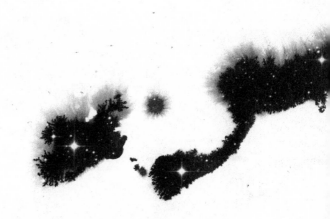

The smallest spark of light: that was all that was left
of him.

His mortal body was gone, all burned away.

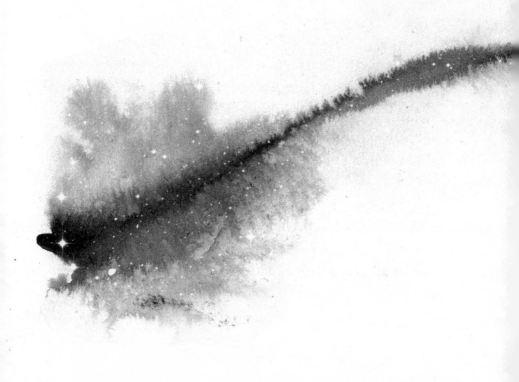

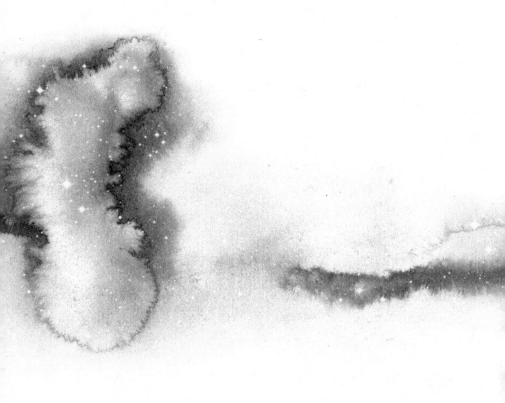

But now that it was gone — something new was growing around him.

A new body, brighter than fire, lighter than air.

The body of a star.

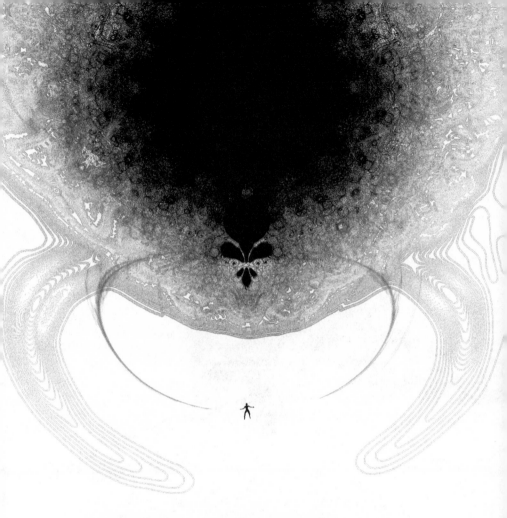

And Lucky came into his power at last.
He rose.
He flew.

Like a phoenix, he soared up into the sky, into space, into the stars and constellations.

He rose higher and higher in his new, weightless, astral body — all the way to the Wolf That Eats the Stars.

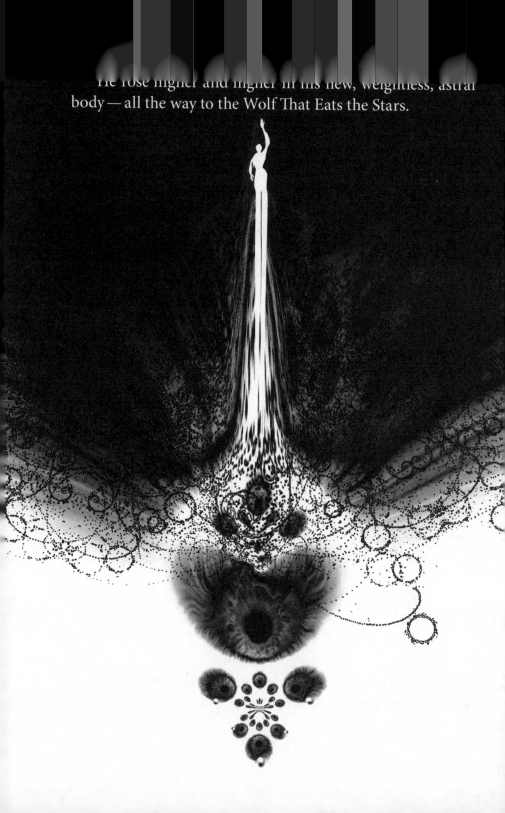

As he reached it, the Nothing whispered in his heart once more.

What matters? it hissed as it surrounded him in darkness. *Nothing matters anymore.*

But Lucky's heart of starlight burned too bright to feel despair.

"*You want to know what matters?*" he roared at the Nothing. "*I'll tell you what matters! ALL OF THIS! EVERYTHING MATTERS, AND IT ALWAYS WILL!*"

He couldn't destroy it; he knew that now.

But there was another way. Not destruction, but creation.

As he entered the heart of the black hole, as he became one with it — he let loose the power of creation —

— and with it, he filled the void.

He filled it with his own being: with everything that he knew. With all the feelings that he'd felt, all the places that he'd been, all the people that he'd met, all the stories that he'd seen. With everything that made him what he was — Lucky filled the void.

And there in the darkness that was the end of all things, he shone, and shone, and went on shining.

With his life and light and power, he healed the rift in space. He stopped the Nothing, and sealed it up behind the sky.

Looking down, he could see everything spread out below him. All of it was beautiful, and all of it alive.

He could see the Dark Matter connections holding it together: those swirling lines of silver light, like the view inside the astrolabe.

Except now ... those lines of silver light were coming from *him*. They were streaming out from the center of his being, radiating in every direction, illuminating the galaxy, spiraling to infinity.

Space and time were all one to him now. He could see past, present, and future: all at once, all together.

And those who had died, and those he had lost, and those he'd been forced to leave behind: he was connected to them still.

For everyone was connected. Everywhere was connected. Everything was connected.

This was who he was now, and where he was meant to be.

He had returned to the sky, as Gala had foreseen. For to be the star, he could be the boy no longer.

But what she hadn't said was how it would feel to become all that he could be.

He'd felt so homesick for so long. Now at last he was home.

He was flying high and free, higher than he'd ever been. Open space stretched out ahead of him, unboundaried: the living sky.

He was going places he'd never seen, never even dreamed of seeing. And he was part of it; he was part of everything, and it was part of him.

He danced in his new place in the sky. He was up, and away, and free.

And they were all around him, as they'd always been. They welcomed him back with joyful waves of silver sound.

He was singing, smiling, laughing as he danced among the stars.

I am alive, he sang.
I am alive. I am home. And I am free.
And I am free.
And I am free.

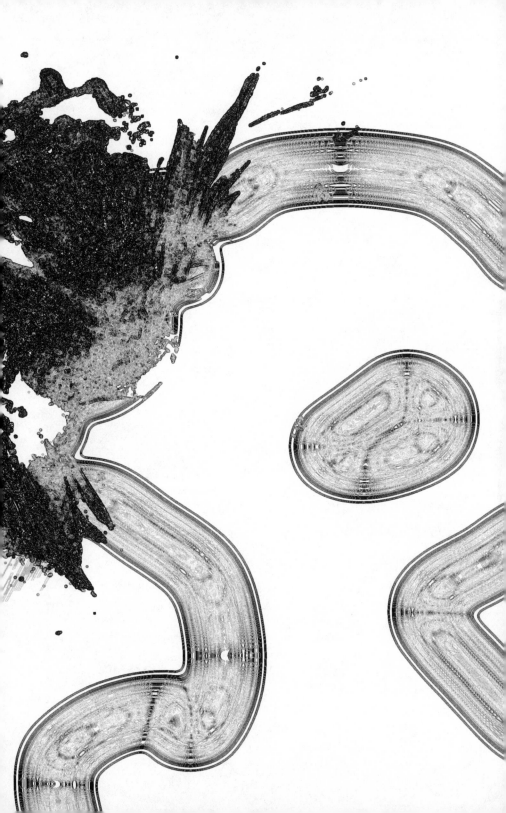

CHAPTER FORTY

Down below the mountainside, Humans and Axxa alike were holding each other's hands, sheltering from the broken sky, preparing for the end.

Bixa Quicksilver thought she heard something.

A small, soft, silvery sound, like the chime of a faraway bell.

The sound grew. It surged and swelled. Bixa felt her blood surge with it, felt her head lighten and her fears fall away from her shoulders.

For it was a song. A song of freedom, a song of love. She heard this song in her heart — as clear and true and near as the thoughts in her own head.

She looked up, and saw that the rip in the sky was healed, no longer torn. The crack in space was sealed up. The black hole was gone. Reality was restored.

And in her heart, the song was still growing. It was like the music of life, endlessly renewing itself. Like an ember of light in the dark; a spark of silver in the black.

And I am free.
And I am free.
And I am free.

That was the song she heard. And as she realized that she was hearing a star, her star, singing in her heart — she came into her power at last.

"You?" she yelled up at the new star that blazed bright and beautiful where the black hole had been. "It was you all along?" Her heart filled with feelings she didn't have names for. And then her voice rang out, bringing the truth to everyone. "He did it!" she cried, eyes shining like starlight. "Lucky saved us all!"

Far in the distance, the Spacewall flickered out and was gone. The galaxy was open and free again. The War was over. The peace had just begun.

The new Startalker took the needles from her hair, one by one, and let them fall. She didn't need them anymore.

And all around her, the mountain shone as a new day dawned. A new morning.

A new sun was shining down on them.

A new star was born.

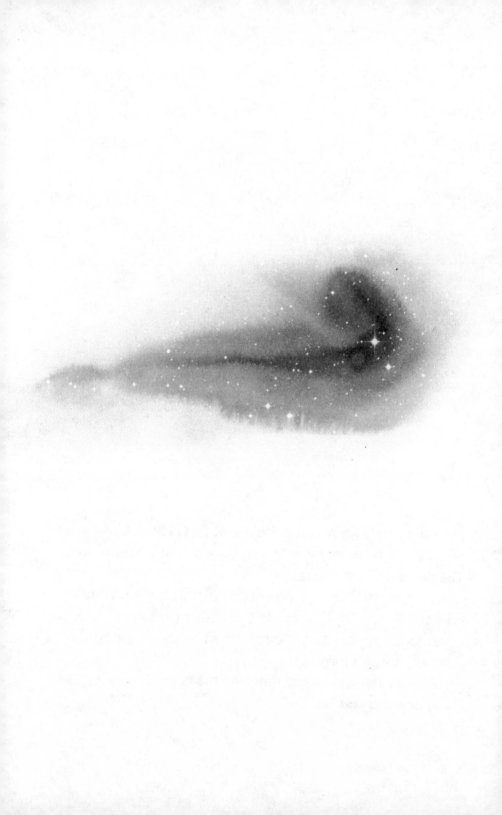

ACKNOWLEDGMENTS

This book took almost seven years to write. Like Lucky, I couldn't have done it alone, and there are many people I would like to thank.

My agents — Celia Catchpole, James Catchpole, and Val Hoskins — supported me every step of the way, in every way that I needed, from the very earliest drafts. My publisher, David Fickling, never stopped believing in this book, or helping me make it the best book it could be. I owe huge thanks to him, as well as to Bella Pearson, Tom Fickling, and Sophie Nelson for their invaluable editorial contributions, and to Hannah Featherstone, Ness Wood, and Tilda Johnson for their parts in bringing it into being. I am also enormously grateful to Philippa Dickinson and the team at Random House Children's Publishers for all their support over the years. For this beautiful Candlewick edition, I would like to thank the brilliant editor Carter Hasegawa for taking on the book and making it even better, and I'd like to thank Sherry Fatla and Rachel Smith for interior design, Nathan Pyritz for cover design, Hannah Mahoney for copyediting, and Martha Dwyer for proofreading. I would also like to thank the Candlewick sales and marketing teams for their support.

Once again, Dave McKean transformed my work with his amazing illustrations. I asked him to imagine things that are unimaginable, to depict things that are impossible — and somehow, he succeeded, producing art that takes my breath away and gives me the sense of awe and wonder I always hoped my story would have. He also gave me vital thoughts on the penultimate draft. There's not enough chocolate in the world to repay what I owe him!

I was fortunate to have many wonderful readers commenting on various drafts, offering ideas and feedback that helped to shape the book: Sophie Mayer,

Andrew Killeen, Rebecca Porteous, Ali Fahmi, Toni Kearton, Emily O'Brien, Félix Lajeunesse, Alison Coles, Tom Mitchell, Freddie Poser, Asa Thomas, Helen Thomas, Katie Broderick, and Mabel Baxter Dalrymple. I would also like to thank the CLPE (Campaign for Literacy in Primary Education), as well as the teachers and students I met through them, not only for allowing me to test out passages and titles but also for consistently supporting my work; and Jeff Roberts, who helped me to survive the process, and provided many important insights along the way.

Much of this book was written in libraries. I am eternally grateful to the public libraries of North London, without whose excellent facilities I could never have done my work, and to the staff of the BFI Library, whose Stephen Street premises meant more to me than I can say. Thanks also to Mal Og Mening in Reykjavik and La Tetería in Barcelona, where crucial parts of the book were written.

I owe a great debt to Sigur Rós, the Cure, British Sea Power, and Godspeed You Black Emperor, whose music formed a constant soundtrack to the writing. Eminem's "Lose Yourself" also helped me out of many dark corners.

I would like to honor the memories of Alia Al-Askari, Zina Al-Askari, Nehleh Carol Bailey, Dania Allemi, and Elijah Kunuk, all of whom passed away during the writing of this book, all of them too soon.

My biggest thanks are due to those who supported me personally through this journey. There are too many names to list here, but I'd particularly like to thank Andrew Killeen, Nick Bradshaw, and Rebekah Polding for some crucial conversations; my mother, Nahla Al-Askari, whom I can never repay for introducing me to books in the first place; and my partner, Sophie Mayer, whose own writing is a constant inspiration to me. Much of this book has its origins in conversations with her, and I cannot thank her enough for her support.

This book is for Sophie and LT.

SF Said

Thanks to Liam for pretending to be Lucky.
This one's for you.

Dave McKean